AVA

Jill Todd

First published in 2025 by Blossom Spring Publishing
Avalon Sky © 2025 Jill Todd
ISBN 978-1-917938-21-1
E: admin@blossomspringpublishing.com
W: www.blossomspringpublishing.com
All rights reserved under International Copyright Law.
Contents and/or cover may not be reproduced in
whole or in part without the express written consent of the publisher.
Names, characters, places and incidents are either
products of the author's imagination or are used fictitiously.

To Pete, both Marks, and Justyna, for their hours of reading and invaluable criticism – and to Dad, for his optimism and encouragement.

ACKNOWLEDGEMENTS

As well as thanking family and friends for their tolerance and unfailing support, I am grateful to all those who maintain the UK's dwindling treasure-trove of small airfields, which give pleasure to so many, and which supplied the inspiration for parts of this story.

My appreciation also goes to everyone involved in making Lundy Island such a special place to visit – but the island staff mentioned, like all other characters, are my invention. Any similarity to actual staff, past or present, is coincidental.

PROLOGUE

I could have been in another century. No lights. No phone signal. Not even a building this far south, and the cloud cover obscured any glimmer of moon or starlight.

Without the headtorch I would never have found the way, let alone been able to run, and speed was what mattered now. I set a fast pace, the rhythmic beat of my trainers on the uneven ground hardly louder than the wind gusting over the heathland or the murmur of waves breaking far below.

If I could reach her in time, she might still be alive.

To my left, a stone wall bounded the path. Beyond that, the land stretched away towards the cliffs. I kept turning my head to light the slopes, but there was no sign of her.

An obstruction checked my progress: two gates, the narrower one for walkers. Closing it behind me, I shouted her name into the darkness.

A cold wind flattened clumps of taller grasses inland, and a sheep looked up from grazing, eyes eerily reflecting the torchlight. Nothing else stirred.

I ran on, keeping in mind the hand-drawn map in the guide book. The path was now on the seaward side of the wall. With growing, icy certainty, I guessed where she would be, and knew the place must be close.

There was no comfort in the knowledge.

If she was there, I might already be too late.

ONE: Sixteen days earlier

My sister was only trying to help. She was worried about us. Nothing that happened later was her fault.

Near the end of October 2019, I took her call while dishing up muesli and fruit juice for two, and responded to her deceptively casual questions in the usual way: yes, all good, we were ticking along.

But this time Robyn was on a mission. 'We wondered if you'd like to visit next week? Maybe for a couple of days? Wednesday onwards would be good. I'm taking time off to do Hallowe'en stuff with the kids, and Ian will be around after work.'

'Appreciate the offer, Robbie, but we're pretty booked up.'

'Oh ... I thought this might be the moment to ask, with your new contract not starting till January, and Lissa ... well ...'

My wife was still on maternity leave. Technically.

'Sorry. We're, um ... feeding a cat. The old guy in Flat 4 is away, staying with his daughter.'

This feeble lie silenced her briefly, but she rallied. 'Whenever you feel ready, then. You know we'd love to see you.'

'Yeah. Thanks.'

Ending the call, I turned to find Lissa standing in the kitchen doorway, arms folded, her stance as indignant as she could make it while swathed in a fluffy sky-blue dressing-gown.

'Feeding Malcolm's cat?' she queried.

'I had to say something.'

'How about, *I'll check with Lissa and get back to you?*'

'I didn't think you'd want to go.'

She came and put her arms around my waist, looking up at me with those huge dark eyes, aware that I couldn't refuse her anything. 'I miss them, Kit. We want them in our lives, don't we?'

I flinched inwardly. 'Guess I was thinking, at Christmas …'

'How would that be easier?'

It wouldn't. Stifling a sigh, I promised to talk to Robyn again. But after breakfast I went for a run instead, pushing through the pain barrier, running to escape from a flat full of memories, from Lissa's reproaches, from the weight of trouble and doubt and grief.

Running from life.

It was a coward's option. Lissa was right; everything had to be faced. Lungs heaving, I flopped down on a bench and messaged my sister that the cat was sorted and we were free after all.

Her reply arrived within a minute. *That's great – Wednesday pm works for us. Jenny's holding the fort at the gallery. You can help carve pumpkins! Bring costumes for trick-or-treat!*

The gallery must be doing well if she could afford to give her obliging assistant more hours. I was pleased for her, as well as relieved. Opening a fine arts outlet on the High Street had been a risk.

I replied, *Cloak packed, fangs sprouting.*

Committed.

So on Wednesday, after an early lunch, we locked up the Maidstone flat and headed for Herefordshire, a journey of nearly two hundred miles. Our Mercedes hatchback – a decent second-hand model, bought with a baby in mind – was comfortable on long trips, and we shared the driving.

Robyn's and Ian's new home was a black-and-white house outside the village of Colwall, between the Malvern Hills and the Welsh border. Set amid climbable fruit trees, it had a long side-lawn, a wooden playhouse, a rabbit hutch and a wonky swing. A kids' paradise.

As I parked on the drive, Lissa was winding a coil of her dark hair around her finger, a sure sign of nerves.

'OK, sweetheart?' I asked.

She forced a smile, putting on a brave face. She was good at that. 'We'll be fine,' she said.

My brother-in-law Ian, with little dark-haired Imogen on his hip, opened his front door and called a welcome, then waited on the step to keep his socks dry while we unloaded the luggage.

His son was not the waiting type. Samuel Pevensey-Threlfall, a stocky redhead like his dad, charged to meet us, grabbed my hand and swung from it. I groaned convincingly and pretended to stagger, making him chuckle.

'We've been tidying up,' he said.

'Oh, no! We love mess.'

'*You* do,' Lissa corrected me drily. 'Hello, Sam.'

'I'm three-and-a-quarter,' he informed us, bracing his slippered feet against my leg and starting to climb. 'Have you got us a present?'

Ian exclaimed, '*Sam!* That's rude – and get down!'

Sam dropped his feet and grew helpful, insisting on dragging our wheeled suitcases indoors. Lissa's was a challenging size. While he battled with it, Ian clapped me on the back and kissed Lissa, prompting Imogen to burst into tears. In the hall, we gave out light-up Hallowe'en mugs, hoping to appease her, but her howls increased in volume, which inspired Sam to make a great show of thanking us.

'*I'm* polite,' he said.

Robyn emerged from the kitchen, stepping around a pushchair to start another round of hugs. Her dark curls were cut in a new, boyish style that accentuated her height and slenderness. I knew that Lissa always felt short and fat beside her, which was nuts. My wife had the sort of curves that some women paid to achieve.

'You're all looking well,' I said.

Ian grimaced, patting his straining shirt buttons with his free hand. 'Too well, in my case.'

'We could go for a run later, if you like.'

Before he could think of an excuse, Robyn rescued him.

'If you want exercise, little brother, I'm sure the kids will oblige.'

I smiled at her with affection. At five-eleven, I was taller than she was, though not by much. These days she only used the old epithet when feeling sentimental.

Sam dumped his new mug on a pair of shoes and leaned his elbows on my case, regarding us solemnly. 'Baby Emily died,' he said.

He stopped my breath, but Lissa replied evenly, 'I'm afraid so, Sam.'

'*And* my rabbit died.'

'Oh dear,' she said. 'I'm sorry.'

'I was sad. Were you sad?'

'Yes, we're very sad, Sam.'

Ian stepped in. 'Pizza time! Come along, monsters!' Still holding Imogen, he ushered Sam in the direction of the kitchen, from where we heard the little boy demanding pepperoni and no coleslaw.

Robyn turned to us in anguish, her innate composure shattered. 'Oh, my God, I'm so sorry.'

Lissa shook her head. 'It's OK, honestly. We don't mind talking about Emily.'

I wasn't so sure about that. My sister sighed, still upset. I knew how it would be; as parents of two healthy children, she and Ian would never complain to us about tantrums or broken nights, or even about Sam's embarrassing honesty, for fear of sounding crass and ungrateful. Our friends and work colleagues were the same, but this felt worse.

Oh Christ, I thought, *we shouldn't have come,* but I patted Robyn's arm and raised a smile to reassure her. 'Lead on, then, let's see our room.'

The guest bedroom boasted an ensuite shower and a window facing east. I recognised the distant summit of the Worcestershire Beacon, brown and gold with autumn bracken, a view familiar from childhood.

'I've applied for a researcher's job with the BBC,' Lissa was telling Robyn, 'at the Bristol studios, as Kit will be based there.'

I turned round, making the effort to be sociable. 'So we'll be moving nearer to you. We might buy instead of renting.'

'We feel brave,' Lissa said. 'I'm sure Kit didn't tell you, but they actually head-hunted him to front the *Enigmas* series, so they're likely to renew his contract beyond next year.'

Robyn was impressed. I had been pretty pleased myself. After several years of writing and presenting niche-audience history shows for a production company based in Kent – the same one that Lissa had later joined as a researcher – neither I nor my agent had expected a call from the BBC. But here I was. From January, I would be shooting *Enigmas* for release in the autumn: six episodes about unsolved murders and disappearances.

'You could stay here longer and do some house-hunting,' Robyn suggested.

'That's really kind,' Lissa said, taking a sudden interest in a willow-pattern jug and ewer on the dressing-table, 'but it's early days. We need to decide what sort of home we're looking for.'

Quick to sense the change in atmosphere, Robyn glanced from one of us to the other. Lissa wouldn't meet her eyes, and my apologetic shrug was no help.

'Well,' she said breezily, 'you know it took Ian and me nearly a year to find somewhere we both liked.' She moved to the door. 'We'll be eating later, when the kids are in bed. A friend's joining us – David Macrae. He's an auctioneer, so we'll have to try not to talk shop. You don't mind, do you?'

Neither of us did.

On her way out, Robyn delivered a mischievous parting shot. 'Just a heads-up, Kit. You're his celebrity crush.'

As the door closed, I commented to Lissa, trying to dispel the tension, 'He must have a thing for Z-listers. Lucky you're not the jealous type.'

'Lucky you've never tested me. I'm going to take a shower.'

I must have brightened visibly, because she added, 'Alone.'

So that was that. Feeling restless and disconsolate, I joined the family in the kitchen, drinking coffee while the kids tucked into pizza with raw carrot sticks. Imogen acted up and refused to eat her carrots, so I played aeroplanes with them, making engine noises, until she consented to let me fly them into her hand one at a time.

Sam claimed my attention, asking with his mouth full, 'Want to see my drawing?'

'Eat your dinner first,' Ian said.

Sam stuffed the last chunk of pizza into his mouth, slid off his chair and ran from the room. Ian frowned, Robyn rolled her eyes, and I kept a straight face with difficulty. Sam returned with his artwork and slapped it down on the table.

'That's you and Auntie Lissa.'

Two moon-faces smiled up at me, framed respectively by a cap of luminous yellow and a long black scribble. My hair in real life was admittedly nearer blond than brown, but not actually fluorescent.

'Wow,' I said.

Sam reached up and stroked my jawline. 'I forgot this.'

'Stubble is hard to draw,' I said.

'Dad says you'll mend our swing.'

'I said *might*,' Ian protested, his freckled skin colouring. Neither he nor Robyn were fans of DIY. 'But I've bought new bolts, if you're interested, and there's a toolbox in the shed.'

'Sure, why not?'

Sam celebrated with a yell of delight and rushed off to grab his coat and boots. Once Imogen had finished eating, she warily let me guide her feet into pink wellies.

Watching them run towards the swing while I laced my trainers, I conceded privately that Lissa had been right. There could be no excuse for shutting the family out of our lives. I loved them dearly and was glad to see them happy and settled, thriving in their 'forever home'.

That was the easy part. Harder to admit, even to myself, that being around them flooded me with shameful emotions like jealousy and bitterness and sheer bloody rage at the unfairness of life ... but unless I could deal with those feelings and set them aside, we would all be the losers.

I zipped up my leather jacket against the penetrating cold and went out into the garden.

TWO

Sam helped me replace the rusty bolts, and Lissa came outside to stop Imogen from using the new ones as teethers.

We were trying out the rejuvenated swing when David Macrae arrived. His car was a new red Audi hatchback, from which he unfolded his lanky frame gracefully, almost with a flourish. He wore a three-piece suit in powder blue and looked immaculate from gelled brown curls down to polished shoes.

'Excuse the fancy attire! I'm here straight from work,' he called.

'Bloody hell,' I muttered to Lissa. 'I was less smart at our wedding.'

She treated me to a sparkling look, a rare glimpse of her old self. 'Not true. And watch your language in front of the kids!'

David Macrae ducked back into the car and emerged carrying a white, wriggling West Highland terrier puppy.

Sam shouted, 'Maisie!'

Within seconds, he and the puppy were chasing each other noisily around the lawn, with Imogen in squealing pursuit.

The auctioneer's grin showed off a set of professionally whitened teeth. 'David. You must be Lissa.' He bent to kiss the air near her cheek. 'So lovely to meet you. And Kester.' He shook my hand and pushed his black-rimmed glasses up the bridge of his nose to study me more closely. 'Huge admirer. Robyn calls you Kit. Do you prefer that?'

I was Kester Pevensey on my birth certificate and for television, but seldom in private life.

'Kit's fine,' I said.

His gaze lingered on me as if questioning my other preferences; then he indicated the bottle of Chablis in his hand. 'Straight from the fridge at Waitrose. Shall we hunt down a corkscrew? Maisie! Here, girl!'

We ushered the children and dog indoors. Robyn took Sam and Imogen off for a bath and bed, amid loud protests, while Ian insisted that Lissa, David and I relax with the wine while he prepared the meal. We retired to the living room, whose neutral tones were complemented by bright, Clarice Cliff ceramics displayed at child-proof height in an alcove, while glowing landscapes in oils adorned the walls.

'Eighteenth century, Flemish School,' David noted. 'Robyn has such an eye for quality.'

'Always,' I agreed.

'The gallery will be a spectacular success.' The wry twist to his mouth implied that he knew the background. My sister had learned her trade in the family antiques business. Dad was gone now, but Mum and our two brothers had been outraged by Robyn's decision to leave. In my cynical view, they regretted losing her specialist expertise; but either way, they had obligingly bought her out.

Ian came in then, to leave us a bowl of pretzels before dashing back to the kitchen, and David grabbed Maisie's collar to restrain her from scoffing them. The puppy lay down with what sounded like a resigned sigh.

'She's learning,' Lissa said, amused.

'I take her everywhere. You're family, aren't you, my lovely?' He fondled Maisie's ears, slanting us an oddly shifty look. 'My human family is in Somerset. A tiny village called Netherzoy, at the back of beyond. Of course you know it, Kit.'

'I do. We were filming down that way six or seven years ago.'

David looked pleased that I remembered. 'For *Ghosts of Avalon*. There's a theory linking Glastonbury to the mythical Isle of Avalon,' he told Lissa, unnecessarily. Although we hadn't worked together then, she had watched the programme, and we had both known the Arthurian legends since childhood.

David was watching us doubtfully, for the first time seeming unsure of himself. 'Of course I was dying to meet you both, but I do have an ulterior motive. I'm hoping you'll be interested in doing me a favour.'

'Depends what it is,' I said, smiling to sweeten the words.

'Well ... our mum passed last year, and we encouraged Dad to take up a hobby. He decided to write a history of the village – the years within living memory. It became quite a passion. But then ... to cut a long story short, he needed a heart bypass. It's practically routine these days, but he was fretting about the project, so I promised to finish it if he couldn't. And ... he died under the anaesthetic.'

'Oh, David,' Lissa said, 'I'm so sorry.'

'Very tough,' I said, 'losing your mum and dad so close together.'

'Yes ... and now I feel terrible because I can't keep my word. I did try, but Dad's filing system was totally random, and I simply don't have time to spend every weekend down in Somerset, sorting piles of old photos and newspaper cuttings and quizzing the neighbours.'

'And that's where we come in?' I hazarded.

'If you have other commitments, please forget I asked.

I only thought of you because of Robyn. I confess I was unloading on her, and she mentioned that you were between contracts and might jump at the chance of a holiday.'

Robyn had set us up. She must have decided that we, like David's dad before us, needed a hobby, a distraction from grief, to fill in the weeks between now and January.

Saving my true feelings to vent on Robyn later, I contented myself with showing mild scepticism. 'Sounds a long job.'

'Not for you, I'm sure. And of course I wouldn't want you to write the book for me. I'll enjoy that. I plan to self-publish and recoup the investment with local sales, but ... well ... this is embarrassing, but I'm hoping you'll consider payment in kind. I certainly couldn't afford your rates, Kit.'

Like most people, he imagined that all TV presenters were paid the astronomical salaries that regularly made headlines, but that was like assuming that an intern at a major company earned the same as the CEO. In those terms, I might have been at the level of junior management.

'What's the deal, then?' I asked.

'My uncle – great-uncle, really – has a holiday let in the village. You'd be welcome to stay there for as long as necessary. It's his old home, and newly renovated, although the garden still needs work. Unc won't let it till the spring, so you'd be the first to sample its delights. Are you tempted?'

Lissa and I exchanged glances. She would never make a poker player; I could read in her eyes which way she would vote.

'We'd like a private chat,' she told David, 'before we decide.'

'Of course.'

We went as far as the hall and shut the door.

'Oh, Kit, let's do it!' she said. 'It would be a proper break. I know we went to the Canaries and we were just really sad, but this is different. We'd be doing something constructive, and helping David.'

I could see the appeal, but was still annoyed at Robyn for interfering.

'It'll take longer than he thinks,' I warned.

'But not *months*, and we can fetch more clothes from home if we need to.'

I tried to weigh the pros and cons, but cons were hard to find. Neither of us would be homesick. Lissa felt as I did about the flat, which we had prepared with such excitement for Emily's homecoming.

Seeing my hesitation, she said, 'We could look on it as a second honeymoon. Perhaps that's what we need.'

Wow, I thought. Since Emily had died four months ago, we had been each other's lifeline; but for the past three weeks, Lissa had often been distant or irritable, and she was avoiding sex altogether. I knew why, but that only made our lack of intimacy harder to bear. If she believed that a stay in Netherzoy might help, that was good enough for me.

'OK,' I said.

Her face showed as much relief as delight, and she kissed me with more passion that I would have dared to expect. We returned to the living room, all smiles, and asked when we could start. David beamed, hands clasped theatrically, as if we had answered a prayer.

'That's marvellous! I'm so grateful. I can't tell you …'

'Looking forward to it,' I said. 'We're not tied for time. Lissa's taken some leave, and I'm free till the New

Year.'

'Fantastic! Robyn has told me about your new series. *Enigmas with Kester Pevensey.* Quite a step up, having your name in the title.'

I grinned. 'They can blame me if it tanks.'

He waved a hand dismissively. 'There's always an appetite for true crime – though I must say, it's a departure from your usual fare. You'll be quite the private investigator.'

'Not me. I'm just the front man.'

'Don't kid a kidder. I know you'll both do me proud with the research.' He leaned down again to rub Maisie's ears, leaving a pause before adding, 'You do need to be aware, Great-Uncle Alf ... his mother took her own life when he was a child. This past year, ever since Dad started his project, Unc has been having nightmares about her. He's hoping they'll stop once it's finished. I suppose that might give him some sort of closure.'

'Poor man,' Lissa murmured.

'Don't get me wrong, you can talk to Unc about your progress. But if your interviewees mention his mum – her name was Barbara – it would be kindest to keep that to yourselves. Of course, I'll exclude anything insensitive from the book.'

I felt an uneasy sense of déjà vu. Four years ago, Lissa and I had dug into the history of our shared family and uncovered more than we had ever wanted to know. We had chosen to keep the more damning secrets, to avoid causing pain to people we loved, but had still ended up estranged from most of our relatives. There had been no suicide in our family, but even so ...

'Alf's mother ... She definitely took her own life, right?' I asked.

'She was deeply depressed and eventually hanged herself, poor thing. Why do you ask?'

'Just curious. And there's no one else, apart from your uncle, who'd be sensitive about us opening old wounds?'

'Oh, no. The older villagers will enjoy reminiscing. They'll remember *Ghosts of Avalon*, too. If they're a bit star struck, they'll be falling over themselves to chat.'

Lissa laughed shortly. 'They'll hardly be star struck by *me*.'

'You're gorgeous, darling. Their hearts will melt.'

She blushed, embarrassed as always by flattery.

'Well, then,' he said, 'if you're both happy, we'd better exchange contact details. I also have a Google Sheet that you'll need …'

The spreadsheet was his dad's list of about thirty suggested interviewees. Some addresses were idiosyncratic, such as *second house down from the church,* and *bungalow on corner of Peat Cutters' Lane,* but the locations were specific enough. Lissa and I agreed to split the interviews between us.

'We could start this weekend,' she said. 'You always say I pack enough for a month, Kit. Now I feel completely justified.'

'Perfect,' David said. 'I'm driving down to Netherzoy on Friday to spend the weekend with my brother Ben and Uncle Alf. Why not join us for dinner? Your cottage – look at me, calling it yours already! – is actually next door. And of course, the Bridgwater Guy Fawkes Carnival is this Saturday. It's quite something. People come for miles. That's why I picked this weekend to visit.'

'That would be lovely,' Lissa said. 'So your uncle lives with Ben now?'

'Sorry, didn't I say? Ben asked him to move in after Uncle Alf was widowed. That's when Unc decided to turn his own cottage into a holiday let – or rather, he asked Ben to do it. My baby brother is extremely capable. He's also a keen cook. He won't mind two extra guests.'

Over our own dinner, a succulent beef casserole, we were given some more background on the Macraes. Ben was only twenty-two, and an aircraft mechanic at Sedgemoor Aerodrome, helping to maintain the flying school's small fleet as well as planes for charter. In a junior capacity, he also worked with the team that restored vintage aircraft for the on-site museum.

'I know the aerodrome,' I said. 'Is Jackson Naylor still in charge?'

'Lives for the place, especially the museum, though he's training his kids to take over. The whole site was quite run down at one point, but then Avalon Sky – Jackson's company – bought it, and he's completely turned its fortunes around. Of course, he was already a big name locally. The Naylors have been lords of the manor in Netherzoy for three generations – though no title, unfortunately. If anyone deserves a knighthood, it's that dear man.'

'Jackson certainly treated us well,' I said. 'Gave up his time to fly us around personally, for aerial shots of Glastonbury Tor and the Levels.'

'Then you'll be glad to hear his name is on Dad's list.'

I agreed that it would be good to catch up with Jackson again.

The rest of the evening passed pleasantly. We finished four bottles of wine between the five of us and exchanged anecdotes about our different professional worlds. To my relief, David didn't ask whether Lissa and I had children.

If he knew about Emily, he kept that to himself.

Sometime after midnight, he accepted Robyn's offer of the sofa, while the rest of us went tipsily upstairs. From our blue-quilted bed, I watched Lissa undress, enjoying the smooth sheen of her skin and the play of lamplight over her curves. As she slid under the duvet, I kissed her shoulder, and she smiled into my eyes.

'I'm so looking forward to our working holiday,' she said. 'Don't you dare have a go at Robyn about it!'

I grinned at her bossy tone. 'No, ma'am!'

'I'm glad we came, aren't you? Sam is such a little character, and Imogen is adorable.'

As often, her strength left me humbled. I whispered into her hair, 'You're amazing,' and started to kiss her in more interesting places.

She gently withdrew. 'Goodnight, Kit,' she said, turning away to switch off the light. Within minutes, her breathing was even and steady. Asleep or faking it.

Ah, well. Not long till the start of our second honeymoon.

I lay staring up into the darkness, thinking about us ... and Emily. Lissa and I had been lovers in our teens, but later I had kept my distance for five years, uncomfortable with the fact that we were cousins. In the end, after much soul-searching and a few short-lived relationships, I had loved her too much to stay away, but burying my doubts had required a conscious effort.

Lissa's view had always been straightforward. Our marriage was legal, therefore it wasn't incest. Other people could think what they liked.

Nothing was straightforward any more. The risk of our children having an abnormality was about six per cent – twice the rate for an unrelated couple of our age (Lissa was twenty-nine, I was thirty-one), but the same as for any new mother over thirty-five. Before trying for a family, we had had blood tests and seen a genetic counsellor. We were both healthy, with no hereditary conditions.

When Emily was born at twenty-five weeks, she was perfect. We were told that sometimes premature labour had no obvious cause or trigger. Our genes were not to blame, but there had been unpleasant whispers among those supposed friends who had quietly disapproved of our marriage. That may have explained why a work colleague had 'accidentally' leaked the story.

The internet trolls had called us disgusting. Perverted. Some expressed the opinion that we shouldn't be allowed to breed. Online death threats had landed daily. For me at least, during the twenty days that our baby daughter fought for life, the doubts sown by our accusers had added a whole new dimension to suffering.

I had no religious convictions, no certainty of an omnipotent God shaping our fate, but in my darkest moments I feared that the trolls were right.

Maybe we had been irresponsible to risk having children, and losing Emily was our punishment.

THREE

Next morning I was downstairs before seven. David Macrae was already seated at the table with a mug of tea, while Maisie watched him with concentration, silently begging for a treat. I bent to scratch the puppy behind her ears and was rewarded by an ecstasy of snuffling and tail wagging.

'I helped myself, I'm sure they won't mind. Maisie, sit!' David said, to no effect. He lifted her onto his lap. 'Work in progress, aren't you, my darling?'

I made myself a black coffee and a round of toast. 'How was the couch?' I asked.

'Slept like a log. You've lifted a weight off my shoulders.'

'Glad to be of service.'

'I've told Ben you're on board. He's delighted, obviously.'

'And your Uncle?'

'Sleeping in. Another nightmare last night.'

I grimaced sympathetically. 'I was thinking, if we'll be going through old photos, a Macrae family tree would help.'

'Good point. I'll make you one. To fill you in until then, our grandad – he's passed on now – was Uncle Alf's brother. Their parents were Freddie and Barbara, but he was killed at Dunkirk in 1940, and she took her own life two years later.'

So Freddie Macrae had been a casualty of war, and Barbara had hanged herself. It was a start. I typed their names into the Memo app on my phone, then brought up the Google Sheet of proposed interviewees. Above Jackson's name was his mother's, alongside the address and phone number of a care home called Cedar Lawns, near Gloucester.

'I never met Ursula Naylor,' I said. 'She must be a fair age.'

'Late nineties. She'd have been nearly forty when Jackson was born.'

'What's her health like? Can we interview her?'

'If she'll agree. Ben's close to Jackson's daughter, who says her gran has had episodes of confusion recently, but most days she's sharp enough to cut diamond. I did try calling her myself, but she was appallingly rude. She doesn't seem to like men, outside of family.' His lips quirked. 'And certainly not me. I don't think she embraces the Pride flag. She might tolerate Lissa.'

From the doorway, my wife said, 'I might not tolerate *her*. Who are we talking about?'

Once David had explained, she was happy to accept the challenge. Gloucester was only forty minutes away, so it would make sense to visit Ursula Naylor before we left for Somerset.

By the time the three of us had finished breakfast, the family was up. Sam conducted a debate with both parents consecutively about his need for frosted flakes instead of toast and egg, then reacted to defeat by making a flamboyant performance of every mouthful, looking around to see who was watching. Imogen joined the rebellion by refusing to eat at all – and David made his escape with Maisie.

After breakfast, we spent an hour carving pumpkin faces with the kids before excusing ourselves to ring Cedar Lawns. The website gave the general manager's number for all enquiries, and her voice on the phone matched her warmly smiling photo. Having taken Lissa's name and business, she asked her to hold, explaining that each resident had an extension in their room.

After a minute of Debussy's New World Symphony, the music cut off and a thin, acerbic voice said, 'Ursula Naylor speaking.'

'Good morning, Mrs Naylor,' Lissa said. 'I'm –'

'Lissa Pevensey. So I've been told. And I'd prefer Ursula. For some unfathomable reason, you want to talk about Netherzoy. What possible interest can you have in the history of that God-forsaken backwater?'

'Er ... my husband and I are helping David Macrae compile a village history. I think David may have spoken to you about it?'

'He did.' She managed to endow those two words with a weight of censure. 'The village featured in a TV programme a few years ago. The presenter was a Kester Pevensey.'

'My husband.'

'I suspected a connection. Is he involved in this project too?'

'In a p-private capacity.' The childhood speech impediment afflicted Lissa rarely these days. 'Our research is exclusively for David's book. 'Would you be happy for me ... or us, to visit you for a chat?'

'Will I receive any remuneration for my trouble?'

'Oh ... I'm afraid not, but I'm sure David would be happy to credit you in the acknowledgements.'

'That won't be necessary.' A brief, thinking silence. 'You may visit, if you wish. On your own.'

We high-fived silently. Into the phone, Lissa said, 'Thank you so much, Ursula. I wonder ... I appreciate it's short notice, but we're in your area today and tomorrow morning ...'

'I'll check my diary. Give me your number. This

archaic telephone has no screen.'

Lissa complied, and Ursula immediately rang off.

'Quite a character,' I said.

'She's clearly determined to frighten me.' Lissa's confidence was reviving. 'I'll have to disappoint her.'

Ursula rang back ten minutes later. 'I'm free on Saturday morning. Nine-thirty. Take it or leave it.'

Tomorrow would be Friday. We had planned to drive to Somerset in the afternoon, arriving in time for dinner with the Macraes at eight.

Screwing up her face at me, Lissa said pleasantly, 'Perfect. I'll look forward to it.'

Ursula ended the call without saying goodbye.

The change of plan obliged Lissa to stay with the family an extra night and drive down to meet me on Saturday, but Robyn and Ian assured her that was fine and we were both welcome, always. Lissa sent David her apologies for missing dinner.

She opted to keep our own car. She was a good driver but more comfortable with a familiar vehicle. I hired a similar Mercedes, arranging for it to be dropped off at five o'clock tomorrow. Then we all went to a local farm park, where the kids held a selection of rabbits and guinea pigs, and even Imogen rode a donkey, steadied by her dad.

While I was leaning on a fence, watching Ian and Lissa introduce the kids to a sheep, Robyn drifted over to me, as if casually.

'Hope the rain holds off,' I said, frowning at the sky, 'or we'll need waterproofs for trick-or-treating.'

'Kit,' she said, 'I've been wanting to tell you ... we do appreciate you coming. We know it's not easy.'

I nodded, concentrating on Imogen feeding the sheep.

Robyn was silent for a while, but I knew her. She had something else on her mind.

'Problems, Robbie?'

She turned to face me squarely. 'Tell me to mind my own business if you like, but is everything all right between you and Lissa?'

'Sure.' I contrived a puzzled smile. 'Fine.'

'She seems ... Is it about moving to Bristol?'

'Not really.' I hadn't intended to confide in her, or anyone, but for some reason found myself saying, 'Lissa wants us to try again.'

'For a baby? Oh ... well, I suppose ...' Robyn floundered, searching my face. 'Are you thinking it's too soon?'

'I don't want to. Now or ever.'

She was very still, her expression studiously blank.

'Guess you think that's pretty unreasonable.' I tried not to sound desperate. 'So does Lissa.'

'Is it worth waiting a few months? Putting off the decision?'

I shook my head miserably. Waiting would solve nothing.

'Oh, Kit.' Tentatively, she patted my arm. 'Hang in there, little brother. You'll work it out.'

'Yeah.' I breathed deeply. Even managed to grin. 'Anyway, I'm glad we came. We might start using your guest room more often.'

She smiled back. 'I should hope so,' she said.

FOUR

Auntie Lissa and Uncle Kit, vampire-fanged, took the kids trick-or-treating in nearby Colwall, and the small skeleton and fairy in our charge then picked me to read their bedtime story.

Soft Brown Dog, Sam's nighttime companion, chose *Hairy Maclary from Donaldson's Dairy*. With Sam and Imogen both installed in his bed, I duly bounced around on all fours, accompanied by "Soft", while imitating the various canine breeds in the story. The kids were shrieking with laughter and barking maniacally when their mother walked in, rolling her eyes and saying they'd be awake till midnight.

Retreat seemed the best option. I slunk off with Lissa to our own bedroom, where we googled Jackson Naylor. He was sixty but looked older in recent images, his thinning hair uniformly silver, jawline sagging a little.

'He has sad eyes,' Lissa said.

The Jackson of six years ago had smiled easily and often. Since then, his company, Avalon Sky, had taken Sedgemoor Aerodrome from strength to strength, but he had also lost his wife to cancer.

His son and daughter, Alex and Chloe, were now young adults, both with white-blonde hair and haughty eyebrows. They had joined the business straight from university. Alex was listed as assistant manager of the flight training school, while Chloe organised weddings in the grounds of Zoyland House, the family home. The Lodge, beside the main gate, was available to honeymooners, and the reviews were glowing – but there were only three, all from September this year.

'A new venture,' Lissa commented. 'Chloe's idea, do

you think?'

'Could be. She's listed as HR manager as well. Looks like she and Alex are keen to earn their inheritance.'

Lissa scrolled down Jackson's Wikipedia page. 'Father, Oscar Naylor, DSO, DFC. He died a couple of years before you were there.'

'Pity he's not still around. He'd have been worth talking to.'

I messaged Jackson there and then, and to our gratified surprise, he responded within the hour. *Kester, great to hear from you. Would you and your wife like to join me for coffee at the aerodrome on Sunday morning? How does ten-thirty sound?*

'Friendlier than his mother,' Lissa said.

Having accepted the invitation, we went to bed that night feeling motivated and upbeat. Lissa said goodnight quite affectionately before turning over to sleep.

Ian took Friday off. We all ventured to the hills for an increasingly wet walk and returned to the cottage soaked, trying to keep the kids laughing instead of grizzling. We were hanging our coats over radiators and bannisters when David rang me.

'Sorry to be a pain, Kit.' The background noise sounded like motorway traffic. 'Are you on your way yet?'

'No. Why – aagh! *Sam!*' The little wretch was pushing a cold, wet "Soft" up my back, under my clothes. I grabbed the dog, plonked it on Sam's head, and escaped into the kitchen, closing the door behind me. 'Sorry about that. Everything OK?'

'Absolutely fine, I was just … A guy from the village wants to meet me at five-thirty, at Merlin Park, to value an antique for him. I was hoping you might join us, but obviously that's a non-starter.'

It was four-fifty already, and Netherzoy was a hundred miles away.

'If you want a second opinion,' I said, 'Robbie's the expert.'

'Actually, I was after your body – and no jokes, please, I'm not flirting. To be frank, you look as if you can handle yourself in a scrap.'

'What? Jesus, David! If you don't trust this bloke, don't meet him!'

'Well, ordinarily I'd agree, but it's only Conor Yandle. He's a bad boy, but I've known the family all my life ... I just suddenly felt that I was taking a chance. Never mind, I'm over-dramatising.' He chuckled. 'No change there.'

'Can't Ben go with you?'

'I haven't bothered him. He'll be rushing home after work to start dinner.'

I grimaced; dinner seemed secondary. 'Where's this park? How public is it?'

'It's not an urban green space. It's a small industrial estate out in the sticks, with an airfield at the back. Completely private, after hours.'

'For Christ's sake –'

'That's why Conor wants us to meet there. Netherzoy is such a hive of gossip. The item is alleged to be gold and could be rare. It belongs to a friend of Conor's, who doesn't want his grasping family to find out he's selling.'

'So he says. What is it?'

'He wouldn't tell me. In fact, he was oddly cagey in general. That's really what's making me think twice.'

'It's most likely nicked.'

'Then why contact me? He must know more than one

disreputable type who'd be happy to fence stolen property.'

By the sound of it, long acquaintance with Conor Yandle was no basis for trusting him an inch.

'You could reschedule for tomorrow, in daylight,' I said. 'I'll come with you then.'

'No, it has to be tonight. Conor's involved with the carnival tomorrow, and I don't want to pass up the chance to acquire a genuine find. Think of the commission!'

'Not much use if you wake up in a ditch, minus the Audi.'

'Now who's being melodramatic? Forget I called, Kit! I'll see you at Ben's.'

'No! David –'

But he had already disconnected. I rang him straight back, but it went to voicemail.

Seriously worried, I relayed our conversation to the others, which achieved nothing except to wind them up as well. I went upstairs and started packing, to be ready to leave as soon as the car arrived. I couldn't reach Netherzoy until long after David's meeting had ended, but it felt wrong to delay unnecessarily.

Lissa kept me company and found Merlin Park on Google Maps. It was three miles outside of Netherzoy. The satellite view showed a small cluster of buildings and a grass airstrip surrounded by fields. Less than half a mile away, two semi-detached cottages stood at the end of a short track. Too far off for David to call for help if Conor turned nasty.

'You're thinking of going to the park,' Lissa said anxiously.

'I'll pick up our key from Ben first,' I said, stuffing underwear into the corners of my case. 'If there's still no sign of David – and it's a big if, he's probably fine – I'll drive over there with Ben.'

'But if he's that late ...'

'He won't be.' I kissed the top of her head. 'Fingers crossed, eh?'

The car arrived promptly, and the satnav calculated a journey time of two hours plus, door to door. Amid a flurry of hugs and waves from the family, Lissa leant into the car to give me a parting kiss, and to murmur that I should keep the bed warm for tomorrow night.

I was therefore feeling better about life in general as I left Herefordshire behind and followed the M5 south. Around six-thirty, caught in slow-moving traffic, I tried David's mobile, but it was switched off.

Nothing sinister in that. He might still be with Conor Yandle – but I kept my foot on the gas and my eyes alert for speed cameras.

South of Bristol, a call came in from another mobile. I had my phone on handsfree. As I answered, a young male voice asked, 'Is that, um ... Kit Pevensey?'

'That's me.'

'It's Ben. Ben Macrae. Dave's brother.'

My stomach tensed. 'Is there a problem?'

'I don't really know. Is Dave with you?'

'No.' The clock on the dashboard read seven-ten.

'He messaged from Gordano Services,' Ben said, 'to say he had a meeting at five-thirty, so he'd be with us about six.'

I had passed Gordano a mile back. 'He was meeting Conor Yandle at Merlin Park,' I said.

'Conor? What, at the caravan? What for?'

'A valuation. He didn't mention a caravan.'

'He didn't say anything about Conor. Where the hell is

he, then?'

'They could still be chatting, catching up on local gossip.'

'They're not mates.' Ben sounded increasingly panicked. 'Have you got Conor's number?'

'Oh ... yeah. I'll try him. If he doesn't answer, I'm going over there.'

That seemed a bad idea. It was already dark.

'Look, I'm twenty minutes away,' I said. 'Wait for me! We'll go together.'

'I don't want to wait –'

'I mean it, Ben, don't go on your own! I'm sure David's fine, but ... is Conor the type to kick off if his antique was worth less than he hoped?'

Or if he fancied a brand new Audi.

'He wouldn't hurt Dave,' Ben said. 'Conor's mum was friends with ours. She'd kill him.'

Impossible to know whether that argument was valid.

I said forcefully, 'Just sit tight, OK?'

A pause. If he resented a stranger dishing out orders, I couldn't blame him. After a second he muttered, 'See you,' and rang off.

I swore creatively and continued to push my luck with the cameras. Leaving the M5 south of Bridgwater, I turned east, along narrowing country roads where speed would have been insanity. The night was black, the route devoid of streetlamps. Pockets of fog drifted and coalesced along the lanes, forcing me to brake every time my lights bounced off a wall of invisibility. Around me, I knew, were the flat fields and intersecting drainage ditches of the Somerset Levels, but it was hard to make out anything beyond the nearest hedge.

I hoped to God that Ben would stay at home until I got there.

FIVE

It took longer than the satnav's revised estimate before the sign for Netherzoy materialised out of the fog. I saw Peat Cutters' Lane just in time to make the turn. It was a straight, gravelled byway, with a row of semi-detached cottages to the left and a hedgerow to the right. The modest homes had slate roofs, and cream-rendered walls that gleamed in my headlamps' light like apparitions from a vanished century.

The name of the Macraes' home, Spindlewood, was painted on a boulder beside an ungated driveway. The sign for the adjoining property hung from a chain beside its gate: Yew Tree Cottage. Our holiday home.

No red Audi. The only vehicle on Spindlewood's drive was a sporty Kawasaki motorcycle, lovingly polished. Unless Uncle Alf was less frail than I had envisaged him, Ben was a biker, unusual for his generation.

Since Yew Tree Cottage lacked a drive, I parked alongside the hedge opposite.

Ben Macrae had his front door open before I reached it. He was recognisably David's brother, with the same curly brown hair and lanky build, but where David was thin, Ben looked wiry. He also sported a row of metal studs in each ear, while a flock of tattooed bluebirds took flight from under the collar of his sweatshirt, disappearing into a short beard which failed to age his boyish features.

'Thanks for waiting,' I said. 'Nothing from David?'

'His phone's turned off. Conor's too.' He looked me distractedly up and down, measuring my five-eleven frame from his own height of around six-two. 'You look taller on TV.'

'Sorry,' I said flippantly. 'What you see is what you get.'

'Shit! I don't know why I said that.'

'It's fine, Ben.' I indicated the Kawasaki. 'Yours?'

'Yeah. Can we take your car, though? If Dave's run into a ditch, he'll need a lift –' Ben broke off and sniffed the air. *'Shit!'*

He dashed back into the house and through a doorway at the end of a hall adorned with family photos. I closed the front door and followed him into a small 1970s kitchen, all shiny orange units and chipped Formica. The aroma of roast chicken sent my salivary glands into overdrive.

Ben was removing the well-browned bird from the oven. 'Sod it!' he groaned.

'Smells wonderful.'

He thumped the roasting tin down on the table, stabbed the chicken with two forks and lifted it on to a plate. His big hands bore several nicks and minor cuts at various stages of healing, the inevitable scars of his trade. He wore a distinctive ring on his right hand, the wings of the RAF's insignia in line with his middle finger.

I watched him drain most of the meat juices into a bowl.

'For dripping,' he said. 'Unc likes it for breakfast, on toast. Reminds him of when he was a kid.'

'Is your uncle in?'

'Nipped to the shop for beer.'

While he was transferring potatoes from a pan to the roasting tin, I took in details of the room. Marigold-patterned curtains framed a windowsill swarming with miniature vases, all from West Country seaside resorts.

Among the ornaments stood a photo of a smiling middle-aged couple, their heads tilted together.

'Your mum and dad?' I asked.

'Yep.' He put the potatoes in the oven and then checked the contents of a simmering saucepan. 'I've messaged everyone I can think of, in case Dave's called in to see an old mate. And ... well, I rang the local hospitals, and two in Bristol as well, in case he's crashed on the motorway or something. I've left them my number.'

'Right.' There was no hope of eating yet, but quenching my thirst might stave off the hunger pangs. 'Can I get a glass of water?'

'Course. I'll do it.' He filled a pint glass for me and smiled fleetingly, dimples showing through the beard. 'What a rubbish host.'

I grinned back. 'Demanding guests, who needs 'em? This Conor character ... David said he's got a reputation?'

'I told you, he wouldn't hurt Dave. Apart from our mums being friends, Conor's out on licence. He might go out on the rob now and then, but he wouldn't chance getting violent.'

'Sounds like a prince.'

'Honestly, I'm just scared Dave's pranged his car in the fog. We might find him on the way to the field.'

'Can you leave all this?' I waved my glass at the cooker.

'Soon as Unc gets back.' He went to the front door and peered along the lane. 'I asked him not to go, but he said he wanted a walk. Course, he's on edge, too.' Ben gave up and shut the door again with a sigh. 'I wanted to ring 999, but Unc said it wasn't an emergency, so I called the station at Bridgwater instead.'

'Any joy?' I asked, guessing the answer.

'No, they were crap. They said eighty per cent of people reported missing turn up safe within twenty-four hours, and Dave's an adult, not vulnerable or anything. He can go off if he wants, and he's not even two hours late yet.'

Ben's disgust was understandable, but I could see their point.

'Why does David keep a caravan at the industrial estate?' I asked.

'Oh ... it's Unc's, really. He was going to dump it after Auntie died, so we bagged it for the airfield instead, to use when we take people flying.'

'You've got your own plane?' Jackson must pay his employees well, I thought.

'A third share, with Dave and Unc. She's a Jabiru microlight. Two-seater. Want to see?' He passed me his phone.

The photo on his home screen showed a scaled-down version of a regular light aircraft, its white bodywork adorned with abstract red and blue curves evocative of a bird in flight. The plane was so small that Ben and David, posing with grins behind it, were visible from their chests up.

'Pretty,' I said.

'Dad and Unc bought her as a home-build twenty years ago. A kit, you know?'

I whistled. 'Big project.'

'Three years, give or take. Dave helped but I was too little.' Ben's brown eyes were alight, his pride in the tiny aircraft glowing in his face. 'I was six the first time she flew. Dave got his licence as soon as he could and bought in. Then I got an apprenticeship at Sedgemoor, and Jackson gave me a brilliant discount to take flying lessons there. I passed my test two years ago.'

'You're a talented guy. Pilot, aircraft mechanic, chef.'

He ducked his head shyly. 'She's so light, I only needed a microlight licence. And I'd been flying from the passenger seat ever since I could reach the pedals. Dad left me his share in his will – and it costs less to run than you'd think. Unc says he used to spend more on fags before he gave up.' He stopped. 'Sorry to ramble on. Trying not to think about other stuff, you know?'

He must still be grieving for his parents, I thought. No wonder he was panicking about his brother.

We heard a key being fumbled in the lock, then the door opened and Alf shuffled in. His thin silver hair glistened with damp, and his oversized coat suggested a recent loss of weight.

'Any news?' he asked Ben.

'Not yet. Here, let me have that wet coat.'

'I'm not an invalid.' But the old man spoke indulgently and fixed me with a pale gaze while allowing Ben to take his bulging carrier bag, help him out of the coat, and drape it over the hall radiator. 'You'll be Kester,' he said. 'Recognise you off the telly.'

'Kit. Good to meet you, Mr Macrae.' I shook his outstretched hand. It was dry and cold, veins knotted like ancient tree roots.

'Alf,' he said. 'You're staying in my house, eh?' He inclined his head in the direction of the adjoining cottage. 'Shame your wife can't join us for dinner.'

'Yeah, sorry to mess you about. She's coming tomorrow.'

He grunted. 'You two had best get off, then. I'll plate

up some dinner, keep it for you. Got to hand it to the boy,' he added to me. 'Best roasties in the village.'

'Unc! Stop embarrassing me!'

'Someone has to sing your praises, son. It's certain you never will.' Alf saw us out, being doggedly optimistic. 'You'll find Dave's still at the field. That's the nature of flying. Doesn't matter if you're fixing a hangar door or planning a few circuits before sunset, it always takes longer than you think. *Time to spare, go by air,* that's what they say.'

I wasn't sure this applied to meeting a dodgy acquaintance to value an antique.

From the look on Ben's face as we hurried to the car, he was not convinced either.

SIX

The three miles to Merlin Park seemed further, owing to the fog and narrow, snaking roads. David would have driven through Netherzoy to reach the park, so we were following his route, but there was no sign of the Audi having ploughed through a hedge or into one of the roadside ditches.

Ben was constantly fiddling with his ear studs or twisting the ring on his finger. I thought of a way to distract him, although partly for selfish reasons.

'Any chance of a ride on the Kawasaki sometime?'

He looked startled. 'You mean pillion, right?'

'Wouldn't expect to be allowed in the hot seat. But I do have a licence, if you're the trusting type.'

He avoided committing himself. 'You've got a bike?'

'Did have, once. Sold it to pay off a debt in my first year at uni. And none of my mates were bikers. Same for you, I'm guessing.'

'I don't mind that. It was Dad's thing. I helped him rebuild a trail bike – when I was a kid, like – and that was that.'

'Addicted?'

'Yep. Course, the Kawasaki's on lease. Unc thinks I'm pissing money down the drain, but saving up would've taken me till I was over thirty.'

'Geriatric,' I agreed, straight-faced.

Feeling his eyes on me, I flicked him a glance. He was looking pensive.

'What?' I said.

'Don't take this the wrong way, but I thought you might be a bit of a dick, being on TV and all that. But you're all right.'

'Thanks. I think.'

Although the entrance to Merlin Park was signposted, there was no mention of an airfield on the site. Ben jumped out to deal with the padlock on the waist-high gate. I drove through and waited for him to lock up behind us, my lights showing two rows of single-storey industrial units, all dark, no one working a late shift.

Ben slid back into the passenger seat and shut the door. 'Straight on to where the concrete ends,' he said.

As we passed the first row of buildings, a security light flared. A CCTV camera was mounted high up, facing the gate, above a sign: *Please report any suspicious activity.*

'Get much crime out here?' I asked.

'Not so far, but there's a black market in aircraft parts – specially for the Rotax 912 engine. A lot of microlights have those.'

'Does yours?'

'Jabiru engine. Niche market, so the big gangs can't be arsed.'

Had David and Conor interrupted engine thieves?

The road widened into a car park, bounded by an eight-foot bramble hedge and a similarly high metal gate. Ben once again did the honours, this time for a combination lock.

We drove onto an expanse of grass. The fog and darkness cloaked everything beyond a line of three small single-aircraft hangars nestling against the hedge. At Ben's request, I parked alongside the furthest hangar, illuminating an algae-covered caravan as well as a portacabin with a metre-high "C" painted on the side. I switched off the ignition, and the night clamped down. No security lights here – and no sign of David or Conor, or the Audi.

We got out of the car. The silence, the fog and the darkness seemed one entity, as if the night itself were holding its breath.

'Is there a control tower?' I asked.

'Only the C-hut. C for Control. We record aircraft movements there.'

Using our phones as torches, we paused to check that his hangar was secure. Heavy tarpaulin curtains across the front acted as double doors, fastened at the centre by vertical metal strips threaded through loops and padlocked together. As a locking mechanism, it was eccentric but functional.

Just as well that Jabiru engines were not in demand, I thought. The doors might act as a deterrent, but they wouldn't stop anyone with serious intent and a sharp knife.

Having satisfied ourselves that the lock had not been tampered with, we headed to the caravan, where David and Conor would have met. The silence felt oppressive. Maybe the fog was muffling the usual sounds of night creatures going about their business. Ben found the right key on his fob, fitted it in the lock, and opened the door.

We recoiled from the stench, swearing explosively. After a brief hesitation, I edged closer, trying not to gag, and stepped inside to shine my phone light around the interior. To my right were kitchen units, to my left a table with sofas either side. All clean and bare – but that stink was of urine and faeces, and something else. Metallic, rusty. Blood.

Ben climbed the step and stood beside me. We both saw at the same instant the red smear across the fridge door, as if someone had tried to wipe it clean. As I swung my phone downwards, Ben moaned a curse. The tiled floor showed similar marks around our feet and by the table.

Under the table, in shadow, lay a small white shape.

I groaned, 'Oh Christ!'

'What?' Ben pushed past me to see. 'Oh no, no, no.' He crouched beside the puppy's body, starting to lift her, clinging to some shred of hope; but her head lolled from a broken neck, and blood matted the fur on her left side.

Fear crawled in my gut. I turned to face the doorway. Beyond it, blackness and silence, but to anyone watching, we'd be clear targets, outlined against the light.

I checked my phone, but the signal was non-existent.

'She's still warm,' Ben wailed. 'Who'd do this? What kind of sicko?'

'We need to go,' I said.

He stared up at me, his eyes full of horror. 'Where's Dave? Where is he?'

'The police will find him. We need to get out of here.'

'The sick bastard could be hurting him.' He laid Maisie down and surged to his feet. 'We have to find them.'

'Ben, he's got a knife.'

'Piss off, then! I don't need you.' He shoved past me and jumped down the step, yelling his brother's name as he sprinted into the night.

Swearing, I started to follow, but he was already gone. My phone's light bounced off the fog, creating an impenetrable dazzle.

From behind me came a soft clink, like metal knocking against wood.

I whipped round, senses at full stretch, heart thumping against my ribs. The noise had come from the hangar. I shone my light on the tarpaulin curtains, searching not only the padlocked centre this time but all around the perimeter.

Along the top and bottom of each curtain, a row of karabiners, such as rock climbers use, served as hooks for the tracks. In the bottom left corner, three of them were open, the curtain hanging free.

Maisie's killer could have ducked inside when he heard the car.

I flexed my left hand, feeling the pull of old scar tissue, just one memento of the last time I had come up against a knife-wielding assailant – a consequence of Lissa's and my ill-advised digging into our family's secrets. Even now, nearly four years later, I sometimes dreamed of that night and woke up sweating.

Contempt at myself for being so craven fed my anger. Breathing carefully, I advanced towards the hangar, trainers quiet on the wet grass. An owl hooted, far off, and another answered.

Maybe I was wrong. The curtain hooks could have been missed when the plane was put away. The intruder might be nothing more sinister than a rat.

But it wasn't. The lower edge of the curtain moved, and a hand slid into view.

SEVEN

I gasped. The hand was an eerie point of focus in the silent night. The sight of those pale fingers lifting the curtain scattered goosebumps along my arms and between my shoulder blades.

The flap lifted higher, and a slight, hoodie-clad figure slithered out and stood up, facing me, shielding his eyes from the light.

No sign of a knife. I lowered my phone a fraction.

'Empty your pockets!' I said.

Instead, he pushed back the hood.

He was a she. Early twenties, big eyes, hair long and pale. Not your average killer, and not an obvious threat – but I wasn't taking any chances.

'I said, turn your pockets out!'

'Oh, for God's sake! You're Kester Pevensey, aren't you?' Her tone was superior, with barely a trace of a Somerset accent. 'Ben told me you were coming. Where is he?'

'Looking for his brother. Who are you – and what the hell are you doing here?'

'Bit rude. I saw Ben's message in the group chat. I came to look for David too.'

'By hiding from us?'

'I heard the car. I thought you were thieves or something.'

'Didn't you recognise Ben's voice?'

'I couldn't hear properly, until he ran off swearing at you. Why did you let him go – and why was he so upset?'

I told myself to make allowances. If she was a friend of Ben's, she was probably worried for David herself, and I was about to give her a nasty shock.

'We found David's puppy,' I said. 'I'm sorry, there's no easy way to say it. She's been killed.'

If her blank expression was an act, it was a good one. She turned her head slowly towards the caravan's open doorway. 'Maisie's ... dead?'

'Some bastard stabbed her and broke her neck.'

'No ... no, she can't be ...' And without warning the girl turned and vomited on to the grass.

She couldn't have faked that, but something was off. If she had come in a car, it wasn't here now. Had she walked three miles from the village, alone? Or was she involved, at some level, in whatever had happened between David and Conor?

It wouldn't hurt to check that the hangar was empty. Leaving the girl to her woes, I strode to the opening, unhooked two more karabiners and ducked under the tarpaulin. Standing up inside, I used my phone again to light the interior.

The T-shaped hangar was made to measure, with the plane's tail and the rear half of its fuselage occupying the stem of the T. I stooped under the port wing. Behind it stood a cluttered workbench and a chest of drawers, along with six fuel cans, a plastic bucket, a bundle of rags and a fuel pump. The single storage bin on the far side of the hangar was too small to conceal a person, dead or alive.

There was one other possible hiding place.

The fuselage had a fitted cover, fastened with bungees. I unhooked the nearest two and, bracing myself for the worst, lifted the cover to peer inside the tiny cockpit.

No corpse.

I refastened the bungees and turned sharply at a rattle of curtain hooks. The girl was crouched in the hangar opening, watching me.

'Nothing?' she asked.

'No.'

'You really don't know who I am, do you?'

I held my phone to one side, to illuminate her pale face and wide blue eyes without blinding her. She was wearing no make-up, and her long hair was rumpled from dragging off the hood, but I recognised her now. She looked very different from her posed and glamorous online images.

'You're Chloe Naylor?'

'Finally.' She moved aside for me to duck out of the hangar, and I stood upright outside.

Still no sign of Ben. He had been gone far too long.

Chloe's thoughts must have been similar. 'There are a lot more hangars,' she said. 'He could be checking if any have been broken into.'

'I tried to follow him, but this fog is a bastard.'

'All right, don't get defensive.' She stood listening to the silence, then yelled into the night, 'Benji!'

I didn't tell her to be quiet. If Maisie's killer was still on the site, we had already made enough noise to alert him.

Someone was running towards us. Instinctively, I thrust an arm across Chloe, pushing her behind me. She batted my arm aside with an indignant, 'Oh my God, *seriously*?'

I shouted, 'Ben?'

He materialised out of the fog, and Chloe ran into his arms.

'Benji, thank God! Kester told me – I'm so sorry –'

'Chloe, what the – how did you – where's your car?'

'At Harry's. I walked from there.'

'Harry's here too?'

'No, he got held up. I was tired of waiting for him, and I wanted to help.'

If she had walked from Harry's house, presumably he lived in one of the two nearby cottages along the turning before Merlin Park.

Ben regarded me bleakly over her head. 'There's nothing. All the hangars are locked.'

'Let's move, then,' I said. 'Chloe, we'll give you a lift.'

She made no objection, and Ben nodded miserably.

'I'll fetch Maisie,' he said.

Bad idea. The killing of a dog might not usually merit a full-scale investigation, but the link to David's apparent disappearance would change that.

'We can't take her,' I said. 'Sorry, Ben, but it's a crime scene. We need to leave everything the way we found it.'

'I'll stay, then. I can't leave her. Dave would hate that. What if that bastard is still here, waiting to destroy the evidence?'

Chloe threw out her hands in frustration. 'That's exactly why you mustn't stay. David wouldn't want you to put yourself in danger.'

'Absolutely right,' I said. 'We'll just go far enough to pick up a signal and ring the cops, OK? Then we'll come back here and wait for them.'

Ben looked from one of us to the other. Then, without another word, he turned and ran to the caravan.

I reached him before Chloe did. As he leapt up the step, I gripped his arm. 'Ben! I know it's hard, but we have to –'

'Piss off!' He tried to shrug me off, failed, and swung a wild punch. It landed hard enough to send me staggering back. I skidded on the wet grass and sat down heavily, my phone flying out of my hand.

'Jesus, Ben!'

He stopped dead, staring at me. 'Shit!'

My phone lay with the torch uppermost, throwing the scene into relief. As I reached to pick it up, Chloe added another curse to the mix. My left eyebrow was stinging. I touched it gingerly and brought my fingers away wet. Ben's ring made a wicked knuckle duster.

Chloe said urgently, 'You won't press charges?'

'Probably not.' Ben had enough problems, and it had been an accident. Kind of. But I needed to deal with the blood dripping into my eye. 'Got a tissue?'

She drew one from her hoodie pocket and handed it to me, along with my phone. 'Are you OK?'

'Never better.' I dabbed at the cut.

Ben said gruffly, 'Sorry. But I'm still taking her.'

'Actually, we could,' Chloe said. 'I watch a lot of true crime. There's no way to lift fingerprints from animal fur.'

Chloe Naylor was full of surprises, but fingerprints were not the only issue. The forensics team would want to assess the whole picture.

On the other hand, we had to leave the site to call the police, and splitting up was too dangerous – and judging from Ben's truculent expression, he was not about to compromise.

I picked myself up. 'Sod it. Bring her.'

At my insistence, Ben wrapped Maisie in a tea towel from the caravan, which concealed her injuries as well as masking the worst of the smell. We made our way to the car, Ben cradling the puppy, and all of us alert for a dark figure rushing us with a knife; but if Conor or a third party was still here, they were lying low.

The youngsters chose the back seat, Chloe jumping out to open the inner and outer gates and lock them behind us.

The fog was thicker than ever in the lane. Driving with care, while using the tissue to mop persistent trickles, I glanced in the rear-view mirror. Ben and Chloe were talking inaudibly, heads close together, a phone lighting their faces from below.

'Harry lives near here, right?' I asked her.

'We just passed the turn.'

'Want to pick up your car?'

'No, I'll stay with Ben. I'll get a lift tomorrow to fetch it.'

Her reflected face was all innocence. Surely Jackson's daughter could not be implicated in whatever had happened at the airfield tonight? And yet ...

'Must have been a lonely walk,' I said. 'Why not drive?'

'No gate key. It's too big to keep on my fob. I squeezed through the gap next to the gate post.'

Ben muttered, 'I thought you'd dumped Harry sodding Diment.'

'It's complicated.'

'He's a twat.'

'Benji! I'll forgive you this once, but you mustn't be mean about him.'

Ben scowled; but their body language, the way they mirrored each other with a tilt of the head, a shrug of the shoulders, implied a more intimate connection than platonic friendship. I hoped for Ben's sake that Chloe was not playing games.

'Any signal yet?' I asked.

'One bar,' she said. 'I'll wait for two. We're going to ring Ben's cousin Tommie first. Dr Moss – she's the local vet. The police will want a necropsy done. That's what they call an autopsy for animals.'

Another snippet from the annals of true crime, no doubt.

Ben's phone rang, playing the old motorcycle anthem "Born to be Wild". Since he was holding Maisie, Chloe plunged her hand into his jeans pocket to retrieve it. She answered it on speaker, and a woman's voice spoke into the car, low-pitched and calm.

'Ben, I thought I'd ring, as you hadn't picked up my message. Any word from David yet?'

'Tommie, it's me,' Chloe said. 'Something horrible has happened.' She put the vet in the picture, though she allowed Dr Moss to assume that we had all found Maisie together. No mention was made of hiding in the hangar.

The vet was quick to take control of the situation. 'Bring her straight to the surgery. I'll meet you there. Have you contacted the police, or would you like me to do that?'

Chloe held the phone up for Ben to answer for himself. 'I'll do it, thanks,' he said. 'They'll want to ask me about Dave.'

'Of course. I'm so sorry about Maisie.'

Since he was unable to answer, Chloe ended the call, giving Ben time to compose himself before she tapped in a call to Bridgwater. This time, the police took his concerns for his brother seriously. After keeping him on hold, the duty officer informed him that Detective Sergeant Lampert would meet him at his home address within the hour.

The last phone call was to Alf, to save him from

thinking the worst if the police arrived before us. The old man reacted with gruff monosyllables, keeping his emotions under wraps. His final comment was a kindly instruction to Ben. 'Hold up, lad, and get yourself home!'

For the rest of the journey, we barely spoke. No one said aloud what we must all have been thinking.

We no longer expected David to turn up safe and well.

EIGHT

Netherzoy was at the northern edge of the Levels, its narrow High Street sloping uphill to where the vet's clinic stood alone, set back from the road.

The lights were on when we got there. On the drive, a yellow van bore the logo 'Netherzoy Vets', the V curved like a heart.

Dr Moss strode to meet us, buttoning her white coat over a flowered skirt. Her age was hard to determine. Late thirties, perhaps. At close quarters she had a steady gaze and an air of authority, along with an abundance of coppery hair that shimmered under the security light.

She might have stepped straight out of a Pre-Raphaelite painting, like a queen from some Arthurian romance, sprung to life on a foggy night in Avalon.

My imagination was running riot. There was no excuse, but despite the grim circumstances, my pulse rate doubled.

She dispensed with greetings but gave me a nod and a peremptory 'Kester? Thomasina Moss,' before focusing her attention on the puppy. Ben opened the tea towel, and the vet drew a long breath. When she looked up, her face showed as much anger as sorrow. 'You didn't see anyone, at the field or in the lane? And no sign that David or Conor had been there?'

Dejectedly, we acknowledged our failure. Thomasina put her arm around Ben.

'My dear, I know you can't help worrying, but the police will be checking every camera along David's route. We'll soon know where he went.'

Even if that were true, the news might not be good. None of us said so.

'We'll start the necropsy tomorrow,' Thomasina added.

Chloe protested, 'Can't you do it now?' in the tone of a young woman accustomed to dictating terms.

'It will take time,' the vet replied, with admirable restraint, 'and I'll need an assistant.'

Ben transferred the puppy into her arms. 'What will happen to her ... afterwards?'

'I'll arrange a cremation. David can decide what to do with her ashes.' Thomasina regarded him with compassion. 'Say your goodbyes, Ben.'

He kissed Maisie's head before turning blindly to Chloe, and the girl gathered him in like a mother.

I asked Thomasina quietly, 'Guess you'll be working closely with the police?'

'It won't be the first time. Not many vets are qualified pathologists, and most of those work in industry or education.' She suddenly frowned, moving to one side so that the light fell on my face. 'That looks sore. What happened?'

'Fell over in the dark.'

She eyed me quizzically as if sensing a lie, but let it go. 'I can glue it, if you like.'

'Thanks, but we need to get back to meet the cops.'

'Ah, yes.' Her eyes were the deep grey-green of a stormy sea. A man could drown there. 'I'm glad you were with the young ones tonight, Kester. It was good of you.'

I didn't ask her to call me Kit. Self-preservation, maybe.

'David wanted me to meet him at the field,' I said. 'I couldn't make it in time.'

It wasn't much of an explanation, but she understood. 'You can't blame yourself,' she said.

'Just wish things had turned out differently.'

She slowly nodded, as if making a professional assessment. 'I'll take Chloe home, then you and Ben can go straight back to Netherzoy.'

I accepted the offer with gratitude, relieved to shed some of the responsibility. It had been a long day, and David's mild-mannered brother had packed quite a punch. My head was throbbing.

Before we left, Chloe kissed Ben goodbye with a tenderness that must have given him hope, false or otherwise. The two women watched us drive away, Thomasina cradling her sad little burden.

On the short journey to Spindlewood, Ben tried both David's and Conor's phones again, but they were still switched off.

We made it back before the police got there, and Alf directed me to the upstairs bathroom to clean myself up. The cut was clotting, though raising my eyebrow threatened to open it. I pinched a couple of Steri-Strips from an oil-stained first-aid pack on the windowsill and went down to join the others.

My plated dinner, courtesy of Alf, was waiting on a lap tray, in a living room with a pale green suite and flowered scatter cushions. The fireplace looked original but was now filled by a gas fire, nineteenth century character blending with modern comforts.

Above the mantelpiece, a photo montage showed David, Ben and their parents at home and on holiday, Ben a small child in many of the pics. The smiles were spontaneous, unforced, body language casually affectionate. A united family, at ease with themselves and each other.

I flinched from thinking that Ben might be the only

one left. My appetite had deserted me, and I gave up as soon as Ben abandoned his own dinner. He poured us all a triple whisky, neat, which eased my headache a bit.

When the police knocked, Alf jumped as if he had been shot. With astonishing speed, he gathered up reading glasses, whisky and a magazine, bade us a muttered goodnight, and stomped upstairs. Ben went to answer the door, saying over his shoulder, 'Unc got collared for shoplifting as a kid. The cop had hold of him but he wriggled free. I swear he thinks they're still after him.'

The visitors wore jeans and casual tops, as if dragged away from an evening at home. Detective Sergeant Catherine Lampert had a severe haircut, a wrinkled forehead and no laugh lines. Detective Constable George Bailey was a well-built black man of around my own age, with a haircut sculpted to the shape of his head and a passing resemblance to Denzel Washington in his prime. His good looks were enhanced by a sympathetic expression.

The phrase *good cop, bad cop* popped facetiously into my head, the result of too much whisky on an empty stomach, and for the first time I realised that we were not only witnesses but suspects.

Having established our identities and the fact that the absent Alf had not been with us at the airfield, DS Lampert explained that they would take our statements in separate rooms. To prevent collusion, she meant. Leaving her DC with Ben, she suggested to me that we use the kitchen.

'Been in a fight?' she asked, closing the door behind us.

I stuck with the fell-over-in-the-dark story. After

holding my gaze impassively for a second or two, she sat down and motioned me to do the same, giving me a printed template to complete, specifically about the events at Merlin Park. It took a while, but she was patient. She also asked if I preferred her to use my forename. I agreed readily, thinking some informality might thaw her out a bit.

'How do you know the Macraes, Kester?' she asked, taking a notebook from her inside pocket.

I explained about the village history project. I also mentioned David phoning me from his car, though it was hard to recall the conversation word for word. Lampert pressed me on the important points.

'David stated that this antique belonged to an acquaintance of Conor Yandle's. You're certain of that?'

'Yes.'

'And it was Mr Yandle who chose Merlin Park as the location?'

'Definitely.'

'At the field, did Chloe Naylor say why she'd hidden from you?'

'She said she got scared when she heard my car.'

'Expecting some kind of trouble?'

'Just freaked out, I think. It was creepy as hell out there. Thick fog, and no one but the owls for company.'

If the girl had held anything back, to protect Harry, she would have to decide for herself what to tell Lampert.

The DS frowned over her notebook, then tucked it away in an inside pocket. 'Will you be able to call into Bridgwater Police Centre tomorrow, to give a DNA sample for elimination purposes?'

'Sure. What's the legal penalty for killing a dog?'

She tilted her head back, literally looking down her

nose at me. 'Unless it's self-defence, anything from a hefty fine to a five-year prison term.'

In my view, Maisie's killer would struggle to justify his brutality. I couldn't imagine the puppy giving anyone more than a nip.

'Have you spoken to Conor yet?' I asked.

'Talking to Mr Yandle is a priority.' She was bristly, making me wonder if her colleagues were having trouble tracking him down. 'We'll share any new developments with Ben tomorrow.'

Meaning that, from this point onward, the progress of the investigation was none of my business. Fair point.

We re-entered the living room to find Ben and DC Bailey debating the relative merits of British and Japanese motorcycles. Bailey stood up when his boss came in.

'All done, he said, indicating Ben's statement. Ben himself seemed calmer. He even met Lampert's stiletto gaze to ask what would happen next.

'We'll check ANPR cameras on the M5 and elsewhere along David's planned route,' she said, 'but our primary focus will be the area in and around Netherzoy and Merlin Park. In particular, we'll view the CCTV footage from the industrial estate, village shop and fuel station. The airfield has been sealed off, and two officers will stay there overnight. A forensics team will go in tomorrow.'

Ben saw the detectives out. He shut the door behind them and leant against it, staring at me blankly. He looked in shock. I had planned to go next door as soon as the cops left, but I couldn't leave him like that.

'Want a cuppa?' I asked.

'You sound like my dad, thinking tea can cure

anything.' His face suddenly crumpled, and he slid down with his back against the door and sobbed, arms wrapped around his raised knees.

I abandoned the tea idea and sat down at right angles to him, not speaking, just keeping him company. He could always tell me to piss off, I thought – but he didn't. After a minute or two, he quietened down and wiped his face on the cuff of his hoodie.

'Shit,' he said. 'Sorry.'

'Don't be daft.'

'I haven't given up hope. I won't.'

'Good,' I said, not sure that was the best answer. 'How did the chat with Bailey go?'

'I know George.' Ben hiccupped, and took a moment to steady his breathing. 'He went out with Tommie for a while. Gorgeous George, she calls him. He's restoring a vintage Norton.'

Lampert had been clever, choosing the constable to take Ben's statement – the fellow biker instead of the stern detective sergeant.

'There's stuff I need to do,' Ben said.

'Tonight?'

'George thinks I should get the locks changed at Dave's house. In case Conor's got his keys and … and something with his address on. I want to go up there anyway, in case … well, I just want to, you know?'

'The cops won't be searching there?'

'George doesn't think so. He asked if Dave keeps a list of contacts at home, but they'll be in his phone and laptop, and he'll have those on him.'

'In any case,' I said, 'Conor will be keeping his head down tonight, so the locks can wait till tomorrow. Do you work Saturdays?'

'No – and I don't have to go in till Dave comes home. Jackson rang while I was with George.'

'How about the carnival? Are you meant to be on a lorry?'

'They're called carts. No, I don't do acting and stuff.'

'OK, so you can ring a locksmith in the morning, and we'll drive up and meet him at David's place.'

'You mean ... you'll come with me?'

'It'd make sense. Take one vehicle to Bridgwater, go on from there.'

He seemed relieved at being presented with a plan, but then frowned as another thought occurred. 'A locksmith will cost a bit. Emergency call-out, on a weekend.'

It would cost hundreds, probably. I hoped he could afford it.

But that was tomorrow's problem. I clambered wearily to my feet. It was nearly eleven o'clock. Less than six hours ago, I had been saying goodbye to Lissa and looking forward to a second honeymoon in a rural idyll.

'Think I'll turn in,' I said. 'Happy to leave around nine-thirty?'

'OK.' He looked at the key rack near my head. 'The keys to Yew Tree are on the puffin fob.'

I hooked them down.

'Sorry about your eye,' he said.

I grinned ruefully, indicating his ring. 'That's quite a weapon.'

He turned his hand so that the RAF wings caught the light. 'It belonged to my Grandad Thomas. I always liked it. Dave says pilots gave brooches like this to their wives and girlfriends back in the day, but he's never seen one made into a ring. It's unique.'

'Your Grandad was in the RAF?'

'No, he was head gardener up at Zoyland House. The Naylors' place. Jackson's dad – old Mr Oscar – he was a Spitfire pilot in the war. He might've given it to Grandad as a keepsake, like.'

'Unusual gift to a member of staff.'

'Yeah.' Ben hesitated, as if inclined to say more, but then he shrugged. 'S'pose we'll never know for sure, will we?' he said.

NINE

Although Yew Tree Cottage was structurally a mirror image of next door, the paintwork inside was pale cream with caramel-coloured feature walls, while oak kitchen surfaces matched the drop-leaf table and chairs. Inoffensive and relaxing, perfect for a holiday let.

A glance inside the cupboards revealed full canisters of tea and coffee and even a bottle of Merlot. There was also fresh milk in the fridge and ice cubes in the freezer. Quite a welcome pack.

I made coffee while checking my phone. Lissa had left three voicemails, sounding increasingly anxious. Half an hour ago she had resorted to texting, *Are you OK? Call me. I'll wait up. x*

When I called, she answered fast. She had been waiting, as promised. 'Kit! I'd almost given up on you.' Her voice was taut, but she would hear my excuses before blaming me. 'Did David arrive OK?'

I brought her up to date, glossing over the more gruesome details, but the facts were shocking enough. As I had feared, she was very upset. Sometimes it seemed as if losing Emily had flayed our hearts raw, so that other people's sorrows hurt more than they used to. Although Lissa often showed a strength and resilience that I struggled to emulate, tonight she said she had been feeling sad anyway. I wanted to leap in the car and drive back to her, but was way over the alcohol limit.

'I'm sorry,' she said at last, gasping slightly, still trying not to sob. 'I haven't even asked how you're feeling.'

'I'm fine, sweetheart.'

'Do you think Conor lied ... about having an antique

to sell? Did he just want to get David somewhere lonely, to steal the car?'

'No, it's too complicated. He could have nicked the car overnight, from next door's drive. I'm sure you can clone keys from outside the owner's house with a phone and a transmitter.'

'Oh. I've just thought ... Should we make a start on David's project, as if nothing has happened?'

'I think we have to. We can't assume he's not coming back.'

'You should ask Ben and Alf. It has to be their decision.'

We agreed on that, and Lissa pointed out that I could leave the hire car at Robyn's house, as Ben and I were coming as far as Ledbury anyway. Then we could all drive back to Netherzoy together.

'Let's call in at Gordano Services on the way down,' she added. 'It'll be around teatime, so the same staff might be there. Even if the police have spoken to them already, we might pick up something they've missed.'

'Guess so.' I was past making the effort to think positive.

'Kit ...' she said. 'In spite of all this ... I meant it, about the second honeymoon.'

'We're not giving up on that,' I said, adding impulsively, 'I love you, Amphelisia.'

I only used her full forename in especially tender moments. She made some small sound. Perhaps a sob, quickly stifled.

'Love you too,' she said.

After she had rung off, I felt too restless to go straight to bed. There were logs, kindling and matches beside the hearth in the living room, so I lit the wood-burning stove, seeking comfort in warmth.

Three raps on the front door made me start. Fearing the worst, I dashed to open it.

On the doorstep stood Dr Thomasina Moss, carrying a stack of photo albums. Clearly she had not come with bad news, but that failed to slow my heartrate. Water droplets, condensed from the fog, glistened in her coppery hair, and she wore a lace-edged green and grey shawl that looked Victorian and matched her eyes.

'Any news?' I asked.

'Afraid not. I'm staying at Spindlewood tonight, to give the lads some support. I wouldn't have called so late, but your lights were on, and I'd brought these.' She handed me the albums. 'They're Mum's. She won't mind you borrowing them, though I'll check with her when I visit. She's in residential care since her stroke.'

'Oh ... thanks.'

Instead of leaving, she leant forward a little, breathing in the warm air from the hall. 'You've lit the stove. There's a sandalwood candle on the coffee table, if that's your thing. It's said to dispel negative energies.'

Unconvinced that a scent would raise my spirits, I smiled politely. 'So you helped get the place ready for us?' I said.

'Just finishing touches.' She frowned at my left eye. 'Ben confessed, by the way. Thank you for lying to the police – and for not hitting him back. He's such a pussycat, I wouldn't have believed he'd do such a thing.'

'Mitigating circumstances.'

'You're very generous.' She tilted her head, looking past me towards the kitchen. She was a few years older than I had first thought. The beginnings of wrinkles fanned out from the corners of her eyes. 'Do you have everything you need?' she asked.

I began to suspect her motives. It was nearly midnight, and she could have left the albums next door.

'Ben thought of everything,' I said. 'Even wine.'

That was a mistake.

'He's a dear boy,' she said. 'I wouldn't say no to a nightcap.'

It would have been churlish to refuse, or so I told myself. I stood aside, and she stepped past me, slipping her feet out of her pumps and heading for the kitchen. The shawl and skirt rippled with the sway of her hips, and her musky perfume lingered in my nostrils.

I followed her. She was opening and closing the fridge and cupboards. 'Coffee, tea, sugar, milk. Perfect.' She picked up the bottle of Merlot and asked, if daring me to accept, 'Shall we?'

We moved to the warm living room, but I remained standing. Thomasina sank into an armchair and crossed her knees, bending to massage an instep. 'I've been on my feet since eight this morning. I was at home for a grand total of twenty minutes before Ben rang. Occupational hazard, of course.'

'How is he?'

'I persuaded him to get his head down.'

'And you?'

She slanted me a rueful look. 'Oh, I'm the proverbial tower of strength. Ask anyone.'

'Tough role.'

'Is that the voice of experience?'

I shook my head. 'I wish.'

'To be honest, I don't think it's sunk in yet. Who would want to hurt David, of all people? And poor little Maisie …' She drew breath shakily and sipped her wine, green eyes watching me over the rim. 'You're different in real life, aren't you? Quieter.'

'Not always.'

'I must rewatch your programme about the Levels. *Ghosts of Avalon.*'

'I'm flattered you remember it.'

'You were compelling. Passionate. I remember that.'

The subtext was unmistakable. I said firmly, 'I'm married, Thomasina.'

'Good. I'm allergic to commitment.'

'Happily,' I added.

'Ah.' She finished her wine quickly and set down the glass. 'Thank you for that. I do feel better. Or at least, marginally less sober.'

'Don't knock it.'

In the hallway, I opened the door as she slipped her shoes on. A floorboard creaked on the landing, and she glanced up the stairs.

'Did your wife drive down after all?' she asked.

'No. She'll be here tomorrow.'

Thomasina wrapped the shawl more securely around herself, and her teasing smile flickered. 'All old houses have their own sounds, don't they? A creak here, a sigh there. As individual as a fingerprint.'

'Nice analogy. I might use it in the new series.'

'You're welcome.'

She left in a swirl of diaphanous skirts and heady perfume. Closing the front door behind her, I looked up the stairs myself, but there was nothing to see, and nothing to hear except the sighs of an old house settling for the night.

I damped down the wood burner and took my suitcase upstairs. The four-poster bed was a pleasant surprise. I visualised Lissa lying naked there, huge dark eyes smiling an invitation ... imagined burying my hands in her hair and my face between her breasts ... knew so well her curves and the smell of her skin that I could close my eyes and almost feel her.

I sent her a photo of the bed, alongside a heart emoji. No words were needed. She pinged a heart back.

Before turning in, I explored the other upstairs rooms. The bathroom was newly fitted out. When I flicked the light on, my reflection in the cabinet mirror stared back at me: grim, bruised and dishevelled. There were splashes of dried blood on my shirt. Thinking selfishly of how Lissa and I had dreamed of a relaxing break, I found myself scowling, which didn't improve the image.

The second bedroom was a small twin – and cold, owing to the sash window being raised a few centimetres. I opened it fully and leant on the sill. The garden, as David had warned us, was overgrown, though with newly dug borders awaiting plants. At the far end was an old tree, the yew for which the cottage was named.

This was the last house in Peat Cutters' Lane. Over the back fence, the bare branches of an orchard clawed upward out of a sea of low-lying fog. Beyond that, the silhouette of Netherzoy's church tower showed black against the overcast sky.

My hand brushed something on the sill. A brass bowl, decorated around the rim with a repeated motif – a pentagram inside a circle, flanked on either side by a crescent moon.

I was familiar with the symbols of most religions. This one was used in Wicca, the modern incarnation of paganism. Interesting. Although nearby Glastonbury remembered its Christian roots – Jesus and his uncle were said to have visited, a legend which had inspired William Blake's "Jerusalem" – these days the town was a spiritual hub for every belief system imaginable. Ornaments like the one in my hand would be sold all along the High Street. Probably this was another of Thomasina's finishing touches.

Shivering in the night air, I lowered the sash to the point where it stuck fast, and went to bed.

It was impossible to sleep. I couldn't stop thinking about David and Conor. Had they fallen out over the valuation? If the argument had grown heated and Maisie had perceived a threat and bitten Conor, he might have lost his temper. David could have reacted to that.

Then there was Harry Diment. Chloe had been firmly against us collecting her car from outside his house. Did she suspect that he was involved and want to speak with him in private before Ben or I did?

Too many unanswerable questions. Silence settled around me, accentuated rather than broken by the occasional creak or sigh, the sounds that old properties make as the outside temperature changes.

My bedroom door, which I had left ajar, clicked shut. A draught from the open sash in the other room, no doubt. Ben or I would need to fix that. I didn't want Lissa to feel spooked. She was sensitive that way.

I was more of a sceptic, though my TV scripts sometimes implied otherwise; but tonight, perhaps because of the evening's traumatic events, the air seemed to move around me like the whisper of old memories.

Almost as if the cottage itself had a story to tell.

TEN

In the morning, suffering from a mild hangover and too few hours' sleep, I was still in my dressing-gown when there was another knock at the door. This time I refused to anticipate bad news and walked at normal speed to open it.

Ben stood there, holding a large pack of croissants and a jar of strawberry jam. 'Unc's still in bed and Tommie's gone to work. Want to share breakfast?'

In other words, he needed company.

'Sure, why not?'

In the kitchen, he sat at the table and stretched out his long legs, as he must have done countless times when his great-aunt and uncle had lived here.

'Still no word from David?' I asked.

'Nope.'

I poured him a coffee (black, three sugars), set it down in front of him, and caught him staring at my chest, the neck of my dressing-gown having fallen open.

He blinked and averted his gaze. 'Sorry, I wasn't ...'

'It's fine.'

I was used to the occasional curious stare at the beach or swimming pool. Not many people my age carried the long vertical scar of open-heart surgery, let alone the puckered mark of a puncture wound alongside, souvenir of the blade which had nearly killed me.

'Four years ago,' I said. 'Family issues.'

'I remember that, kind of, 'cause Dave went on about you being in the news. I don't really watch live TV. How did –'

'How many croissants do you want?'

He took the hint. Aside from occasional nightmares

and an aversion to bladed weapons – surely a pretty normal hang-up – I had recovered and moved on. End of story.

We talked instead about motorbikes, and Ben enthused about flying. Many of the airfields he had visited were named for obscure villages rather than the nearest major town, so he brought up Google Maps to show me. Since the conversation brought a smile to his face, I was happy to encourage him.

'Where next, then?' I asked.

He shrugged, grimacing. 'Chloe wants me to fly her to Lundy Island. She won't risk landing one of her dad's planes there.'

I should have anticipated that Jackson's daughter would be a pilot too – but I had only the vaguest idea of Lundy's location, somewhere off the North Devon coast.

'What's wrong with it?' I asked, starting on my third croissant.

'What isn't? Ten miles offshore, no fuel on site, sheep grazing on the runway – plus it's lumpy enough to break the nosewheel. I'll talk Chloe into going on the ferry next spring. It's her favourite place in the world.'

I raised incredulous brows. 'Must be special.'

'It's nice. We've been loads of times ... Mum and Dad and Dave and me.' He stopped and shook his head, fiercely in denial. 'He's not gone. He can't be.'

Not wanting either to raise his hopes or dash them, I stood up and went to the window, resting a hand fleetingly on Ben's shoulder in passing. I drew the curtains back, letting in the grey dawn light. The yew looked taller and more ominous than it had from upstairs. Too dense for light to penetrate, it cast a deep shadow over that end of the garden.

'I'd like a closer look at the old tree,' I said.

'OK. It's got some history, if you're interested.'

Aware of time constraints, I bounded upstairs to dress, and then we went down the garden together. Although the yew was mainly on our side of the boundary, it had long since encroached on next door. The last panel of the boundary fence was missing to accommodate its immense girth.

'It's a thousand years old, Unc says.' Ben had lowered his voice to a respectful murmur. 'But yews can live three times that long.'

I laid a hand on the gnarled trunk. The past was not only my bread and butter, it was a passion. This tree had been alive since William the Conqueror's time. A youngster, compared to those which had seen the building of Iron Age hillforts, but still a witness to centuries of forgotten lives.

Directly above us, just out of reach, a single bough stretched horizontally over the lawn.

'I wouldn't tell a proper paying guest, like,' Ben said, 'but Unc's mum hanged herself from that.'

I turned to him, shocked. 'David didn't say where it happened. And Alf chose to go on living here, even after he was married?'

Ben shrugged. 'Him and Grandad Thomas were happy as little kids. That was all Unc remembered, before the nightmares started – and they were asleep when she did it. A neighbour found her next morning and made sure the kids didn't see. After that, an aunt brought them up and this place stood empty. Old Mr Oscar, Jackson's dad, he never even tried to let it. But then, when Unc and Auntie May got married, he offered it to them at a crazy low rent.'

In Alf's place, I would have paid good money *not* to live here.

'And then Grandad Thomas wanted to be next door,' Ben added, 'so Mr Oscar moved Spindlewood's tenants along the lane, and Grandad and Grandma moved in.'

'Spindlewood's tenancy passed to your mum and dad, and now you?'

He nodded.

'And Jackson doesn't mind Alf sub-letting this place?'

'Jackson funded the renovation. Said it'll pay for itself in the end.'

'He sounds like a dream landlord.'

'Yeah, he's an old softie. The Naylors have always been good to our family, 'cause Great-Grandad Freddie was Mr Oscar's valet. His personal servant, like.' Ben shot me a look. 'Unc says his mum slams doors.'

I raised my eyebrows. 'Barbara's haunting her old home?'

'You haven't had trouble that way, then?'

'There's a draught. The sash in the second bedroom is stuck open.'

Ben looked relieved. He wouldn't want a door-slamming ghost to erode his uncle's profits. 'I'll fix that,' he said.

As we walked back up the garden, he suggested we take the bike to Bridgwater and Ledbury, since I could wear his dad's old helmet and leathers. Regretfully, I explained that the hire car needed to end up at my sister's.

Ben went home to check that his uncle was fit to be left alone all day. Last night Alf had seemed pretty able, but Ben confided that he was often edgy and restless in the mornings. The disturbing dreams had become a nightly occurrence.

I asked the hire company to collect the car from Robyn's house after three, and Ben returned at nine-thirty as arranged. He had booked a locksmith to meet us at David's house at one, and Alf had insisted that he was fine and we must 'go and do the necessary'.

But during the journey to Bridgwater Police Centre, our first stop, Ben grew increasingly nervous and started fidgeting with his ear piercings.

I tried to reassure him. 'The cops will have watched the camera footage by now. If there was any news, George would have been in touch.'

'Chloe says when someone disappears, the people closest to them are always the prime suspects.'

Thanks for that, Chloe!

'Lampert will soon chuck that theory out,' I said. 'What did you make of Chloe's story? Think she saw anything suspicious at the airfield before we got there?'

'Course not. She'd have told me.'

Not if she was shielding Harry Diment – or Conor.

'How well does she know Conor?' I asked.

'Outside of work, you mean? She must see him now and then, 'cause he's Harry's mate. Harry and the Yandles are next-door neighbours.'

I whistled. 'Conor and Harry, eh?'

'Wait a minute!' His voice rose angrily as he realised where my questions were headed. 'You're not thinking Chloe could be involved?'

'Just kicking ideas around.'

He was silent for a couple of miles. Finally, he said, 'Look, I trust Chloe, all right? She'd never lie to me. And she's a Grail Knight.'

'A what?'

'It's our friendship group from school. Like in King Arthur's knights, who went looking for the Holy Grail. The girls got into all that after your show went out. They had this thing about us all being loyal forever, not judging, always having each other's backs.'

It gave me a lift, my programme having encouraged a group of youngsters to embrace the legends, even owning them to help cement lasting friendships.

Ben sank again into his own thoughts, perhaps working out how to cajole the truth out of Chloe. Honesty may not have been a required virtue among the knights of history and legend, but courage and honour had been high on the list.

For Ben's sake, I hoped Chloe would remember that.

ELEVEN

With a frontage displaying a lot of glass, the police centre resembled a prestigious company HQ. It also had a decent-sized car park.

I reminded Ben not to fiddle guiltily with his studs as we strolled in like the innocent witnesses we were. The desk officer, a young woman with a peachy complexion and a serious manner, took our names, and another uniformed officer escorted us to have our cheeks swabbed for DNA, unlocking interior doors and securing them again behind us. Ben grew more jittery than ever.

'Chill, OK?' I murmured. 'We're the good guys.'

'Hope Lampert knows that.'

After the swabs were taken, the detective sergeant herself turned up to take Ben to watch camera footage from last night.

'Can Kit come as well?' he asked.

'If you'd like his support.'

She ushered us into a bare, functional room in the interview suite. A camera mounted near the ceiling watched impassively. There must have been a microphone too. We sat facing Lampert across a desk, and she opened her laptop.

'The ANPR cameras have been helpful,' she said, clicking away. 'The fog was an issue, but we do have footage of David's car leaving the motorway at Junction 24, southbound, shortly before five pm yesterday. CCTV outside the convenience store in Netherzoy shows his car again at five-nineteen, driving east along the High Street.'

She turned the laptop to show us. The camera was angled downwards at the shop entrance, but the pavement was narrow enough to leave some of the road in shot. An

Audi could be seen driving past, the number plate briefly visible.

'Eleven minutes before David was due to meet Conor,' I said.

'Indeed. His phone was last active at five-twenty-seven.'

Ben put in, 'It would've gone out of range along Merlin's Lane, before he reached the park.'

'That's correct. Also, Ben, the cameras inside and outside the shop recorded you buying vegetables at five-twenty-eight, which confirms your statement.'

'And gives you an alibi,' I added.

'Precisely,' Lampert said. 'I'd like you to identify this male, if you can.' She brought up another video clip, this time of the Audi stationary outside Merlin Park's outer gate while the driver opened the padlock. Thanks to the security light, it was a clear shot.

Ben drew a startled breath. 'That's Dave. Hundred percent.'

Lampert's finger was poised over the mouse. 'Before I show you the next clip, I need to warn you not to jump to any conclusions.'

Ben stared at her, then at the screen again, wild-eyed, terrified of what might be coming next. I felt a few qualms myself.

Lampert clicked the mouse. The new image showed a time of 19:24, less than half an hour before we had reached the park ourselves. This time the Audi was inside the site, facing the gate. A hooded man, averagely tall, got out of the driver's door and opened the padlock.

I went cold. Ben leapt up so quickly that his chair fell over, thudding onto the thin carpet. 'That's not Dave.'

I stood up myself and put a hand on his shoulder. 'It

might not be bad news, Ben. It could mean anything.'

'Is it Conor?'

'Do *you* think it's Conor?' Lampert said. 'Take a good look, Ben.'

'I can't see past the hoodie, can I? Can't *you* guess if it's him? You must have his mugshot. And why is he driving Dave's car?'

'We don't yet know that, but David may have been a passenger.'

'But he couldn't have been OK, or he'd have been driving. And he'd have taken Maisie's body.'

'We're not making any assumptions.' Her voice had lost its abrasive edge. She sounded quite kindly. 'The male in this footage is not necessarily the same person who killed David's dog. One possibility is that Conor and David surprised one or more intruders. If David was injured, Conor may have driven him to a hospital. We're checking that.'

'I rang the hospitals before we went to the airfield. If he was brought in later, they'd have called me.'

'Shifts change, things can slip through the net. We're seeking information on any unidentified males brought in last night, especially those with injuries that could have delayed identification.'

The colour drained from Ben's face. 'You mean, like ... their faces bashed in?'

'I meant they could be unconscious.'

I righted the fallen chair and gently urged him to sit down again. He complied in shaking silence. I sat beside him, as before.

'I'm sorry, Ben.' The frown lines between Lampert's brows had deepened. 'I know this is difficult, but I want you to understand that we're exploring every avenue.'

He didn't reply.

'George may be the local man, born and bred on the Levels,' she said, 'but living in Bridgwater doesn't make me a foreigner. This is my community, too.'

She was telling us, I thought, that she was not the 'bad cop', and that her cool demeanour didn't imply lack of feeling.

'Have you spoken to Conor Yandle?' I asked.

She hesitated, then answered carefully, 'He didn't go home last night.'

From the sour twist to her mouth, I gathered she was aware of the rumours surrounding Conor's night-time exploits. 'Out on the rob', as Ben had termed it.

'Today,' she said, 'Conor has not been at work but hasn't called in sick. Yesterday he and Harry Diment knocked off at five. Does that tie in with what you remember, Ben?'

'I don't know.' He raked a hand through his curls, clearly struggling to think straight. 'I left after that, and I'm in the workshop, not the kitchen.'

'Harry's lying,' I said, 'or leaving something out. He didn't go home at five. Chloe was still waiting for him at seven. That's when she got bored and walked from his house to the airfield.'

Lampert tapped her fingernails on the desk in a fast, impatient rhythm, her face giving no clue to her thoughts – but she would have known already that Harry's statement didn't tally with Chloe's.

'When we got to the field,' I said, 'we didn't see another car. Conor's must be on the footage as well, arriving and leaving – and if Conor took David's car, somebody else drove his away.'

Lampert pursed her lips, seeming to debate inwardly

how much to tell us. Eventually, she replied, 'All of the units at Merlin Park closed at five. The Audi was the only vehicle to enter the site after that, and Chloe was the only pedestrian. The male in the footage that you've seen, who may or may not be Conor, was either already on-site when the park closed, or he gained access via another route. We'll be consulting with Mr Naylor, as the landowner, about that.'

'There's a stile,' Ben said, 'on the south side of the airfield.' He was still pale but didn't seem in imminent danger of keeling over. 'A footpath starts from there.'

Lampert's sparse eyebrows rose. 'And leads where?'

'Round the fields, to the far end of Honeysuckle Row, where the Yandles and Harry live.'

'I was in Honeysuckle Row last night,' she said, 'and again this morning.'

'You saw the gate, then.'

'I did. You're saying there's a path all the way from those two cottages to the airfield, so you'd never touch Merlin's Lane or the main entrance to the park?'

He nodded. 'Chloe's used it. Not last night, 'cause of all the rain. She doesn't like getting her Gucci trainers muddy, but it's safer at night than walking along the lane.'

Lampert turned her laptop to hide the screen from us and began typing. 'Also convenient,' she said, 'if someone didn't have a key to the park or the combination to the inner gate.'

'Or,' I murmured, 'if they didn't want their face on camera.'

Lampert raised her eyes from the screen. 'Agreed. The path could be significant.'

If Conor had gone that way, I thought, Harry might

have been with him, having locked his own car in his garage after work. Whatever Harry had been up to, he hadn't wanted Chloe to know about it.

'Have forensics come up with anything?' I asked.

'We should have the report this afternoon. It's not helpful that you two removed the dog from the scene.' She glanced at Ben, who avoided her eyes. 'However, the blood on her fur is being analysed, in case any is human. There is also a chance that she bit her attacker, in which case their DNA may be in her mouth.'

Ben put a hand to his stomach. 'I don't feel well.'

That ended the interview fast. Lampert escorted us as far as the door to the toilets, but once inside, he didn't actually throw up.

'None of this seems real, Kit,' he groaned, leaning on a washbasin. 'I keep thinking I'll wake up any minute.'

I wondered how he would cope with going into David's home. 'If you'd rather I dropped you back,' I said, 'I can meet the locksmith.'

'No.' He took a deep breath. 'It's down to me. If anything looks out of place, some sort of clue or whatever, I'm the one who'll know. You don't even have to come.'

'I'm the chauffeur. You're lumbered with me.'

'Oh … yeah. Thanks. I need to keep telling myself it'll all be OK. If Dave wasn't coming back, I'd know.'' He splashed cold water on his face, dried it on a paper towel, and squared his shoulders. 'Let's go to Ledbury, then.'

Lampert took us back to the desk, performing the unlocking and re-locking routine personally. 'George Bailey will stay in regular contact,' she told Ben. 'We don't have a dedicated family liaison officer available, but he'll fill that role and keep you updated. If you have any questions, George will be the person to ask.'

I mentioned our plans to change the locks at David's house. She approved and asked the desk officer to give Ben a crime reference number, along with George's contact details, to enable David to claim the cost against his house insurance at a later date.

Or Ben as his executor, I thought.

As we walked back to the car, hunched against the persistent rain, Ben shot me a puzzled look. 'Why are you doing all this?' he asked. 'Don't get me wrong, but we don't even know each other, really.'

It was a fair question. The truth was, I was angry – at Conor Yandle, and at Lampert's failure to track him down. Angry at life. Ben and his family had suffered enough grief, without this. He needed all the support he could get.

'You're doing me a favour,' I said lightly. 'How else was I going to fill the day?'

He snorted. 'You do talk some bollocks,' he said.

TWELVE

Since Ben had sought my company earlier, I judged that he would prefer conversation to silence. Half an hour later, having exhausted my limited knowledge of modern motorcycles, I had also established that we had little in common beyond some practical skills. He read nothing except flying and bike magazines, had never been to the theatre, and had little awareness of the arts generally but loved Avengers movies – most of which I hadn't seen.

I gave up on shared interests and risked a more personal topic. 'You said the Grail Knights were all mates at school, right?'

'Yep. But we started using that name in Year Eleven, after your show went out.'

'Chloe didn't go to private school?'

Ben shook his head. 'Don't think their mum felt strongly, but Jackson was dead against it. Chloe says he wanted her and Alex to stay grounded, you know? Mind you,' he added, 'Alex is still an entitled little git. He talks to us mechanics like we're shit on his shoe.'

'You report to him? I thought he helped run the flight training school.'

'Yeah, but he's never got enough to do. He's always sodding about, getting in the way. We reckon he'll run the workshop as well when Jackson retires.'

'Will you move on if that happens?'

'Nah. Chloe won't leave, will she?'

'Think you're in with a chance, then, with Chloe?'

He was silent for so long that I added, 'Sorry. None of my business.'

'It's OK. Actually, we dated for three months last year, but we'd got really close before that. After Mum died, and then Dad ... she got it, you know? Because of her own mum. But then Harry Diment got out on licence and Jackson gave him a job in the café kitchen, and that was it. Couple of weeks later, I'm dumped.'

I grimaced.

'She's not playing me.' He was defensive, having accurately gauged my opinion. 'She's confused. Her and Harry, they're kind of on and off, you know?'

'Yeah, well, hope it works out for you.'

'Least I can avoid Harry. I couldn't stay if I had to work with him.'

'He and Conor are not Grail Knights, then?'

'You're joking! Anyway, the Knights are all from our year group. Harry was three years above us, and Conor must be pushing thirty. Chloe wanted to bring Harry in, but there's no way. He's a loser. He'd jump off a cliff if Conor told him to.'

Since the conversation had drifted onto the subject I had hoped to avoid, it seemed worth asking a question that had been niggling at me. 'Could it have been Harry, rather than Conor, driving the Audi away from Merlin Park?'

Ben fell silent again. At last he admitted, 'S'pose so. They don't look alike, but in a hoodie, and from the back ... they're both about your height, and not fat or thin. But Dave was meeting Conor, not Harry, and Conor's the one who's gone to ground.'

All the same, I couldn't stifle the sense that we were missing something, and it had to do with Harry, and Chloe's reluctance to let us anywhere near him last night – plus her visceral reaction to the news of Maisie's killing. She could have a sensitive stomach, but she could also have been panicking about her boyfriend's involvement.

We passed the rest of the journey listening to the radio, channel-hopping in search of music we both liked and groaning in mock despair at each other's favourites – hard rock in my case, techno in his.

Having lived in the Malverns until I was eighteen, I knew the nearby town of Ledbury well, its black-and-white frontages evoking nostalgic memories of teenage mischief. My best mate from school had lived here. This was where we had flashed fake IDs in pubs, with mixed results, and smoked weed in his dad's shed to avoid parental outrage.

David's Victorian terraced house was on the edge of town. The front garden was a neat, low-maintenance square of lawn adorned with a large stone Buddha and two spherical shrubs in pots. We parked on the drive and were relieved to find no evidence of a break-in. Ben picked up the day's unopened mail and sorted a utility bill from the marketing junk, laying the former reverentially on a side table.

'Dave will see it there,' he said.

We checked for windows left open or chargers plugged in, but David had locked up efficiently. Ben coped bravely, concentrating on practicalities. I felt like an intruder. The antique furnishings and rich colours expressed their owner's personality, but the place felt echoingly empty, not helped by the loud ticking of a pendulum wall clock.

The locksmith, a solemn-eyed Pole, arrived early and managed to imply with few words that he preferred to work uninterrupted. He had even brought his own refreshments. He was fast, too. Before two o'clock, we were on our way to Colwall.

Since it was a Saturday, the whole family was at home. Robyn briefed us discreetly that Sam knew nothing about what had happened, which made for a difficult few minutes while we waited downstairs for Lissa to finish packing. My sociable nephew introduced Ben to Soft Brown Dog and chattered about throwing sticks for Maisie and how she was friends with Soft, while Ben fidgeted with an ear stud and glanced longingly at the front door.

Luckily, Sam then noticed my blue and purple eyebrow and wanted to touch the Steri-Strips, returning the favour by showing me a microscopic graze on his elbow; but when Lissa appeared, Ben couldn't hide his relief. I greeted her with a kiss, endured another eyebrow inspection, and carried her oversized case downstairs. She hugged Ben and said kind things about David, almost bringing him to tears.

'Will you drive back?' she asked me. 'Then Ben and I can get to know each other.'

She therefore passed most of the journey twisted round in the passenger seat, and they discovered a shared passion for cooking and gardening. The subject of holidays came up, and Ben mentioned his plan to take Chloe to Lundy Island.

'I was talking to Chloe's grandmother this morning,' Lissa told him. 'She mentioned Lundy too. She said it was like stepping back in time.'

'Chloe and her both love it,' Ben said. 'That's about all they've got in common. They don't get on, really.'

Before we reached the slip road for Gordano Services, Lissa explained to him about calling in there, warning him not to expect too much. Nonetheless, he was quiet as we strolled into Starbucks.

The coffee shop was not too busy. We queued for barely a minute. I asked the young woman who served us whether she had been on shift at this time yesterday. She only worked Saturdays, she said, but Brandon had been here. She pointed out a stocky lad with a scrubbed-clean complexion, adding that he was at university so did regular lates during the week, then the day shift on Saturdays.

We chose the table that he was wiping down, and he flashed us a smile of practised warmth.

'Brandon, is it?' I asked.

He stood up, revealing the name badge at the top of his green apron. 'Hi. Can I help?'

'Our friend David was in here yesterday, between four-thirty and five. We're hoping you might remember seeing him.'

'I'm his brother,' Ben added, showing Brandon a photo on his phone. 'He's gone missing.'

Brandon nodded. 'The police had the same pic. I can only tell you what I told them.'

'That's fine,' I said. 'It'd mean a lot.'

'I remember him because he ordered a puppucino. It's on the secret menu. Free-of-charge cup of whipped cream for dogs. He asked me to give it to his little Westie while he made a call.'

'Did you hear the conversation?'

'Sort of. I didn't mean to listen, but I was right there. I think it was someone he'd talked to earlier. Like he was following up on stuff.'

Ben asked urgently, 'What sort of stuff?'

'Business. Buying and selling.'

'Did you hear the name Conor?' I asked.

Brandon's brow cleared. 'Yeah, that's who he was

calling. He – David – asked him who the seller was. I couldn't remember for the police, but now ... I think it was Fogle, like the guy on TV. Yeah, Mr Fogle. David repeated it back, like he was thinking, wondering if he knew the name. He may have asked if the guy was local.'

I looked a query at Ben, who shrugged. The name meant nothing to him either.

'Know what this Fogle was selling?' I asked Brandon.

'No. Of course, I couldn't hear what Conor said. Sorry.'

'You've been brilliant,' Lissa assured him.

'No problem.' Brandon regarded Ben with sympathy. 'I hope your brother's all right.'

Ben nodded, turning away in depression.

'Thanks, Brandon,' I said. 'We're grateful for your time.'

The barista's face brightened. Gratitude in his line of work was expressed in cash. Lissa gave him ten pounds, and his pleasure left us in no doubt that we had made his day.

I wondered what to make of Fogle. Conor must have rung David earlier to arrange the meeting, then David had had second thoughts and rung him back for more details. If the seller wanted to remain anonymous, Conor would have given David his name in confidence, to reassure the auctioneer that he was acting in good faith; but the name itself could be genuine, or an alias used by the seller, or even Conor's invention.

In the car, we quizzed Ben. He was too crushed to talk much, but stood by his initial reaction. He knew nobody called Fogle or anything similar. Despite his disappointment, he insisted on refunding Lissa for the tip.

There was nothing we could do to help him. Although

hope was sometimes a saviour, having it ripped away could be a route to the abyss. I met his eyes in the mirror. 'Don't despair, Ben,' I said.

'I won't,' he said, defiantly. 'Dave's alive.'

Lissa turned to look forwards again, not wanting Ben to see her face.

Neither of us believed that David was coming home.

THIRTEEN

Back at Spindlewood, we asked Ben and Alf how they felt about us making a start on the research. Both were in favour, although Alf frowned when Lissa asked them to write out a basic family tree.

'Thought this was a village history,' he said, 'not a family memoir. Dave should've told you, I don't want my mum's name dragged in.'

'He did mention that,' Lissa said, 'and he'll write the book. We'll only be sorting the files and doing some interviews.'

The old man was still uneasy. 'I've been having dreams about Mum, ever since Mike – Dave and Ben's dad – starting digging up old stories. Thought I hardly remembered her, but it's like the dreams are bringing things back.'

Lissa asked tentatively, 'But you're still happy for us to go ahead?'

He shrugged. 'Dave's keen. Once it's all done, this old brain' – he tapped a finger against his temple – 'might settle down. Mum might be at peace too. I like to think so.'

We murmured agreement, and I moved the conversation on, not wanting Alf to tell Lissa that Yew Tree Cottage was haunted. As a child, she had once seen what she thought was a ghost.

Ben needed time to gather his dad's research together. He promised to bring it to us at four o'clock, along with the family tree. He was also eager to help us match names to faces and guide us through his dad's filing system, but we agreed that could wait until tomorrow.

Lissa and I were about to leave when he received a

call from Thomasina. He took it in the hall, for privacy, and returned pale and shaken.

'They've finished the necropsy on Maisie,' he said. 'There was blood on her teeth. Tommie thinks her neck was broken to stop her biting.'

'So they've got her killer's DNA,' I said.

'Looks like it.' He flopped down into a chair. 'She's been cremated. Tommie's going to bring me her ashes, to keep for Dave.'

Alf looked at us meaningfully. We needed to leave.

'We'll see you later, Ben,' Lissa said, and he nodded.

Returning to Yew Tree, I felt guiltily relieved at being away from the Macraes for a while. It was selfish and shameful, but I was longing for a respite from the weight of their dread, if only for the hour remaining until four o'clock.

On a practical level, I wanted to bring Lissa up to date on our chat with Lampert, as well as hearing about her interview with the acid-tongued Ursula Naylor. I was also hungry. Lissa had had lunch with Robyn and Ian while I was in Ledbury.

Having nipped to the village shop for a sandwich, we warmed up in front of the wood burner. Lissa raised her eyebrows at the half-empty bottle of Merlot, so I confessed to a therapeutic drink with 'Ben's cousin, the vet'.

I may have left out that the vet in question was a flame-haired cougar with a predilection for married prey.

'Never mind,' Lissa said. 'There's enough for a glass each when we get back from Bridgwater. It's my turn to drive. That's if you feel like going?'

'To Bridgwater?' I said blankly. 'What for?'

'The carnival.'

'Oh, Christ! I'd forgotten that was tonight.'

'We can stay in if you're tired.'

I was tempted. The weather was awful ... and we could have an early night ... but Lissa's offer to drive implied that she would enjoy an evening out, and she had been feeling so low yesterday that I hadn't the heart to back out.

'I'm easy,' I said.

'It might be fun. The rain's meant to clear up later.'

'OK.' I relaxed into the sofa. 'How did you find the prickly Ursula?'

'No less prickly in person. She said one of the few advantages of old age is the luxury of saying exactly what you like. Apparently, I was privileged to be granted an audience. She's choosy about visitors but tolerates Jackson and Chloe coming because it "makes them feel virtuous" – though she waited to say that after I'd stopped recording.'

'Didn't Alex get a mention?'

'Ah, he's special. There's a framed photo of him next to her bed. Dear Alex visits every week.'

'Thoughtful. And surprising. Ben reckons he's an entitled little git.'

'Oh! Perhaps gittishness is in the eye of the beholder.'

She picked up her phone from the coffee table and played me the full interview. The first half-minute consisted of formalities, Lissa introducing herself and Ursula by their full names, for reference, and checking with the old lady that she was happy to be recorded. Ursula stiffly consented.

Thank you for agreeing to meet me, Ursula, Lissa said.

Shall we skip any further niceties? You said on the phone that David Macrae asked for your help, to research a history of Netherzoy. I gather you feel bound to include me in this scintillating memoir?

He gave us a list of people who may have stories to tell. You're near the top.

Alex tells me that David has gone missing and the police are concerned for his safety. Is there any point in continuing with this fiasco?

Unless or until his family calls a halt, yes.

There was a silence, then Ursula said, *Better get on with it, then.*

Since Lissa had been closer to the mic, her indrawn breath was audible, but her voice betrayed no sign of nerves. *So, when did you first come to Netherzoy, Ursula?*

December 1938. I was eighteen. Oscar arranged everything. We had met that summer in St Helier, Jersey – I was born there – when he and his valet were on a cycling holiday. Oscar and I had an immediate connection.

I hit "pause" and interrupted, 'Ursula was eighteen in 1938. That makes her ninety-nine.'

Lissa nodded. 'She seems quite frail, though you wouldn't know it from her voice.'

'Nor her wits.'

'That's deceiving. The care manager warned me that she can sometimes become confused. She's at her best in the mornings, but I was asked to end the visit if she seemed to be getting tired or losing focus.'

'Early stage dementia, do you think?'

'I couldn't exactly ask.'

'No.' I tapped "play" again.

Was it love at first sight? Lissa asked.

Chemistry. And I was eager to leave home. Our dreary

parents were stifling me.

Ours? You had siblings?

One. Guy was much younger, but I told Oscar I wouldn't come without him.

Your parents gave permission, then, for you both to move to England, and for you to marry Oscar?

Not immediately, but we won them round. It helped that my father was concerned about Hitler's ambitions. He said the Channel Islands were strategically insignificant, so the British government would never defend them. He was right. Nine months after Guy and I moved to the mainland, Britain was at war. By the summer of 1940, France had surrendered and the Germans occupied the islands.

In a way, you were evacuated before the war even started.

You could put it like that, Ursula said.

And when you and Guy arrived in Netherzoy, did you stay at Zoyland House?

Of course not. There were standards to maintain. Oscar arranged temporary lodgings for us, and he and I were married the following spring. She chuckled, and added sarcastically, *The end.*

But the beginning of your life in Netherzoy. What were your first impressions of the village?

Boring.

I suppose St Helier had more going on,' Lissa said. *Did you like the village any better once you'd settled in?*

Not much.

How about Guy? Did he make friends at school?

I taught him at home. He was a shy boy. Luckily, he was too young to be called up to fight. Military discipline wouldn't have suited him. He likes to paint. Birds, mainly.

He's still alive?

Yes, but his life has been uneventful. Wouldn't you prefer to hear about my illustrious husband? Her tone was contemptuous of Lissa or her husband, or both.

I'm interested in whatever you'd like to tell me.

Oscar was a decorated RAF pilot. He was ten years older than me, intelligent, handsome, and moderately kind. But we were not mentally compatible. Fortunately, the house was big enough for us to live separate lives ... for the most part. Jackson made an appearance when I was nearly forty. Ursula broke off, then stated abruptly, *That's enough, I think.*

Well, thank you very much for your time, Ursula.

You're being polite, Lissa Pevensey. I'm sure you think me a cantankerous old bitch. You're wondering why I agreed to meet you in person instead of fobbing you off or answering your questions over the phone.

No, I –

Face to face, it's easier to ensure that we understand each other. You will be interviewing many elderly people, most with imperfect memories. Errors could creep in. I wouldn't like any inaccuracies about me, or my family, to appear in print.

Eyebrows raised, I paused the recording. 'Did she just threaten us?'

'No, she was only making a point.'

'Sounded more like "See you in court",' I said wryly, tapping "play".

Of course not, Lissa was assuring her. *Kit – Kester – and I will flag up any discrepancies. And David hopes to sell the book locally, so he won't want to upset his readers.*

I'm glad to hear it. In that case, we appear to have finished.

Er ... I do have one more question, if you're not too tired?

When you reach my age, staying alive is tiring enough. But ask, if you like.

Where did you and Guy stay in the village before you were married?

With an elderly couple in Peat Cutters' Lane. The same cottage that was let to David Macrae's grandfather twenty years later. Spindlewood.

'Coincidence,' I murmured.

Lissa stopped the recording and turned to sit sideways, drawing her knees up to her chin. 'Freddie Macrae may be described as Oscar's valet, but he didn't live in at Zoyland House, did he? He and Barbara lived here at Yew Tree with their two boys. And Freddie would have met Ursula and Guy while he was with Oscar in Jersey.'

'You think Oscar lodged them next door so that Freddie could support them, make them feel welcome?'

'It would make sense. Ursula and Guy would have had to share a room, but they'd have known it was temporary. By the way, I checked David's Google Sheet. A Guy Finch is listed under Jackson and Ursula. He must be the brother.'

'Was Ursula's maiden name Finch?'

'I don't know. I should have asked that. She flustered me a bit.'

'You did a great job.'

'Mm. I wish I'd recorded her comments about family holidays, but that was after she said we'd finished. She talked quite a bit about going to Lundy with Jackson and his late wife, and the grandchildren. I don't think her brother went with them ... Anyway, Guy Finch lives in Heron View. There are roads called that, but nowhere near here. If it's a house name, I think that would only come up if it was officially part of the address. I tried including Netherzoy in the search and still got nothing.'

'Ben will know.' Although interested in tracking down Ursula's brother, I was wondering, with increasing urgency, when we could start our second honeymoon. I looked into Lissa's solemn dark eyes and risked a smile, raising my eyebrows hopefully.

'Definitely not,' she said. 'Ben will be here in fifteen minutes.'

'Long enough.'

She smiled wickedly. 'That's nothing to boast about.'

I studied her face, thinking how much I loved her and how desperately I wanted to go back to the way we had been, before we had ever talked about trying for another baby.

'After the carnival,' I said, 'we'll have all night.'

She uncurled herself and wriggled along the sofa to kiss me on the mouth. A promise, lingering and sweet.

'So we will,' she said.

FOURTEEN

Ben arrived at four o'clock, as promised, laden down with filing boxes, ring binders and photo albums.

'There's more,' he said, 'but this'll do for starters.'

He transferred his burdens into my arms. On top was a sheet of A4 – the promised family tree, which I read after stacking everything else in the living room.

Yew Tree Cottage
Freddie Macrae, died 1940
Married to Barbara, died 1942
Two sons, Thomas and Alf, taken in by relatives
Uncle Alf moved back there with Auntie May, 1950s
Spindlewood
Grandad Thomas and Grandma moved in, 1950s
Two children, Jessica and Mike
Auntie Jess moved out. Married/divorced Jake Moss. One daughter, Tommie.
Mike was our dad (Dave's and mine). Him and Mum took over renting Spindlewood. Grandad and Grandma went to live with Auntie Jess and Tommie.

'Is it all right?' Ben asked. 'Couldn't think how to do a tree.'

'It's great. Thanks. Good idea to group the families by property.'

At this point, Lissa came downstairs, combing her hair and complimenting him on looking smart. He frowned, rotating his shoulders inside the cream-coloured parka as though testing the fit.

'Present from Chloe last Christmas,' he said. 'I'm always scared of getting it dirty.'

'You'll show us up,' I grinned, tucking Ben's list into an album.

Lissa, looking beautiful in a crimson quilted jacket and skinny jeans, slapped my arm in mock indignation. 'Speak for yourself, Pevensey!'

Under duress, I swopped my well-loved leather jacket for a navy quilted one which Lissa had bought me. Having been promised some fun later, I wasn't about to risk an argument.

'Alf didn't want to join us?' I asked.

'Nah, he says he'll enjoy the peace while I'm gone. He's holding up better than me. I'm only going 'cause Harry will be there. Chloe's meeting him in Wetherspoons.'

'Not planning to confront him, are you?' The police would be out in force, and the last thing Ben needed was to be arrested for a public order offence.

'Not to pick a fight. He'd thrash me. But I want to know where he went last night after work.' Ben raked a hand through his already tousled curls. 'What if Conor roped him into some dodgy scheme? Dave deals in some pricey stuff. Conor might've thought he'd have antiques in the car.'

'I don't think that'll fly,' I said. 'Did you tell your workmates that David was coming down for the weekend?'

'Course.'

'Then Conor and Harry knew it was a social visit. They wouldn't expect him to bring valuables, other than his phone and laptop, and electronics can be nicked from anywhere with a lot less effort.'

Ben scowled. 'I still want to talk to Harry.'

I didn't relish the prospect of trying to keep him out of

trouble. Lissa looked from one of us to the other and tactfully changed the subject.

'Where does Guy Finch live, Ben? Chloe's great-uncle. We know it's Heron View, but we can't find it on Google Maps.'

'You won't.' He was still grumpy with me but did his best to be pleasant to Lissa. 'That's the house name. If there's a number, it must be "One". There's no other houses down there.'

'Down where?' She could be extremely patient.

'It's a track, like Honeysuckle Row. Chloe took me once.'

'Could you find it on Maps?'

'Later, if you like. We ought to get going.'

Once we set off, he stopped sulking and told us more about the event. The town, he said, had become known in some quarters as the 'home of carnival'. I thought Rio held that honour but refrained from saying so.

We learned that the carts for the procession were built in sheds on a dedicated local site by the members of various clubs, whose unpaid graft was funded by charities and the council. Sedgemoor Carnival Club had been instigated ten years ago by Jackson himself. Some of the volunteers were his employees, while another two were Grail Knights. Ben had been involved two evenings a week for the past year but had never wanted to perform on the night.

We used the Park and Ride and queued for the shuttle bus into town, to find the place already awash with people. The pub owned by Wetherspoons was the half-timbered and appropriately named Carnival Inn.

After spending a couple of minutes weaving through the closely packed throng inside, checking every nook and alcove, we concluded that neither Chloe nor her boyfriend was there yet. Ben bought us a round, Lissa and I choosing soft drinks. Although I wasn't driving, I preferred to keep my wits about me for an encounter that might require peaceful intervention.

We found standing room beside a square pillar, with a view of the main doors. I asked Ben if he was meeting any friends besides Chloe, but it transpired that only three other Knights still lived locally, and he was vague about their plans.

I began to suspect that he had asked them to steer clear, in case he could persuade Chloe to dump Harry once and for all. If so, it shortened the odds of Lissa and me being caught in the middle of a drama.

'I really appreciate all you've done,' Ben told me earnestly. 'The Knights have been supportive in the group chat, but Ed's the only one living local who's got a car, and you were kind of involved by that point, so …'

'Told you, it's fine,' I said. 'Speaking of cars, did Chloe collect hers?'

'Someone gave her a lift over there this morning. Harry wasn't home. He was working on the Sedgemoor cart. She said he'd finish at four.' Ben glanced at the doors. 'They should be here any second.'

In fact they arrived ten minutes later. Chloe saw us almost at once, grabbed her companion's hand, and dragged him through the mill of people to be introduced. As Ben had said, Harry Diment was around my height and build, though he carried two or three extra kilos around the middle. He was also square-jawed and narrow-eyed, with a spider tattoo at the base of his throat – a hard-man image at odds with the message *Save the Bees* on the front of his hoodie.

He and Ben glowered at each other, as if even a simple 'Hi' would have caused them physical pain. Chloe overcompensated, hugging all three of us and gushing to Lissa about how lovely it was to meet her, and how grateful she and Ben had been for my help last night.

The way she bracketed herself with Ben, in effect speaking for them both, was either thoughtless or mischievous. It did nothing to improve Harry's mood. He said directly to Ben, 'Didn't think you'd be here.'

'Bet you didn't.'

'Don't piss about, say what you mean!'

'Hey!' I said. 'Let's keep it civil, shall we?'

Harry transferred his glare to me, clearly tempted to ask how it was any of my business, but Chloe hissed his name warningly and he backed down with a growled, 'Whatever.'

Since no one had introduced us, I did the honours, adding pleasantly, 'My round. What're you having?'

Harry stated aggressively, 'Doombar.'

The brand lent itself to being spoken like a threat, which amused me. I kept a straight face, took the rest of the orders, and pressed Ben to join me in the hustle for bar service, ostensibly to help carry the drinks but in reality to separate him from his love rival.

'Get a grip, OK?' I warned him. 'You say fighting's not your thing. Try to remember it.'

He looked sullen but kept his eyes down, which I took as reluctant compliance. When we returned with the drinks, Lissa was asking Harry how he liked working at Sedgemoor Aerodrome.

'It's all right,' he conceded. 'Jackson's not a bad boss.'

'Kit and I have been invited there tomorrow. We

might see you.' She gave him a smile. 'Chloe says you've been doing a lot of work on the Sedgemoor carnival cart.'

Harry's eyes flickered. 'Every night this week.'

She was pushing his buttons so that Ben wouldn't have to. I caught her eye and shook my head. She ignored me.

'Oh, so that's why you were late home last night,' she said. 'I'm sure the cart is amazing. We can't wait to see it.'

Disconcerted, Harry turned to Chloe. 'What've you told them?'

'Just that you were held up and I got tired of waiting.'

'That was a private conversation.'

'Oh, Harry, don't be so touchy! What's private about that?'

Ben interrupted, 'Two of the Knights work on the cart. Ed and Amber.'

'So what?' Harry said, but the cogs of his brain must have been creaking into gear as he realised that Chloe or Ben could check his story. 'OK,' he confessed with a sigh, 'so I wasn't there, all right? An ex wanted to meet me for a drink – and I didn't tell you because I knew you wouldn't like it,' he added to Chloe as her mouth fell open.

'You total bastard!' She punched his upper arm, the nearest available body part. 'Why do I ever believe a single word that comes out of your lying mouth?'

He raised his hand to fend off another blow. 'It was one drink. Nothing happened.'

'Who is she?'

'Nobody. She doesn't matter.'

'Just like me, then.'

When I had worried about a fight, I hadn't envisaged

Chloe starting it. Harry might not be prepared to hit a woman, but I didn't intend to take the chance.

Lissa must have been thinking along the same lines. In a piece of neat but unplanned teamwork, she put an arm around Chloe, murmuring soft words and trying to edge her away, at the same moment that I placed myself between the combatants.

Harry pushed his chest up against mine. 'You can sod off!'

Out of the tail of my eye, I saw one of the bar staff stop mid-pour to watch.

'You want to end up back inside?' I hissed at Harry.

There was no need to spell it out. Any hint of a bruise on Chloe, and losing his job would be the least of his problems.

He took a half-pace back. 'I wasn't going to hit her, was I?'

'Never entered my head.'

'Tosser!' he said, then turned and shoved his way out of the pub, causing a bystander to slop his beer and splutter a protest.

I called to the watching barman, 'No problem, all sorted.'

Lissa still had her arm around Chloe. The girl was dry-eyed. She had wept for Maisie, but not for her boyfriend's departure – a fact not lost on Ben, who was looking pensive.

'Think he was telling the truth?' I asked them.

From Chloe's startled expression, she had assumed he was. Ben shook his head, but Lissa was undecided.

'Has he done that before?' she asked Chloe. 'Lied about meeting his ex?'

'Once.' She was defensive, from which I deduced that

she might forgive him.

'Then it didn't take much imagination to use that story again,' Lissa said. 'Convenient that he didn't give the woman's name.'

'Why say it if it wasn't true?' Chloe said. 'He knew how I'd react.'

I was unwilling to share my thoughts. There was no point torturing Ben with every wild theory that occurred to me.

But he said it anyway. 'Because the truth could be worse. If Harry was at Merlin Park last night, he saw what happened … or did it himself.'

FIFTEEN

Far from being over-hyped, the carnival procession was truly impressive. The larger carts were around thirty metres long and were marvels of engineering wizardry. Ben said they had been built from the chassis up, over the twelve months since the last event.

One of my favourites was a pirate ship that pitched and tossed on its painted seas, while the lighted coils of a sea serpent writhed around the hull. Another displayed the whirling giant cogs and gears of Brunel's inventions. Each creation had its own high-decibel music and sound effects. To children staying up past their bedtimes, it would be an experience to remember – although many of them must have been locals, privileged to see the spectacle every year.

An hour into the procession, the Sedgemoor Carnival Club entry passed us. It didn't disappoint. The volunteer team of artists, engineers and mechanics had re-imagined an aerial dogfight from World War Two. Scale models of a Spitfire, a Hurricane and two German Messerschmitts on lever arms flew arcs over the heads of 'families' in costume, who stood outside cottage façades and pointed upwards, waving and cheering. From the sound system, the noise of the planes' engines mingled with the strains of "Jerusalem".

Ben pointed out a young woman in a calf-length dress and pinafore. 'That's Amy, Conor's sister,' he said, and slithered through the press of people between us and the cart.

The floor of the vehicle was waist-high. Avoiding lights and chunks of fake landscape along the side, he clambered aboard, which startled the performers, but

Conor's sister abandoned her role to talk to him. Chloe, Lissa and I were obliged to edge through the crowds to keep up with the cart.

Finally, he jumped down to rejoin us, almost into the arms of a female police officer. Before he could say anything that would get him arrested, I apologised on his behalf.

'He's with us, officer. He's had a few too many. We're taking him home now.'

She looked me up and down as if assessing my own blood alcohol level, before saying drily, 'Good decision. On you go, then.'

We shepherded Ben into the comparative peace of a nearby shop doorway, where Chloe exclaimed crossly, 'Honestly, Ben! There's such a thing as messaging.'

'That was Amy Yandle.'

'I know. You still shouldn't have –'

'The family haven't heard from Conor since Dave went missing. Lampert has been on their backs, thinking they're lying to protect him, but Amy says he'd never bugger off without telling their mum. So him and Dave have *both* vanished, while Harry claims he was with his ex.'

'Don't keep talking as if Harry's done something awful! He couldn't hurt a fly. He might get into a fight now and then, but he wouldn't make two people vanish – and he certainly couldn't have killed poor little Maisie.' She was so passionate, I wondered if she was trying to convince herself.

'He's still a cheat and a bloody liar,' Ben said.

Chloe squeezed his arm. 'He is, Benji. Let's forget about him!'

He allowed her to steer him back towards the kerb,

where she made a point of commenting on each cart, encouraging him to take an interest. To some extent she was successful, and he obviously found her presence a comfort.

Before the final cart passed, she returned to our side, dragging Ben by the hand as she had done with Harry earlier. 'Shall we leave now to beat the rush?' She was shouting from necessity. 'You'll give me a lift home, won't you? I came with Harry.'

Her assumption that we would comply raised Lissa's eyebrows, but we saw the wisdom of leaving early. There would be a shorter queue for the bus. We escaped down a side street and walked to the pick-up point.

Ben was dragging his feet with exhaustion. It was just over twenty-four hours since we had discovered Maisie's body, but even to me it felt like twice as long.

Reminded of the families I would interview for *Enigmas*, I could not imagine the agony of those whose loved ones were missing for decades or never found at all.

Lissa, walking silently beside me, looked up to search my face, as if catching a hint of my thoughts. I hugged her into my side, and she tilted her head briefly against my shoulder.

The simple gesture twisted something inside me. If staying with me meant she could never have a child of her own, would she look elsewhere, for a man with no shared genes?

'Kit,' Ben said, insistently.

'Sorry, miles away.'

'I'm going to message George Bailey.'

'About Harry's alibi, or lack of one?'

'He needs to know, doesn't he?'

Chloe pretended not to hear this exchange. She had become more subdued since we left the carnival. Perhaps her row with Harry would prove to be the final break after all.

During the bus ride and our drive back to Netherzoy, she continued to be abstracted, silent even with Ben; but as we approached the village, she said, 'Please don't take me home yet.'

Ben was quick to see an opportunity. 'Want to come to mine instead?'

'Yes. To talk. Alf should be there too. And you two,' she added to Lissa and me.

'What's this about?' Ben asked.

'I'll tell you at home.'

The fact that Chloe referred to Ben's place as home boded well for his chances long-term; and while her dark hints were a concern, they also gave me hope. Maybe she really had seen or heard something at the airfield.

We left the car outside our lodgings and trooped next door to Spindlewood. Alf was in the living room, watching a quiz programme.

'Don't get up, Unc,' Ben said as he struggled to rise.

The old man sank back with a grunt of relief. The resilience which Ben had claimed for him was nowhere apparent. His pale eyes were sunk deep in shadowed sockets.

'Had your dinner?' Ben asked.

'Not yet, son. Waited for you.'

It was nearly ten o'clock. Lissa ordered pizzas, which we could eat from our laps, while Ben made hot drinks. We found ourselves seats, mine being a scuffed vinyl footstool.

Ben and Chloe shared the sofa. As the girl began

speaking, a hot mug clasped between her hands, she glanced at him every now and then as if seeking approval.

'Last night,' she said, 'I wanted to come to Harry's and stay over, but he was really off with me, as if he was desperate to keep me away.'

Ben nodded. 'You thought he was cheating.'

'I didn't know what to think. I drove to his house and waited ... but then I thought, what if an OCG had paid Conor to steal some aircraft engines, and he'd talked Harry into helping him? Merlin Park is so close to their house, and the airfield is completely unlit and can't even be seen from the lane.'

'What's an OCG?' Ben asked.

Alf huffed tolerantly. 'Organised Crime Group, son, as you'd know if you'd ever watched *Line of Duty*.'

'Harry's desperate to make a fresh start,' Chloe said, 'but Conor's always there, trying to reel him back in. I thought, if they were at the airfield, I'd tell Harry to come with me.'

'Pretty brave,' I said, 'going on your own.'

'Harry wouldn't hurt me, and Conor wouldn't dare. I *am* the boss's daughter. But I was wrong. They weren't stealing engines.'

'But you saw them?' I guessed.

'While I was walking along Merlin's Lane, David's car passed me.'

Ben drew a sharp breath, and Lissa and I exchanged startled glances.

Alf asked, his voice hoarse with urgency, 'Was Dave driving?'

'No, Harry was. He was looking at his phone and it lit up his face.'

We were all shocked, but for Ben it must have felt like a betrayal. He stared at Chloe as if he barely recognised her.

Alf set down his mug with a bang. 'Did you tell the cops that?' he rasped.

She shook her head.

'Why not?'

'Because,' Ben said, 'she was protecting her sodding boyfriend.'

Chloe's face crumpled. 'I thought he'd just stolen the car and was taking it home, and Conor had put him up to it. That's why I didn't want us to drive there to pick up *my* car. I'm so sorry, Benji.'

'Have you seen the footage from the park?' Ben asked. 'Black Hoodie getting out of Dave's car to open the gate?

'DS Lampert showed me when I went for the DNA swab.'

'Did you tell her it was Harry?'

'I couldn't be certain –'

'Like hell you couldn't! He drove past you seconds after he was caught on camera.'

If they continued in that vein, Ben could forget winning Chloe back. They wouldn't even have a friendship.

I interrupted, 'If you want to make this right, Chloe, call George Bailey. Ben's got his number.'

She looked like a condemned prisoner receiving a life sentence. 'He might think I'm involved.'

I drove the message home. 'Right now!'

Her hunted gaze flicked from one of us to the other. What she saw must have been daunting: Alf glaring ferociously, Ben disenchanted, Lissa and I stony-faced –

and none of us about to back down.

Ben took out his phone, tapped his screen to bring up the number, and passed it to her. 'Here. I've made it easy for you.'

Refusal at that point would have cost her more than a tricky interview with Lampert. She would have lost Ben forever and undoubtedly knew it.

She hesitated another second, then made the call.

SIXTEEN

The conversation with George was brief, and his boss called Chloe straight back. We gathered that she wanted Chloe to meet her at Zoyland House.

'In half an hour?' the girl faltered. 'Can't – can't you come tomorrow instead?'

Lampert's reply was inaudible, but Chloe flinched. Ending the call, she informed us, hardly above a whisper, 'DS Lampert says they need to move fast. I think she meant I've wasted enough of their time.'

Ben avoided her eyes, but Alf's glare spoke volumes.

Chloe messaged her dad to collect her. Jackson replied at once; he would be here in ten minutes.

The pizzas turned up first. Chloe and Alf had lost their appetites, and Lissa took a slice without enthusiasm, but my stomach was protesting about the number of hours since my sandwich from the village shop. I was grateful to find Ben equally famished. Between the two of us, we demolished both large pizzas before Jackson arrived.

Ben showed him into the living room, and his daughter threw herself into his arms, sobbing that it was all such a mess and everyone hated her.

Jackson's recent photos online were brutally accurate. He looked older than his sixty years, despite piercingly blue eyes and a full head of well-groomed, though thinning, silver hair; but even in jeans and a casual sweater, his authority was undiminished.

He patted the back of his daughter's head. 'Let's get you home, and I'll hear all about it,' he said, surveying the rest of us over her shoulder. 'Ben, Alf, we're all thinking of you and praying for David's safe return. The whole community is behind you. DS Lampert has been hugely impressed with the levels of cooperation.'

'Appreciate that,' Alf muttered, but Chloe moaned. Her level of cooperation had left a lot to be desired.

'Kester,' Jackson said, 'and Lissa? I wish we were meeting in better circumstances. Can you still come to the café tomorrow morning?'

I assured him that we would be there, although Lissa added superstitiously, 'All being well.'

Jackson exchanged a few more words with the Macraes, then steered his daughter out. Chloe was still sniffling. We said a subdued goodnight to Ben and Alf and returned to our own lodgings.

While we were getting ready for bed, Lissa barely spoke. I deliberately left the lamp on and lay down beside her, hoping she was not too tired for lovemaking – but she pulled the duvet up over us and turned on to her back, frowning at the ceiling.

I traced the line of her collarbone with one finger. 'What are you thinking, sweetheart?'

She sighed. 'David asks for our help, Ben makes no secret of it in the village, and within forty-eight hours, Conor Yandle asks to meet him on a dark, deserted airfield, and they both vanish.'

'You think there's a connection?'

'It's possible, isn't it?'

'David going missing hasn't stopped the project. If that was the aim, they should have made *us* vanish.'

'Don't joke, Kit!'

'I'm not,' I said grimly. 'If we're looking for a catalyst, my money is on the mysterious Mr Fogle and his alleged gold artefact.'

'If Fogle is his real name.' She relapsed into silence, ignoring my efforts to distract her. After a minute she said, 'Chloe might be wrong about Harry. He didn't seem all that harmless this evening, did he? David and Conor could have been in the Audi, unconscious or worse, when he drove past her.'

That had occurred to me too, but even if Harry had gone with Conor to Merlin Park and attacked him and David in order to make off with Fogle's artefact, I couldn't see him taking on two men and a dog and escaping without a scratch. I pointed this out to Lissa.

'All right, I know it sounds far-fetched,' she said. 'Have you got a better idea?'

I was pondering some options, all of them more appealing than a debate about Harry Diment.

'Let's not talk any more,' I said.

She snuggled closer. 'Help me forget, then.'

I didn't need telling twice. She proceeded to dispel all of my fears about our relationship, even if only temporarily. She was still my Amphelisia. I wouldn't let myself wonder if she was merely giving in to a physical need, leaving emotions aside for another day.

As we lay side by side in the small hours, fingertips entwined, she suddenly turned her head to listen. 'What's that rattling noise? I heard it earlier.'

I hadn't noticed. My mind had been on other things.

'The sash in the back bedroom,' I said. 'Ben's going to fix it.'

'Couldn't we secure it somehow? It's annoying.'

We put on dressing-gowns against the chill and went to struggle with the sash. After a minute, I gave up and fetched some paper from downstairs, to fold as a wedge to stop the rattle. I returned to find that Lissa had raised the window fully and was leaning on the sill, as I had done last night. She pointed to the silhouette of the old yew tree.

'That's how the cottage got its name, then,' she said.

I wrapped my arms around her, enjoying the feel of her bottom against my thighs. 'It's a thousand years old, according to Alf.'

She went on gazing at the tree, which was creaking a little in the wind. We had never made love in a window, I thought. Worth considering, for another day ...

'It does have a presence, don't you think?' Lissa said. 'I wonder what secrets it could tell?'

The old yew certainly had an atmosphere, especially at night. I couldn't entirely dismiss the notion that dramatic or tragic events might leave an energy trace on the landscape – the well-worn but still popular 'stone tape' theory.

Despite my resolve not to mention Barbara's ghost, there was no reason not to tell Lissa how she had died.

'Alf's mum hanged herself there,' I said.

'What?' She stood upright, turning to face me. 'From the yew? Oh, my God! But ... Alf lived here afterwards. His wife too ... Are you sure? I mean ...'

'Long story. Tell you tomorrow.' I kissed the end of her nose. 'Do you mind?'

'What, staying in a house where a woman killed herself?' The question was ironic, but then she paused to consider. 'Actually, no,' she said. 'I like it here. It feels ... I don't know. Friendly.'

'I think Alf and his wife were happy here,' I said.

'Their memories must have seeped into the walls.'

On this comfortable thought, we returned to bed and switched off the lamp. Then, while I was feeling peaceful and content, she asked, 'Do you think you'll change your mind, Kit, about another baby?'

My breath caught. It was the last thing I wanted to talk about.

'I'm sorry, sweetheart,' I said.

She was silent for a while, then asked quietly, 'Is it just that you'd rather wait a bit longer? Because I'd be fine with that.'

'No, Liss. If something went wrong ...'

'Emily didn't die because we're cousins.'

'But that doubles the risk of a problem,' I said.

'Six per cent instead of three. You've taken bigger risks for an hour's fun.'

I wasn't sure how the figures stacked up, but it was true that I had sampled a few extreme sports.

'That's different,' I said.

'You're right. It's not about percentages.' She rose to one elbow, looking down at me in the dark. 'All the time, you hear couples say *we're* expecting a baby. I've even heard *we're* pregnant. But we weren't. *I* was. I used to talk to Emily. Just chat away about nothing. How we'd been painting her room, or choosing a mobile for her cot. Silly things.'

The pain in her voice made me want to take her in my arms and comfort her; but the comfort she wanted, I couldn't give.

'You never told me that,' I said.

'No.'

But through the months of waiting, I had known that our baby was more real to Lissa than to me. Even when I had placed my hand on her bump and felt the first flutters of movement, my main emotion had been awe.

Only after Emily was born, and she looked up at me with those dark-blue unfocused eyes, which a nurse had said might turn grey like mine ... that was when I truly became her dad. It had seemed wonderful, and terrifying, that our lives from now on would be all about nurturing her and keeping her safe, helping her grow up healthy and strong enough to follow her own path, her own dreams.

But we hadn't done that.

'I loved her too, Liss,' I whispered.

'I know.' She was holding tight to control. 'Are you saying we'll never have a family now?'

'We could think about adoption ... couldn't we?'

She didn't answer. All the same, I knew. She longed to feel another child stir inside her; yearned to talk to her, or him, as she had with Emily; wanted more than anything else in the world to give birth to our own healthy baby.

'The past three weeks,' she said, 'it wasn't that I didn't want you.'

'You just proved that.' I stroked her shoulder.

'I needed to take a step back. To think.'

My stomach dropped. 'About us?'

'It didn't get me anywhere. I just felt more and more desperate. But then David offered us the chance to come here, and I thought ... a second honeymoon might help us find the solution, together.'

It seemed pretty clear what that meant. 'You were hoping some holiday sex would change my mind? Am I that shallow, then?'

She flinched away from me and sat up, hugging her knees. I sensed that she was making a huge effort not to bite back, afraid of escalating the argument and saying something we would both regret. Not usually slow to speak her mind – to me, at least – she wouldn't risk a row that could drive us even further apart.

The realisation fuelled my anger. She was the one who had forced the issue, but suddenly it was my fault.

'So now I'm getting the silent treatment,' I said bitterly.

She lay down and turned her back on me, pulling the duvet up high, using the mound of feather-stuffed cotton to shut me out.

I lay there seething, feeling misjudged and manipulated, and only gradually became aware of small snuffling sounds from beside me. She was crying quietly, not wanting me to know.

I couldn't bear that. I still resented having being played but now felt like a heartless pig as well. Tentatively, I reached out and stroked her hair, running the soft tumble of curls through my fingers.

'I'm sorry, Liss,' I said.

Not sorry enough, evidently.

'Just go to sleep!' she said.

SEVENTEEN

In the morning, Lissa was cool and polite, so I responded in kind, anxious not to make things worse. Verbal sparring over day-to-day disagreements was one thing. This could break us if we let it.

We had to put on a good front in public, partly because we were due to meet Jackson at Sedgemoor Aerodrome, but also for Ben, who darted outside to catch us before we drove away. Since he was in short sleeves, our attention was caught by the 'ripped skin' tattoo on his left bicep, which gave the illusion of his skin having been clawed apart to reveal a black panther's face glaring out.

'Thought you'd like to know,' he said, 'Harry's been arrested. Amy Yandle saw it from next door.'

Ben felt positive about this development, so we reacted accordingly, but the reality was grim. If Harry gave a 'no comment' interview, Ben would be none the wiser about David's fate. If he came clean, the facts could be devastating.

To change the subject before he pressed for an honest opinion, I indicated his tattoo. 'Quite a work of art.'

'Thanks.' He smiled wryly. 'The beast within.'

Lissa said teasingly, 'I thought you weren't the aggressive type.'

'I'm not. I used to get bullied at school. Even at college, a bit. So I got this, to change my image. I call it the Beast of Netherzoy. Like the old stories of the Beast of Exmoor, see?'

We saw, but I wondered whether the tattoo really was just a bluff by a gentle soul, or whether the rage of the bullied teenager was still in there, waiting to erupt. He had been quick enough with his fist on Friday night.

'Course, our family's more about witches,' Ben said. 'People thought Great-Grandma Barbara was one. It's in Dad's notes. And Tommie was in a coven before she went away to university. Dr Moss,' he added, for Lissa's benefit.

I thought of the pot on our upstairs windowsill, and Thomasina saying that the sandalwood candle dispelled negative energy, and was not totally surprised.

'So do witches meet to dance naked under the full moon,' I asked flippantly, 'or is that just a male fantasy?'

'Dunno. Maybe it's just yours.'

I hadn't got as far as visualising Thomasina that way. Now, of course, it was impossible to think of anything else.

'Lissa's my only fantasy,' I said.

My wife gave me the withering look this remark deserved. 'Isn't that rather a contradiction, a witch becoming a vet?' she asked Ben. 'Magic versus science?'

'Not really. Tommie's got this "healing hands" thing. Her hands get hot when she does massage treatments on animals – but that's as well as the normal meds, like. And she had a crush on the local vet, before her A-Levels, so she was always helping out there. She joined the practice straight after qualifying.'

'To be with the vet?' Lissa asked.

'Nah, she'd lost interest in him by then. Tommie's a free spirit.' Ben shivered suddenly. He was not dressed to linger outdoors. 'Can I come round later? Help you go through Dad's stuff?'

We told him that we would be free after lunch. As we drove away, Lissa asked pleasantly, 'What's Thomasina like?'

'Fortyish. Capable.'

'Attractive?'

I was driving, which gave me an excuse to watch the road. 'Guess so. Is this about me inviting her in on Friday night?'

'Should it be?'

Her lack of faith in me was a shock. Tempted or not, I had resisted Thomasina – but I wasn't stupid enough to try that defence.

'She asked for a drink because she needed one,' I said. 'That's it. Nothing happened.'

Lissa was silent. I took a risk and placed my left hand over both of hers. She didn't pull away. A minute later she said shakily, 'This isn't us.'

She was right. Until now, I had thought we trusted each other enough not to be jealous of chance encounters and imagined flirtations. I removed my hand from hers to change gear and pulled up at a T-junction, frowning left and right.

She said quietly, 'I know you haven't cheated. You wouldn't be this good at hiding the guilt.'

Acquittal was a relief, but I was still smarting from the implied accusation. 'I haven't and I won't. Not with Thomasina. Not with anyone.'

She didn't answer, but this time she was the one who reached out, laying her hand on my thigh and keeping it there until we turned in through the gates of Sedgemoor Aerodrome.

The visitors' car park was half full. We parked close to where a couple of families with kids were leaning on a picket fence, watching a light aircraft taxi over the grass towards a tarmac runway.

From outside, the place was much as I remembered it. The two largest hangars were listed buildings dating back over a century. These days they housed the Sedgemoor Aviation Museum, but in themselves they were a poignant memorial to the men and women who had lived and sometimes died for the cream of flight, even before the First World War had given its development an urgent and solemn focus.

Alongside Hangar One was a red-brick building with two pairs of glass doors. One of these, the entrance to the museum, was propped open. The other bore the blue and white logo of Avalon Sky. Behind this, I knew, was a suite of offices, where the TV crew and I had convened with Jackson six years ago.

Beside the museum entrance, a sign with the words, *Spitfire Café – open every day, 10am-4pm,* invited us up a flight of metal steps to a separate entrance, allowing people to buy refreshments without paying to see the exhibits.

As Jackson had suggested meeting there, we went straight up. At the top of the steps, a glass door opened into a room that seemed full of light even on that sunless day. Floor-to-ceiling windows along one wall gave a fine view of the runway, while the colour scheme (new since my last visit) was reminiscent of green fields and summer skies, with tables and chairs in natural pine. Along two other walls, metre-wide prints told the story of more than two centuries of aviation, from the Montgolfier brothers' balloon to the Eurofighter.

Tempted by the food photos on the website, we had skipped breakfast, and now delectable aromas lured us to the counter to order fresh coffee and bacon rolls. There were some other customers but no queue, and we chose a free table next to the window to await our order – and Jackson.

He arrived promptly, in the company of a young man whose white-blond hair and superior expression I recognised from online, as well as from his resemblance to Chloe.

Jackson introduced him. 'Lissa, Kester, this is my son Alex, assistant manager of Avalon Sky's flight training school. He was keen to join us.'

'Hi, TV people,' Alex drawled, not sounding keen at all.

Ben's description of him as an entitled little git was misleading. Though marginally shorter than the lanky Macrae brothers, Alex Naylor was over six feet tall and had his father's solid build, scaled up. He had also inherited Jackson's blue eyes, minus the twinkle.

Jackson flicked him a warning look and sat down heavily, as if feeling his age. Since we were no longer meeting professionally, I told him that friends called me Kit. He seemed quietly pleased by the compliment and managed a smile for the waitress as she brought four coffees.

'Is that my Americano, Poppy? And a skinny latte for Alex? You're a quick learner. How are you liking the job?'

'It's great,' she said, beaming.

'The usual breakfast for Alex and me, please.'

She hurried off. Alex watched her go, with a smirk that hinted at private knowledge of her faults.

Trying to ignore the tension between father and son, I commented on the new décor. Jackson praised the talents of his interior designer and told us, with evident pleasure, that the wall art had been his son's idea. Alex's response was a grunt that defied interpretation. After that, Jackson gave up on small-talk and said in a low voice, ensuring that his words would not carry to the next occupied table, 'You'll have heard, Harry Diment is being questioned under caution?'

I nodded. 'Think they've got enough to charge him?'

'Hard to know. It might hang on whether Chloe can ID him from when he passed her in the lane.'

'And whether she *will*,' Alex said.

Jackson neither defended his daughter nor agreed with Alex. Poppy's return with the breakfasts – bacon rolls all round – supplied a brief diversion, during which I caught Alex watching me closely, as if he suspected I knew more about Friday night than I was saying. As soon as our eyes met, he looked away.

Having missed this odd moment, Lissa was pursuing her own line of thought. 'If Harry killed Maisie, he might have left his DNA in the caravan, or on Maisie herself. DS Lampert told Ben they've found traces of human blood.'

Jackson shook his head. 'Harry's not a violent man. If he was, I wouldn't tolerate him chasing Chloe.'

Alex chuckled derisively 'I think you'll find she's doing the chasing.'

'Hm. Well, Chloe's not a child, as she constantly reminds me.'

'Shame she acts like one.'

It was hard to tell whether Alex was angry with his sister or in a foul mood for some other reason, but his sneer was annoying me. I changed the subject. 'What's your view of Conor Yandle?'

Although the question was directed at them both, only Jackson answered. 'Conor's had his challenges, but he's able enough. I'm hoping for great things.'

It was the most positive statement about Conor that I

had yet heard. Alex did not appear to share his father's optimism. He had tipped his chair back and was staring at the ceiling, whistling through his teeth.

'If Conor is hiding from the police,' Lissa said, 'it doesn't look good for David.'

'Too true.' Jackson bit into his bacon roll. 'I should have checked on Conor yesterday morning. Unfortunately, my mother was unwell.'

Alex brought his chair down with a bang. 'Tell it like it is, Dad. Gran went missing from her care home.'

'Thank you, Alex,' Jackson said sarcastically, before admitting to us, 'Mum walked out through the front door while the desk staff were welcoming a visitor. It was a concern, as Mum has a serious heart condition, but luckily she was found twenty minutes later. The manager notified me at that point. I drove straight there.'

'Is she all right?' Lissa asked anxiously.

'She was tired, but fine otherwise. By the time I saw her, she was quite lucid, even telling me that she'd recently signed a DNR instruction. Do not resuscitate.' Jackson frowned, distracted by the memory. 'I must confess, I'm a coward about discussing such matters.'

'I visited her yesterday morning,' Lissa said, 'to interview her for David's book. Do you think I may have upset her somehow?'

'I'm sure not.' Jackson's smile was warmly reassuring. 'Mum has had some memory issues lately. The staff will be on the alert after this.'

'Easier for all of us if she wasn't in Gloucester,' Alex muttered.

'Cedar Lawns was your gran's choice.'

'Because she couldn't live alone anymore and *you* didn't want her living with us, so she moved far enough away to make visiting more difficult. Saying "Sod the lot of you", basically. Probably stuck a pin in a bloody map.'

Lissa and Jackson looked as uncomfortable as I felt. This was a discussion they should have as a family, not with near-strangers.

'Mum is well looked after, that's the important thing,' he said.

'Bet she will be from now on. They found her sitting on a bench at the side of the road.' Alex sounded more upset than his father at the staff's oversight. 'She was phoning for a taxi to take her to the Marisco Tavern.'

'Is that local to Cedar Lawns?' Lissa asked.

Alex laughed bitterly. 'You're over a hundred miles out, and no one ever got there by car.'

Jackson enlightened us. 'It's the village pub on Lundy Island, in the Bristol Channel. When I was a child, we holidayed there every year. My late wife loved wild places, so we continued the tradition with Alex and Chloe.'

'There are puffins.' Alex sounded wistful. 'I wouldn't mind another trip sometime.'

The glimpse of vulnerability and nostalgia for happier days gave me a twinge of remorse. I had no right to judge him. He and Chloe had been teenagers when their mum had lost a long battle with cancer. Despite the trappings of wealth and privilege, the young Naylors hadn't had it easy, and Alex seemed genuinely fond of his grandmother and angry with Jackson for not offering her a home with the family.

Jackson brought the conversation back on track. 'Be that as it may, I was out of the loop yesterday and didn't realise Conor had gone missing. The café manager left a message on Chloe's voicemail, but she was in Bridgwater for her DNA swab. When I got back, she asked me to ring the Yandles' landline.'

Alex interrupted, 'So much for her being the HR manager.'

Jackson flashed his son another quelling look. 'With Ben so distressed over David and Maisie,' he said, 'Chloe couldn't trust herself to remain professional with Conor, but in fact it was his mum who spoke to me. After work on Friday, Conor asked her to keep his dinner hot, then rushed out at five-fifteen and didn't come back. His mum was putting off ringing us, hoping he'd turn up with a good excuse.'

'Sounds like he didn't plan whatever kicked off at Merlin Park,' I said. 'Unless his mum is covering for him.'

'I'd say she's genuinely frantic, and I'm a fair judge of people. How are Ben and Alf holding up?'

'Struggling, I think.'

'Mm. It's been a bad year for them, and now this.' Jackson put down his bacon roll as if he had suddenly lost his appetite. 'I'm very fond of the Macraes. Our families have always been close.'

'Ben told me their grandad was head gardener at Zoyland House,' I said. 'And *his* father, Freddie, was your father's valet.'

'Ah, yes. A story in itself.'

At this point, Lissa said diffidently, 'Jackson, do you mind if I record this? It would help us get to grips with who's who.'

'Not this time, please. With so much going on, I'd prefer to exercise discretion. I suspect that we've already made a couple of forays into slanderous territory. But by all means take notes.'

He waited while she took out a pen and her shorthand notebook.

'In the 1930s,' he began, 'Dad was young, single and bored. He had heard of other youngsters cycling across Europe – those privileged not to work for a living – and the idea appealed. He started taking two or three trips a year. Freddie Macrae went with him, officially as his valet, but also because Dad wanted a companion. His friends were either unavailable or not keen on the cycling aspect.'

'When war broke out,' Lissa said, 'I suppose Freddie left your father's service and joined up? We know he was killed in action in 1940.'

'Then I expect you also know that Barbara, Freddie's widow, took her own life two years later. A tragic business. Their sons were so young. Alf was five. Thomas – David's and Ben's grandad – was seven.'

'You know their family history very well,' Lissa said.

Alex grunted again, this time in amusement. Jackson twinkled at her, ignoring his son's reaction.

'Our destinies are linked,' he said. 'Dad made certain that Freddie's descendants were never in hardship. There were monetary gifts from time to time, larger than might be required for necessities. I understand that one of those gifts purchased the Jabiru kit.'

'Your father was a generous man,' Lissa said.

'Especially to Freddie Macrae and his offspring.' Jackson's eyes glinted. 'Chloe is adamant that Dad and Freddie were lovers. If Dad was still alive, I suspect she would ask him. I'm not sure how I feel about that, but none of us will ever ask Mum. Not even my forthright daughter would have the nerve. Eh, Alex?'

Alex rolled his eyes. 'Grandad and Freddie were a

couple, Dad. Live with it. You only have to look at the photos from those cycling trips. Their body language says it all.'

'Could we borrow the photos?' I asked.

'If I can find them,' Jackson said. 'But you can see copies in the museum. Would you like a guided tour? It's grown since you were last here, Kit.'

We leapt at the chance. Alex excused himself, mumbling about getting back to work. Considering his attitude throughout, I couldn't think why he had wanted to meet us, unless to vet the people who had been questioning his grandmother. Ursula might have put him up to it. Either way, I wasn't sorry to see him leave.

Jackson, by contrast, was glad to share his passion for aviation history with an interested audience.

Unlike the café's wall art, the museum focused solely on aircraft from the World Wars. Hangar One housed, beside table displays and a recreated trench, two biplanes which had flown over the battlefields of Ypres and the Somme. The second hangar, once the home of a solitary Spitfire, now also boasted a Hurricane, along with four other planes that were less immediately familiar. All had been painstakingly restored.

'They're a credit to my team,' Jackson said, his voice echoing through the high-domed space. 'The collection is complete now, but I admit I indulged myself for a few years. An old man's privilege.'

A rich man's privilege, I thought, but I couldn't begrudge him that. Reading between the lines of his online biographies, Jackson had increased the value of his inherited assets rather than live off them – no doubt by clever investment as well as hard work. Nor had he ploughed all of his profits into the museum. His support for local good causes was well documented.

He stopped beside a display dedicated to the life and career of his father: Wing Commander Oscar Naylor, DSO, DFC. A life-sized cut-out of Oscar in RAF uniform, from a blown-up photograph, stood alongside a board telling his story in images and bold text.

'All placed with care,' Jackson pointed out, 'beside the door to our small cinema, which screens a rolling movie. Visitors waiting for the next showing have plenty of time to read about Dad's life and illustrious career.'

A couple of paying visitors hovered within earshot. Jackson had a clear, carrying voice, and locals would recognise him.

'So this is Freddie,' Lissa said, bending to view a cluster of four black-and-white images on the display.

'Ah yes, I had to include the cycle tours. They were a big part of Dad's life before the war.'

In one of the photos, Oscar Naylor, his resemblance to Jackson barely disguised by a luxuriant moustache, stood beside a taller, curly-haired young man, captioned as Frederick Macrae. Their bicycles, with minimal luggage strapped to the racks, were propped against a tree.

Another pic showed Freddie alone in an Alpine meadow, wearing a short-sleeved shirt and lederhosen and glancing over his shoulder at the camera. His dimpled smile hinted at flirtation. If Oscar had been behind the camera, that smile had been for him.

Both men had fathered children with their wives, but that didn't preclude an affair with each other. The marriages might also have provided a useful smokescreen. In that era and for decades afterwards, gay or bisexual men in a same-sex relationship had risked arrest and a maximum of ten years' imprisonment.

Jackson said, lowering his voice to exclude the wider public, 'Alex has little time for all this. He'll be a safe hand on the tiller of Avalon Sky when I step aside next year. In fact, he's chomping at the bit, telling me twenty-five is old enough. But he's an accountant at heart. Chloe's more like me, an incurable romantic. I'm sure she'll make a success of the events management side, but she'll also be the beating heart of the museum one day. And speaking of Chloe,' he added, 'she's traced our family tree back a century or so. She was the one who gave Mike Macrae – David and Ben's dad – the idea of writing a village history.'

'She knew Mike well, then?' Lissa asked. 'Not just his sons?'

'Oh, yes. Our families have always shared summer barbecues, and the occasional fly-out, not to mention holidays when my two and Ben were little. Alex and Ben have grown apart since, but that happens.'

I wondered how Jackson and Ben had managed the transition to boss and apprentice; but since Ben had nothing but praise for his CEO, the arrangement must have worked well so far.

As I drove us away from the aerodrome, Lissa commented that she was looking forward to going through Mike's notes. 'I hope it includes more about Oscar and Freddie,' she said. 'Their story could show how far attitudes have changed. I'm sure David will like that.' She broke off and corrected herself in a whisper. 'He would have liked it.'

'Yeah.' I sighed. 'What d'you make of Alex?'

'Born with the proverbial silver spoon. Enjoys chewing on it for effect, but definitely won't be spitting it out.'

'You didn't feel sorry for him, then?'

'Well, yes, he and Chloe must have had a really rough time growing up. But that doesn't excuse his snide attitude. Let's face it, he doesn't have much to complain about now. If Chloe wants to concentrate on weddings and keeping the museum ticking over, it sounds as if he'll be CEO of Avalon Sky in a year's time, overseeing the village properties and running the aerodrome.'

Bad news for Ben, but Alex himself was apparently eager to embrace his fate. My siblings and I had faced a similar choice, though in more modest circumstances. Robyn and our two brothers had happily joined the family antiques business straight from university, and only Robyn had eventually felt the need to forge her own path.

I had been the rebel, pushing against constraints of any kind, and most of all against having my future decided for me. In Alex's place, I would have hated owing every achievement, every promotion, to my father. Maybe a part of him did resent it. That could account for his need to feel superior, to convince himself that he deserved his fast-track to the top, even while he was impatient to step into Jackson's shoes.

That didn't make Ben's analysis of his character wrong. Alex Naylor might deserve compassion – but he was still an entitled git.

EIGHTEEN

After lunch, Ben turned up with the rest of his dad's research, including a laptop. He was determined to help us sort everything out.

Two hours later, upon discovering that a binder labelled *Austria 1937* was mainly filled with cuttings about ten years of Netherzoy fêtes, he groaned loudly and plunged both hands in his curls as if preparing to tear them out by the roots.

'Is this what you do for work, Lissa?' he asked incredulously. 'Trawl through acres of random crap?'

She gave him an indulgent smile. 'We don't mind if you want to go home. Or you could give us some background on your dad, to pass the time?'

Mike Macrae, it transpired, had been most at home in his garage-cum-workshop or maintaining the Jabiru. Before starting the project, paperwork of any kind had been a chore. He had read only motorcycle and flying magazines for pleasure, like his younger son.

His filing system was therefore whimsical at best. A teacher's obituary shared a page with a mention of her pupil's English prize, while a 1934 article on a local footballer was stapled to one on a post-war angling competition.

Luckily, the photo albums were dated. The oldest included a solemn black-and-white portrait of Freddie and Barbara in their wedding finery. Smiling for the camera had been a new notion at that time, not universally fashionable. Barbara's veil was turned back to reveal a serious, heart-shaped face framed by loose curls.

We were interrupted by a door slamming upstairs, which reminded us about the window. Ben leapt at the chance of a break and dashed home for his toolbox, then bounded up the stairs. I was tempted to join him, but Lissa put on a mock-stern frown and commanded me to stay focused. We continued with our painstaking task, cataloguing and labelling everything, gradually seeing order emerge from one small section of the chaos.

I found an album devoted to Oscar's and Freddie's European cycling holidays, from 1935 to 1938. In one shot, Oscar was seated with other men at a table, all of them looking at the camera with tankards raised. A sign saying *Kneipe* had sneaked into shot.

'German for pub.' Lissa was hot on languages. 'So the Fatherland was still welcoming British tourists, even the year before the war. I suppose that makes sense. Hitler never wanted to fight us, did he?'

The Führer, in fact, had seen Britain as his natural ally against Communism. Well into the war, he had continued to hope for a negotiated peace. Since he had never grasped the essential bloody-mindedness of the British, our refusal to back down in the face of terrifying odds must have bewildered him.

Lissa had turned to the final pages of the album, which contained shots of a seaside town with white-painted buildings and a yacht harbour, plus a pub called La Folie Inn.

'Look!' She pointed to a disdainful blonde and a sullen boy posing on a causeway that wound away behind them to a sprawling castle. 'This could be Ursula and her brother.'

A Google search confirmed it. Elizabeth Castle was in the parish of St Helier, Jersey. La Folie Inn was a centuries-old pub, now closed and derelict, in the same town.

'Ursula's still got that to-hell-with-you expression,' Lissa said.

I laughed. 'Like her grandson.'

At this point, Ben joined us. 'All sorted. There was a little coin poked deep in the frame. By a kid, I s'pose. Could've been Unc.' He showed us an old farthing with the head of King George VI.

We were duly appreciative. He dumped his tool bag in the hall and took an interest in the album of Freddie's and Oscar's adventures.

'Chloe lent that to Dad,' he said. 'Her grandad took the photos.'

After he had gone home to cook dinner, Lissa and I leafed through an album containing snaps of Barbara and Freddie with their sons in the garden. One of them captured Barbara sitting in a tyre swing strung from the yew's horizontal bough, with her little boys peeping from behind the trunk.

It gave me a shiver. She might have used that rope to hang herself.

Lissa, drawing the same inference, said, 'No, too sad. That's enough for one day.'

She retreated to the kitchen to cook, refusing my offer of help. So I went for a run. Without the focus of a shared task, we were awkward with each other again, last night's bitterness still festering.

Over dinner and a glass of wine, I suggested watching a movie, thinking that would give us an excuse to snuggle up and might lead to other things. Lovemaking wouldn't solve our problems, but it seemed a good place to start.

Before Lissa could reply, a banging on the door made us jump. The urgency had us scrambling to answer the summons, and Lissa flung the door open.

'What's happened?' she asked.

Ben took a step back, looking startled. 'Nothing. I mean ... Is it OK if I fetch Unc?'

'Alf's not here,' I said.

'He's gone through into your garden from ours, between the yew tree and the fence.'

'Why would he do that?' Lissa said.

'It's his thing, kind of. I could've fetched him back the same way, but it seemed rude not telling you. Can I come in?'

We followed him through the cottage to the back door, exchanging quizzical looks behind his back.

'Do you think Alf's confused, Ben?' Lissa asked.

'No, it's not that. After Auntie May died, he started going down the garden to think. About his mum and stuff. The old tree draws him, kind of. I know that sounds weird.'

We went outside. It was fully dark. The light from the kitchen cast a glow across the garden, where Alf and his brother had played as children, and which he and his wife had later tended through decades of marriage.

At the end of the overgrown lawn, beyond the pool of light, the yew tree was black against a dimly ragged sky.

Ben called softly, 'Unc?'

A torch flicked into life, and we made out Alf's bent figure about three metres from the yew. He was directing the light downwards, onto an area that was mostly dirt. The dense foliage overhead admitted too little light for grass to grow.

A cold breeze whispered, and the tree's great horizontal bough groaned, as if remembering Barbara's hanging weight.

I shook myself. Best to save my imagination for TV scripts.

Ben went to his uncle. 'Your mum's not here, Unc. You know she's buried next to Mum and Dad and Auntie May.'

'I'm aware of that,' the old man rasped. 'Haven't lost my marbles yet. But this'll be where they laid her when they cut her down.' He twitched the torch upward to light the horizontal bough. 'I'm sick of the dreams, son.'

Ben sighed. 'I know.'

'Memories. Stuff rising to the surface that I never knew was buried.'

'Come indoors, eh? You're cold.'

'Tell you something. The times I dream about, when it was just Mum and Thomas and me, sometimes she's happy. *Don't you worry, my boys,* she says. *Better times are coming.* But then it's night-time and she starts screaming, on and on, like she'll never stop. Thomas and me, we put our heads under the covers and pretend we can't hear. Then it goes quiet, and I go to the window ...' He shrugged helplessly. 'Then I wake up.'

'Was that the night your mum died?' Ben asked.

'No ... I'm sure it wasn't. But there's this name in my head. Daphne. She might've been a friend, though Mum didn't have many.' He turned to Lissa and me. 'Scoff if you like, but I think Mum's trying to tell me Daphne knows the truth.'

We didn't scoff. I ventured carefully, 'David spoke as if it's fairly certain, what happened to your mum.'

'She took her own life, you mean? Yes, she did that. They said it was grief for my dad, like Thomas and me didn't count. But if that's true, why do I dream of her being full of hope? And what did Daphne tell her that night to make her scream like the world was ending?'

'You can't be sure they're real memories, Unc,' Ben said.

'No ... but you two,' he pointed at Lissa and me, 'if you interview someone who remembers a Daphne, you need to tell me, and I'll be paying that family a visit.'

We both nodded, but Alf's commitment to finding answers sounded borderline aggressive. I thought privately that if anyone recalled a long-dead relative named Daphne, it might be kinder to all parties if we questioned them ourselves.

Alf consented to go home with Ben. They took the short cut between the tree trunk and the end of the fence. On their way up their own garden, we heard Ben promising his great-uncle a hot chocolate with marshmallows, just the way he liked it.

I resolved to ask all of our interviewees about a contemporary of Barbara's named Daphne. Netherzoy was so small, someone would remember her, if she had ever existed outside of Alf's dreams.

When we went to bed, Ben's window repair proved disappointing. Sometime after we turned off the light, our bedroom door once again latched itself firmly, startling us both awake, but draughts were inevitable in old houses. In future we would close the door ourselves.

Trying to fall asleep again, I couldn't stop thinking about what Alf had said. Almost imperceptibly, amid the shocking events of the past forty-eight hours, Barbara's fate had become important to me. If she had been happy and optimistic about the future, even after she was widowed, that made her suicide all the more tragic.

Whatever hopes Barbara had cherished for herself and her sons, better times had not come soon enough to save her.

NINETEEN

On Monday, we telephoned the handful of villagers whose phone numbers were alongside their names on the list. Most sounded pleased to be asked for an interview. One declined owing to poor health, but I asked her my question anyway. She had known two Daphnes – an aunt who had lived all her life in Yorkshire, and a school friend who had died of pneumonia in 1935, aged eight.

Not a promising start, but I would persevere.

We had booked only one appointment for today, at one o'clock, to allow time for shopping first and more paper-shuffling in the afternoon. Google flagged up a major store in the town of Lamport, which was smaller and closer than Bridgwater.

The trip proved quite enjoyable. Walking up and down the aisles, we bickered good-naturedly about meal planning and steered clear of other topics. We needed a respite from brooding over the Macraes' troubles, as well as our own.

Returning to Netherzoy with a week's supplies, we made a salad to compensate for the recent instant meals and takeaways. Since I was short of clean clothes, having only packed for a short stay with Robyn and Ian, we also ran the washing machine.

Then we strolled along Peat Cutters' lane to meet our first interviewees. Ted and Gladys's bungalow smelled of furniture polish, every hard surface gleaming. I saw a duster stuffed down the side of a sofa cushion and felt a bit guilty that they had cleaned in our honour, but they seemed pleased to see us. Gladys, warmly clad despite the snug indoor temperature, settled herself in a self-riser armchair while her husband plied us with tea and Hobnobs.

They had both been primary school age when the war started, but they remembered it vividly.

'We were lucky, down here,' Ted said. 'Yeovil was bombed ten times, and Bristol and Bath caught it, but Hitler wouldn't waste bombs on sheep and cows. People were evacuated here from the cities.'

'Of course, our young men did their bit,' Gladys put in, 'Mr Oscar, Jackson's father, he paid for a plaque with the names of the fallen, to be added to the old village cenotaph.'

'Great man,' Ted added. 'Heart and soul of the village. Jackson's the same.'

'We don't think so much of *Mrs* Naylor,' Gladys said.

'Jackson's mother?' Despite her use of the present tense, I wanted to be sure that she didn't mean his late wife.

Gladys tapped the side of her nose knowingly. 'A very clever woman. Ursula and Guy Finch came here from Jersey in the December of '38 with nothing but a little suitcase each and the clothes they stood up in. Then we heard she was Mr Oscar's intended. Three months later, they were married and she was installed at Zoyland House, along with her brother.'

'Bringing Guy was a good decision,' I said. 'Two years later, the Channel Islands were under Nazi occupation.'

Gladys gave us a sweetly satisfied smile. 'Clever, see? But that Guy, he's a strange one. We barely saw him, right from the outset. Home-schooled by his sister, my mum heard.'

'He lives at Heron View now, doesn't he?' Lissa prompted.

'That's it. All alone at the back of beyond, down by

the King's Sedgemoor Drain. We used to see him out with his easel, didn't we, Ted? Painting birds. Of course, he'll be ninety-odd now. Not so keen on standing about in the cold.'

'Does he ever come into the village?' Lissa asked.

'Never, to our knowledge. I think Jackson visits every week or so. Isn't that right, Ted?'

Ted nodded. 'Him or one of the kids. The son, mostly. Alex. Bit above himself, but he's got a soft spot for old Guy.'

'And for his gran,' I said.

Gladys sniffed, as if that was no recommendation. Ted declined to comment.

On the short walk back to Yew Tree Cottage, we resolved to track down Guy Finch, who had somehow slipped down our list of priorities.

There was an unmarked car outside Spindlewood, a silver Volvo SUV. As we drew nearer, George Bailey emerged from the cottage, looking relaxed and not like a bearer of bad news. We exchanged friendly greetings, and I introduced him to Lissa.

'Any developments?' I asked.

'Fewer than we'd like. David's car didn't pass through Netherzoy again after it left Merlin Park, but that's not much help. The driver could have headed north or south from the end of Merlin's Lane.'

Harry might equally have turned into Honeysuckle Row and gone home, but unless he had a garage big enough for two cars, he couldn't have hidden the Audi there. The police would not be ignoring that option, but their enquiries could have ruled it out. They would have acquired the record of Harry's phone locations by now.

'South is Netherzoy,' I said.

'Plus a whole network of lanes and tracks leading to farms, hamlets, and clusters of cottages. The farms have security cameras, but no one's confessing to sight of a red Audi.'

'You think David could be concealed in a barn, if Harry or Conor has a farmer friend?' I asked, having baulked at saying *David's body*.

'You're not the first to wonder. There's been speculation online, and two farmers have reported trespassers in their outbuildings. Amateur sleuths can trample all over a crime scene and never know it. By the time they've finished, any evidence is compromised.' His dark eyes narrowed in sudden suspicion, tempered by an apologetic smile. 'You two haven't been joining in the fun, have you? Ben said you were out interviewing villagers.'

'For David's book,' Lissa said. 'Hand on heart, we haven't done any trampling. Is Harry still in custody?'

George responded tolerantly to this shameless fishing. 'No comment. But as a general rule, we can hold a suspect for twenty-four hours. Extensions are possible in some circumstances.' He glanced back thoughtfully at Spindlewood. 'Ben asked about a helicopter search. If our local leads come to nothing, that might happen tomorrow. He wasn't too pleased about the wait. I think he might try playing Poirot himself. Can you make sure he doesn't?'

That was a big ask. Once Ben dug in his heels, he wouldn't listen to anybody, as Chloe and I had discovered on Friday night.

'We can try,' Lissa said.

George then informed us that the forensics team had finished at Merlin Park, and I relayed our chat with the barista at Gordano.

Lissa added quickly, to pre-empt an accusation of interference, 'It was on our way back from Ledbury. We know DS Lampert had already spoken to Brandon, but we thought it couldn't hurt – and talking to us did seem to jog his memory.'

George was fine with that. He admitted that Mr Fogle might provide a new lead, and we parted on friendly terms.

Lissa and I knocked at Spindlewood to check on Ben's plans and found him looking excited. His eyes were sparkling, and he radiated nervous energy.

'Saw you with George,' he said, showing us into the living room. 'I've had an idea.'

Alf looked up from his armchair. 'A bad one.'

I guessed what that meant. 'You want to use the Jabiru?'

'Exactly!' Ben said. 'A mate from school lost a drone once. It went out of range and crashed, so Dave and me took the Jabba up to look for it – and there it was, plain as day, in a field of cows. If Dave's Audi is parked outdoors, we'll see it.'

The car was one thing, but if David's body was out there, Ben shouldn't be the one to find it.

'You could be jumping the gun,' I said, feeling like a hypocrite. In his shoes, nothing would have kept me on the ground. 'George said they're following local leads.'

'Sod that! There's a gap in the weather this afternoon. The viz won't be great but it's legal.' He searched Lissa's face and mine. 'Either of you want to come? Unc has trouble getting in and out of the plane, and if I'm on my own I can't see through the passenger window, so it'll take longer and I might miss something.'

There were other considerations. If he saw David's

body, having a passenger might give him a reason to stay calm and focused – but I didn't want Lissa to volunteer. He might become too emotional to make sound decisions, putting them both in danger.

Seeing her about to reply, I said quickly, 'I'll come.'

She rounded on me, eyes flashing. 'I was about to ask Ben what he meant about the viz being poor. I suppose that's visibility? It doesn't sound safe for any of us.'

'Ben's the best judge of that, sweetheart.'

'I think we should trust our own judgement.'

Ben was too relieved to notice the insult. He thanked me effusively, before suggesting we ride the Kawasaki to Merlin Park.

'You've been dying for a go,' he said, 'and you can borrow Dad's old gear.'

'Love to,' I said – and Lissa folded her arms and glared at me.

Ben glanced uneasily from one of us to the other. 'We won't take off if the viz is bad,' he said. 'Flying is really safe, honestly. There's only one fatal accident in every hundred thousand hours, and I do fifty hours a year, give or take. To rack up enough, I'd need to live, um ...'

Lissa got there first. 'Two thousand years.'

'There, see?' he said. 'We're more likely to be killed riding to the airfield.'

I rolled my eyes. 'Jesus, Ben!'

'Shit! Sorry.'

Lissa shook her head helplessly, still angry but also trying not to laugh, which was encouraging.

I took her hands, putting on what I hoped was a persuasive expression. 'If there's any doubt about the conditions, Liss, I won't get in the plane. And we'll only be on the bike for five or ten minutes each way.'

'Oh, stop wheedling, Pevensey! You'd better go and get ready, the pair of you, before you dig yourselves a deeper hole.'

But she was squeezing my hands so hard, I knew that she shared my concerns. I couldn't leave without making up ... just in case.

I kissed her forehead. 'I love you,' I said. 'Thank you for letting me go.'

Only after the words were out did I realise, with a superstitious qualm, that they sounded like a final farewell.

TWENTY

Ben checked that Alf didn't mind being left alone, then brought down his dad's biking gear from the loft. The helmet and gloves fitted me, and the jacket was wearable, though baggy around the middle, but the boots were too small and the trousers were useless.

'Dad was on the plump side of chubby, bless him,' Ben said. 'Still, it's only ten minutes down the road.'

Lissa was unhappy about the lack of protection. When we were finally about to leave, she kissed me goodbye, whispering in my ear, 'Be careful, love!'

We climbed aboard the Kawasaki, which started with a satisfyingly throaty roar. Once through the village and the thirty speed limit, Ben began demonstrating the bike's capabilities. As we dipped and swooped along the lanes, I found myself grinning with nostalgic delight.

Since it was a weekday and within working hours, the outer gate to Merlin Park stood open. At the inner gate, I hopped off to open the combination lock and bin a drifting ribbon of police tape that still hung from one hinge, and we rode onto the airfield and parked beside the Jabiru hangar.

While Ben was swopping his boots for trainers, which were better suited to using rudder pedals, I walked across to the caravan and opened the door. It had been shut up for too long; the stink lingered. I pushed the door back to its full extent, against the outer wall, just as Ben wandered over.

'I should clean up properly in there,' he said.

'Get a professional company in. I bet Jackson would pay. It's his land, and his security that was breached.'

'I s'pose.' He leant back against the open door, gazing

across the field to the runway. 'This was our special place, you know? Even after Mum and Dad died. When Dave came down, him and Unc and me used to come out here with one of those portable barbecues. Chloe too, sometimes.' He drew a shaky breath. Despite his determination not to give up hope, he must have been fearing those times were gone forever.

'What d'you make of the viz, then?' I asked.

He stood upright and turned a full circle, staring at the misty horizon. 'Good enough. Shouldn't be wasting time, though.'

In the portacabin known as the C-Hut, he estimated our take-off time for the flight log. Then we unfastened the hangar's tarpaulin curtains and dragged them aside, revealing the aircraft in all its miniature glory.

Ben grasped the propeller hub, leaning back for leverage as he pulled. I gave him a hand, but he could have managed alone. Once the Jabiru was outside on the grass, it looked even smaller than in the close confines of the hangar.

'Nice paint job,' I said, indicating the red and blue abstract image of a bird in flight.

'Dave designed that. I won't chat while I do the walk-around. Don't want to miss something and fall out of the sky.'

I kept quiet, unsure whether or not he was joking. He began a detailed inspection of the plane, big hands moving lightly over the propeller first, then the leading edges of the wings, then the tail and every part of the fuselage, before he stooped to check the tyre pressures. He was patient and thorough.

'Can't rush this,' he said.

'Anything I can do?'

'No, you're OK.' He took a fuel sample from a drain underneath the fuselage, nodding with satisfaction before throwing the phial's contents onto the dried mud floor of the hangar.

I closed up the caravan while I was waiting. Eventually, Ben wiped his hands on a rag and studied the clouds, which had turned a more dismal grey in the past few minutes.

'We need to get airborne or lose the weather window,' he said, opening the Jabiru's passenger door. The right-hand door, unlike in a car. 'Sit in, and mind your head. Feet in last. It's a knack.'

I followed his advice, ducking to miss the top of the aircraft's doorframe and dropping into the moulded bucket seat. Ben slid into the left-hand seat and shut us in, untangling some thin cabling to don a headset and offer me one.

'Less cramped than I expected,' I said.

'Yeah. I wouldn't fit if I was much taller, though.'

This was true. His unruly curls were touching the roof.

We strapped ourselves in, and he opened the door briefly to shout 'Clear prop!' before starting the engine. Obviously a routine precaution, as the only other sign of life was one elderly guy polishing his yellow two-seater a hundred metres away.

The engine fired readily, and after an impressive number of instrument checks, we taxied to the end of the runway, bumping over the uneven grass. There we paused for what Ben called 'into-wind checks'. Outside, the colours were draining from what passed for daylight, while a line of trees beyond the next field had developed a blurred and ghostly aspect.

As we lined up for take-off, I said casually, 'Keeping

an eye on the weather?'

'Yep.'

We moved forward, gaining speed rapidly. Although I had flown in a few light aircraft for work, this was my first experience of a grass strip. I was unprepared for our increasingly teeth-rattling progress, but the juddering eased as the aircraft began to lift. Then we were airborne and climbing smoothly.

I looked out of the side window, surprised at the number of drainage ditches – the rhynes – intersecting the flat expanse of pastures and ploughed fields. Where shafts of sun split the cloud layer, the water gleamed. The nearest ditch ran straight and broad as if pointing the way ahead, a sword of light slicing through the land.

The sunlight died, clouds ominously close above us as we levelled off at six hundred feet. A hundred above the minimum legal altitude, Ben informed me. He banked steeply to the right. There were farm buildings directly below, then a field, then another farm. I could see every detail. If we spotted a hastily dumped body, we would know what it was.

Watching the rotating landscape through my side window was dizzying. Feeling mildly nauseous, I glanced ahead to orientate myself. We were near the higher, wooded land at the eastern edge of the Levels.

'Zoyland House,' Ben said, pointing. 'Half a mile ahead at one o'clock.'

It looked closer. The Naylors' home was an elegant mansion in the local stone, complete with a swimming pool and tennis court.

'Merlin Park is off to our right now,' he added, turning away from the rising ground.

I took his word for it. All I could see were fields

intersected by full ditches. 'Does Jackson own all the land between the airfield and his house?' I asked.

'Most of it.' He turned a slow half-circle so that we overflew the airfield again, then banked left, allowing him to scan the fields himself. 'That's Honeysuckle Row. See the two cottages where Harry and the Yandles live?'

I craned forward against my harness, peering past him to glimpse them before Ben levelled the aircraft.

'Harry lives on his own?' I asked.

'Since his auntie passed on. She brought him up. His sister's moved away, got a job and her own place in Bristol. We ought to turn back. The viz is getting marginal.'

In every direction, we were looking into a milky haze. Only the land directly below was clear, giving it the unnerving appearance of a hole in a fog bank.

'Can't you fly on instruments?' I asked.

He laughed shortly. 'The Jabba's a bit basic for that, even if I had the rating. We have to fly VFR. Visual Flight Rules. Minimum legal viz is five kilometres. Three miles.''

Looking again at his simple dashboard arrangement, I got the point. There was no artificial horizon, for a start.

'I'll give us another ten minutes, max,' he said.

Through my headphones I heard another pilot requesting 'joining instructions' and a woman's voice responding, 'Runway 27, right-hand, no other traffic.'

'Yeovilton,' Ben said. 'They won't bother us here.'

We were alongside the broad, straight rhyne which I had seen the first time around. A dozen white cows grazed a neighbouring field, seeming undisturbed by our engine noise.

'That's the King's Sedgemoor Drain,' Ben said.

Near the rhyne, a red-brick house stood at the end of a gravel track.

'You'll see a house on its own,' Ben said. 'Heron View.'

I was barely listening. In the rhyne itself, not far from the house, a patch of reddish mud showed beneath the water.

Unless it wasn't mud.

'Ben!'

'What? What is it?' Panic in his voice.

I pressed my cheekbone against the window, squinting for a better view, but that section of the drain was already fleeing out of sight.

'Not sure. Turn around.'

He hadn't needed the prompt. The plane was descending, banking through a tight arc. The ground filled my vision, clear and alarmingly close. The rhyne swung back into view, then Guy Finch's house … and there was the patch of red, the edges sharp, unnatural. Not like mud at all.

'Is it Dave?'

'No.' But I felt cold inside. 'Looks like the roof of a car underwater.'

'Shit! *Shit!* Is it the Audi?'

'Can't tell.'

He increased the power, flying fast away before completing another steep turn, describing a figure of eight this time, to put the rhyne on his side of the plane.

I looked ahead, checking the visibility. Beyond the flicker of the revolving propeller, there was no longer much to see, just a ghostly patchwork fading into whiteness. With the drone of the engine in my ears, it was like being suspended in time, circling between earth and sky, delaying the descent to knowledge and grief.

A glance at my watch showed we had passed the ten-minute deadline.

'Ben, we need to head back,' I said.

He was twisting sideways for a final look through the side window.

'Right.' He started the turn, hand steady on the joystick. Whatever he was feeling, it didn't affect his flying. I had been wrong to doubt him.

The weather was deteriorating fast. There was no longer a definite cloud base. All around was greyness, our one reference point the small circle of green below. Not usually a nervous flyer, I fervently wished we were on the ground.

The GPS in the dashboard showed us as a luminous plane tracking across a back-lit map, but we were flying nearly blind. Locating the airstrip precisely enough to start our descent at the right time would be tricky at best. Every field, hedge and ditch looked the same as the last.

We could pick a different field. They were all flat, and some would be long enough … although that would be hard to gauge in the mist …

Ben asked abruptly, 'Not scared, are you?'

'Should I be?'

'Airfield is dead ahead. We'll come straight in. No point flying a circuit.'

He had chosen not to answer my question. I didn't ask again.

The descent was controlled and gradual, the GPS track encouraging. Still just whiteness where the airfield ought to be.

Suddenly, magically, the grass strip materialised. Dead ahead, as Ben had promised.

I glanced at him. His jaw was set, his whole being focused on the demanding job in hand. *David would be proud*, I thought, with piercing regret.

We came in at what seemed a high speed but turned out to be perfect. Ben flared the nose at the last second and we touched down with barely a bump, the Jabiru rumbling over the grass until he applied the brakes and we slowed to a walking pace.

'Neat,' I commented, trying for nonchalance.

'A greaser. I was lucky.'

In more ways than one. I now understood why three miles' visibility was the legal minimum. It sounded a long way. It wasn't.

'Sorry I cut it fine,' he said. 'You were right, though. It *was* a car.'

'Yeah.'

'That's it, then. Dave's in the King's Sedgemoor Drain.'

'We don't know that.'

'Shouldn't have kept hoping, should I?' He was unnaturally calm. The shock hadn't hit him yet. He unbuckled his harness, turning to me with dry eyes, his face wiped of all expression. 'It's right by Guy Finch's house.'

'Does Guy know Harry? Or Conor?'

'He doesn't know anyone.' Ben shrugged wearily. 'Best put this plane away,' he said.

TWENTY-ONE

I copied George Bailey's mobile number from Ben's phone and walked along Merlin's Lane to ring him while the Jabiru was being put to bed. In light of our discovery, George could hardly accuse us of interference. He passed his phone to his boss, who had evidently been listening.

She came straight to the point. 'The King's Sedgemoor Drain is several miles long. Can you give us a specific location?'

'It's near a house called Heron View. Jackson's uncle lives there. George is local, he might know it.'

'George is shaking his head. Do you have the GPS coordinates?'

'Sorry, I should have asked Ben. I've come down the road to pick up a signal.'

She muttered a frustrated exclamation, which I didn't quite hear.

'We can be outside the gate in ten minutes,' I said, not totally confident that Ben would be finished that soon. *Time to spare, go by air.*

'Perfect,' she said. 'We're four miles away. We'll see you there.'

I messaged Lissa that we had landed safely, then jogged back to the airfield. I found Ben struggling to fasten the hangar padlock. His hands were shaking and he looked white enough to faint, reaction setting in with a vengeance. I put a hand under his elbow and told him to sit on the grass and put his head between his knees.

'Get off, I'm all right,' he said.

'Take some deep breaths, then!'

Surprisingly, he obeyed orders while I told him the plan.

'I'll lead them there,' he said. 'I need to see for myself.'

'Lampert won't want us anywhere near a potential crime scene.'

He glared at me as if I didn't understand, but I did. For him and Alf, waiting at home for a call would be unbearable.

'If we go,' I said, 'we'll have to keep our distance from the rhyne. But you're in no state to ride. Want to be the pillion?'

He studied my face suspiciously. 'You won't be a nutter and write it off?'

'Give me a break! I'm not eighteen. Will your insurance cover me?'

'Only needs my permission. I checked that when Dad wanted a go.' He hesitated, then gave in. 'OK – but be careful, the track's a bit rough. Chloe took me down there once.'

'If it's impassable, we'll get off and walk.'

That satisfied him. We togged up and straddled the Kawasaki, and I managed a reasonably efficient exit from Merlin Park. Outside, Lampert and Bailey were waiting beside their silver SUV. We raised our visors but stayed on the bike.

Lampert's thin face had a pinched look, and her throat was pink as if with heat rash. A reaction to stress, I suspected. She could hardly berate us for handing them what might be a major lead, but she gave it her best shot.

'It's highly likely that you saw some scrap metal, but we need to follow it up. I hope you haven't posted anything about this online?'

Ben looked bemused at the suggestion. We must have had a signal while we were airborne, but chatting on social media would have been the last thing on his mind.

'Other things to think about,' I said. 'Don't worry, we'll be discreet.'

She gave a restrained nod of approval and turned to Ben. 'Do you have the coordinates?'

'Didn't note them,' he said, all innocence. 'But I know where it is.'

'Show me, then.' She came towards us, holding out her phone, clearly intending him to point to the location on Google Maps.

Her request was a gift to Ben. 'OK,' he said, and dug me in the back; a prompt to go.

We rode away, the engine noise muting any protests from Lampert. I kept the speed down at first, letting the detectives catch up – but when I opened the throttle along the first straight section, the acceleration was impressive.

I've missed this, I thought.

With the Volvo following, we passed Honeysuckle Row on our left, then turned right at the end of Merlin's Lane.

Ben leant close, his open visor bumping against my helmet. 'Next left!'

The track had once been gravel, but now had grass tussocks along the centre. Not the best surface for a road bike but negotiable at low speed. Behind us, the SUV was having no trouble.

After the first bend, however, there were deep runnels veering off at angles. Some were still full of water. The Kawasaki bucked and jolted, forcing me to put a foot down for balance every few metres.

Unless I made a decision now, this would end badly. Glancing in my wing mirror to meet Lampert's unforgiving frown, I picked the next firm spot near the hedge, waved her past and kicked the side-stand down. She drove another fifty metres or so, with mud-caked tyres and wheel arches, then stopped where the track ended.

Leaving our helmets on the bike, we trudged to meet the detectives as they were pulling on blue polythene overshoes. Beyond a stretch of long grass, the rhyne was as grey as the sky, ripples obscuring whatever lay beneath.

DS Lampert wore her chilliest expression. 'I wasn't requesting an escort,' she snapped, 'as you knew perfectly well.'

We had no defence to offer. Looking humble seemed the best plan.

She jabbed a finger at a narrow gate set in the hedge. 'So Jackson Naylor's uncle lives here,' she said to Ben. 'That would be Guy Finch, am I correct?'

'Yeah.' He was barely listening, his haunted gaze fixed on the water.

'Ben!' I said. 'Don't even think about it!'

'I have to see,' he said, and ran forward.

Swearing, I raced after him, with George on my heels. From behind us Lampert shouted, 'Ben! Stop right there, or I'll arrest you for obstruction!'

He halted, but not on her orders. Where the grass began giving way to more mud, parallel tyre marks led down a shallow slope to the edge of the great rhyne. We hadn't noticed them from the air; all of our attention had been on the water.

Even in the fading daylight, from here I could make out a red area near the surface, like some exotic algae bloom.

Ben had seen it too. He stepped sideways, clear of the

tyre tracks.

I gripped his arm. 'They've got this, OK?'

Lampert caught up with us. 'One more step,' she said, her voice taut with fury, 'and you'll be spending the night in a cell.'

'That's not scrap metal,' Ben said, with equal force.

'It looks like a vehicle,' she conceded. 'That doesn't make it David's. We'll arrange for its urgent recovery –'

'How urgent?' Ben said. 'It'll be dark soon.'

And with no more warning, he lunged forward, shrugging out of the leather jacket, leaving me holding it as he tore himself free and staggered through the mire to the water's edge.

George and I both shouted, but he didn't even look round. Lampert let out a string of surprising curses, followed by a command to George.

'Fetch him out and cuff him!'

The constable nearly caught him, but Ben lashed out. George ducked aside and skidded on the mud. Before he could recover his balance, Ben plunged through the shallows and threw himself forward, right arm arcing over to begin an efficient front crawl.

He wasn't thinking straight. If he meant to search inside the car, he could snag himself on something and drown. There was a reason divers worked in pairs.

While George hesitated, looking back at his boss, I stripped off my own jacket and waded in. The water was painfully cold. I clenched my teeth and started swimming.

Ben was already beside the car. Between strokes, I saw him reaching down, as if to find the handle of the rear passenger door. When my head tilted that way again, he had dived. An eddy swirled as the door opened.

By the time he surfaced seconds later, I was standing neck-deep beside him.

'Not there,' he gasped, blinking water out of his eyes.

'For Christ's sake, Ben, let the cops do it!'

His answer was to swim around to the back of the car and dive again. I followed, then ducked underwater myself, seeing nothing but swirling brownness, totally opaque. My eyes felt full of grit. A hard corner jabbed my arm – the hatchback opening. Ben would have no better vision. He must be feeling his way.

I came up for air. Saw his back in front of me, still submerged. He had been under too long. I grabbed his shoulder, and he surfaced, crowing for breath. His eyes were bloodshot. Like mine, no doubt.

'Dave's inside,' he gasped. 'I felt him. Help me!'

'No! We can't –'

He was gone again.

Inwardly cursing his obstinacy, I took another breath and went under, trying to orientate myself by feeling around the edge of the boot space. Ben was on my left. He jerked twice, as if pulling something heavy and resistant. I ran my hand down his arm and found what he was holding. Some sort of fabric.

I pulled with him. Whatever it was, it came free. Shifting my grip, clutching blindly, I was suddenly clasping an icy, flaccid hand.

I must have gasped. Then I was choking. In a panic, I found my footing and broke the surface, coughing up brown water. The corpse bobbed up, mercifully face down as it nudged against me. The head was partly concealed by a hood, but I glimpsed white, disintegrating skin, amid a drift of what looked like brown waterweed.

I thrashed backwards, desperate to put distance

between myself and … David. Ben had come up too. His face was empty of emotion. I was still breathing raggedly, too shocked to speak.

George appeared beside us. 'Get out! Both of you!'

Ben stirred, focusing on him with an effort.

George added more quietly, 'You don't want to see David like this. You can identify him later.'

When a mortician has made him presentable.

Ben shook his head fiercely, reaching out to turn the body over. 'I need to see him. He's my *brother*.'

George wasted no time on debate. He grabbed Ben's sweater and yanked him towards the bank, ignoring a flurry of curses and flailing fists. I struck out after them, finding it quicker to swim than to wade.

The instant that George had him on dryish land, he brought him to the ground and straddled his back to apply handcuffs. As I clambered out, he dragged Ben to his feet and passed him to a visibly irate Lampert. Then he strode past me, back into the rhyne.

We watched him guide the floating corpse to the bank. Ben had stopped fighting. He was staring at the body.

'George!' he yelled hoarsely. 'Take off his hood!'

George failed to comply. Lampert turned Ben away but he was still twisting round, trying to see. I moved to block his view.

'It's not Dave,' he said.

Lampert stopped dead. So did I.

'What?' she said.

He made some sound between a laugh and a sob. 'Dave's got short hair.'

George pulled the hood back. The lank, straight, light-brown hair which I had taken for weed was nothing like David's cropped curls, and this man had the words 'Self

Love' tattooed above his right eyebrow.

'Do you recognise him?' Lampert asked Ben.

I guessed the answer before he spoke.

'That's Conor Yandle,' he said.

TWENTY-TWO

All three of us who had been in the water were shivering. Ben was as pale as a corpse himself. Lampert had a restraining hand on his arm, but despite her earlier threats, we didn't seem to be under arrest. Neither of us had been cautioned, and there was no mention of handcuffing me as well. Ben's cuffs, I suspected, were intended simply to keep him under control.

Dragging Conor's body, George stumbled up the shallow bank, feet sliding in the mud and catching in flattened reed stems. Then he turned the corpse on to its back.

Decomposition had begun its grisly work since Friday night. Winter clothing left only his face and hands exposed, but that was more than enough. He was grotesquely bloated, white skin blotchy and threaded with dark blue lines. Worse, though, was the pinkish foam bubbling from mouth and eye-sockets.

I had seen plenty of skeletons, mostly from archaeological digs, but never a recently dead body recovered after three days underwater. My stomach heaved.

'Fetch the blanket from the car,' Lampert snapped at George.

'Thanks,' I said, through chattering teeth.

'It's for Ben,' she said.

Ben, to be fair, was shuddering uncontrollably with cold and shock.

'Got a spare?' I asked.

'Sorry.'

But she did relent far enough to retrieve our leather jackets from where we had slung them down. Having extracted a promise of good behaviour from Ben, she uncuffed him, enabling him to put his jacket on. George then returned to envelop him in a large woollen blanket.

'Started carrying it in December 2013, when the floods hit,' he said. 'It's come in handy a few times since.'

Zipping up my own borrowed jacket was immediately comforting. I hoped that Ben and I would be allowed, or ordered, to leave, but Lampert was staring pensively at Heron View. The old house had a newish door and windows, and the fruit trees had been shaped by an expert – probably Jackson's gardener. Sadly for Finch, the feeders for his beloved birds were empty. Perhaps, these days, he found refilling them too much effort.

The hall light was on, shining through glass panels in the door. A glow through the curtains in a downstairs room could have been from a lamp, or diffused light from the hall. If the latter, that meant no rooms were lit at all.

Lampert must have reached the same conclusion. 'If Mr Finch is in bed already, that might be a concern,' she said to George. 'I'll check. I want a chat with him anyway. This hedge would block his view from downstairs, but if sinking the car triggered an alarm, that might have brought him to an upstairs window – and if our luck's really in,' she added, 'the perpetrator used the headlamps or a torch to light the scene for our convenience.'

George snorted. 'If he did that, boss, you should buy a lottery ticket. And I'd hope Finch would have called it in.'

'I've heard he's a recluse, minds his own business. Wait in the car with these two, or I'll have three hypothermia cases on my hands.'

While Lampert made her way up the garden path, we squelched to the car. Ben was muddy from head to foot, having been forced to lie on the bank, but he had the blanket to sit on. George dragged a supermarket bag-for-life from a door pocket for me.

'Don't want the next occupant complaining of a soggy backside.' He installed himself behind the wheel and started the engine, turning the heater and fan up to maximum. 'This seat will have to lump it.'

Lampert was gone long enough for the heater to have some effect. The warmth was blissful.

'D'you think Harry killed Conor?' Ben asked.

George twisted round in his seat, his expression more sympathetic than his reply. 'You know I can't answer that.'

Ben chewed at his lip. Finally, he said, 'Dave could still be alive, couldn't he?'

George grimaced. 'Nothing is a given, Ben, but I won't lie to you. We're very concerned for his safety. Finding Conor won't change that.'

Ben shrank deeper into the blanket and changed the subject. 'I can't leave the bike here. It'll get nicked.'

'You're not fit to ride. You can come back later.'

He was too cold to argue the point, but he wasn't happy.

The solution seemed obvious. 'I'll ride it back,' I said.

George scanned my soaked jeans and trainers. 'Sure?'

'It's no distance.'

Ben thanked me gruffly. I stayed put for a few more minutes, partly to continue warming up but also to hear what, if anything, Guy Finch had witnessed. Outside, twilight had descended.

Lampert returned, talking into her phone. The light

showed her features set in their habitually severe lines. As George wound his window down, she ended the call.

'No joy,' she said. 'He might not like answering the door after dark. There's a broken window at the back, but it's been boarded up from the inside.'

'Must be recent,' George said, 'or Jackson would have had it fixed.'

'If he knew about it. We'll knock again tomorrow, in daylight. You'd better go and drop these two off.' She gave us a peremptory nod. Our antics seemed to have put her off using our names. 'Then find yourself some dry clothes and meet me back here. I've briefed the pathologist. She'll be here in twenty minutes. What's happening about that?' She pointed to the Kawasaki.

George told her the plan, which seemed to satisfy her. She tilted her head to see us better through the open window.

'We're grateful that you spotted the car,' she conceded stiffly. 'Ben, I understand how difficult that must have been – but you put George at risk. Kester, you shouldn't have got involved. You're both lucky that I'm not charging you with obstruction, or with perverting the course of justice – a serious criminal offence. I won't be so lenient again. Is that clear?'

Ben muttered something short but fortunately inaudible.

'We get it,' I said. 'Can I ask a favour?'

Lampert's thin eyebrows rose high, making plain that I had a lot of nerve.

'When you release a press statement,' I said, 'please could you keep my name out of it?'

She huffed with sour amusement. 'Gladly. The last thing we need is a TV personality attracting even more interest.' Her tone made my job sound vaguely distasteful. 'Tell the public too little, and they say we're dragging our heels. Too much, and suddenly innocent people are being libelled and trolled online, while wannabe Poirots start poking around and destroying vital evidence.'

I was relieved that we were in accord, for once, despite her numbering Ben and me among the wannabes.

She stalked off to stand guard beside Conor's body. I then had to steel myself to leave the increasingly humid warmth of the police car; but bringing the bike home would cost me nothing worse than a few more shivers, and it would give Ben some much-needed peace of mind.

All the same, the three-mile ride was quite long enough. The wind chill through my wet jeans was brutal. I also started to wonder if Ben's dad had been covered by the insurance solely because he had owned and insured a bike himself ... but it was a bit late now.

By the time I reached Netherzoy, my legs were aching with cold. At Spindlewood, I parked on the drive, dismounting stiffly as the police car stopped outside and Ben came to join me. I passed him the borrowed biking gear and bent to rub my freezing thighs.

'You were in the best place,' I said.

'I thought that.' He regarded me solemnly. 'Thanks. Again.'

Before I could reply, Lissa emerged from Yew Tree Cottage and came to greet us, her strides quick and purposeful. I would have warned her not to touch me, but it turned out that a hug was not on offer.

'Where the hell have you been?' she said.

I blinked. 'I messaged you.'

'Two hours ago!' She stopped, anger giving way to

disbelief as she noticed my soaked jeans and the brown water oozing from my trainers. She switched her attention to Ben's equally bedraggled and far muddier figure. 'Tell me you didn't ride into a ditch!'

George wisely saw no reason to get involved. He sketched a wave, drove off, and left us to it.

I clenched my chattering teeth. 'Can we talk indoors?'

She drew closer, sniffed curiously, and flinched. 'Oh, my God, what is that smell?'

It might have been the mud, but I recalled Conor's hand drifting through mine, his fragile skin sloughing off ... then his corpse nudging me, almost as if trying to communicate.

A wave of nausea brought me out in a cold sweat. I thought the smell on my clothes was death.

TWENTY-THREE

Lissa steered me into the warmth and privacy of Yew Tree Cottage. 'Shower first, explain afterwards!' she said.

Not usually a fan of obeying orders, I had no issues with that one. It took an overdose of shower gel and several luxurious minutes under the steaming spray before I felt clean as well as warm, and even then I was glad to have packed a thick sweater and jogging bottoms. Lissa came into the bedroom while I was tugging a comb through my hair.

I checked her expression in the mirror. Finding it friendly, I risked a smile. 'Sorry, Liss.'

'You should be. You couldn't spare thirty seconds to warn me you were delayed – and TV critics reckon you have a way with words.'

'Pack of liars.'

'Quite.' But the corners of her mouth twitched upward.

Encouraged, I sat on the bed and drew her towards me. She took my head between her hands, bending to sniff my wet hair.

'My midnight fig,' she said. 'Glad to see you're exploring your feminine side.'

'I aim to please.'

'You have your moments.' She kissed the top of my head and asked seriously, 'What happened, love?'

For the second time that day, she had called me 'love' as if she meant it. Horror was still suppurating near the surface of conscious thought, but I suddenly felt better equipped to deal with it.

'Any wine left?' I asked.

'Half a bottle.'

'Let's drink it.'

I hadn't wanted to think of food but found my appetite when Lissa brought out crackers and cheese with the wine. Curled up with her on the sofa, I brought her up to date, omitting the stomach-churning elements. She heard me out, then simply cuddled me – a favour that I willingly returned, sensing that she needed it as much as I did. There was hope for us, I thought, while we still cared enough to set grievances aside and provide comfort instead.

After a while, she picked up her phone to check the local news, but there was no mention of our discovery.

'DS Lampert must be keeping the press at bay.' She put down the phone with a sigh. 'Ben should never have done what he did. I know he's going through a lot, but that's no excuse for stupidity. If he'd got into trouble, you or George could have been injured, or worse, trying to rescue him.'

I hugged her close. 'He's just lost, sweetheart. And desperate.'

'He's reckless, thoughtless and pig-headed.'

'Ah.' I grinned. 'Not like me at all, then.'

'Like you at eighteen, maybe. He's twenty-two. He needs to grow up.' She kissed my shoulder. 'I feel horribly selfish saying it, but this is not the peaceful respite that Robyn planned for us. I'm not sure we're in a good place to deal with it all.'

I didn't want to leave Ben in the lurch, but Lissa had to be my priority. 'Have you changed your mind about going home?' I asked.

'No.' Another heartfelt sigh. 'I don't know. Shall we take some more time out tomorrow? Street is just down the road, isn't it?'

I didn't understand the question. 'Which street?'

'The Clark's Village in Street. It's a huge retail outlet. Last season's fashions at discount prices.'

'Shoes?' I was less than keen.

'Everything! Dozens of stores. Robyn mentioned it. Weren't you listening?'

If I had been within earshot, the information hadn't registered, but clothes shopping was not my favourite pastime. Left to my own devices, I would happily have lived in my old leather jacket and a pair of Levi's, keeping a couple of suits and a black-tie outfit to dust off for weddings, funerals or the occasional glitzy work event.

But I was a bit of a sucker for designer T-shirts. Lissa promised that would be enough to keep me motivated while she indulged in some intensive retail therapy.

'We could have lunch there,' she said, regarding me solemnly. 'And we won't talk about any of ... this.'

'No,' I said, adding apologetically, 'Tomorrow, definitely not, but ... I can't stop thinking, Liss, why dump the car by Heron View, rather than any other remote stretch of rhyne?'

'You think it's a weird coincidence because Conor worked for Jackson, and Guy Finch is Jackson's uncle?'

'Don't you?'

'Not necessarily. Most of the area's population must be linked to the Naylors somehow, and that spot might have ticked all the boxes. A shallow gradient, near Merlin Park and far from prying eyes. Old Mr Finch can't have recognised anyone in the dark and the fog, even if he went upstairs to see over his hedge. And the killer would know there'd be time to escape across country if they heard a police car coming along the track. Anyway,' she finished, 'DS Lampert will have plenty of new questions for Harry Diment.'

A search online revealed that, with permission from a superintendent, Lampert could hold Harry for up to thirty-six hours without charge. He had been in custody for that long already. Any further extension would require a warrant from a magistrate.

Lissa drew her knees up to her chin and tucked it between them, one of her favourite thinking poses. 'Ben's right, you know. David really might still be alive. Suppose there was an argument and Maisie went for Conor, protecting David. Might David have hit him, then panicked and gone to ground?'

'He'd have called Ben. And he wouldn't have left Maisie's body behind.'

'No,' Lissa agreed sadly. 'You're right, he'd never do that.'

Beginning to regret the lack of a substantial evening meal, I opened a pack of custard creams and scoffed most of them while leafing once again through Barbara's and Freddie's family album. Near the end, Thomas and Alf were older, so these snaps had been taken a year or so after their father died – and all on the same date, judging from their clothes. Barbara wore a smart blouse and skirt, and lipstick. I wondered who was behind the camera.

'She looks happy there, doesn't she?' Lissa commented, then leant closer, pointing. 'Is that what I think it is?'

On the lapel of Barbara's blouse was a detail, almost certainly a brooch. Two outstretched wings, one each side of a circle. Impossible to see the lettering, but I would have laid a bet on what it said.

R-A-F. The type of brooch given to pilots' wives and

sweethearts.

Ben's unique ring had come to him from his Grandad Thomas, one-time gardener at Zoyland House – and Barbara's elder son.

'Thomas must have kept his mum's brooch as a memento,' I said, 'then had it made into a ring when he grew up.'

'Who gave it to Barbara?' Lissa said. 'Oscar Naylor? Do you think they had an affair, after Freddie died?'

'She thought better times were coming. Oscar might have intended to divorce Ursula and marry her.'

'Oh, that's a leap! And he'd have needed Ursula to divorce *him*.'

'Mm. The flaw in my theory.'

In the 1940s, the only legal grounds for divorce had been adultery, cruelty, desertion or insanity. As far as we knew, none of those accusations had been levelled at Ursula; and whatever Barbara's hopes or Oscar's promises, the privileged Lady of the Manor might have preferred to stay married.

'Even if it's true,' Lissa said, 'David wouldn't include it in the book.'

'No. Interesting, though.'

The mysterious Daphne could have been a messenger, I thought. A friend of the Naylors, or of Barbara herself, asked by Oscar to tell her the affair was over because Ursula refused to divorce him. That wouldn't say much for Oscar's moral fibre, but he wouldn't be the first to rush headlong into battle, while ducking out of ending a relationship face to face. Cowardice could come in many forms.

But I kept that theory to myself, because an early night beckoned. Lissa was strangely turned on by what she saw as my delivery from danger, even though she hated me taking unnecessary risks.

I would never completely understand her, but would be more than happy to spend the rest of my life trying.

We drove to the Clark's Village next morning. It was set in the midst of the village of Street, its pedestrian walkways crossing the original roads. There was certainly a great selection of stores. I steeled myself for a long day.

In the first ten minutes, I bought three T-shirts, all from the same outlet, then spent two hours waiting while Lissa flitted in and out of various changing rooms with armfuls of clothes, periodically twirling in front of me to ask my opinion. I thought she looked stunning in everything, or out of it, which was obviously no help at all.

I broke before she did.

'That's it,' I said, as we emerged into gloomy November daylight with another full bag. 'It's lunchtime. Feed me!'

She laughed. 'I've had enough for one day, anyway – and I know you have. We've certainly spent enough. Shall we go back to Yew Tree after lunch?'

Sweet words. We took our logoed carrier bags to an Italian restaurant. On that grey, chilly Tuesday, we had our pick of vacant tables, and Lissa chose a window seat. Over pasta and salad, she scanned the passers-by with more than casual interest.

'What's up?' I asked.

'I thought a man was watching us from across the road. He's gone now.'

'Must have fancied you. Good taste.'

'It wasn't like that. Actually, he looked quite angry.'

I felt a flicker of unease, thinking of the online death

threats of a few months ago. We had never been accosted in real life, but for a while, we had both been looking over our shoulders.

'Probably some guy waiting for his partner and longing for lunch,' I said.

Lissa chuckled. 'My heart bleeds.'

We were halfway through our own lunch when she froze, staring at a point behind me. 'Kit! He's here.'

I whipped round in time to spot a large, shaven-headed individual with a pumped-up physique slide behind a pillar, which failed to conceal his bulk.

This was no innocent diner in search of a table. From his new position, all he could have seen was yellow paint. I felt a surge of indignation. Whatever this prick was up to, he had no right to interfere with our day off.

'Sod it,' I said, 'I'm going to find out what his game is.'

As I stood up, he happened to sneak a glance from behind his pillar, revealing a tattoo of a sheathed knife on the side of his neck. Our eyes met. His were fierce, but then his gaze flicked around the other diners, all potential witnesses to any confrontation.

He silently mouthed at me, 'Bastard!' and stormed out.

Lissa jumped up and grabbed my arm. 'Don't follow him!'

There was no point. He had a head start and was moving fast. Besides, I didn't want to catch up with him in an empty side street. He looked the type to think with his fists – or a weapon of choice.

We sat down again, but the odd encounter cast a shadow over the day, even though the man had done nothing overtly threatening and had almost literally run away.

Lissa thought he was a troll with vigilante leanings, who had recognised me by chance. I suspected a link to Lampert's investigation. Although the DS had agreed not to mention my name in connection with the case, my presence in Netherzoy was no secret, and social media might once again have become our enemy. The Macraes and Naylors were aware that I, as well as Ben, had discovered Maisie's body. Who knew how far that news had spread?

But why that should trigger anyone's anger was a mystery.

TWENTY-FOUR

Returning to Yew Tree Cottage, we decided to sacrifice the rest of our day off in exchange for peace of mind. If the village's social media groups were well informed about my recent activities and were becoming abusive, Ben would know.

We messaged him. When he had failed to reply an hour later, Lissa began fretting. She wanted the answer quickly, before we had to think about unpleasant characters hanging around the cottage after nightfall.

So we went next door, and found Ben more subdued than usual. I wondered whether that was solely down to the uncertainty over David, or whether, like me, he kept flashing back to Conor's bloated face.

He asked us into the kitchen and apologised for missing our message, adding in an undertone, 'I don't want to keep on about this in front of Unc – he's having a bad day – but they've got the car out. Had to use a crane, George said, from the other bank. More solid ground there.'

'Did he say if it gave up any clues?' I asked.

'Like DNA, you mean? No, but Chloe reckons that's possible, even after three days underwater. But there's something else. Mr Finch still wasn't answering his door this morning, so DS Lampert called Jackson to let them in. They found him in bed, passed away.'

We exclaimed in shock, and Lissa asked, 'Was it … natural causes?'

'Think so. There'll be a post mortem, but Jackson told Chloe he looked peaceful, like he'd gone in his sleep. No one's been since Alex was there a week ago, so he might've been gone three or four days before the car was dumped.'

'Poor old man,' Lissa sighed. 'Dying all alone like that.'

'Yeah, Chloe's upset, but Alex has always been closer to the oldies. He's going to drive up to Gloucester and break the news to their gran.'

My opinion of Alex rose a few notches.

'I think,' Ben added, 'Chloe's more worried that her precious boyfriend might've lied to her – about everything.' Seeming suddenly to realise that he was being a poor host, he waved a hand vaguely at the kettle. 'Want to stay for a coffee?'

The invitation suggested that he would be glad of company, so we sat down with him at the kitchen table.

'There's one good thing,' he said. 'Jackson's going to get the caravan cleaned.'

'Lets you off the hook,' I said.

'Yeah.' But he barely sounded relieved. There was too much else weighing him down.

'Is Harry still in custody?' I asked.

'No – worse luck! They charged him with taking a car without the owner's consent. Lampert could've refused bail, Chloe says, because of Harry's record, but her dad spoke up for him, argued that Harry was doing well at work and trying to turn his life around.'

'Aside from nicking cars?'

'Exactly. Jackson's too soft sometimes.' Ben was disgusted.

'In fairness,' Lissa said, 'Harry might have a chance without Conor's influence.'

'We'll see, won't we? He actually confessed to taking the car. Claims Conor messaged him at home, asked him to walk across the fields, pick him up at the airfield, and drive the Audi off-site. His own car was in his garage, so Chloe wouldn't have known he'd got back and gone out again.'

'Why couldn't Conor drive himself?' Lissa said.

'He'd been in a fight, got bashed over the head.'

'A fight with who? David?'

Ben shrugged. 'Conor never said.'

'Or Harry ran out of fairy tales.'

'I s'pose ... but I can see him helping Conor out, no questions asked. Conor wouldn't have hurt Dave because his mum would go ballistic, but Harry was frightened of him. Whatever Conor threatened, Harry wouldn't report it. There'd be no witnesses, and Conor would've half-killed him for grassing him up.'

'You believe he went to collect Conor and the Audi,' I said, 'like a good little car thief?'

'Dunno. But he says they left it in Honeysuckle Row and next morning it was gone. He thought Conor had got rid of it. And he swears he never saw Dave.'

'And Lampert bought that?'

'Must have.'

'Or she couldn't prove Harry was lying,' Lissa put in. 'He can't be the person whose DNA was on Maisie, or he'd have been charged with killing her.'

'Maybe. They got two sets of footprints from near the rhyne, by the tyre tracks,' Ben said. 'They don't match Conor's trainers, so he wasn't killed on the bank. Lampert is going to release the information that they're looking for two perpetrators.'

But even if one set of prints belonged to Harry, that wouldn't prove his guilt. The track was a public byway. We had no trouble listing other likely visitors, starting with Jackson, Alex and Chloe, and amateur detectives searching for David. Then there were bin collectors, posties, and even delivery van drivers, any of whom might have parked clear of the muddy section and walked to Heron View, then gone as far as the rhyne for a smoke or a cheeky piss.

Having exhausted all possibilities, I felt justified in changing the subject, to tell Ben about our inept stalker. He looked startled at my description, and then nervous.

'You know him?' Lissa asked.

'Nathan Yandle's got a tattoo like that. Conor's brother.'

'Oh! But why would he be angry with us?'

'Not you, just Kit and me. Chloe says Harry's got a theory that Conor did for Dave and Maisie, and then we clobbered Conor for revenge. He might've told Nathan that.'

'Great!' I said. 'So he's decided to shift the heat on to us.'

'He might have. Nathan can be a bit ... well, he's all right, but I wouldn't want to cross him.'

I laughed shortly. 'Looks like he feels crossed.'

'We'd best avoid him, then, till Lampert nails Conor's killer. Watch out for a green and white van with *NTY House Clearance* on the side.'

'Has Harry been sounding off online as well?' I asked, thinking that Nathan Yandle might not be the only villager baying for our blood.

Ben shook his head. 'He can't afford to put Lampert's back up.'

'Thank Christ for that!'

'Yeah. S'pose you haven't seen all the crap about Dave on *Spotted Around Bridgwater*?'

'We don't look at social media. What crap?'

'About people who've disappeared on purpose or faked their own deaths. Like he would ever do that. A few sickos are saying he killed Maisie to avoid vet bills.'

'Trolls are bullies with too much time on their hands,' Lissa said. 'Don't let them get to you.'

He tried a smile, but his eyes were haunted. 'I'm as bad. When I saw Conor's long hair, I was so happy 'cause it was him and not Dave. How sick is that?'

'You're only human, Ben,' I said. 'I felt the same. Stop beating yourself up.'

Lissa put her hand on his arm across the table. 'You're not sick. You're doing brilliantly, the way you're keeping everything here ticking over, taking care of Alf, and trying to support Chloe. It's amazing you can even think straight.'

'That's bollocks,' he said, squirming, but he was clearly grateful for the show of support. I was glad that Lissa had forgiven him for his idiocy at the rhyne, or at least had refrained from mentioning it.

She smiled and withdrew her hand. 'End of lecture. Can we say hello to Alf before we go, if he's awake?'

When we opened the living room door, Alf looked up morosely, but roused himself to be sociable. 'Suppose you heard Guy Finch has snuffed it?' he said. 'Poor old sod.'

It turned out that he had only met Finch once, as a child. He and his brother had thought the older boy odd. Finch had barely spoken, and then in a whisper.

'Mrs Naylor – Ursula – visited on her own, mostly,' he said. 'She liked playing Lady of the Manor, showing how caring she was to a war widow. When Mr Oscar came instead, we'd be told to make ourselves scarce. I think him and Mum liked sharing memories of Dad.' Alf leant back, closing his eyes to end the conversation. 'All gone to dust. All except *her*.'

As Ben showed us out, I told him about the brooch. 'Think your Grandad Thomas inherited it from his mum and had it made into your ring?' I asked.

'Oh ...' He was embarrassed at being caught out. 'Yeah, he did. I nearly told you when you asked before, but it seemed wrong, spreading rumours about my great-grandma. Because of Unc.'

'Sorry. Looking through the albums is making us nosey.'

'Nah, we're mates now. Mr Oscar might've had the hots for Great-Grandad Freddie, but he liked women too. I think him and my great-grandma had a thing going.'

'We wondered that,' Lissa said.

'Don't tell Unc I said so. He'd hate me slagging off his mum.'

We assured him of our discretion and went back to our lodgings. Lissa occupied herself typing notes from the Macraes' paperwork, but the family's anguish was affecting us both. She was quiet and withdrawn all evening, tears sliding down her face as she worked.

Seeing her like that tore at me. Our grief for Emily was always there, but there were times when our daughter's absence – the life she would never have, and the memories we would never make together – became unendurable.

I tried to offer comfort, but Lissa didn't want that. She said she was fine, 'just being silly'. I feared that she saw me as another source of pain. At home she would have gone for a walk, finding peace in solitude; but with Nathan Yandle a possible menace and darkness falling by five o'clock, she stayed indoors, trapped and suffering.

A series of distant explosions reminded us it was November the fifth. We watched the local display from the doorway. When I put an arm around her, she didn't shrink away, but neither of us felt like going to the village green for a close-up view.

She went to bed early and was asleep by the time I joined her. I lay awake for a long while, remembering our baby. The first time I had touched Emily, through the hole in the incubator, she had moved her limbs as if startled, screwing up her face; but the next time she had been quiet and calm, getting used to the feel of me stroking her skin. We had needed to be so careful not to over-stimulate her fragile nervous system.

When she was a week old, her hand had closed around my finger for the first time.

I took some deep breaths and tried not to think at all, concentrating instead on the creaks of the old cottage settling for the night. Once, the sounds were like footsteps ascending the stairs – so much so that, imagining Conor's brother breaking in, I went to investigate.

No one was there. All that met me was that light, cold breeze, which still wafted around despite Ben's window repair. It was as gentle as a sigh, mourning for all the sorrows those old walls had witnessed.

My low mood was making me prone to morbid imaginings. I went back to bed, but for some reason felt more at peace and was able gradually to sink into a dreamless sleep.

I woke to another grey morning to find Lissa's side of the bed empty and cold, and a message on my phone. *Gone out to clear my head. Back for breakfast. xx*

Dressing quickly, I shrugged into my leather jacket

while walking to the gate. The lane was deserted, the only sounds a cawing of crows and the distant drone of a propeller aircraft. In the field beyond the hedge opposite, four white cows were grazing.

I turned left, away from the village. The lonelier route. I broke into a run. Nathan Yandle could have nothing against my wife personally, but he might hurt her to get back at me.

Beyond the last cottage, the tarmac gave way to a grassy byway, trampled by regular use. Glimpsing the church tower behind a clump of pines, I crossed a stile and followed the track to where it emerged on to a minor road – Church Lane.

Saint Peter's stood on a raised bank, with a flight of steps leading up through the graveyard. There were new headstones in one corner, two with fresh flowers, but elsewhere many were weather-worn and tilted, their inscriptions lost to time, like the relatives who must once have tended them.

The Naylors' plot was alongside the path. Oscar's stone bore a Bible quote below his name and dates.

I have fought the good fight. I have finished the race. I have kept the faith.

A good epitaph. I wondered whether Oscar had chosen it himself.

I decided to jog the long way back rather than use the cut-through. If my sense of direction was true, Church Lane would meet the High Street. I knew my way from there.

When I reached the entrance to Peat Cutters' Lane, there was still no sign of Lissa. She could have extended her walk in another direction, but no route would be safe. There was little traffic and few pedestrians at this hour. I had seen one dog-walker, from a distance, and been passed by two tractors and a van delivering groceries.

I phoned her and felt a surge of relief when she picked up.

'Morning, darling.' Her tone was cheerful but with an edge of frustration. 'Didn't you see my message?'

In other words, *Why are you invading my 'me' time?*

'Where are you headed?' I asked.

'Back to you. I'm five minutes away.'

She assumed I was at the cottage. I didn't tell her otherwise. With hindsight, mooching around the village in the hope of meeting her seemed over-protective and rather pathetic. Returning the phone to my pocket, I kept walking.

A vehicle pulled up alongside me. A green and white van, emblazoned with the words *NTY House Clearance*.

I stopped. The van's approach had been stealthy. The driver must have been watching and waiting for either Ben or me to emerge from one of the cottages. Through the passenger window, I glimpsed his shaven head and ferocious expression before he got out, slammed the door and advanced around the bonnet with fists and jaw clenched.

'Kester sodding Pevensey!' he said.

TWENTY-FIVE

It seemed unwise to enquire whether he was Nathan sodding Yandle. I stood my ground, met his belligerent glare as neutrally as possible, and asked without heat, 'Is there a problem?'

He advanced to stand too close for comfort, six-foot-three of muscle and rage. His van must have had an efficient heater; he was bare-armed, displaying tattoos in which knives, snakes and skulls featured prominently, in contrast to the scent of lavender that was filling my nostrils. Whoever did his washing was generous with the fabric conditioner.

'What the fuck did you do to my brother?' he snarled.

A denial might fuel his anger, but the alternative was retreat. That would only postpone the confrontation till another day, or a dark night, and next time Lissa might be with me.

At least he carried no obvious weapon, although with that physique he hardly needed one.

I stated emphatically, 'Absolutely nothing. I never saw Conor until he was pulled out of the rhyne.'

'Liar!' He grabbed a handful of my jacket and shoved me back against the side of the van, while his other fist slammed into my side.

My ribs shuddered. I grunted involuntarily, which pleased him. He leered, his face so close that I could smell his breath. Bacon, mostly, blended with the continuing wafts of lavender. Delightful.

'You'll tell me,' he grated, reinforcing the message with another savage body blow, 'or you'll wish you'd gone in the rhyne with him.'

Since I had nothing to tell, he was likely to pulverise

me, but I wasn't going down without a fight. I stamped on his foot, regretting that my trainers were not designed to cause damage. He reared his head back in surprise more than pain, and I used the moment and both fists to deliver two quick, hard stomach punches.

His breakfast finished the job. He groaned, retched, reeled backwards, and turned just in time to deposit it over Spindlewood's low garden wall.

I pushed myself upright, gasping for breath. 'I've got an alibi ... on the M5. On camera.'

He was in no position to reply.

'We found the dog dead,' I said. 'Never saw Conor or the car. Harry's talking crap. Even the cops don't buy it.'

Nathan straightened painfully, clutching his stomach. 'You and Ben ... you're thick as thieves.'

'I'm here with my wife ... renting Alf's old cottage.'

He shook his head. 'You led the cops to the car.'

'We saw it from the air. From Ben's plane.'

He scoffed incredulously. 'So you're James sodding Bond now?'

I needed to keep the upper hand – or get him on-side, a safer option long-term, and he might know more than he had told Lampert. Conor could have let something slip about Fogle or the antique in the days or hours leading up to David's disappearance.

'Finding David,' I said, 'alive or dead, could lead the cops to your brother's killer.'

Nathan glared. He was still pale and sweating. 'So what?'

'We're on the same side. Want to compare notes?'

'Piss off! I don't know sod all.'

'What've you got to lose?'

He sat down heavily on the garden wall. 'You're

bloody nuts.'

He hadn't actually refused. I leant against the van and felt my ribs gingerly. They seemed to be intact. Considering the size and power of Nathan's fists, I could have fared worse.

'Why were you following us in Street?' I said.

'See where you went. Who you met. What your game is.'

He was desperate for answers, still winding himself up with Harry's crap and baseless theories of his own.

'When d'you knock off work?' I asked.

'Cancelled today's jobs, didn't I?' He averted his face, as if struck afresh by the reality of his brother's death.

'How about a chat now?' I said.

He went on sitting there, looking along the lane, but then his shoulders slumped. 'What's it matter? Everything's gone to shit.' He stood up slowly. 'But you'd better not be pissing me about.'

I kept my distance on the short walk to Yew Tree Cottage, in case he had a violent change of heart.

'Your wife's coming,' he said.

Lissa was walking faster than usual, her expression focused and frowning. We waited for her at the gate, and I wondered how much she had seen.

'Gonna tell her about … back there?' Nathan asked.

'Why not?'

'Don't want people thinking I'm a loose cannon. Bad for business.'

'I'm sure.'

'And I'm bloody not.'

'Good to know.' As Lissa reached us, eyeing our visitor with alarm, I said breezily, 'All's well, sweetheart. I've asked Nathan in for a cuppa.'

She looked into my eyes, seeking answers. If she had seen the scuffle, she would have said so, but she could tell something was off. I shrugged and grinned. She gave up the silent interrogation and treated Nathan Yandle to her sweetest smile.

'Pleased to meet you, Nathan,' she said.

In the living room, our guest sank into an armchair, stretching out his legs in their oil-stained jeans as if glad to sit down. I hoped his bruises were as tender as mine.

'Tea or coffee?' Lissa asked him.

'Earl Grey if you've got it. No milk or sugar.'

So much for stereotypes. While Lissa was offering condolences for the loss of his brother, I headed to the kitchen, leaving the doors between us open in case Nathan stoked himself up again.

'Ben's done this up nice,' I heard him say. 'Caramel Latte feature wall. Very restful.'

'You used to visit Alf and his wife here?' Lissa asked.

'Just the once. Me and Conor quoted for a new kitchen. Jackson's idea, but the old 'uns backed out. Didn't want the upheaval. Heard it's been done since.'

I took in the refreshments, including our open pack of custard creams, and sat down next to Lissa. She offered Nathan the pack. There were only three left after my binge the other evening. Temptation overcame courtesy and he took them all, popping one in his mouth whole and placing the others delicately on one massive thigh.

'You don't just do house clearances, then?' Lissa said.

'Mostly I do. Kitchen-fitting is for a bit of extra cash, like.' He made a shameless under-the-table gesture, before adding to me, 'You gonna cut to the chase? What were you and Ben doing at Merlin Park that night?'

Lissa barely blinked. She would have guessed Nathan

was here to talk about his brother. I explained briefly why we were in Somerset and what had happened at the airfield. At my description of how we had found Maisie's body, he was clearly discomfited.

'Lampert came to tell us about Conor,' he said. 'Thing is ... This doesn't go any further, right?'

That would depend on what 'this' was, but we nodded.

'He wasn't into pets, OK?' he said.

Lissa and I exchanged looks, and I asked bluntly, 'You think he could have killed the puppy?'

Nathan stuffed the remaining two biscuits in his mouth in quick succession, and chomped and swallowed them before saying, 'We had a little mutt as kids. Conor used to wind her up, till she bit him one day. He picked her up and slammed her against the door.' Nathan flinched at the memory. 'Killed her stone dead. Reece – our little brother. Half-brother, like – he went for him, shrieking and kicking, but Conor didn't give a shit.'

Conor Yandle had been a real charmer. Although his family would mourn him, others might be breathing a sigh of relief at his demise, including whoever had murdered him.

My disgust may have shown on my face. Nathan added quickly, 'He wasn't all bad, you know? Just saying he could've lost it with a dog.'

'Of course you don't want to tell DS Lampert that.' Lissa's voice was soft, inviting confidences.

Nathan was not immune to feminine charms. He smiled at her sadly. 'Wouldn't help catch whoever killed him.'

'But you can't seriously suspect Kit and Ben? The camera at the village shop showed Ben there after work, and Kit was driving down the motorway from

Herefordshire.'

Nathan grunted. 'Sodding Harry,' he muttered, shifting the blame for his own aggressive impulses.

'Could someone have had a grudge against Conor?' I asked.

'No one that'd act on it.' Nathan put down his mug and started picking at a broken fingernail. Admitting his dead brother's faults wasn't easy for him. 'He did a bit of dealing. Might've roughed up a few poor suckers that couldn't pay their debts, but not the sort who'd dare get back at him.'

'Did you know he was trying to sell an antique,' I asked, 'for a guy called Fogle?'

Lampert would have asked the same question. He shrugged. 'Name doesn't ring a bell, but Conor helps ... helped out with the house clearances when my regular bloke pulls a sickie. He could've found something. There's often stuff down the backs of drawers, like.'

Any such finds would be a perk for Nathan's crew, not Conor's sole property.

'When did he last help out?' I asked.

'September. Old Mrs Naylor's place.'

The Naylors again.

'She'd been living at The Lodge for years,' he said, 'but she'd been ill, had to go into residential care.'

'The Lodge at Zoyland House?' Lissa asked. 'The one that Chloe Naylor's started letting out for weddings?'

'That's it. Jackson hired us and let Conor off work to give a hand. As it was for his own family, like.'

'Did Conor find something valuable there?'

Nathan hesitated before saying carefully, 'Not that he showed me. I reckon Harry knows more than he's letting on. He was thick with Conor.'

It was an evasive answer. I stored the knowledge away.

'Jackson and Chloe don't see Harry as a killer,' I said. 'Do you?'

'Always thought he couldn't swat a dying fly on a dung heap, but now he's spouting all colours of shit, pointing the finger at you and Ben. Makes him look guilty as hell.'

'Or he's innocent,' Lissa said, 'and tired of having the finger pointed at *him*.'

Nathan rubbed a hand over his shaven head. 'Whatever, that's me done. What've you got?'

'Not much,' I confessed ruefully, 'but that might change.'

'What kind of deal is that? I warned you ...'

'What about?' Lissa asked, before I could respond.

His bemused expression was priceless. It appeared that his moral compass pointed away from threatening women, or perhaps just pretty women who offered him tea and biscuits.

'Just saying,' he floundered, 'Kit and me agreed to swop information. You haven't got any.'

'But we soon might have,' she said. 'We'll be doing a lot of interviews. Something relevant may turn up.'

Not that we would rush to share it, I thought, with a man who preferred private vengeance to the due process of law.

The bluff seemed to work, however. Nathan leant back, cautiously allowing himself to relax. 'You've picked a good base for looking up history.' He waved a hand at our surroundings. 'Most haunted house in Netherzoy.'

'Really?' Lissa was immediately interested.

'My old nan, she used to say Oscar Naylor wouldn't walk down this lane for any money after Barbara Macrae died here. Can't swear it's true – Nan could tell a tale – but she said Oscar's plane got hit over France one time. He made it back, but he caught some shrapnel. Put him out of active service for a few weeks. Story goes, he started visiting Barbara Macrae, keeping her company while the kids were in bed.'

'Company?' I queried.

'Yeah, well. Next thing you know, Barbara hangs herself. After that, her kids were always getting into fights, taking on anyone who said a word against their mum.' Nathan rubbed his midriff abstractedly, as if in sympathy with the boys' victims. 'And people would see her ghost after dark, staring out the window, or they'd hear her screams.'

'Oh!' Lissa shot me a startled look. 'Barbara hasn't bothered us, I'm glad to say.'

'Is your nan still alive?' I asked Nathan, wondering if her name was on our list.

'Nah, she passed four years ago. But it was Tommie that told me about the fights.'

'Thomasina?' I said. 'The vet?'

'That's her.' A secretive smile tweaked at Nathan's mouth. 'She likes to educate me. Spend time with Tommie Moss, and you'll learn a lot of stuff you never knew you were missing.'

His meaning was unmistakable. My mind conjured the memory of Thomasina's grey-green eyes locked on mine as she held out a bottle of Merlot and murmured suggestively, 'Shall we?'

'You two are an item?' I asked, avoiding Lissa's eyes.

'Nothing regular, like, but I take what's offered. A

woman like that doesn't cross a man's path too often.' He smiled at Lissa with unexpected gallantry. 'Mind, I'm easily tempted. No beauty of my own at home, unlike some.'

Lissa returned the smile. 'I can't wait to meet her.'

It seemed a good time to pull the conversation back on track. 'So what do you make of it all, Nathan?' I asked. 'Could what happened to Conor be linked to Ursula's house clearance?'

'Doubt it,' he said, wincing as he heaved himself out of the armchair. 'I'd best be off.'

We exchanged phone numbers and email addresses. As we closed the front door behind him, Lissa said thoughtfully, 'He knows something. Not about Conor's murder, or he wouldn't have believed Harry's theory ... but something.'

'Yeah. Not sure how we'll get him to open up. Still, look on the bright side. He's not gunning for Ben and me anymore.' I lifted my sweater and shirt to inspect the reddened area over my ribs. 'Just as well.'

Lissa gasped. 'Nathan did that?'

'Don't fret, sweetheart, I returned the favour.'

'He punched you and then had the bloody nerve to scoff our last three custard creams?'

'What can I say? The man's an animal.'

'It's not funny, Kit.'

'No.' Straightening my face, I caught her hand and laid it against my side. 'Want to come upstairs and kiss me better?'

She did laugh at that, though unwillingly. I studied her face to find the truth, not joking any more.

'Did walking help, Liss?' I asked.

She nodded. 'Today will be better than yesterday,' she

said, a mantra for courage that brought a lump to my throat – and without another word, she led me up to our room with the four-poster bed.

TWENTY-SIX

That evening, we walked to the village shop and treated ourselves to a chocolate bar each. I had met the cashier, but today we were served by the owner, an older man with a missing front tooth and a genial manner.

Although he was not on our list, in the absence of other customers he had time to chat. Lissa steered him into talking about the Naylors.

'I used to work for Mr Oscar, as a nipper,' he said.

'Good boss?' she asked.

'Pretty fair. Moody, though. He could break off talking and look straight over your shoulder, like he saw something you couldn't. Gave me the creeps. People said he suffered with his nerves, 'cause of the war. PTSD, they'd call it now. Not so sure, myself.'

The museum displays had not mentioned that; but during the war, and long afterwards, mental health issues had been regarded as shameful. Jackson may have been respecting his father's wishes – and, I thought cynically, preserving the legend intact.

'What do *you* think traumatised him?' Lissa asked.

'I'm with those that think he was haunted.'

'By Barbara Macrae?'

'There've always been stories. A face at the window, screams in the night. Some won't walk their dogs down Peat Cutters' Lane after dark. One pound thirty-two, please. Don't need a bag, do you?'

We didn't. I scanned a card.

'Heard you're staying at her cottage,' he said. 'Not been bothered by the ghost yourselves, then?'

'Not yet,' I said. 'Ever hear of a woman called Daphne, from Barbara's time?'

He thought, squinting in concentration, then shook his head. 'Sorry. Course, I'm not that old, but if she was still alive after, I don't recall her.'

On our way back to the cottage, Lissa said thoughtfully, 'If Barbara's neighbours heard her screaming one night – while she was alive, I mean – and word got around, that might have led to the stories after she died. People could have started to interpret … I don't know … owls calling, as her ghost.'

'I thought you believed in ghosts,' I teased her gently.

'I believe in common sense as well.'

'If the neighbours heard screams, Alf doesn't recall them rushing to help,' I commented.

'No … but Barbara had kept to herself, hadn't she, after Freddie died? No friends except Oscar and Ursula.'

'And possibly Daphne.'

'A woman that Thomas and Alf never saw, and no one else seems to remember. She's as elusive as Mr Fogle.' Lissa hugged herself as if suddenly feeling the cold, though her coat was warm. 'Are we focusing too much on the Naylors and Macraes?'

'Hard not to. Every conversation seems to lead back to them.'

'Mm. I suppose, if Barbara's story is within our reach, we ought to keep digging, even if the truth is too scandalous to pass on to Alf.'

'OK.' I drew her closer as we walked. 'As long as *you* won't find it upsetting. I don't want you fretting that she's not at peace.'

Lissa didn't reply to that, but she held my hand all the way back to the cottage.

Next day we had five interviews lined up. In the morning we saw a widow and two couples. As baby-boomers, none remembered Barbara, but we garnered a lot of material about post-war village life, before strolling back for a late lunch.

We didn't get that far. As we walked up the front path of Yew Tree, Ben accosted us from his own doorway.

'Unc's in your garden again,' he called. 'He's forgotten his coat – he'll catch a chill. OK if I go through the fence?'

We said he hadn't needed to ask, and he ducked inside his own cottage and shut the door.

'Shall we go down there?' Lissa said. 'I'd like to know Alf's all right.'

We walked through our cottage and down the garden. As before, the old man stood three metres to the right of the yew's spreading boughs, staring at the ground. Ben was guiding his uncle's arms into his long coat, the old man seeming hardly aware of his presence.

Lissa suggested brightly, 'How about a cup of tea, Alf?'

He raised his head, blinking at her as if coming out of a trance. 'I dozed off in front of the TV.'

'Did you dream again?' she asked.

'Same as before. I got out of bed and looked out of the window. But this time I didn't wake up before …' His voice tailed off, but his eyes held the memory of some unguessable horror.

A shiver went through me. 'What did you see, Alf?' I asked.

He indicated the ground at his feet. 'I've told Ben to dig. Right here.'

'What for?'

He wrapped the coat closely around him. 'I won't say it. Might have been an ordinary nightmare, meaning nothing. You could help, though. My digging days are long past.'

Thinking of our afternoon appointments, I asked bracingly, 'How about tomorrow morning, early as you like?'

He shook his head. 'I can't face that dream again, son. Not without knowing.'

That settled it. Besides, we had half an hour to spare. Ben fetched his uncle's spade from the shed and another from Spindlewood. Then he and I, being the strongest, set to work. Lissa brought out two kitchen chairs, to keep Alf company until one of us wanted her to take a turn.

The earth there had been undisturbed for decades, but it was soft after a wet autumn. In ten minutes, following Alf's instructions, we had created a shallow hole two metres across and found nothing but stones and snails, plus a major root that we were careful not to damage. The discarded earth was piled up beside the yew.

Despite the chilly temperature, I was starting to work up a sweat. 'How deep do you want us to go, Alf?' I asked.

'Till you find it, son.'

Even Ben protested at this. 'Come on, Unc, you have to tell us what we're looking for.'

'If you find it, you'll know.'

We began putting in more effort. By the time we were a metre down, I was wondering how much longer Alf would hold out before he felt obliged to concede there was nothing here to find.

'Either of you want a break yet?' Lissa asked.

Neither of us would be the first to admit to tired muscles. We called a cheery negative.

I was the one who hit metal. A curve of rusted enamel,

bulging from the side of the hole. Alf's directions had not been quite accurate. We had dug more deeply than necessary and had nearly missed it.

Ben and I sliced more earth away, while Lissa and Alf stood up and drew closer. A handle was exposed, at the side of some kind of tin, with a domed lid in which we could now see moulded dimples.

Ben straightened up. 'It's an old enamel casserole dish. Mum had one. Hey, Unc, you didn't bury your savings here, did you?'

But I had seen the change in Alf's face. It wasn't his savings.

Kneeling, I pulled at the handle, jerking it back and forth while Ben chopped away with the spade. In a few seconds I was able to lift the pot free.

It was oval, and big enough to cook a family meal for three days, or a Christmas roast. The lid had once been secured by what might have been a leather belt, but all that remained of that now were fragile scraps, along with a shard of rusty metal that could have been a buckle.

I pushed aside the disintegrated fastening and lifted the lid.

My breath caught. Reality fractured. I was looking down at Emily's body, my chest tight as if a great weight was crushing my heart. I was dimly aware of Ben's whispered oath and his hand on my shoulder.

'What is it?' Lissa asked urgently, from above me. 'Move, Kit! I can't see.'

'Don't!' My voice didn't sound right. 'Sweetheart, don't look!'

The skeleton was curled inside the oval cooking dish like a foetus in the womb, on a bed of what looked like damp dust, or fine compost. Perhaps there had once been a blanket. I needed to believe that the baby had been lovingly laid to rest in her makeshift casket, which had stayed intact for eighty years.

'My sister.' Alf's rasping voice sounded oddly far away. 'Daphne.'

I sat down and lifted the dish carefully onto my lap. There was so little of her left, she was no bigger than Emily had been. I placed a hand on the dome of the tiny skull, cupping it tenderly.

Lissa was suddenly at my side, her arm around me. She was sobbing helplessly. 'Poor little baby. Everyone forgot her.'

I turned to her blindly and we clung together, oblivious of Alf or Ben, alone in our private grief, while the old bough creaked above us, and Daphne lay quietly in my lap on her bed of dust.

When at last we came to ourselves, the Macraes had gone.

TWENTY-SEVEN

We focused on mundane tasks. Lissa cancelled our afternoon appointments, offering vague apologies and promising to rearrange them for another day. From the kitchen window, I saw Ben collect the dish and take it next door, perhaps fearing that a fox or rat would find Daphne's remains before the police did.

I didn't tell Lissa. She couldn't bear to look through the back windows. For me, it was that pitiful little skull under my hand that I couldn't forget.

Much later, the detectives came to see us. Catherine Lampert's frosty mask was nowhere in sight. She even told George to make us a cup of tea while she went out to look at the grave. They must have seen the remains already; they had visited Alf and Ben first.

We sat in the living room, which mercifully faced the lane. George set our mugs within reach and sank into an armchair.

'You'll have realised,' he said, 'that we had to look into your background, after the events at Merlin Park.'

We gave him some sort of acknowledgement.

'I'm sorry for your loss,' he said, giving the formal words weight and sincerity.

Lissa smiled faintly. 'Thank you, George.'

'Ben and Alf have agreed that we can access the scene via their garden. Even so, there'll be a lot of activity. If you don't want to stay here ...'

'We'll book into a hotel,' I said.

We hadn't discussed what to do in the longer term. All we knew was that, right now, we felt too drained and shaken to face a long drive.

'I suppose you don't know yet,' Lissa said, 'if the

baby really was Alf's sister?'

'Not until we have DNA results. Alf thinks the child was stillborn or died soon after birth, and that his mother buried her. He remembers hearing her extremely distressed and crying the name Daphne. He watched from his bedroom window as she took the dish down the garden. She fetched an oil lamp, he says, to light her work.'

When Barbara's screams had woken Thomas and Alf, she must have been in labour or consumed by grief.

'I gather her husband was killed in action two years earlier,' George added, fishing for our thoughts, but for Alf's sake we didn't want to share our theory about Oscar and Barbara. If Chloe's DNA swab from last Saturday showed a familial match with Daphne's, her parentage would be beyond doubt. Until then, we would keep quiet.

'Even if Barbara had recorded the birth,' Lissa said, 'her baby might still have been buried outside the churchyard, in unconsecrated ground. She must have chosen not to face the shame.'

George nodded. 'According to Alf, she hardly went out, and the Naylors were her only friends.' He paused, watching us, his dark eyes full of compassion. 'Look, we don't have to talk about this now.'

I would have let the subject drop, but Lissa shook her head.

'What does it matter?' she said. 'We won't be able to stop thinking about her. I keep wondering ... Do the police even investigate deaths from so long ago?'

'Anything less than a hundred years, yes, we do. Ben was right to ring me. But if the death turns out not to be suspicious, of course there'll be no investigation.'

Lissa reached for my hand. 'Alf is hoping the truth

will give him closure,' she said. 'I'm afraid it won't.'

'You may be right,' George said. 'It seems likely that his mother concealed her pregnancy. That enabled her to bury the child in secret. A victim of her times – but her child could have been a victim too. Unmarried mother, desperate situation ...' Sensitive to our feelings, he couldn't bring himself to spell it out.

Lissa said it for him. 'Barbara may have smothered her baby and later killed herself out of remorse.'

'Yes.' He looked at me, probably picking up on my silence. 'I'm sorry. We'll leave it there – although I should warn you, the autopsy might not tell us much. We may never know whether or not the child died of natural causes.'

Neither of us asked what types of foul play could be deduced from a baby's skeleton. I didn't want to think about it.

Lampert came into the living room. The bottoms of her trousers were mud-splattered, I noticed inconsequentially, but her shoes were clean. She must have worn polythene overshoes, as if Daphne's grave was a crime scene. I supposed it was, until they knew otherwise.

'Thank you both, for bearing with us,' she said. 'We do appreciate your patience.'

She was a softie, really. Bit of a change from our last encounter, when she had threatened to charge me with perverting the course of justice.

'Will we have to give a statement?' Lissa asked.

'No. We've spoken with Ben, and it's not as if you witnessed a crime. When you found Maisie, Kit, it was in your own interest, as well as ours, to record what you had seen and done. This is quite different.'

They left with apologies for taking up our time. Lampert even asked if there was anyone we'd like her to call, but Lissa assured her that we were fine, we just needed time to process what had happened.

Left alone together in the hall, we were silent for a long moment. I wasn't aware that my fists were clenched until Lissa came to me and stroked the backs of my hands, then laid her head in the crook of my shoulder.

'I still want us to finish the interviews,' she said, muffled.

'Long job. Big hotel bill.' My voice sounded all right but there were tremors inside me. Shudders, almost.

'Why don't we ask Ben if he knows of a nice, cheap cottage or apartment,' she said, 'before we search online?'

I couldn't summon any interest in David's project. All I could think about was the curve of Daphne's skull under my hand.

'Shall we book the nearest Travelodge and sleep on it?' I said.

Lissa tilted her face up, her great dark eyes gazing into mine. 'We can't go home without seeing this through, Kit. Or *I* can't.'

'Because of Daphne?'

'She's been lying out there forgotten, all these years. I can't bear it. I have to find out what happened.'

'Whether Barbara killed her, you mean? Who's going to know that? And even if you got to the truth, you couldn't tell Alf.'

'Not that, no. But if she was innocent, that would help him, surely?'

'It wouldn't help *us*, would it?' I said.

'If we go home, we'll have failed Barbara and

Daphne, and Alf.'

'You think?'

'Why are you getting angry?'

'Why are you putting this on us? We're not responsible for giving Alf closure.'

She stood back a little, calm and solemn. 'If you'd rather go home without me, I'll understand.'

'No! That's the last thing I want. *Christ!*' I turned on my heel, consumed by untargeted fury, wanting to punch the wall, to smash something. I paced the length of the hallway, seething, directionless. 'All we wanted was a fucking holiday. Was that too much to ask?'

'Kit … Kit …' She came and wrapped her arms around me, holding me tightly as if she could somehow contain the rage. 'It's all right,' she whispered. 'My dear love. We'll go and see Ben. He'll recommend somewhere nice for tonight. Not some characterless hotel.'

I took a deep breath. 'I'm not angry at you. If we've got somewhere to stay, maybe we can go on with the project, but that's not the same as focusing on … I can't think about it, Liss. Not right now.'

'I know. Go for a run.'

'What?'

'Punish the road.' She smiled sadly. 'That's your thing. Do it.'

'No. I want to be here for you.'

'I should hope so.' She laid a hand against my cheek. 'We need to be strong for each other. Run hard, come back sane.'

She was immovable. And right.

I ran for three miles along the hedged lanes of the Levels, past fields swathed in mist and beneath bare trees hung with clumps of mistletoe. Crows flew up, cawing.

Some more white cows were walking in line across a field, perhaps aware of the dimming afternoon light, heading willingly for shelter. Before many more days, they would vanish from the landscape, to be housed indoors until spring.

I set a fast pace, impossible to sustain for more than a mile, but even after that I kept pushing, the rhythmic beat of my trainers on the tarmac satisfying and ultimately calming.

When at last I let myself in through the gate to Yew Tree Cottage, Lissa opened the door. She tilted her head, eyebrows raised as I walked slowly up the path on jelly legs.

'How are you feeling?' she asked.

'Knackered.' I gave her a twisted smile. 'Sane. Ish.'

'Good.'

'I'm sorry.'

'Me too. I'll run you a bath.'

While I was soaking, she sat on the edge of the tub. 'Are you OK to talk about it?' she said.

I nodded reluctantly.

'Barbara didn't kill her baby,' she said. 'Alf heard her screaming and crying Daphne's name – the name that Barbara must have given her. Does that sound like a woman who had smothered her own child?'

'Hard to know,' I said wearily.

'Alf thought Daphne was in the house, talking to his mum. That suggests *someone* was. It would make sense, if she was in labour. And who was her only female friend? Ursula Naylor!'

'You want to talk to Ursula again?'

'I'd like us both to be there, if she'll agree. She might know that Barbara was innocent. DS Lampert won't ask her, because officially no crime has been committed, unless the autopsy throws up a surprise.'

I was willing to meet Ursula, but I was worried for Lissa. For both of us, really. She was investing a lot of passion and commitment in an eighty-year-old tragedy, which I would have preferred not to think about at all.

'I wish this didn't mean so much to you,' I said. 'If we fail –'

'We'll have done our best. That'll have to be enough.'

I knew that tone of voice. She had made up her mind. If I refused to go with her to Cedar Lawns, she would go alone.

'OK,' I sighed, and with kisses she tried to persuade me that I wouldn't regret the decision.

But I wondered.

TWENTY-EIGHT

We went to tell Ben and Alf that we were moving out. Ben was fiddling with an ear stud when he answered the door. I was uncomfortable that he had witnessed our raw emotion in the garden, and he knew me well enough by now to realise that.

'OK?' he asked.

'Fine,' I said.

'How's Alf?' Lissa asked him.

'Taking a nap upstairs. Talking to DS Lampert took a lot out of him. Are you, er ... coming in?'

'If that's all right,' Lissa said.

As he closed the door behind us, he squared his shoulders and faced the elephant in the room. 'Look, I – I'm really sorry. If I'd guessed what we'd find, I'd never have let you ... well, you know.'

He had been bound to find out about Emily. Despite our best efforts in closing down social media profiles, the information was out there.

'Please don't feel bad, Ben,' Lissa said. 'We're fine now. It was a shock, that's all.'

'Thing is, I, um ... googled you when Dave said you were coming. I never told Unc about your baby ... I'll put the kettle on.'

The therapeutic qualities of hot beverages were overrated, I thought; but we had coffee with him around the kitchen table, partly for Ben's sake. He needed to see for himself that we were all right.

'Life can be shit, can't it?' he sighed. 'I know .. well, sometimes it helps to talk about stuff. Do you, um ... want to?'

The prospect of a heart-to-heart filled me with dismay.

Our time with Emily had been private and precious. I was not ready to share those memories with anyone except Lissa.

She knew how I felt. She was the one who had seen a bereavement counsellor, while I had shied away.

'Not right now, Ben,' she said, 'but thank you. You're a lovely man.'

He blushed to the tips of his ears but also looked mightily relieved to be let off. 'No,' he stammered. 'I mean ...'

I took pity on him. 'We're hoping you can suggest another local billet.'

'Oh! You're staying on, then?' He was touchingly pleased.

'Still a lot of interviews to get through,' I said.

'Well, you don't want to pay for a place. Tommie's got a spare room. She lives in Burrowbridge, but that's not far, and she'd let you stay for free.'

'You can't know that,' Lissa protested.

'I do know, but I can ask her if you think it's polite.'

Lissa slanted me a questioning look, but I was willing to go along with it. We needed to hold on to our savings. One day, we might find a house that suited us both.

'Sounds good,' I said. 'Thanks.'

He messaged Thomasina there and then. 'She'll have finished work, unless there's some emergency,' he said. 'Bet she'll get straight back to me.'

He was right. She called back within five minutes, and Ben put his phone on speaker. He must already have told her about Daphne's remains, because she didn't ask why we had to move so suddenly.

'They're more than welcome,' she said. 'After the way they've been supporting you, it's the least I can do.'

We took less than an hour to pack, including the food from our grocery shop. Driving through the dark lanes to Burrowbridge, Lissa switched the radio on, and Lewis Capaldi's anguished vocals and heart-rending lyrics filled the car. *I let my guard down, and then you pulled the rug. I was getting kinda used to being someone you loved.*

She turned it off.

Robyn rang. The sight of her name on the screen pricked my conscience and sent my spirits into freefall.

As soon as I answered, she launched into recriminations. 'Oh, you're alive, then! Don't you ever read your messages? Not to mention two voicemails.'

'Sorry. Things have been a bit stressful.'

'Are you both all right?'

'Fine.'

Lissa put in, 'We're moving to the next village. Long story. Can we chat later?'

'Of course.' A tense pause, but she resisted the temptation to question us further. 'I'm sorry the cottage didn't work out. Ring any time after seven. The kids will be tucked up by then, fingers crossed!'

Having deferred the inevitable explanations, I talked myself into a more positive frame of mind before we reached Burrowbridge.

The centre of the village nestled beneath a round hill, quaintly signposted 'Burrow Mump' and topped by a ruined church. We would discover in daylight that Thomasina's side windows had a view of the Mump, but all we saw that evening was a bungalow set amidst a mature garden, with a mobile of moons and stars swaying above the porch and twinkling blue lights strung from the eaves. The name 'Greenways', burned into a piece of stripped bark, hung from an apple tree, while in a corner of the lawn, two man-sized monoliths leant close together, as if whispering the homeowner's secrets.

We walked up a drive lined with solar lights, and Thomasina opened her door. She wore a green and grey Indian-print dress, and her hair was loose and shimmering.

Lissa smiled sweetly at the woman I had described as capable and fortyish. 'This is so kind of you, Thomasina. We really appreciate it.'

'Delighted to have you.' Her gaze held mine a fraction too long, seeming to give the words more than simple meaning, and she stood aside with an expansive gesture. 'Your room is ready.'

We followed her through a dim hall painted purple and cream. A mandala adorned one wall, and a tabby cat hissed at us from a high bookshelf.

'Shut up, Bormo,' she scolded him. 'Don't be such a drama queen!'

At least he wasn't called Grimalkin. Bormo was a Celtic god of healing springs, so the cat might be friendlier than he sounded.

In our room, a candle supplemented the welcoming glow from bedside lamps. The décor here was more restful, with forest-green walls, and a duvet and curtains patterned with ivy stems.

'I've cleared a shelf of the kitchen fridge for you,' Thomasina said. 'I assume you'll be self-catering, but help yourselves to cupboard ingredients – nuts, seeds, and so on. You'll also find various herbal teas, and I keep instant coffee for visitors, if that's your poison of choice.' She gave us a warm smile, the perfect landlady. 'The bathroom is the first door on the left. I'll be in the living room if you need anything.'

She wafted out, opened a door further along the hallway, and closed it behind her.

'Good thing she's not offering breakfast,' Lissa commented. 'You'd be on the menu.'

'Thanks for the heads-up.'

'Like you hadn't noticed, Pevensey.'

'We passed a pub in the village, if you fancy dinner out,' I said, partly to change the subject but also because my stomach was growling.

'I suppose we should eat something,' she said, looking suddenly lost, as if wondering if her crusade was misguided after all; but if I tried again to talk her out of it, that would make her more determined to stay.

Instead I drew her in close, and she laid her head against my shoulder. I stroked her hair for a while, until she pulled gently away, smoothing the long curls back from her face and picking up her bag. Comfort had been offered and accepted. She was herself again, prepared to face the world.

'Let's go,' she said.

The local pub food was great, though we vowed to make the effort to self-cater more often, Lissa complaining that she had gained a kilo in a week. By eight-thirty we were back in our room. She was keen to prioritise the visit to Ursula rather than reschedule our cancelled interviews for tomorrow. Sitting cross-legged on the bed to ring Cedar Lawns, this time she was put through to Ursula's extension with hardly any delay.

'You again.' The old woman's tone was acidic, as if to quash any notion that she had been eager to take the call. 'Are you hoping for more fascinating anecdotes about the Netherzoy metropolis?'

'If you're happy to provide them.' Lissa was friendly

but business-like, nerves well under control. 'My husband is keen to meet you. Would you mind if he joins us? Tomorrow, if you're free.'

'Why should Kester Pevensey be interested in my ramblings?'

'He's a historian, and not many of the older villagers have a memory as good as yours.'

'Flattery never sways me.'

'Truth is not flattery, Ursula.'

She barked with laughter. 'You've found some spark. You assured me, during our first conversation, that your research would be used exclusively for David Macrae's book –'

'Yes, that's –'

'Are you being deceptive? Kester has a new series in the pipeline, about cold cases. He may be looking for material.'

Taken aback, Lissa met my eyes as she replied carefully, 'There's no deceit on our part, Ursula. We'll give all our files to the Macraes. If Netherzoy holds any unsolved mysteries, they won't be featured on *Enigmas*. In fact, the series will never broadcast any family's story without their permission.'

'Good. Not that it's a concern. Do you have specific questions? If I know in advance, I can search my aged brain and prepare some notes.'

She was on her guard, I thought. Recent events may have left her feeling insecure, even vulnerable. Since the previous interview, she had suffered at least one episode of confusion, and Alex had brought her news of her brother's death.

'I'm sorry, we haven't come up with the questions yet,' Lissa said. 'We weren't sure that you would agree to see us.'

'It's now nine o'clock. Not quite an anti-social hour, but close. That implies you have an urgent reason for wanting to see me tomorrow, and that you know precisely what you want to talk about.'

When Ursula was in full command of her faculties, she was formidable. I mimed at Lissa, 'Just ask her!'

She shook her head. 'You're right,' she told Ursula, 'but I'd rather not discuss it over the phone.'

'In case I become bored or take offence and hang up on you?'

Lissa rolled her eyes at me, then took a breath and abandoned caution. 'Exactly.'

The tactic worked. Ursula cackled with mirth. 'I'll see you both in the morning. Eleven o'clock sharp. And if I don't like what you have to say, I'll have you thrown out.'

She ended the call in her usual abrupt fashion, but we agreed that Lissa had won the round.

Since we would be heading in Robyn's direction, I called her and suggested meeting in Ledbury to see the new gallery. She offered to book us a table for a pub lunch, which won my approval, and in return I promised to tell her all the news tomorrow.

'So much for self-catering,' Lissa grumbled, turning in front of the mirror and frowning at her waistline.

'You're beautiful,' I said, truthfully.

'You're biased.'

She sat beside me on top of the duvet and leant back against the pillows with a sigh, meeting my eyes with such sadness that my heart contracted; and she turned to gather me into her arms, holding me close enough that I could feel her heartbeat.

'I love you so much,' I whispered into her hair. 'We'll get through this. I promise.'

But although she didn't reply, I knew her answer.

Love was not always enough.

TWENTY-NINE

The care home was a converted Georgian mansion on the outskirts of Gloucester. Having returned to their website for a second look, I had been newly impressed by the facilities, which included a small indoor pool and mature gardens. The perfect choice for those seeking tranquillity and luxury in their final years, as their site's homepage had stated.

The reception area was decorated in muted greens and cream, with swagged curtains and Chesterfield sofas. Higher maintenance than modern décor, but the oak sidetables gleamed, and portraits of long-dead worthies were complemented by antique gold frames, where no dust was permitted to linger.

The neat, dark-haired woman at the desk asked who we were visiting and indicated the signing-in book. A nurse came downstairs and spoke to a man in an inner office, their voices discreetly inaudible. He made notes on a laptop, and the nurse nodded and smiled. The exchange, simple as it was, spoke of efficient and harmonious teamwork.

'Ursula is expecting you,' the receptionist said. 'Nurse Tamara will show you up.'

The nurse took us up the main staircase and along a corridor. Ursula's was the last of four widely spaced doors. Tamara knocked, and Ursula called from within, 'Come in! I don't plan to get up.'

The bed-sitting room was spacious and bright, table lamps helping along the winter daylight. There were personal touches, too. Aside from the framed photo of Alex beside the bed, a collection of ceramic animals covered the dressing table, all with the distinctive patterns of Royal Crown Derby.

From her leather armchair, Ursula Naylor gave us a piercing stare that contrasted with her obvious frailty. Her appearance was immaculate. The tweed trousers and cashmere sweater looked new, and her nails were manicured, silver hair expertly cut in a bob.

'Hello, Ursula,' Lissa said.

'Hello yourself.' But the stare was aimed at me. 'Don't trouble to introduce yourself, Kester. I've seen some of your programmes. Think you're quite the history sleuth, don't you?'

'I enjoy my job.'

'And now you're here to annoy me with difficult questions.'

'We're hoping for an informal chat, Ursula. If there's a question you prefer not to answer, that's fine.'

'So I should hope.' She suddenly became aware that the nurse was hovering in the doorway. 'If I'd wanted you to keep us company, Tamara, I'd have said so.'

The nurse seemed unoffended. She asked us to buzz Reception when we were ready to leave, and closed the door.

Ursula was twisting her thin hands together, perhaps unconsciously. Considering her wariness in general, I was surprised that she had agreed to the interview.

Lissa must have been thinking along similar lines. 'If you've changed your mind about talking to us,' she said, 'there's no pressure.'

The old woman flapped a hand as if swatting at a fly. 'I'm curious. Sit down and get on with it.'

We shared the sofa opposite her chair. Lissa wanted to lead the interview, in the hope that Ursula would feel more at ease with someone she had met before.

'Do you mind if we record our chat?' she asked. 'Like last time?

'I do mind.'

Lissa folded her hands in her lap, as she often did in challenging situations, to stop herself from fidgeting. 'OK, well ... we wanted to come today because there's been a development.'

'The macabre discovery in the King's Sedgemoor Drain? My grandson has given me the full story.'

Alex would know the details, of course. Ben would have told Chloe all about it.

Lissa sighed. 'No, this is s-something else. David's disappearance, or our research, seems to have triggered his uncle's childhood memories. Ben and Kit ... Kester ... Alf showed them where to dig, in the garden at Yew Tree Cottage.'

Ursula drew a long breath through her nostrils, watching us closely. 'I see,' she said, with no sign of emotion. 'You found the remains of a newborn.'

'You knew ...' Lissa faltered, cleared her throat, and asked more firmly, 'You knew that Barbara Macrae's daughter, Daphne, was buried there?'

'I'd forgotten the name, but yes, of course I knew. Those little boys must have heard more than I realised. I helped deliver the child. Barbara had no one else. I would have dealt with the problem –'

'The problem?' I asked.

Ursula's eyes flicked my way. 'The child. I would have buried her. Barbara was not physically up to the task, and quite hysterical. But the silly woman snatched the infant's body. I left her to it.'

Her off-hand attitude was chilling. I tried to tell myself that she belonged to a stoical generation and must feel more than she wanted us to see.

Lissa asked quietly, 'Was the baby stillborn?'

'She died almost immediately after birth.'

'I suppose ... you don't know what was wrong with her?'

'I'm not a doctor.'

'So ... afterwards ... were you there, when Barbara buried her?'

'Certainly not. I told you, Barbara was hysterical. She wanted me gone. Oscar visited her the following evening and discovered her attempt at a grave. He said she had barely broken the surface. Any animal could have dug it up. Oscar dug the hole to a suitable depth.'

'We've heard,' Lissa said, 'that Barbara became depressed after the birth.'

'She did, but her mental health had been fragile before that. She had barely left the house in months. She even sent her boys out for groceries.'

'To conceal her pregnancy?'

'Naturally, but such isolation was bound to be unhealthy. If she'd had any sense, she would have got rid of it.'

'The baby?' Lissa said.

'What else?'

If Ursula was putting on an act, it was a good one. Could she really be this cold? Had her visits to Barbara been all about image, as Alf claimed? *She liked playing Lady of the Manor, showing how caring she was to a war widow.*

'Did you suggest that to Barbara?' Lissa asked.

'That she should have an abortion? More than once. I would have been happy to find someone with the appropriate skills.'

'But she chose to carry the baby to term.'

'Foolishness. You probably know I became her only female visitor. She didn't like it, but she couldn't shut the door in my face. Oscar and I owned her home.'

'Why did you continue visiting her if she made you so unwelcome?'

'She was a tenant. One has obligations. During the last two weeks of her pregnancy, I made sure to call in every day. One afternoon I found her in the early stages of labour, so I stayed.'

Ursula paused, staring down at her hands with an abstracted frown, as if considering how much to tell us. We waited in silence, giving her time, hoping she was in the mood to divulge everything.

'You two are tenacious,' she said at last. 'I think you're determined to solve every forgotten mystery in Netherzoy.'

'Are there others, then?' Lissa asked.

Ursula raised her eyes, her expression wiped clean, unreadable. I sensed that she had reached a decision, but she didn't answer the question.

'Barbara hanged herself less than a week after giving birth,' she said. 'If the child had lived, she would have been orphaned and dumped on relatives, like her brothers. She was better off dead.'

'Pretty harsh,' I said.

'Sometimes harsh decisions are necessary.'

She couldn't mean what it sounded like. I asked, hesitantly, 'Are you saying you were relieved, for Barbara's sake, when the child died?'

Ursula's faded blue eyes never wavered, but she began adjusting the cuffs of her sweater, tweaking them further down her hands. 'You know perfectly well what I'm saying. Even if Barbara had lived, she would not have been equipped, either emotionally or financially, to bring up a fatherless bastard.'

Lissa made a choked sound. I felt cold to my soul. Barbara, weak from childbirth, had only been able to scream her baby's name as she watched Ursula kill her.

If Daphne had been Oscar's daughter, that gave Ursula a motive, but neither he nor Barbara would have dared to accuse his wife publicly. It would have been her word against Barbara's – the charitable Lady of the Manor against the secretive village woman, who would then have been stigmatised by her neighbours, if not accused of infanticide herself.

'You can tell us what happened, Ursula,' I said roughly. 'No one is listening.'

She fixed me with an icy glare. 'I've told you enough. How you choose to interpret anything I have said is your business. But if I don't like what appears in print, I will sue whichever Macrae eventually publishes their book.'

'None of this will be included,' I said. 'Do you know who Daphne's father was?'

Ursula lifted a shoulder. 'Some clod of a farm hand, I expect, or an inadequate who had failed the army medical.'

'Really? The DNA results on Daphne's remains will be interesting.'

Her eyelids flickered. I didn't know whether Lampert would ask the lab to compare Chloe's DNA with Daphne's, but neither did Ursula.

'You're implying that my late husband was the father,' she said. 'That may be so. Oscar was not immune to temptation, but in this day and age, I doubt anyone would care that he had a fling with a local strumpet.' The outdated insult fell naturally from her lips. 'Even my morally upright son would get over it.'

'Then why do you care what goes in the book?' I said.

Rather than answering directly, she fired a question back. 'What is your interest in all this? We've established that it has no bearing on David Macrae's research.'

'We're doing it for his uncle,' Lissa said. 'To give him closure.'

'For Alf. I see.'

The hint of a tight-lipped smile made me wonder if she knew about Emily. If so, she could guess at our feelings about a baby's murder.

'I suppose you'll go running to that detective sergeant,' she said. 'You needn't bother. I'll deny we ever spoke about it.'

'Why confess to us, then?' I said bitterly.

'Because you need to understand that the dead have earned their rest. Who will benefit if you tell Alf Macrae that his half-sister died under a pillow? Is that the closure he's looking for?'

'We won't tell him,' I said.

'Then you have no reason to continue meddling in affairs that don't concern you.'

'Are you warning us off?'

She smiled thinly. 'I'm an old woman. All I can offer is advice, but I advise you to leave my family alone. The Macraes are entitled to look into their own family history. They have no right to know mine.'

I caught Lissa's startled glance. Ursula might not fear being held to account for Daphne's murder, but she was afraid of *something*.

'What does it matter?' I asked. 'Are you scared of what else we might find out?'

'I don't scare easily, Kester Pevensey. Never did.' She waved her hand towards a button on the wall. 'You can leave now. Buzz Reception.'

If she had not ended the visit there, I would have done. I had had more than enough of Ursula Naylor, and Lissa was sitting close enough for me to feel her trembling.

The nurse arrived promptly, and Ursula informed her that she was too tired to chat any longer.

'Never mind,' Tamara said. 'You can have a nice nap before dinner.'

'I've warned you before about patronising me.'

'Oh yes,' she responded cheerfully. 'You'll get me fired.'

'You think I can't? Keep using that tone and you'll find out.'

We made our escape. As I turned back to close the door, my final view of Ursula was of her sitting with folded hands, tolerating the nurse tucking a rug around her knees. A frail, elderly woman, no threat to anyone.

THIRTY

We didn't speak until we were in the car. I picked the driving seat because Lissa was still shaking.

'Bloody murdering *bitch*!' I had rarely seen her so angry. 'She smothered that little baby out of jealousy, and she doesn't even care if we know it.'

'Why should she?' I said. 'Nothing we can do.'

'For a start, we can tell DS Lampert.'

'She can't do much either, unless the autopsy shows evidence of foul play. Even then, Ursula could claim Barbara killed Daphne herself.'

Lissa leant her head back with a groan. 'Let's go, for God's sake! I can't look at that place any longer.'

I drove more aggressively than usual. When a car pulled out in front of us, forcing me to brake hard, I sat on the bastard's bumper for half a mile – until Lissa told me to get a grip or swop seats. I took my foot off the gas.

'Sorry,' I said.

She didn't nag about it. Instead she said quietly, 'I hate her, Kit.'

I couldn't recall her ever saying that before, about anyone. I laid my hand over hers, and drove the rest of the way to Ledbury without causing a road rage incident or breaking any speed limits.

We found a parking space and walked to Robyn's Fine Arts. The shop front was narrow but impressive, displaying several contemporary rural landscapes by the same artist. They were technically accomplished, with a fishbowl perspective which lifted them out of the ordinary.

This, I knew, was only the High Street face of the business. Robyn earned more from art appraisal, for tax or insurance purposes or as part of an estate valuation – a line of work which required delving into data from many sources. Like Lissa and I, she searched the past for clues to illuminate the present. I would value her thoughts on the Netherzoy situation.

There were no customers when we arrived. Robyn greeted us as usual with restrained hugs but genuine warmth, and we complimented her on the window display.

'We show a different artist's work every month,' she said, alight with enthusiasm. 'A perfect symbiosis. We gain a constantly changing window, and the artist gains exposure. By the way, I've booked a table at The Seven Stars.'

The pub was two or three minutes' walk away, and Robyn had requested a table in an alcove, ideal for a private chat. Although I had promised to pass on any news of David, my sister had begun to fret about our lack of communication generally. This was my fault. Not wanting to relive the discovery of Conor's body, I had let her hear about it via the media.

Daphne's grave was still not public knowledge, though the Naylors knew. In the comparative privacy of our alcove, I told Robyn about that. Even after two days, it was difficult. When I paused, ostensibly for a swig of beer, she let out a long breath.

'I was going to ask how you're both doing,' she said, 'but clearly that would be a really stupid question.'

'We're all right,' Lissa said. 'It was upsetting, but we're over it now.'

Robyn's frown betrayed her scepticism. Fair enough.

'Well,' she said, 'as you're determined to carry on with the research, I'm glad Thomasina has come up trumps. What's she like?'

'Nice,' I said.

Lissa snorted derisively. 'That's one word.'

'Oh?' Robyn queried.

'Try man-eater.'

'Really?' She slid me a mocking look. 'Is my little brother about to be spit-roasted and served with garnish?'

'If I catch him flirting with the Witch-Queen of Burrowbridge,' my loving wife said mildly, 'I'll be the one inserting the spit.'

I winced. 'You know I'm all yours, Liss. Now and forever.'

'Cheesy.'

'But true.'

Robyn moved the conversation onto safer ground. 'Did this all start because David resurrected his dad's project – and recruited you?'

'No,' I said. 'Most likely, someone found out Conor was bringing an antique worth nicking to a lonely location. If so, David was unlucky. Wrong place, wrong time, but nothing to do with us. You don't need to feel guilty for setting us up.'

'I wanted the break to do you good.'

'It's OK, Robbie. Shit happens.'

'But Netherzoy can't be exactly a crime hotspot, and now two murders have come to light within a week. Could they be connected somehow?'

'The Naylors keep cropping up,' I said. 'Of course, Jackson's a local employer and seems to own most of the village, but even so …'

'And now his mother wants you to stop investigating the family. If that doesn't imply a closet full of skeletons, I don't know what does. Mr Fogle could be one of them.'

'Unfortunately, there's nothing to link Fogle with Barbara,' I said.

'If the antique belonged to Ursula,' Robyn said, 'she's the link.'

'Could be, if Conor invented Fogle to cover a theft during Ursula's house clearance. Her dressing-table at Cedar Lawns is covered in small collectables. She may have had a lot more before she moved.'

'If something went missing, it might have gone unnoticed,' Robyn agreed.

'But,' Lissa said, 'once the paperwork was signed, the Yandles would have owned whatever they drove off with. If Conor had pocketed something high-value and planned to sell it on the quiet, he would only have been cheating Nathan.'

'Perhaps Nathan killed him, then,' Robyn said.

'I wouldn't put it past him. He assaulted Kit.'

'He thought *I'd* murdered Conor,' I pointed out. 'If he'd done it himself, why come after me?'

Having mentioned the scuffle with Nathan, we then had to explain and reassure Robyn that the problem was resolved.

'For God's sake,' she said, 'have you had a single restful day since you left us? And I'm not helping, am I?'

'You're an antidote to Ursula's poison,' Lissa said. 'We needed that.'

'Plus,' I added, to lighten the mood, 'you're a natural sleuth. Feel free to carry on bouncing ideas around.'

'Oh ... All right ... Could Conor have stolen the antique from Ursula's brother? After all, you don't know yet how he died. He might be the third victim. The fourth, with Maisie.'

But whether or not Conor had come by the artefact

legitimately, from whatever source, he had ended up dead. Lissa started theorising that Ursula had engineered everything remotely, acting from some dark, hidden motive.

My phone rang. As I pulled it out and saw Ben's name, I feared the worst. He rarely made voice calls, except in an emergency.

'What's up?' I asked.

'George called.' He sounded shocked, his voice unsteady. 'They've found Dave.'

'Oh, Christ. I'm so sorry, Ben.'

'No, he's OK. I mean he's been in a coma, but he's out of it now, and they're saying I can visit –'

'Wait – *what?* David's in hospital? But how … You called them.'

'Not the right one. It's too far away.'

'Jesus! Where the hell is he?'

'Southampton,' he said.

THIRTY-ONE

Ben had rung Southampton General, but the conversation had been frustrating. He knew, from George, that David had been admitted under a false name, but the police had asked hospital staff to give no information over the phone to anyone claiming to be family. Visitors would need photo ID. Thomasina planned to drive Ben and Alf to Southampton that evening, after completing a scheduled surgery.

George had also warned the Macraes to share the news only with close relatives. A waste of breath. Since Ben had included us, he was bound to tell Chloe, who would almost certainly pass it on to the rest of her family and probably the Grail Knights as well. The whole village would soon be buzzing. Lampert's security measures might be tested.

Robyn, however, promised to tell no one except Ian. Lissa and I passed most of the journey to Burrowbridge trying to fathom why the person who had taken David to hospital – most likely Harry – had picked one eighty miles away and then given him a false name, when David himself was bound to set the record straight when he woke up.

Our best guess was that Harry had wanted to keep David's whereabouts secret, in case his attacker came to finish the job. He could have bargained on the police taking over the responsibility if or when David came round.

'Harry must have been confident that David wouldn't identify him,' Lissa said, 'which suggests he wasn't there when David was attacked. That fits with his story, that he was asked to collect the Audi from Merlin Park –'

'But not by Conor, if he was already in the boot.'

'No. The killer may have thought he'd left *two* bodies at the field, or in the car,' Lissa said thoughtfully. 'What if Harry was just told to collect the car, ask no questions and take it to the King's Sedgemoor Drain? He might never have known about Conor. If he found David lying in the car and decided to save him, why would he open the hatchback? So he could have chanced taking the Audi, rather than his own car, all the way to Southampton and back.'

It was a good thought. Harry wasn't built like Nathan Yandle. Moving David's unconscious weight to his own vehicle would have been no easy feat. More importantly, his neighbours the Yandles could have witnessed him trying.

We deduced that Harry would have driven south and east, regardless of his destination, to keep off the major highways and avoid ANPR cameras. After that, he might simply have continued as far as time allowed, before picking the nearest accident and emergency department.

Lissa experimented with Google Maps, bringing up directions from Netherzoy to Southampton General, then moving the waypoints to find a route that avoided major towns and highways.

'It's tricky,' she said. 'And slow. Over three hours … but he may have thought Salisbury wasn't far enough away. That means, allowing time for hospital staff to move David from the car, it could have been an eight-hour round trip.'

I thought back to the footage that Lampert had shown us, of Harry opening the gate to leave Merlin Park. 'He didn't get away till nearly seven-thirty,' I said, 'and the odds are, when he got back, he helped the killer dump the car. Hell of a night. Impressive that he went to all that trouble to save a guy he doesn't know well.'

'So he's a decent human being. He wears a *Save the Bees* hoodie.'

'Not sure that'll stand up in court,' I said.

'Don't be mean! It shows he's not callous and uncaring.'

'To bees.'

'Oh, stop it! He didn't want to feel responsible for a murder.'

'Or be implicated as an accessory.'

'Well, yes, that too. I wonder what he told the killer when he turned up hours late and without David?' Lissa thought for a while, nibbling a thumbnail. 'Harry is loyal to the killer,' she said at last. 'All that time he was in custody, he never gave them away.'

'Loyal or scared.'

'I suppose David will have some of the answers.'

'Depends how hard he was hit,' I said. 'If he's been in a coma, that implies a serious head injury.'

On this sobering thought, we reached Greenways. It was nearly dark, so the blue lights were twinkling a welcome. Bormo the cat, impatient for dinner, rubbed himself against our legs as if he had never hissed at a guest in his life. We opened a can for him, to acknowledge the truce.

Our landlady arrived shortly afterwards, with George Bailey. He had pulled onto the drive as she reached the doorstep. It was an official visit, to catch her before she left for Southampton, but George's tweed jacket and slim-fit slacks might have been lifted straight off a mannequin. His loafers were so new, they were creaking.

'I assume you've heard?' Thomasina asked us.

'Ben rang,' Lissa said. 'It's incredible. We're so happy for all of you.'

'We still can't believe it. George, can you tell us how David is? The hospital's saying almost nothing.'

'The boss is there now,' he said. 'Barring complications, he could be moved to Bridgwater tomorrow and discharged within the week.'

'Oh, that's wonderful.' She turned away quickly. I thought she was struggling with her perceived role as the family's tower of strength. 'I need to change,' she said over her shoulder. 'If one of you could make me a camomile tea, that would be marvellous.'

Predictably, George knew where to find the herbal teabags. Thomasina returned with her gorgeous hair newly brushed and shining. She wore a voluminous green sweater that hinted at her curves, plus skinny jeans that emphasised them.

I concentrated on pouring three coffees. Noticing other women's beauty might be excusable. Drooling was not. George passed her the requested tea, and she sat down with a sigh.

'You should eat something,' he said, taking a seat beside her.

'We'll stop at a services. And don't tell me what I should do.' She smiled at him, taking the sting out of the words.

'But you'll stay in Southampton tonight?' He wisely made that a question.

'I'll book us in somewhere. It'll be good for Ben and Alf to be away from Peat Cutters' Lane. The local news site mentions remains from the war being found in a local garden. The ghouls will start to home in.'

'We're prepared for that. The boss had to give the

media something, and that seemed the least sensational way to phrase it. We'll keep an eye on Yew Tree and Spindlewood till you get back.'

'Thank you.' She patted his hand across the table. Their eyes locked.

Feeling that Lissa and I were gate-crashing a private party, I justified our presence by asking whether Lampert had spoken to David yet.

'For a few minutes,' George said. 'He's experiencing some short-term memory issues, and he still can't separate dreams from reality. The consultant says that's to be expected.'

Thomasina nodded. 'It's not like in movies,' she said. 'Coma patients don't just open their eyes and they're back in the room. The brain wakes up gradually. How long it takes for David will depend on how long he was unconscious and how deep the coma was.'

'He was only out for twenty-four hours. The consultant thinks his problems should resolve themselves in a week or so.'

'Oh!' Thomasina looked down at her mug. 'That's such a relief, George,' she said shakily.

'He might remember who hit him,' I said.

'Less certain, unfortunately,' George said. 'And as things stand, his last clear memory of that day is leaving Gordano Services.'

'Could he still be in danger?'

Thomasina looked up with a gasp. 'Surely not!'

'We can't rule that out,' George said. 'The perpetrator wasn't working alone, or not when the car was dumped. If his accomplice found David alive and drove him to the hospital, he must have lied to the killer. He probably said David wasn't in the car when he picked it up. By now, with no news to the contrary, our perp must be hoping David collapsed somewhere and passed away trying to get back to Netherzoy. That's why we're not making his whereabouts public.'

Thomasina asked calmly, though still with a tremor in her voice. 'But he's safe in the hospital, isn't he?'

'Without a doubt. He's in a private ward, with a local officer stationed outside, and all visitors will be ID-checked and monitored. Similar arrangements will be put in place at Bridgwater. Meanwhile …' George dragged himself out of the depths of Thomasina's eyes and focused on Lissa and me. 'Ben and Alf have no objection to you knowing the DNA results for the remains in the garden. Are you happy with that, Thomasina?'

'I've no strong feelings.'

'OK. Alf and the child are half-siblings, as he thought.'

'How about Chloe?' I asked. 'Was Daphne her grandad's child?'

George smiled crookedly. 'If you want to know that, you'd have to ask the Naylors.'

It had been worth a try.

Lissa asked tautly, 'Do you have the results from the autopsy?'

'We do.' He hesitated. 'You're sure you want the details?'

'Yes. Please, George.'

'Well, in the absence of soft tissue, the pathologist couldn't verify whether the child was stillborn or died soon after birth, but there's no evidence of foul play. The bones show no sign of toxins, fractures, or marks from deep wounds.'

'Could she have been smothered?'

George's eyes narrowed. 'I'm no pathologist, but I think significant pressure can damage the facial bones. They were intact. Why –'

'For a newborn baby,' Lissa said, to me, 'she wouldn't have needed to press hard.'

'Who, the mother?' George sat up straight, the DC back on duty. 'Did Alf witness –'

'No, he didn't see that, thank God. And it wasn't Barbara.'

Lissa relayed an edited version of our conversation with Ursula. George's expression grew troubled, while Thomasina set down her mug and stretched her arms out across the oak table, splaying her fingers and pressing them to the ancient wood, as if to draw strength from the contact.

'Do you believe her?' she asked Lissa and me. 'She couldn't have been confused? Thinking of something she'd seen on TV?'

'She was razor-sharp,' I said.

'It would explain why Grandad Thomas hated her. He used to call her "the harpy". Behind her back, of course.'

'Think he knew what a harpy was?'

'Oh, yes. If he called Ursula a monstrous bird of prey with a woman's face, that's what he meant. I suppose you can't charge her, can you, George?'

'Not a hope. Even if she volunteered a confession, her memory is known to be unreliable. Not to mention the fact that, officially, no crime has been committed.'

'Then we've hit a brick wall.' Thomasina finished her tea. 'When can you release Daphne's remains? Ben has asked me to help arrange a funeral service.'

They discussed the macabre logistics. After that, I thought to ask whether the DNA in Maisie's mouth had been analysed. George said, rather stiffly, that he really couldn't discuss that.

When Thomasina rose to leave, he gave her a peck on the cheek. Lissa hugged her, so I did the same, briefly.

'We'll be thinking of you all,' Lissa said. 'Give David our best.'

Not wanting to delay Thomasina further, I waited until she had gone before asking George whether Conor's, or Fogle's, antique might be the key to the whole investigation.

George twitched his eyebrows upward. 'Fishing again?'

'Give me a break. I'm curious to know your opinion.'

He relented. 'Whether or not it turns out to be relevant, there's still no trace of it. Nor of Fogle.'

'Could it have belonged to Ursula originally?'

'Because the Yandles bought up her house contents? It's doubtful. As Jackson could tell you himself, Ursula took her favourite ornaments to Cedar Lawns. Anything else of value had been sold weeks earlier at auction. Through David, incidentally.'

David being involved made sense, owing to his long friendship with the Naylors.

'How about Guy Finch?' I asked. 'Did *he* die of natural causes?'

'Passed away in his sleep. No suspicious circumstances at all.'

We saw George out. He advised us to take care and stay out of police business, and we promised to be good.

Over dinner – a healthy salad, to help Lissa lose her excess kilo – she confessed to feeling pessimistic about our elderly interviewees knowing anything useful. She wanted justice for Daphne, but knowing the baby would have a decent burial was enough for me. I was trying to forget the feel of her skull in my hand. I didn't want that mixed up forever with my last memory of holding Emily after she was gone.

'I think we could cut ourselves some slack,' I said.

Lissa compressed her lips, engaged in some internal struggle. I feared she would escalate the disagreement into another row, but instead she said firmly, 'I want us to go and see Nathan.'

I whistled. 'Wasn't expecting that.'

'He may not be my favourite person, but his nan told him about Barbara and Ursula. I'd rather talk to Thomasina, but she's got too much going on right now, and we do have Nathan's number.'

I was not averse to another chat. There was an outside chance that he might let slip whatever he had held back last time.

He took a while to pick up the call and sounded startled to hear my voice. 'Kit? I was gonna ring you tonight.'

'What for?'

'You first.'

'We'd like another exchange of ideas.'

He grunted. 'Same. Come round. It's just me and Reece. Mum and Amy are staying with rellies on the coast. Change of scene, like.'

I raised questioning eyebrows at Lissa, who nodded. For Daphne's sake, she would meet Nathan Yandle on his home turf.

'We'll be there in ten minutes,' I said.

THIRTY-TWO

The surface of Honeysuckle Row was little better than the track leading to Heron View. Our headlamps gleamed on puddles that disguised the potholes beneath, while the recent rain sparkled on a central line of grass; but we reached the end of the lane without blowing out a tyre, and parked outside the two semi-detached cottages that I had seen from the Jabiru.

Nathan's van stood outside the right-hand property. As far as we could tell in the dark, both houses were neat and well kept, with a detached garage each, and a picket fence surrounding matching rectangles of lawn. In the Yandles' single downstairs window, light showed through a crack in the curtains. Harry's cottage was in darkness.

I stood still, taking stock. We were alone in a black, hushed landscape, the only sound a distant murmur from the Yandles' television.

'It feels so isolated,' Lissa said. 'How close is Merlin Park?'

'Less than half a mile, by road or across the fields.' I pointed to the gate next to Harry's cottage, which marked the beginning of the path.

'You'd never know it, would you?' she said.

It was true. We could have been miles from anywhere. Nothing stirred but the damp air that chilled my face. The shrouded, silent land was breathing its secrets too softly to be heard.

Nathan must have heard the car. He opened his front door and checked right and left before beckoning us inside.

'Expecting trouble?' I asked, as he double-locked the door behind us.

'Being careful.' He indicated a spindly youth who stood in the living room doorway with a triangle of pizza halfway to his mouth. 'This is Reece.'

We exchanged casual greetings and the lad bit into his pizza slice. He was biracial, his thin face framed by the corkscrew curls known as baby locks. I recalled Nathan saying they were half-brothers. He looked about sixteen but may have been older, judging from the optimistic tufts of beard adorning his long chin.

'Want to see the murmuration?' he asked with his mouth full. 'The starlings. Shot the video today.'

Nathan rolled his eyes. 'They're not interested in that crap.'

'I am,' Lissa said.

Reece's face lit up. 'Cool!'

We followed them into the living room, where Nathan moved two empty pizza boxes from the sagging sofa, freeing space for us to sit. The aroma of melted cheese and pepperoni made me salivate, our salad meal having contained more greenery than substance.

Reece played his phone footage on the TV. It was a continuous shot of thousands of birds moving like one organism against a louring sky, an amorphous black form that flowed, stretched and whirled above the flat landscape. The display was hypnotic. At the end, the birds dropped to roost in a line of trees as if guided by a single mind.

'Scientists think they do it for protection,' Reece said. 'From falcons, mostly.'

'It's amazing,' Lissa said.

'I see 'em when it's dimpsey – after sunset, like – but I'm often out later, watching owls and bats.'

'He's nuts,' Nathan said.

Reece raised a hand as if to cuff him, and Nathan swatted it away with a mock-threatening growl. Reece grinned and perched himself on a faux-leather footstool, looking up at his older brother as if waiting for him to make the next move.

Nathan leant against the wall and crossed his arms, frowning at me. 'I'd have called if you hadn't got in first. We've heard about Ben's brother turning up.'

'My mate told me,' Reece said. 'His sister Amber's a Grail Knight.'

The friendship group chat was a dangerous hotline, I thought.

Nathan was keen to hear the details, obliging us to lie that we were as much in the dark as anyone.

'The cops are keeping his location quiet,' I said, 'for his own safety.'

Nathan flicked his brother an unreadable look, which Reece returned with a shrug.

'Have you heard,' Lissa asked, pursuing her own agenda, 'about the remains we found in the garden?'

'George Bailey was here this morning,' Nathan said. 'He let us know there's no connection with Conor. And he told me Harry's been released, and warned me to stay away from him. Tosser.'

Hard to tell whether this was aimed at George or Harry. I wondered if Nathan saw the handsome DC as a rival for Thomasina's affections, but today he evidently had more to worry about.

'There's stuff we want to tell you.' He looked down at Reece, and the boy nodded emphatically. The dynamic between them seemed democratic, despite the elder brother's bluster.

Nathan rubbed a hand distractedly over his head. 'We

can't talk to the cops,' he said. 'But we've got to do something, before the bastards who did for Conor come after him.'

'Why should they?' I asked. 'Reece, do you know who killed your brother?'

'No!'

'If you have any information at all,' Lissa said, 'you should talk to DS Lampert. She can protect you. We can't.'

'Look,' Nathan said forcefully, almost shouting. 'The cops can't help us. They never do. But you can ask the right questions while you're talking to people about bloody history.'

''What questions?' I said. 'We're interviewing people in their eighties and nineties, not Conor's dodgy mates.'

Nathan started to reply hotly, but Reece interrupted him. 'Even if you can't help, you'll be our insurance, like. It's safer for four people to know than just us two.'

'Surely you've told your family?' Lissa said.

'No way,' Nathan said. 'Mum would go frantic, and Amy would blab all over the village.'

Lissa and I exchanged glances. She was as curious to know Reece's secret as I was. Once he had enlightened us, we could try again to persuade the brothers to see sense.

'All right,' she said. 'We'll be your insurance.'

Nathan sat down abruptly, making the old armchair creak. 'It might've started when we cleared The Lodge,' he said. 'Old Mrs Naylor had moved out, so Jackson lets us in. Conor finds an old coat of Mr Oscar's and tries it on, and there's envelopes in one pocket, all stuffed full of letters. Conor starts shuffling through 'em, says they're love letters. Then Jackson walks in the room and Conor shoves 'em back in the pocket and asks to keep the coat. Jackson's fine with that, so Conor takes the view that he's been given the letters too. Job lot.'

'They won't sell for much,' I said. 'Letters never do, unless they're from a famous name.'

'But if they're rude, like, the old lady wouldn't want 'em made public. Embarrassing for Jackson and the grandkids. I reckon Conor fancied blackmailing her.'

'*Are* they explicit?' Lissa asked.

'Dunno. Conor wouldn't show us. Later on, after he'd had a proper look himself, he starts acting mysterious to wind us up.'

Reece said sorrowfully, 'He was like that. Teasing, kind of.'

Nathan nodded agreement. 'He asks me if I noticed the envelopes, but he'd given me no chance to see shit. Then he says to be patient and trust him, and there could be serious money in it for all of us.'

'Envelopes ...' Lissa tapped her teeth. 'Ursula came from Jersey. We should google the value of Jersey stamps from the 1930s.'

'I did that,' Reece said. 'They're worth sod all. Four for a tenner.'

'We've looked for the letters since,' Nathan said, 'but Conor must've had 'em on him that night.'

Could his killer have stolen them, I wondered, for Ursula's sake – or at her request? That would put the Naylors and their employees in the frame, but saving an old woman from embarrassment was a tenuous motive for murder.

Conor's search history might reveal what he had thought special about the envelopes.

'Have you checked his computer?' I asked.

Nathan shook his head. 'He did everything on his phone, but that wasn't on him when … when he was found. But the letters aren't the problem. We're just thinking they might be connected.' He threw Reece a despairing look. 'Tell 'em.'

Reece drew up his bony knees, visible through the designed slits in his jeans, and hugged them to his chest. 'Like I said, I'm out most evenings. Till late, sometimes. So me and Mr Finch –'

'You knew Guy Finch!' Lissa exclaimed, then blushed. 'Sorry, Reece. It's just that we thought he didn't see anyone except family.'

Reece shrugged. 'Two or three years ago, I was by his garden, taking pics of an egret. We started chatting about birds. He said I could come in for a cake.'

'It sounds as if he was lonely,' Lissa said.

'Yeah. After that, if I found a cookie on the gatepost, that meant I could knock for a chat.'

Here Nathan interjected, 'Reece never said a sodding word about all this till we found out Finch had snuffed it. The old nutter could've been grooming him.'

'Well, he wasn't,' Reece said indignantly. 'He was all right.'

'I'm sure he just enjoyed your company,' Lissa said.

'Right, well … about ten nights ago, there's nothing on the gatepost. It's raining, so I'm gonna head home. But then Conor drives up, so I hide, like, in the garden.'

'Why hide if you recognised him?' I said.

'He'd have beaten the crap out of me, thinking I was spying on him. But I couldn't leave' – Reece squirmed, shooting Nathan an apologetic look – 'in case Conor meant to rob Mr F. But he just knocks, and Mr F opens the door on the chain. Conor says he's my brother, and

Mr F lets him in.'

Reece paused, checking we were paying attention. A knot formed in my stomach as I visualised the old man, alone with his uninvited guest, in a house with barely any phone signal and no help within shouting distance.

'Then the hall light starts swinging,' Reece said. 'I see movement through the windows in the door. A scuffle, like. So I run round the back and lob a stone through a window to make Conor stop.'

'That was you!' Lissa said.

'Why not? It worked. Conor opens the door and looks round. Soon as he goes back in, I sneak round the front again. When he comes out, Mr F is holding on to the doorway. His hair's all messed up. He yells, "Bugger off!" and slams the door. Conor looks down at what he's holding and whispers, *Thanks, old man.*' Reece swallowed; the memory upset him. 'Then he drives off. I should've gone to check on Mr F ... but I went home.'

I did some mental maths. Ten days ago would have been three days before Conor was killed and the Audi was dumped – and after Alex's final visit.

'Been back there since?' I asked.

'Every night that Conor went out. But I never saw him there again.' Reece looked at each of us in turn, his expression set in misery. 'And I never knocked, 'cause there was no cookie. D'you think Conor killed poor old Mr F?'

Guy Finch's death could have been hastened by the stress of his encounter with Conor, but it would be kindest to gloss over that.

'Mr Finch died in his sleep,' I said. 'George Bailey told us. Conor probably just threatened him and gave him a shove to get the message across.'

Reece straightened his thin shoulders. 'It's my fault,' he said. 'He made Mr F hand over his special thing. That's how Conor got it.'

'Hang on,' I said. 'Are you talking about the antique? The one that Conor wanted David to value?'

Reece nodded. 'Mr F said he never normally showed it to people, but as we were friends ... Afterwards I told all the family. It was so beautiful.'

'What was it?'

'Dunno. It was silver, mostly, with weird-shaped gold bits, and a gold dangly thing. And bells. Mr F would only say it was a *special thing* but it'd never really be his. I reckon he nicked it, years ago.'

'What size are we talking?'

'Small enough to fit on my hand.' Reece held his right hand out, palm upwards, as if re-examining the object in his mind's eye. 'Might've been an ornament, but it couldn't stand up. Too many bits poking out.'

We were as flummoxed as Nathan and Reece.

'I think,' Reece said, 'Conor thought up the name Fogle because it starts with F, like Finch.'

'And you believe there's a link between the antique and the letters?' Lissa said.

'We don't know. There could be.'

'You mean Oscar or Ursula could have mentioned the antique in the letters, and Conor wouldn't have told you?'

'Yeah. But he only knew it was at Heron View because of me.'

'Conor made his own choices,' she said. 'You're not responsible.'

To distract Reece from feeling undeservedly guilty, we discussed whether Ursula might have brought her brother with her to England to save him from being arrested in Jersey. Lissa and I assured the Yandles that we would search the news archive and let them know if we found any clues.

They seemed heartened by the promise of action, and Nathan prompted his brother, 'You'd better spill the rest of it.'

Reece was growing accustomed to being centre stage. He sat up straight again, scanning our faces for a reaction as he spoke. 'I was outside Heron View last Friday night. I saw the Audi there.'

Holy shit.

'It was foggy,' he added. 'And really late. I'd stayed in after dinner because Conor hadn't come home and Mum was fretting. She didn't want me going off too. But I was nervous about what Conor might be doing, so when they were all asleep, I sneaked out.'

'What time was that?' I said.

'After two. Mum had waited up ages for Conor. Mr F's house had a light on in the hall, but the curtains were shut. Then I heard a car, so I crouched down by the gate, thinking it'd be Conor ... but it was two other men. Not with long hair like him.'

'Tall, short, fat, thin?' I asked.

'One was tallish, like you. Could've been Harry. The other one looked a bit bigger all round, unless that was his coat.'

Between them, those descriptions fitted half the male population.

'Definitely men?' I asked.

'Think so. They have a look at the rhyne, then the smaller one gets back in the car, opens the windows and drives into the water.'

'Under power?'

'Yeah. First of all, I thought he was trying to drown himself, but that seemed too weird. You don't take a mate to watch.'

'No. The guy on the bank, what was he doing?'

'Just fidgeting about. Then the car cuts out and starts sinking. The driver's holding his door open, then he jumps out and starts swimming. Next second, the water's over the roof. The driver claws his way up the bank, sliding in the mud and swearing non-stop. Then I must've leant on the gate, 'cause the latch clicks down ... and they both stare right at me. And I leg it home across the fields without looking back.'

'Oh, Reece,' Lissa said. 'You were so lucky.'

'But Conor ... he was in the boot all the time and I didn't know. I should've been braver, told them I'd rung the cops.'

'They'd have done for you too.' Nathan's voice was rough with emotion. 'You couldn't have saved him. George Bailey told us he'd passed on before he went in the water.'

Reece nodded, blinking hard. 'I just feel like shit about all of it. First Mr Finch, then Conor. He wasn't the best brother, but he was ours.'

Not a bad epitaph, all things considered.

'Think either of the men recognised you?' I asked.

'Dunno. They never caught me.'

That meant nothing. Reece had had a head start and he knew the terrain, and the men at the rhyne might have chosen to head straight home and establish their alibis, in case Reece had recognised *them*.

'For all we know,' Nathan said, 'they could be out in the lane now, waiting to slit your throat.'

'If they were, they could've got me days ago.'

'Yeah, 'cause every time I turn my back, you're out sodding birding.'

I said mildly, 'Nathan's got a point, Reece. You're the only witness.'

'And that's the problem,' Nathan said. 'If all those bastards saw was a shadow running off, this daft sprog is safe, right? But if he goes to the cops, he paints a sodding target on his back.'

The sprog looked mutinous. 'I'm not giving up my birding!'

Lissa stood up, reaching for her coat, the move effectively timed to stop the brothers from arguing. 'I wanted to ask if your nan had any more stories about Ursula,' she said, 'but I suppose you don't really want to bother with that right now.'

'I don't recall much else,' Nathan said. 'Not about the Naylors, like.'

'Never mind. We'll make a start on the Jersey archives tomorrow.'

'Are you gonna ask David what happened to Conor, when you can visit him?'

'We won't interrogate him. But he might remember, given time.'

Nathan shrugged, looking disconsolate. 'Head injuries can be a bugger. Might be a bloody long wait.'

Lissa regarded him solemnly, biting her lip, then tentatively patted his forearm. 'I don't know if we can help you,' she said, 'but if we can, we will.'

He gave her a wan smile in return and said to me, 'You're a lucky bugger, you know that?'

'My first thought every morning,' I said.

As we left the house, Lissa twined her fingers through mine. 'Is that true?' she asked.

I stopped walking. Nathan had already closed the door; we were alone in the quiet darkness.

'Always,' I said.

The light from the house showed tears glistening on her face. She might have been thinking about Emily or Daphne or feeling upset for the Yandles, but I feared that she was sorry for me, knowing how devastated I would be if she chose to leave.

I kissed her forehead and walked with her to the car, still holding her hand – and despite the Yandles having given us plenty to talk about, we drove back to Greenways in silence.

THIRTY-THREE

We didn't expect to hear from Ben or Thomasina, but Ben texted me around eleven as we were getting into bed. *Talked to Dave, all good!!! Staying over, visiting again tomorrow am.*

Relieved for the Macraes but too wide awake to sleep, we lay comfortably entwined, and finally talked about Reece's revelations. If Harry had been one of the men who dumped the Audi, the other could have been a mate of his, or a work colleague from Sedgemoor, or even Jackson or Alex Naylor. As for the antique, Lissa thought that might be a pocket-sized, highly-decorated book with a bookmark attached, while I favoured a high-end gift edition of a travel-sized game, relic of a bygone generation.

Growing tired of fruitless speculation, I suggested putting our wakefulness to better use, but Lissa elected to cuddle instead – always a tricky alternative. After a few minutes, during which I strove to be unselfishly affectionate while thinking boring thoughts, she giggled in the dark and kissed my nose.

'I'm being mean to you,' she said.

'Never.'

'My darling boy.'

She hadn't called me that in weeks. Originally, it had been a joke between us, because she could cite any amount of evidence that I was basically a child. My occasional yearning for a fast motorbike was only one example.

'I've been thinking,' she said. 'As well as looking up the Jersey records, we should type transcripts of our interviews, for David.'

'Not tonight.'

'First thing tomorrow,' she said, and kissed me properly before turning over, trying to relax into sleep.

I lay awake, thinking that all I had to do was give in, and the barriers between us would evaporate like mist in sunshine ... but if I did that, I would be taking responsibility for whatever might happen afterwards.

In the morning, since we had the place to ourselves, we set up our laptops on the kitchen table. Lissa could touch-type, and from long practice I was nearly as fast with two fingers. We finished typing up the recorded interviews, and Lissa made calls to arrange three more.

I then spent some time delving into the Finches' past. Ursula had been eighteen in 1938, and the site for Jersey births and baptisms showed about twenty female Finches born within a year of 1920 – but only one with the correct forename. She was listed as having a father and mother, unnamed.

Our best clue to Guy's birth year was the photo of him with his sister in 1938. I widened the search filter, assuming he had been ten to fourteen when the shot was taken. There was one Guy Finch, born in 1926, making him twelve in the photograph.

We were both registered with the British Newspaper Archive, so the Jersey Evening Post was the natural next step. Ursula was mentioned once, in 1925, as one of the infant cast of a school nativity play. Disappointingly, however, the paper's 1938 editions contained no reference to the theft of a valuable silver and gold artefact, either as an unsolved crime or linked to a juvenile suspect.

'This is hopeless,' I said. 'We need to ask George if he's checked the police computer.'

I texted him, but we were prepared to wait hours or even days for a reply. The Finches' early years would not be high on his list of priorities.

Ben sent me a brief, almost curt message around lunchtime, to say they were halfway home and he would call in to see us later. Concerned by the change of tone, I rang him. He answered quickly, but his greeting sounded flat and weary.

'Everything OK, mate?' I asked.

'Think so. Get my message?'

'Yeah. We'll be in all evening.'

Lissa leant forward to speak into the phone. 'Or we can come to you?'

'Oh ... hi, Lissa. If you could, that'd be great. I'm a bit knackered, to be honest. It's been all up and down today. Dave's OK but ... I'll tell you later.'

In case he felt obliged to offer us dinner, we said we would eat at our lodgings and come to Spindlewood around six.

Our first interview that afternoon was with a couple in their mid-eighties, who recalled Barbara only as a frightened face at a window. All the kids their age had believed she was a witch, and had dared each other to throw stones at her house and run away.

The couple also recalled that Mrs Naylor, courtesy of her industrious gardeners, had taken eggs and home-grown vegetables to the war widows, and the village kids used to scrump apples from the estate – until a rumour spread that Ursula would shoot trespassers personally. They had been more scared of her than of 'the witch', but no one had actually been shot.

The other two interviewees were women, both living alone. The elder, unprompted, mentioned rumours of

Barbara's affair with Oscar, but said the baby's remains in the garden had come as a shock. The younger offered some sporty anecdotes, useful for David's book.

Before returning to Burrowbridge, we stopped at the Netherzoy shop for salad and two pizzas. The owner gave us his gap-toothed grin.

'Buying enough for your landlady?' he asked. 'Better choose a Margherita for her – she's a vegetarian. Heard she's been to Southampton and back. Good news about David Macrae, eh?'

We were past being surprised by how fast secrets could travel through a small community.

Thomasina came home wearing one of her floaty dresses under a practical raincoat. She looked as tired as Ben had sounded, though her face lit at the prospect of pizza.

'You're angels. I was going to settle for soup.'

'David doing OK?' I asked.

'Making progress. They're being cautious about recovery times, but that's always the case with brain injuries. The good news is that he's being discharged tomorrow, instead of being transferred to Bridgwater. We reassured the consultant that he can stay at Yew Tree Cottage for a week or two, where Ben and I can keep an eye on him.' She smiled wearily. 'He's looking forward to seeing you two again.'

We drove back to Netherzoy straight after dinner. As we drew up on the verge opposite the Macraes' cottages, I hesitated, suddenly unwilling to get out of the car.

Lissa slid her hand into mine. 'We're going to Spindlewood,' she said, 'not Yew Tree.'

'Sure.' I took a breath. 'Sorry.'

'Don't be.' She leant across to kiss my forehead. 'I

feel the same.'

We walked up the path together. Ben welcomed us with enthusiasm, thumping me on the back and hugging Lissa so tightly that she squeaked in protest.

'Thanks so much for coming over!' he said. 'It's been a bit of a ... well, I'm getting it sorted but –'

'How can we help?' I asked.

But all he wanted was someone to talk to. We sat in the chintzy living room, keeping our voices low, Alf having opted for an early night.

'It wasn't like I expected,' Ben said. 'Last night Dave seemed fine. Normal, you know? We were over the moon. But this morning he didn't remember we'd been.'

'It's early days, Ben,' Lissa said.

'I know. It's this thing called PTA. Post-traumatic amnesia. It can make you really confused at first.' He raised a desperate smile. 'The consultant told us you don't wake up all at once. It might take Dave a week or so. He was never in a really deep coma, which is good. They've got some sort of scale they use to measure ...' His voice tailed off.

'Hang in there, mate,' I said. 'It sounds like he's doing well.'

'It's hard, seeing him like that.'

'Yeah. George says he doesn't remember being attacked.'

'No, nothing after he left the services. Next thing he knows, he's waking up in hospital and a nurse is calling him Jake.'

'Poor David,' Lissa said.

'He couldn't make sense of anything. They told him he'd fallen off a shed roof, and his brother Charlie had brought him in. And then the wanker had the nerve to ring them on Tuesday to see how "Jake" was.' Ben broke off as I swore explosively. 'Yeah, can you believe it? But after that Dave remembered his real name and that actually I was his brother, and that's when the hospital called the cops.'

According to the ward sister, Hampshire Constabulary had contacted Avon and Somerset. DS Lampert's visit had been brief, and the consultant had asked her not to prompt David. Apparently, it was better for his recovery if he was given time to remember for himself.

It had therefore fallen to Ben to break the bad news about Maisie.

'That was the worst,' he said, his eyes welling up.

Lissa sat on the arm of his chair and stroked his shoulder. He fumbled in his jeans pocket, but pulled out only a set of miniature screwdrivers, so she produced a clean tissue from her own pocket and handed it over.

'Sorry,' he said. 'It's just … It's all been …'

'We know, Ben.'

'If David will be staying next door,' I said, trying to be bracing, 'you can pamper him with your superb cooking.'

He raised a smile. 'Don't know about superb, but yeah, that's the plan.'

'He's lucky to have you,' Lissa said.

Ben squirmed a little and failed to come up with a reply. I asked if he wanted us to stay, or if he'd rather have some space.

'Oh, you get on back,' he said. 'I'll be fine now. Just wanted a chat, you know? I tried to ring Chloe, but she's not answering.' A shadow crossed his face. 'It's a bit odd. I haven't talked to the Knights much, what with visiting Dave, but Chloe hasn't been online at all.'

In different circumstances, I would have thought nothing of this, but Chloe's boyfriend was Harry Diment.

'I've tried ringing her,' he said. 'I know she'll want to hear how Dave is, but her phone's switched off.' He shrugged. 'Ed said Alex is throwing a party tonight, because Jackson's gone steaming off up to Gloucester again to see his mum.'

'So Chloe will be at the party,' I said.

'She could be. We don't often hang out with Alex's crowd, but Ed's going this time, so Amber was tempted as well. Actually, that's a thought. I'll call them.'

Ed's phone went to voicemail, but Amber answered hers. She was at home, having decided against a night out, but while they were chatting, a message buzzed through to Ben. He read it without ringing off, sucked in a startled breath, and told Amber, 'OK, I've tracked her down. Ed says she's there … Yeah, I'll let you know.'

Ending the call, he turned to us. His usually gentle brown eyes were full of fury, the Beast of Netherzoy surfacing. 'That tosser Alex! He's taken Chloe's phone and locked her in.'

'In her bedroom?' I asked.

'Dunno. Upstairs somewhere.'

'Bastard!' Lissa exclaimed. She and I had been on the receiving end of many pranks by my older siblings, including my now caring and suitably remorseful sister. Locking us in the dark cellar had been a favourite.

'You're going over there?' I asked Ben.

'Bloody right.' He strode into the hall, grabbing his jacket from the coat rack in passing.

'Shall we come with you?' Lissa asked. 'If Alex's friends are involved, you might need some support.'

The thought gave him pause. 'Might be best if it's just

Kit and me.'

Her eyebrows shot up. 'What does that mean?'

'If it all kicks off, you don't want to be caught in the middle.'

'Nor does Kit.'

I hugged her into my side. 'It'll be fine. You stay here with Alf.'

'Like a good little wife?'

'No, sweetheart. When have you ever been that?'

'Really?'

'OK, that came out wrong. But one of us should be here, in case Alf wakes up and wonders where Ben is. You'll be able to reassure him.'

She narrowed her eyes, still simmering, then reached a decision. 'If I stay, then your job is to keep Ben away from Alex.'

Ben protested, 'I'm not stupid enough to thump the boss's son.'

'Good! And Kit,' she added with fierce intensity, 'don't you get into another fight, either! Are you listening?'

'Always.' I zipped up my hoodie and dropped a kiss on her cheek.

'Take care,' she said.

'It's only a party, love.'

'I know.' Her smile didn't reach her eyes. 'Be careful anyway.'

THIRTY-FOUR

The gates of Zoyland House stood open. Passing The Lodge, we drove along an avenue lined with beeches and stopped on a broad sweep of gravel, outside the porticoed mansion that I had glimpsed from the air. Built from the local yellow-grey stone, its tiled roof punctuated with gables and slender chimney stacks, the house was a young partygoer's dream. No close neighbours and plenty of bedrooms.

There was a clutter of randomly parked cars. Small runabouts, mostly, the type driven by youngsters wanting reliability and a low insurance group. I turned the Mercedes around for a swift exit if Chloe's departure should prove contentious – assuming that she wanted to leave at all.

The front door, like the gates, was invitingly open. We were met by the smell of weed, along with the distant thump of an electronic dance track. A couple were snogging on the wide, crimson-carpeted staircase, oblivious to the music and to us.

Ben strode across to them. 'Is Chloe upstairs?'

Without looking up, the young woman gave him the finger, but her partner offered half a nod.

We took the stairs two at a time. On the upper landing, a guy was preoccupied with snorting coke from a Regency chest of drawers, amid a welter of empty cider cans, while three more women in their mid-twenties sniggered at some private joke.

I said urgently, 'Hey!'

They gave us their startled attention. One said with a giggle, 'Who's your friend, Ben?'

'Hi Gemma. Where's Chloe?' he said.

She pointed to a narrow, curving stair. 'Alex dragged her up there. They were having a steaming row.'

Ben ran ahead of me up the stairs, to a dark, equally narrow landing edged by a thin bannister, at odds with the luxury below. These must once have been the servants' quarters, I thought.

A door at the end of the passage stood open. Inside the room, Alex Naylor stood at the open dormer window, shouting through it, 'That's not my fault, you silly bitch!'

He wasn't looking down, but upwards and sideways, to the roof beside the gable.

Ben groaned a curse. Alex turned just as Ben pushed past him to see out of the window himself. Swearing, Alex flung him back with little effort, sending him staggering against the bed.

'What's going on?' Ben thrust himself upright. 'What've you done to Chloe?'

'Bloody nothing! *She* did it.'

'Ed said you locked her in.'

'Yeah, and then she started screaming I couldn't keep her here, and it all went quiet, so I opened the door ...' His eyes slid to the window.

I beat Ben there by a scant second and leant out, peering to the right as Alex had done, around the edge of the dormer. My eyes needed time to adjust to the dark. All I could see was a shadow huddled against the base of the nearest chimney stack, three metres away and slightly above my eyeline.

Jesus Christ!

'Don't move, OK, Chloe? Keep absolutely still!'

She said in a small, shaky voice, 'Is Ben there?'

He was already pushing his head and shoulders out of the window. It was a tight fit; his chest was pressed against my back. 'I'm here, Chloe.'

I could see her a little now. Her right arm was around the chimney, her left hand pressed flat against it. To some extent, that was a relief. Her body language shouted terror, not a suicidal impulse, but the drop to the patio was horrifying. We were three storeys up. If she fell, she'd be killed outright or broken beyond mending.

From behind us, Alex grated, 'You pair of tossers want to sort this? You can tell Dad when it all goes to shit, then!'

I looked back in time to see the dread in those blue eyes of his, before he turned and ran from the room. If his sister died, he was facing a lifetime of blame and regret, but that didn't excuse his trying to make it our fault.

Not important now. With difficulty, wedged against the window frame, I reached the phone from my pocket and shone the torch to check Chloe's position. Her knees were drawn up, feet in dolly shoes braced against the wet roof tiles. She wore jeans and a T-shirt. Indoor clothing.

'Stay where you are,' I said, tapping the first of three nines. 'We're calling Fire and Rescue.'

'Don't!' She was shivering almost too much to talk. 'D-don't call anyone!'

'It'll be fine, they'll have you down in no time.'

'No!' She must have moved. Her foot slipped and she gasped, hugging the chimney stack more tightly.

'Chloe, listen to me!' I strove to keep my voice calm and steady. 'You'll be all right if you keep still.' Looking over my shoulder, I added quietly to Ben, 'Keep her calm and keep her talking. I don't want her to know I'm calling them.'

His eyes were stretched wide. He was no actor; Chloe would see his panic ... but he was also honest and self-aware, and he loved her.

'You'll do it better. I'll make the call,' he groaned, and

ducked back into the room.

I prayed he was right. Given more space, I adjusted my position and leant out of the window again. In the room behind me, Ben was on his phone, speaking in an undertone.

I hitched my backside onto the sill, gripping the frame. That way I could talk to Chloe face to face, even if obliquely, rather than peering around the dormer.

'Where's Alex?' she said.

'Gone.' Shining my phone's torch up at her again, careful not to blind her, I spoke as casually as my galloping heart would allow. 'You had a row, right, and he took your phone?'

'How do you know that?'

'Ed messaged Ben. Did Alex hurt you?'

'No.' A sob escaped her. 'He l-locked me in. I had to get out ... to get to Ben. I've done it before.'

'Done what?'

'Walked across here ... and in through that window.' She nodded towards the next gable. 'We used to do it as kids ... Alex and me ... but not ...' She glanced down at her feet.

Not in smooth-soled dolly shoes.

Ben returned to the window, trying to see past me. 'It's OK, Chloe, it'll be over soon.'

'What?' She stared down at him, eyes huge, wet hair clinging around her face. 'You didn't call them? Oh, Benji! Oh, no!' Her voice caught on another sob. 'It'll be on the news and Dad will see ... and everyone else ... and I can't tell them why ...'

From below, a flash. I looked over my shoulder. Several partygoers were on the terrace, clustered between the house and the swimming pool, now covered for the winter. The lights from indoors glinted off phones tilted upwards. Gathering material for YouTube, no doubt.

Various obscene epithets occurred to me, and Chloe screamed most of them. We were both equally keen to avoid that kind of publicity. I pulled my hood forward.

Ben suddenly yelled, 'No! Chloe, *don't!*'

I jerked to face her again. She was edging sideways and down, away from the comparative safety of the chimney stack.

'Help me!' She stretched out her left hand, never taking her eyes from the drop.

'No! *Stop!* I can't reach.' I tried, but there was a two metre gap. 'Keep still! Hold the chimney!'

'I need to get inside before they come.' She was ignoring me, inching her way diagonally downwards.

Her left foot slid on the wet roof and she moved the other quickly, scrambling for purchase. My stomach plunged. Ben was groaning, 'No ... no ... no ...'

My trainers would grip. The roof was steeper than some, but roofers walked on tiles every day of the week. Chloe had done it herself in different footwear, probably countless times.

I climbed out through the window and squatted on the sloping tiles beside the dormer, shifting my grip from the window frame to the edge of the bricks.

Ben moaned, 'Don't! *Please!*'

'She's not going to wait for the cavalry.'

'Fuck's sake, you're both gonna die –'

'Shut up!'

She was between me and the chimney, moving crabwise towards me. If she fell now, she would miss the dormer. Momentum would carry her over the gutter and straight down to the paved terrace.

I needed to be where I could catch her.

Not so easy. The wet tiles were slick with moss and algae, making my trainers little better than Chloe's treacherous footwear.

'Wait!' Straightening my left leg, I placed my foot on the guttering. It seemed firm but was never intended to take a man's weight.

I had to be crazy.

Slowly, I stepped to the left, along the gutter, moving my right hand down to grasp the windowsill.

From the terrace, someone yelled, 'Go, Spiderman!'

Chloe shrieked, 'Bastards!' – and in that instant her foot slipped again and jerked downward. This time she couldn't stop. She screamed, and slid uncontrollably past me.

Too fast for thought, I caught her wrist with my left hand, bracing my arm to take her weight. A futile effort. Falling at that speed, she would take me with her.

At the last second the guttering caught her. I felt it shudder, heard a crack, but it held. She teetered there a second, unbalanced – then went over the edge with a shriek that would haunt my nightmares.

I tensed every muscle to hold her, but the jolt was brutal. Somehow my left hand was still clamped around her wrist, but my right lost its grip on the windowsill.

Without Ben, we would both have fallen. He grabbed my right forearm and the back of my hoodie, and I flung myself flat on the tiles, both feet on the guttering. Above me, Ben's face was contorted with exertion and terror.

I looked down. Chloe was dangling from my left hand, her face white as death in the light from the window. Her wrist was slipping through my fingers, wet with rain or sweat. I clenched my hand so hard that she cried out, but

I couldn't hold her much longer, much less pull her to safety.

The hoodie's fabric tightened under my armpits. Ben was swearing and gasping. My back and shoulders were on fire.

We were going to lose her.

I yelled, 'Grab the gutter!'

For a second she didn't react ... but then she pushed one foot against the wall, raising herself enough for her free hand to reach the guttering.

Lying on my front was no use. I turned sideways. Heard and felt a seam rip.

'Ben, I need to let go. Hold me!'

'What? *No!*'

I had to trust him, and the hoodie's seams. And the guttering. I took a breath and let go of the sill. Twisted round to clamp both hands around Chloe's wrist.

'Climb!'

She began scrabbling at the wall below. Found a foothold and lost it, swinging free again. Another frightful jolt. Another protest from my outraged muscles.

They made it look easy in the movies. Lying bastards. Jackson's daughter was going to die because I wasn't strong enough to save her...

Suddenly her foot found purchase against the wall — enough for her to swing her other knee over the gutter. I pleaded with her, groaning her name as I hauled her up, telling her she was doing great, begging her to climb, just bloody climb ... and finally, incredibly, I dragged her up far enough for her to roll over the edge, onto the tiled slope below the dormer.

She lay on her stomach beside me.

'You're OK,' I managed to croak. 'You're all right now.'

It wasn't over, but the rest was nothing by comparison. In fact it was Ben who pulled Chloe in through the window. I could scarcely even help myself. Inside, I slid down against the wall beside the window and just sat there, watching Ben wrap Chloe in the duvet from the bed, soothing her while she sobbed and whimpered.

A skinny ginger-haired guy rushed in, all wide eyes and theatrics. 'Oh God ... Oh Jesus!'

Ben and Chloe barely glanced at him.

'You were *awesome*,' he said to me.

I tried a grin. 'Are you Ed?'

'Yes, I was on the terrace, so of *course* I came up to help.'

A bit bloody late.

I became aware of a rising clamour of voices, distant but getting closer. Alex's friends apparently cared less for his sister's welfare than for shooting pics and videos to share online.

We would soon have another problem, too. With the emergency services on their way, the local press wouldn't be far behind – and my involvement would raise their interest level. Chloe's troubles could end up splashed across the tabloids. *BBC presenter in rooftop rescue.*

My new bosses would be ecstatic.

Too bad. Promoting the series via pre-arranged interviews was all well and good, but the last thing Lissa and I needed was sensationalist reporting. *Kester Pevensey, whose baby daughter tragically lost her fight for life four months ago ...*

Time to make a move.

I picked myself up. A muscle in my lower back twinged sharply, and my arms and shoulders ached. Running and the odd gym session had been no preparation for tonight's workout.

'Are you OK?' Ed asked.

'Just about. Chloe's heavier than she looks.'

'I still can't believe you did that.'

'Yeah, well ... could you do me a favour? Keep my name out of it, if the media pesters you?'

'Of course. Whatever.'

No telling whether he would, but he was one of the Knights, after all. I took a slow breath, trying without success to calm the internal tremors, and walked on unsteady legs to Ben and Chloe.

'We need to go,' I said.

Chloe raised her head from his shoulder. 'I'm coming with you.' She wiped her eyes with the heel of her hand, making a fair show of taking charge. 'We'll use the back stairs, avoid everyone.'

Too late. The door flew open and crashed back against the wall. The small room was suddenly full of about six more people, all of them hyped-up on the drama and calling Chloe's name, trying to startle her into looking their way. Before the first phone flashed, I pulled my hood forward again and held it there.

To Ed's credit, he acted fast, spreading his long arms to corral the crowd as he tried to shout over their protests, forcing them to retreat towards the window.

For two precious seconds, the route to the door was clear. We reached it ahead of another outbreak of yells and flashes. A hand snatched at Chloe's arm but she wrenched herself free, with a noise less like a cry than a snarl. For an instant, her face was transformed – a wild animal cornered. The guy who had grabbed her backed off hastily.

'Chill, all right? Jesus ...'

We fled down the attic stair. Someone started in pursuit, ignoring Ed's shouts, but then the voice of the guy who had tried to stop Chloe drifted after us, more shocked than mocking.

'Let them go, mate! She's a total psycho.'

THIRTY-FIVE

Whatever Chloe's mental state, physically she had suffered nothing worse than a sore wrist. Ben noticed it was swollen, but she shrugged off his sympathy as if embarrassed, which was understandable. Having stopped crying, she kept her composure, though she must have felt as shaky as I did.

Reaching the first floor landing, we stepped over an unconscious young woman. Ben, always the carer, went back to roll her into the recovery position. Everyone else must have been out by the pool or mobbing Ed for answers. I began to hope that we would escape unphotographed.

Once outside, however, our troubles were not quite over. On the floodlit drive, Alex was leaning against the wing of the Mercedes. Far from showing gratitude, he was fixing us with a belligerent stare.

I walked ahead of Chloe and Ben, saying pleasantly, 'Off my car, please!'

He folded his arms. 'What, you're abducting my sister now?'

'Her choice.' I kept my tone amiable. 'The emergency services are on their way. We'll leave you to deal with them.'

'Piss off! Chloe, you need to stay here.'

'I don't think so.' She stalked to the passenger door, which her brother immediately blocked.

I unlocked the car, telling Ben and Chloe, 'Get in the back.'

Chloe stepped sideways, opened the door, and got in. Ben stayed with me, making the odds two to one, in theory, but the last thing I wanted was a fight. Too many aches, for a start; and although the BBC might cheer a rooftop rescue, they would look less kindly on an arrest for assault.

'Chloe needs some space,' I said. 'You can talk to her tomorrow. Ben, get in the car.' As he hesitated, I added, 'It's fine. Get in.'

Good sense won. He did as he was told, keeping his rebellious mutterings too quiet to be heard. A good decision. Alex's father paid his wages.

Alex himself, meanwhile, began stroking the handle of the rear passenger door as if tempted to open it and remove his sister by force.

'Try it,' I said. 'I'll enjoy dragging you out.'

'Try it,' he echoed, snidely. 'I'll have a great lawyer.'

I showed my teeth. 'If Chloe wants to press charges for false imprisonment, you'll need one.'

His eyes narrowed, reassessing me as an opponent. Then he bent to look through the window at his sister. 'You wouldn't,' he challenged her.

She opened the door forcefully, obliging him to step back. 'You think?' she said.

'You might not give a toss about our family, but I do. If you repeat one word –'

'You'll what, Alex? Do you actually care about any of us, or is it all about you and Avalon Sky?'

'Don't be so bloody self-righteous! I didn't see you refusing Dad's cash for your little events project.'

Glaring, she slammed the door.

'OK, Alex, that's enough,' I said. 'Sod off and annoy someone else!'

He swung round. I thought he might throw a punch, but instead he said fiercely, 'Whatever she tells you, it's crap. She's a spoilt attention-seeking little cow.'

'Thanks, we'll bear that in mind.' I held out my hand. 'We'll take Chloe's phone, too.'

He froze. For a second it really did seem that I had pushed my luck too far – but whatever the cause of his row with Chloe, he may have recognised that standing his ground now could weaken his version of events later. In one swift movement, he pulled out the phone and tossed it contemptuously onto the gravel between us.

I toed it to one side, far enough to pick it up without appearing to grovel. Then I walked around the car, being careful to keep him in my field of vision, and slid into the driving seat. As we moved off, he kicked the tyre once. A childish parting shot, unlikely to have caused damage.

'Twat!' Ben growled.

I glanced in the rear-view mirror and passed Chloe her phone. 'OK?' I asked her.

'Yes.'

I accelerated along the gravel drive, which was still free of emergency responders. There were questions that needed to be asked, before she had time to raise her guard and concoct a plausible fiction.

'Feel like telling us about it?' I asked, alternately watching the road and checking the mirror to gauge her reaction.

In her dimly reflected eyes, I caught a glitter of tears. 'No. It's family stuff.'

Ben immediately said, 'But you'll tell me later, won't you?'

'Some of it, Benji. Can I stay at Spindlewood tonight?'

'With me?'

'Not like that.'

'Oh … You can have my bed, then. I'll sleep on the sofa.'

'It'll only be for one night. Dad will be home tomorrow.'

'You could stay forever if you wanted.'

'Benji.' She stroked his shoulder. 'You're so good to me.'

He cleared his throat. 'Where's Harry tonight, then?'

A bloody good question.

'We broke up,' she said.

'Oh! Like ... properly, this time?'

'Properly. Permanently.'

'Oh,' he said again. 'I'm sorry.'

'No, you're not.'

A charged pause, then he replied cautiously, 'You're right. He's a shit.'

'Is that the only reason you're glad?'

He leant in close to whisper in her ear, and she turned her head and kissed him on the mouth. I stopped looking in the mirror and didn't bother asking any more questions. Whatever had happened between Chloe and her brother, she would confide in Ben. Whether it was any of my business, or Lampert's, would need to be his decision.

Halfway to Spindlewood, Lissa rang. Alf had woken up and insisted that he didn't need a babysitter, so Thomasina had given Lissa a lift back to Burrowbridge, then returned to Netherzoy herself to stay with Alf – whether he liked it or not.

I dropped Ben and Chloe outside Spindlewood and drove on to Burrowbridge. It seemed further than usual. I had to grip the wheel to stop my hands from shaking, but at long last the fairy lights of Greenways twinkled a welcome.

Lissa opened the door as I reached it. 'You've been

gone ages,' she said, before noticing the streaks of algae on my clothes. 'Are those *grass* stains? You haven't been fighting again?'

'No.'

'Is Chloe all right?'

'Fine. Disaster averted.' I headed for the living room, flopped onto the sofa, and closed my eyes. 'God, I'm knackered.'

She made us both a coffee and sat down next to me, handing me a steaming mug. 'Tell me,' she said.

There was no need to dwell on the scarier aspects. In my edited version, Chloe, for reasons we had yet to discover, had been sitting on the roof outside the window after her row with Alex, then had lost her nerve and needed help to climb back inside.

My wife, however, was no fool. 'You're making it sound easy. I can see it wasn't.'

'There was a dodgy moment.' I smiled. 'All's well, sweetheart.'

She leant her head against my shoulder. Her hair smelled of her favourite midnight fig shampoo. If she left me ...

I must have sighed involuntarily, because she sat up to see my face. 'You're really all right?'

'Yeah.' I forced another smile. 'Want to watch a movie in bed?'

Bormo was asleep on the duvet, pushing his luck. Lissa put him out in the hall, and he stalked off to the kitchen to find his food bowl, tail lashing.

We heard Thomasina let herself in around eleven, which implied that she had spoken at length with Ben and Chloe before leaving Spindlewood. We put the light out soon afterwards. Within minutes, Lissa's breathing slowed to a near-silent rhythm. My heart rate was still too fast for sleep, brain relentlessly active, trying to guess what Chloe and Alex had rowed about, and why Chloe had suggested that it could affect either Alex's inheritance or his burgeoning career at Avalon Sky, or both. What had he done, to risk losing that?

Killed Conor Yandle to retrieve his great-uncle's antique?

But I couldn't suspect the guy just because he was a git. With luck, Chloe would consent to Ben passing on some answers.

I fell into a sleep marred by dreams full of fear and threat, and woke at first light. Lissa had burrowed deep into the duvet, only the top of her black curls visible. I swung my feet to the floor and sat on the edge of the bed. Every muscle in my upper body was stiff, but that seemed a fair price to pay. I felt good about last night. Proud, in a way. Because of Ben and me, Chloe Naylor hadn't died.

I stood up – and pain gripped my lower back in a vice. I bit back a groan, clutching at the windowsill for support.

'What?' Lissa muttered, still half asleep.

I couldn't justify waking her.

'Nothing.'

Gritting my teeth, I eased a dressing-gown on over my sleep shorts and hobbled to the bathroom. The cabinet was depressingly bare of painkillers; but I had heard a chink of crockery from the kitchen, so Thomasina was up and about.

I found her emptying the dishwasher, wearing a cream silk kimono that clung to her curves. Catching movement from the tail of her eye, she stood upright and turned.

'Oh, my dear!'

I shook my head to discourage the rush of sympathy, and sat down gingerly at the table. 'Have you, um ... got any paracetamol?'

'Of course.' She reached down a blister pack from a high cupboard, poured a glass of water, and set both in front of me. 'Why are you embarrassed?

'Making a fuss. Sorry.'

'For goodness' sake!'

I thanked her for the pills and swallowed two, aware of her watching me with what may or may not have been clinical appraisal.

'Any nerve pain?' she asked. 'Numbness? Tingling?'

'No.' I managed a rueful grin. 'Could be worse, right?'

'In more ways than one. Ben told me the whole story. You're a brave boy, aren't you?'

'Instinct. Didn't have time to think.'

'And modest.' She sighed wistfully, mocking herself. 'Irresistible.'

'Thomasina ...'

'I'm teasing. Lose the dressing-gown, and we'll see if I can help the meds along.'

A startling offer, to say the least. She laughed out loud at my expression.

'Stop looking like a rabbit in the headlights! As a vet, I also offer my own alternative therapy. It seems to work. Imagine you're a labrador.'

I nearly laughed, but anything was worth a try. I removed the gown and, following her instructions, sat sideways on the chair. Thomasina knelt behind me. Her hands moved over my waist, pressing gently here and there: a professional examination. She was wearing a new fragrance, spicier but no less alluring. At that precise moment it hardly mattered, but I folded the dressing-gown on my lap as a precaution.

'Not at the practice today?' I said through clenched teeth.

'I worked last weekend. We have a rota, and I'm collecting David from Southampton at one. Ben will be preparing Yew Tree and buying in groceries … There's some slight inflammation here. I'm not qualified to make a diagnosis, obviously.'

'How about if I was a labrador?'

She chuckled. 'It's probably a mild strain.'

'Is that all? I'm a fraud, then.'

'Absolutely not. Even a minor back injury can cause excruciating spasms.'

I grinned at her over my shoulder. 'You don't say.'

She laid her palms flat against my skin. I felt them growing warmer.

'Ben says you've got healing hands,' I ventured.

'I call it massage therapy, but I don't quash the rumours. My pet owners seem to enjoy a hint of magic.'

'Fair enough. This is Avalon, kingdom of Morgan Le Fay.'

'Mm. Three or four centuries ago, I'd have burned at the stake.'

Her hands were acting like a heat pack. The rigid muscles were starting to relax, the breathtaking pain gradually lessening.

'Wow,' I said. 'How are you doing that?'

'I've no idea. Some oddity of circulation, or a reaction to skin-to-skin contact. A gift from my great-grandmother.'

'Barbara?'

'Haven't you heard she was a witch? People came to her with their aches and pains, until she was widowed and hid herself away. Poor girl.'

Since Thomas Macrae, Barbara's elder son and one-time head gardener at Zoyland House, had been Thomasina's grandad as well as David's and Ben's, I asked if she had heard stories of the Finches' lives in Jersey.

'Ah, their allegedly misspent youth,' she said. 'Barbara warned her boys about Ursula and her brother. She said the tales about them would chill you to the bone.'

'Bloody hell. Such as?'

'Grandad said his mum mentioned a burglary. She would have known, I'm sure. His dad would have been in Oscar's confidence.'

'Was it *just* a burglary?'

'Not sufficiently bone-chilling? I agree, the stories are contradictory. If violence had been involved, and the Finches came here to escape arrest, as Grandad thought, surely they would have been extradited back to Jersey?'

'Unless the war and the Nazi occupation intervened. Records may have gone astray. Ever hear if the Finches stole a valuable antique?'

'Ah, in case Conor acquired his artefact from one of them?'

'Yeah. If he knew he was nicking stolen property ...' I chose my words with care, to avoid betraying Reece's confidence. 'He might have bargained on them not reporting it. And after eighty-odd years, he could have felt it was safe to sell through legal channels. Enter David.'

'Not a bad theory. What do the police think?'

'We've asked George to check their database for Jersey criminal records from 1938. Got any more stories?'

'Nothing specific. I suppose you know that Oscar was generous to our family, probably for Freddie's sake. He may have fathered Barbara's child and felt guilty over her suicide, but I'm certain Freddie was the love of his life. And vice versa.'

'Jackson has been generous too,' I said. 'Ben was given cheap flying lessons.'

'I doubt if Jackson feels bound by his father's obligations. More likely, he did Ben a favour as a family friend. Ben should be more discreet. Jackson wouldn't like to be accused of favouring one employee over another.' She took her hands away. 'Better?'

I moved cautiously. My back was still stiff and aching, but the cramps had gone.

'Magic,' I said, adding seriously, 'Thank you.'

'It was only heat, not a cure. Stick with paracetamol if you need painkillers – avoid ibuprofen for the first forty-eight hours – and be kind to yourself. Gentle exercise and no more heroics. See a doctor if there's no improvement in a week.'

'Yes, ma'am.'

She stood up, looking down at me quizzically. 'Shall we have breakfast, if Lissa is still sleeping? I'm not in the habit of waiting on men, but for heroes I make an exception.'

Over toast and marmalade, she told me that Ben and Chloe would be paying us a visit at eight-thirty.

'Any idea why?' I asked.

'Perhaps she wants to kiss your feet.'

'Or to explain what last night was all about.'

'Such optimism. You must be feeling better.'

After breakfast, Thomasina went outside to pull up her dead summer plants. I showered and dressed, but Lissa was still reluctant to wake up. At a loose end, I took my laptop into the kitchen and typed a chronology of events.

1920 Ursula Finch born, St Helier

1926 Guy Finch born ditto

1930s Barbara marries Freddie, healing hands, treats villagers, witch rumours

Summer 1938 Oscar and Freddie on cycling tour. Meet Ursula and Guy, Jersey

Late 1938 Did Guy burgle a house and steal an antique?

Dec 1938 Ursula and Guy sail to England, lodge at Spindlewood

Spring 1939 Oscar and Ursula married. Live at Zoyland House with Guy

Sept 1939 War declared

1940 Freddie killed at Dunkirk

1940-42 Barbara aloof, few friends, witch rumours turn nasty

1941? Affair with Oscar Naylor? Ursula seeking revenge?

1942 Daphne killed by Ursula. Barbara commits suicide

Date unknown: Guy moves into Heron View

1959 Jackson born

2010 Oscar dies, having continued to provide for the Macraes

That provision may have inspired Oscar's epitaph, the words of a man who had finally made peace with himself and his past. *I have fought the good fight. I have finished the race. I have kept the faith.*

I allowed a thought, barely acknowledged until now, to rise to the surface of my mind and linger there. My fingers hovered above the keypad, then I typed at the foot of the list:

Did Barbara Macrae hang herself?
And then, more slowly, the final question.
Or did Ursula kill her?

THIRTY-SIX

I was still pondering that grim thought when Ben and Chloe arrived. Thomasina came in with them, peeling off her gardening gloves as she ushered them into the kitchen. I closed the laptop and offered a cheerful greeting, which they returned more soberly.

Ben sat down facing me and pulled out another chair for Chloe, making himself at home; but the girl stood as if unsure of her welcome, picking a thread from a crepe bandage around her wrist.

'Still sore?' I asked her.

'My own fault.' She was regarding me unhappily. 'Tommie says you've hurt your back.'

'Not much. I'm fine.'

Thomasina touched her shoulder. 'Please sit with us, Chloe. We're all your friends.'

Looking disconcerted, she sat down. 'Have you seen the videos on YouTube?' she asked me.

'I'm saving that treat.'

'They've gone viral. There are some pics on *Spotted Around Bridgwater* as well. Alex's so-called friends have identified Zoyland House, and me.' She sighed gustily. 'I'm such an idiot.'

'Anyone mention my name?'

'No. The local paper rang, and someone from a news agency. They didn't ask about you, but anyway I wouldn't talk to them. I blocked their numbers and then turned my phone off.' She was still watching me, but now with puzzlement. 'You kept your hood up last night. Don't you want good publicity?'

'Yes, on my terms.'

I saw her face change. It was obvious that she knew

about Emily, either from Ben or what she had found online.

'Sorry,' she said. 'I mean, I'm sorry you had to ...' She ducked her head, slanting me a shamefaced look through the white-blonde curtain of hair. 'I'm trying to say thank you. I'll owe you forever, won't I?'

'No.' I was cringing inwardly. 'You should thank Ben as much as me. If he hadn't grabbed my hoodie ...'

'I know.' She smiled at Ben.

'Well, OK,' he said.

'Show Kit the videos.'

He opened the first one before handing me his phone. My initial reaction was relief. The footage was dark and grainy, and although I had been nearer the window than Chloe and therefore better lit, my hood was an effective disguise. Also the caption gave nothing away: *Real-life Spiderman saves party girl.*

But the content was shocking. The incident looked no less perilous from ground level, and in addition was punctuated by the spectators' cries and occasional shrieks, which at the time I had barely registered. Seeing Chloe slide off the edge of the roof and swing from my hand was horrific. One of the onlookers could be heard sobbing.

The second video, entitled *Iron Man eat your heart out!*, was longer, running until we hauled Chloe in through the window.

Finding no words, I gave Ben his phone back.

'There's endless chat online,' Chloe said, 'but most of the witnesses were drunk or high. Some of them think you were Ed.'

From the doorway, Lissa said, 'Morning, everyone. Why would anyone think Kit was Ed?'

She was wearing her sky-blue fluffy dressing-gown, and her hair was wet, the black tendrils clinging to her cheeks and neck. She looked adorable.

'Hi, Lissa,' Ben said. 'Seen Kit's superhero act?'

'His what?'

'Ben!' I growled, trying in vain to catch his eye.

She snatched the proffered phone. After a few seconds, she gasped and nearly dropped it, then held it at arm's length as if afraid to see more but unable to look away. Finally, she raised her eyes to meet mine, shock turning to anger. '*A dodgy moment*? You nearly died.'

Too late to wish I had been straight with her last night.

'It looks worse than it was,' I lied.

She rounded on Chloe. 'And this was all because of some stupid argument with your brother? What the hell were you thinking? Or didn't you think at all?'

'You don't understand. I needed to get to my car, to get to Ben –'

'Chloe,' Ben said. 'Start from the beginning, eh?'

She nodded, taking a deep breath. 'You're right. That's why we're here. You deserve to know the truth – especially you, Kit – or as much as I've told Ben. And I need your help.'

Lissa pulled out a chair next to me and sat down facing the pair of them, her arms folded. 'We're all ears.'

Thomasina served a round of coffees, plus camomile tea for herself, and then took her place at the end of the table as if chairing a meeting.

'Take your time, Chloe,' she said. 'Whatever the problem is, we'll support you.'

I was not sure that Lissa would agree, but she maintained a tactful silence.

Chloe turned her mug between her hands. Her blue

eyes were wide and tragic, which meant nothing in itself. She seemed able to summon that expression at will.

'Alex and I used to play in the attic rooms all the time,' she said. 'The first time Mum had cancer, I was eight. Alex was eleven. When Dad wasn't at work, he was caring for Mum. We did as we liked, really. She was ill for years, on and off, having one course of chemo and radiotherapy after another. In the end there was a paid carer as well, but she didn't bother us.'

The picture Chloe painted was heart-wrenching, but I wondered if Jackson would recall things differently. He and his wife might deliberately have given their children more freedom than most, as a respite from the pain of witnessing their mother's suffering.

'We used to dare each other,' Chloe said, 'to climb out on the roof, touch the chimney, then climb in at the next window along.'

'I never knew that,' Ben muttered.

'It didn't feel all that dangerous. My record was twenty-one seconds, but Alex did it in seventeen once. We broke the catch on the other window on purpose. No one noticed. It stays closed till you pull it.'

'You're not kids now,' I said.

'But I knew I could do it, and I was so upset, I didn't think about my shoes not having much grip – and the tiles never used to have green stuff on them. I just wanted to get to you, Benji.'

She had him in the palm of her hand.

'What did you row with Alex about?' I asked, more sharply than I should have.

'It was because of what Gran said.'

Ursula again.

'What did she say?'

Chloe fidgeted a little, as if having second thoughts about sharing her family's problems with a wider audience, but she had claimed to need our help. If that came at a price, she would pay it.

'Sometimes lately,' she said, 'Gran gets confused, like when she walked out of the care home. And she calls us by the wrong names, then pretends it was a slip of the tongue.'

'She's nearly a hundred, my dear,' Thomasina said. 'It would be understandable if she has memory lapses, or even mild dementia.'

'I know that ... but yesterday, I drove up to visit her. She dozed off at one point, and when she woke up, she started talking to herself ... thinking out loud, as if I wasn't there. Then I spoke, and she jumped and said she'd been dreaming. But I know she was awake. And what she'd been saying ... I went home and told Alex, but it turns out he's known for years. So I lost it with him ... and you know the rest. He was scared that I'd tell Ben everything, but I won't. There are things we can never tell anyone. Ever.'

As a confession, it was not exactly enlightening.

'Why not?' I asked. 'What's the worst that could happen?'

She grew still, her haunted eyes fixed on mine. 'We don't want even Dad to find out. It would destroy him.'

There was a ripple of incredulity around the table, mostly raised eyebrows and sceptical looks. Lissa rolled her eyes.

'I'm sure he'd cope,' she said. 'He might actually be able to help.'

Chloe gave a bitter little laugh. 'Not this time.'

'Did your gran talk about the remains we found?' I said.

Beside me, I felt Lissa tense.

Chloe looked bewildered. 'The baby in the garden? Why would ...? I don't understand.'

'She was Barbara Macrae's child,' I said. 'Alf's half-sister. Your gran delivered her.'

'So what? What are you saying?'

'Your grandad was probably the father. We asked your gran about it. She all but confessed to smothering the baby.'

I was prepared for Chloe to be angry, or to insist that we had misunderstood, but instead she drew a deep breath and said quietly, 'You know what? I wouldn't even be surprised.'

Bloody hell.

'When Barbara hanged herself,' I said, 'it was recorded as suicide, but your gran hated her, didn't she?'

Lissa breathed, 'Oh, my God.' There had been no opportunity to share my theory with her.

'You think she killed Barbara too?' Chloe leant back in her chair as if trying to retreat physically from the barrage of accusations. 'The shit just keeps piling up, doesn't it?'

Her reaction stunned me.

'So,' I said, 'even if your gran has committed double murder, that's insignificant, compared to some other secret that would devastate your dad if he found out?'

'I never said that,' Chloe murmured, but she didn't deny it.

'How about the carers?' I said. 'Ursula could let it slip to one of them, or your dad could catch her talking to herself, like you did.'

Chloe's lip trembled. 'There's nothing I can do about that.'

Ben put his arm around her. 'Does your gran know

who hurt Dave?'

'No!'

'But you think it happened because of ... whatever you can't talk about?'

'I don't know. Maybe.'

Into the charged silence that followed this admission, Thomasina said sternly, 'Chloe, if you know anything at all that could help the police, you can't justify keeping it to yourself.'

The girl bowed her head, staring down into her mug. Nobody spoke. All of us, I suppose, were hoping that her feelings for Ben were strong enough to override family loyalty.

At last she looked up. 'I can't help what's happened in the past,' she said. 'I just have to find a way to live with it ... and keep my family from falling apart.'

Seeing how tortured she was, I couldn't totally harden my heart – but whatever she and Alex were hiding, the fallout had nearly killed her. We had to make her see sense before something worse happened.

'This has already gone too far, Chloe,' I said. 'You need to confide in your dad. Whatever your gran has done, he'll get over it.'

She shook her head fiercely. 'No.'

'If you'd died last night, he'd have spent the rest of his life wondering if he could have done something, anything, to change what happened ...' I stopped, because suddenly, out of nowhere, all I could think about was Emily.

I couldn't save her.

Under the table, Lissa slid her hand into mine. 'However bad this problem seems,' she told Chloe, 'your dad would hate to think you and Alex are taking it all on yourselves. He doesn't need that.'

'You're wrong,' Chloe said. 'That's why I'm here. To ask for your help, because I can't go to Dad.'

I cleared my throat. 'Help with what?'

'Dad's bringing Gran back with him today. She was going to come for Uncle Guy's funeral, but that's not for another ten days. Alex wants to fly her to Lundy before that, as a treat. He's booked the plane for next weekend, Friday to Monday.'

Today was Sunday.

'Great. Why do you need us?' I asked.

'They'll be staying in Square Cottage. It's near the pub, so Gran won't have to walk far. Sometimes only the big properties are free at short notice, even in November, but Alex got lucky.'

'Good for him.' I was becoming impatient.

She turned to Ben. 'If you and Kit fly to Lundy as well …'

'In the Jabiru?' The prospect alarmed him; he dropped his arm from around her. 'What for?'

'Because –'

'Actually, I don't care why. We're not going. The strip is rough as hell and the Jabba's not built for that. If I break the nosewheel on landing, the prop will hit the ground and shock-load the engine.'

'I'd ask Dad to pay for the repairs if it came to that.'

'I don't want him to. I don't want the Jabba broken.'

'But I need you and Kit to keep Gran safe –'

'That's Alex's job. We're not your gran's carers.'

'Benji, you have to save her *from Alex*.'

I made some incredulous exclamation, and Ben said, 'What for? He wouldn't hurt her. He loves her.'

'But he's still going to kill her.'

Quite an accusation. We all reacted, but it was Ben

who said aloud what we must all have been thinking.

'That's crazy. Why would he?'

Chloe gave him the full force of those wide blue eyes. 'Haven't you been listening, Benji? I can't tell you.'

'Well, I'm sorry,' Lissa said, with no trace of apology, 'but you can't come out with something that extreme and then refuse to justify it.'

Chloe bristled, gave up on winning her round, and looked at Ben, Thomasina and me in turn. 'You said you'd support me. You have to help. This is life or death. *Literally.*'

We didn't have to do anything, but I suspected that Ben would cave in eventually, whether he thought Ursula was in danger or not.

'Did Alex tell you about this alleged plan?' I asked.

'Of course not,' Chloe said. 'I just *know.*'

Lissa threw out her hands in frustration. 'How can you possibly? And anyway, why involve Kit? Ask one of the Knights!'

'Kit got the better of Alex last night,' Chloe said. 'That's rare. And he's strong. I thought he'd drop me but he didn't.'

Ben immediately protested. 'I'm as strong as Kit.'

'I know, Benji.' She pouted, stroking his hair back behind his ear. 'But you're so sweet. Kit looks a bit more ... dangerous.'

'We're not bruisers for hire,' I said.

'I don't want you to *fight* Alex. He's not stupid. As soon as he sees you there, he'll guess I sent you to watch him, so he won't try anything.'

But her whole rationale was absurd. I couldn't accept that Alex would murder his own grandmother to save his dad heartache over her criminal past – which he was almost guaranteed to find out about, at some point. It wasn't a plausible motive.

If Alex's career had depended on Ursula keeping quiet, that might be different; but despite Chloe's accusations last night, I couldn't see how even a full confession from their grandmother would impact his future at Avalon Sky. If she was convincing, the publicity would be unpleasant, but it would pass.

'Why don't *you* go with Ben?' Lissa asked Chloe.

'I couldn't stop Alex, because he knows I'd never tell on him.'

Lissa laughed shortly. 'That's honest.'

'But he's already learned that he can't bully Kit.'

Ben was increasingly outraged. 'He can't bully me either. And I'm not sweet.'

'I take it back.' Chloe kissed his ear. 'You're an absolute monster.'

He wriggled free. 'I'm still not happy about landing on Lundy.'

'You can't take the tourist helicopter, even if there'd be seats available,' Chloe said. 'Alex could fly Gran off somewhere else once he sees you there, and you wouldn't be able to follow them.'

Ben shrugged helplessly, looking to me for support.

I gave logic a try. 'Surveillance wouldn't work, Chloe. Once they're inside the cottage, Alex can do as he likes.'

'But he won't. Square Cottage is sort of upside down. There's a bedroom and bathroom on the ground floor, so Gran's bound to choose that. The kitchen and living room are upstairs, but they'll eat in the tavern. Alex can't cook. That means Gran won't need to go upstairs, so Alex can't push her down – and he won't risk doing anything that would leave forensic evidence. Why should he, when there are so many cliff paths, and hardly any mobile signal?' Chloe caught at herself. 'God, I can't believe I'm saying this.'

She wasn't alone there.

'What about after they're back home?' I said. 'You can't have your friends playing bodyguard on a rota.'

'I think Gran's pretty safe at Cedar Lawns, don't you? And at our house, she just reads or does puzzles or watches TV, or has a short walk in the gardens with one of us. There are no cliffs or lakes, and she never goes near the swimming pool. That's why Alex is taking her to Lundy.'

It was hopeless. She had it all worked out.

Thomasina tried a different tack. 'Chloe, taking a step back, do you honestly think your brother is capable of murder?'

'People sometimes do terrible things to save their loved ones, don't they?'

Not just to save them from being upset.

'Will you go?' Chloe asked me.

'How about me?' Ben asked. 'I haven't said *I'll* go yet.'

The word 'yet' was a dead giveaway.

'But you will, won't you?' Chloe said.

He shrugged and frowned, keeping her in suspense; but then, inevitably, he nodded. 'But if the nosewheel collapses, *you* can ask your dad to help me get the Jabba back.'

'Oh, thank you, Benji, thank you!'

While he was being thoroughly kissed, Lissa said quietly to me, 'Well, that's that. You won't let him go alone.'

'Do you want me to?'

'No. I don't know. I'm afraid for you.'

'In case the landing gear breaks?'

'That too, obviously. But mainly in case Chloe's right.'

'She's not, sweetheart. Alex will take an uneventful holiday with his gran, and Ben and I will pass the time hiking through drizzle.'

Chloe had put Ben down and was watching me with such intensity that she hardly seemed to breathe. 'Are you saying yes?' she asked.

I grinned wryly. 'Looks like it.'

She burst into tears and hugged Ben again, then made a tour of the table and gave Thomasina and me the same treatment. She came to Lissa last, but checked herself on seeing my wife's stony expression.

Relenting slightly, Lissa handed her a tissue, and Chloe wiped her eyes, blew her nose, and said with determined breeziness, 'Well, if you want to know anything about the island before next Friday, just ask.'

Ben put in helpfully, 'I've got Mum's *Lundy Companion* at home. I could fetch it –'

'No, Ben,' Thomasina said. 'You need to focus on making sure Yew Tree is ready for David, and I need to leave in a few minutes.'

I suggested that we call into Spindlewood later for the book. 'We won't visit David today,' I added. 'He'll want to settle in. Maybe tomorrow, if he feels up to it?'

We left the arrangement open. Meanwhile, having achieved her purpose, Chloe began hassling Ben to leave. They had reached the hall before I realised there was something I had never asked her.

'Chloe,' I called, 'do you know a Mr Fogle?'

She turned sharply. 'Sorry, what? Who?'

Her reaction struck a false note. I was certain Ben would have mentioned the name to her.

'That's a "no", is it?' I said.

'Yes. I mean no, there's no one called that.'

As Thomasina showed them out, I frowned after them. Was I over-thinking it, or had Chloe's choice of words been significant? She hadn't claimed not to know Fogle.

She had said there was no such person.

THIRTY-SEVEN

When the others had gone, we stayed in the kitchen, researching Lundy on my laptop. The island was three miles long and half a mile wide: an undulating plateau surrounded by cliffs, ten miles off the coast of North Devon. During a long history, it had been 'ruled' by various colourful types, including assorted pirates and other marauders – but nowadays it was owned and run by two respectable trusts and was famous mainly for its puffins. The only full-time residents were staff.

Lissa immediately fell in love with the quirky holiday lets, which were mainly converted from historic buildings. Their interiors were reminiscent of the 1950s, all chintzy sofas and dark wooden furniture, with jigsaws and board games but no television.

'I'm a bit jealous now,' she said.

'Come as well, then. There might be a seat in the tourist helicopter.'

'No, take me next summer instead. Clifftop hikes in November don't appeal. I wonder where you'll be staying? If they're fully booked, you'll have to cancel the trip.'

She was still anxious about it, despite Ben having assured her – truthfully or otherwise – that we wouldn't die if the nosewheel snapped. I thought we might flip over, but kept that opinion to myself.

'You really think Alex is a killer?' I asked.

'Well, look at his grandmother! Honestly, Kit, I don't know what to think.'

I drew her close, and we studied the satellite view of the island, a mostly green expanse of nothing much. As a potential crime scene, it was a long way from the mean streets.

There again, it was a long way from anywhere. If there were security cameras, they wouldn't cover the wilderness beyond the one tiny, sprawling village; and with only twenty-three properties for visitors, the island population could surely never exceed a hundred and twenty, including staff.

For a man looking to shove his grandmother off a cliff, it would be easy to pick a spot, and a moment, with no witnesses. I still thought Chloe was wrong, owing to the lack of a sensible motive; but as she was convinced of Alex's murderous intent, I could see why Lundy worried her.

Maps offered no proper street view, but dropping the yellow man icon into any marked spot produced a three-sixty-degree still shot from that location. One such view showed us Square Cottage, a cube-shaped house built of the same grey stone as several of the other buildings. It stood beside the broad, stony main thoroughfare, ambitiously named Lundy Road, and was a short step from the pub.

Lissa was keen to locate the grass runway. We found it crossing a swathe of rough pasture, half a mile north of the village. There was no control tower. Not even a C-Hut, as at Merlin Park. A further internet search revealed that visiting pilots were required to phone in advance for permission to land.

'It does look bumpy.' She was watching a pilot's video of his approach and landing. 'The whole field is very tussocky.'

'The north end of the island is pretty rugged, too,' I said, to distract her. 'Can't see Ursula venturing that far, so it'll be easy to keep tabs on them.' I stretched my back cautiously, wincing. 'Glad we're not flying out today.

Gives me some time to recover from last night.'

'Poor Spiderman.' Lissa was teasing but sympathetic. I even got a kiss. 'I'm proud of you,' she murmured in my ear, 'but never, *ever* do anything like that again!'

'Not even for you?'

'If one of us needs to save the other, let's try to avoid death-defying stunts. Seriously, darling, are you suffering?'

I slid her a smile and winked. 'Might need to lie down.'

She laughed. 'Oh, really? Gymnastics are off the menu, then.'

'Other dishes are available.'

'True.'

We spent the rest of the morning finding satisfying ways to entertain each other and ourselves. Eventually, as we were feeling languorous and disinclined to get up for lunch, Lissa made us a plate of sandwiches each and brought those and our laptops to bed. We sat decadently propped by pillows to continue our research in comfort, trying not to spill crumbs on the duvet.

I showed her the list I had compiled earlier, with the query about Barbara's fate – and on reflection added the name Fogle.

'You think Conor made him up, don't you?' Lissa said. 'But how would Chloe know about that?'

'She could have overheard Conor and Harry talking.'

'But that would mean she knew about the theft … wouldn't it?'

For Ben's sake, we hoped there was another explanation, but realistically it was a dead end, unless or until we could press Chloe for a straight answer.

'Let's forget about present-day stuff for now,' Lissa

said. 'I'm going to look at the archives again. I know we've exhausted the Jersey papers, but I want to try Somerset – in case the rumours are wrong, and there was an unsolved burglary *after* the Finches came to England.'

But Ursula had been engaged to Oscar by then, which removed any financial incentive. Bored with looking over Lissa's shoulder, I pulled up the Jersey death records. My imagination was running riot about what Ursula might be capable of. She could have lied about her parents letting her take Guy to England. What if they had died in 1938, in suspicious circumstances?

Ursula's and Guy's birth records had not given their parents' forenames, but searching for the surname alone brought up a handful of burials, in chronological order, for every Finch who had died in Jersey between 1844 and 1940. I scrolled down the list.

'Holy shit!'

Lissa nearly dropped her sandwich. 'What? What have you got?'

I turned my screen to show her. It took her a second to register what she was seeing, but then she gasped. 'But that ... that means ...'

'We've opened a can of lively worms.'

The dates were shown left of screen. Alongside 7th August 1927 were the names of two children, aged seven and one, both buried on the same day.

Ursula and Guy Finch.

THIRTY-EIGHT

We didn't delude ourselves that the ID theft was Chloe's big secret. After eighty years, it was hard to believe Ursula would be prosecuted for that alone, but it did imply the Finches' need to conceal a darker crime – borne out by Chloe's reaction this morning, when the murders of Daphne and possibly Barbara had seemed the least of her worries.

Lissa wondered about pre-war espionage, but we soon dismissed that. I had never heard of Nazis infiltrating the Channel Islands before the wartime occupation, and we found no hint of it online.

It seemed unlikely that the detectives had checked Jersey's burial records. Even if my text to George had prompted a search of burglaries on the island during the late 1930s, they would hardly have looked at deaths a decade earlier – but we felt that Ben should be the first to hear our news. Following a message from him that David was home and would love to see us, we drove to Netherzoy at three.

By 'home', Ben meant the place prepared for his brother's convalescence: Yew Tree Cottage.

Since Lissa was being calm and resolute, I talked sense to myself. The forensics team had long gone, and Daphne was not Emily. Time to act like a grown-up. Today was about David.

Ben answered our knock. The day's events had transformed him. He was unable to stop smiling, dimples working overtime.

'Dave's really keen to see you,' he said. 'He's bored already, now Chloe and Tommie have gone home. Oh, and this is for you.' He took a slim book from his pocket.

The Lundy Companion was half the size of a standard paperback, its cover protected by a plastic sleeve, which may have been a publisher's hint that the little volume would live up to its title and become a friend for life. Lissa stashed it in her handbag.

We found David reclining along the sofa, watching TV, but he switched it off when we entered the room. He was pale, and wore gold-framed glasses, presumably because his usual pair had been lost or broken. There was no visible wound, though a bar of bruising on his neck suggested a similar head injury.

'Hi guys.' His voice trembled, emotions barely in check.

Lissa bent to kiss his forehead. 'We're so sorry about Maisie.'

He nodded wordlessly, and I shook his hand and clapped him on the shoulder. He raised disapproving eyebrows, making the effort to smile.

'What, no kiss for the invalid?'

'You're not that sick. How are you doing, really?'

His smile faltered. 'I'll get there. It's wonderful to see you both.'

While Ben was supplying beverages, we chatted with David about our interviews. After a few minutes, however, the pauses became more frequent and increasingly awkward. We were running out of topics that wouldn't cause him distress.

It was David himself who called a halt. 'You've made amazing progress and I'm hugely impressed,' he said, 'but honestly, is this *really* what you want to talk about?'

We were not sure how best to respond.

He rolled his eyes. 'My dears, trying to ignore the herd of elephants in the room is wearing me out. I suppose you know that DS Lampert has been haunting my bedside?'

'George Bailey mentioned it,' I said. 'Guess you still don't remember that night?'

'Oh, I remember all sorts of things. Unfortunately for our detective sergeant and Gorgeous George, most of them never happened. Yesterday I woke up convinced that I'd dozed off in the garden at Spindlewood, surrounded by spring flowers.'

'It must all have been a bastard,' I said.

'It was terrifying. Still, I know who I am now, that's the main thing – and everything else has started coming back, apart from that Friday night. And now I'm just livid with whoever dumped me at the hospital. If he'd given my right name, Ben and Unc would have been saved a lot of heartache.'

Ben came in with a laden tray. 'You're the one who got hurt,' he said.

'That's all over and done with. Except, of course, it might not be.' David regarded us with solemn eyes. 'Ben and Unc are trying to keep this from me, but I'm not totally away with the fairies. Conor's killer may try to silence me before I can identify him.'

'Lissa and I have talked about that,' I said. 'Ben, you've told the Knights that David's home, right?'

'Course.'

'You could embellish the story. Say he was confused at first, so now the cops are hacked off because they can't trust his testimony and wouldn't be able to use it in court. Ask the Knights to spread the word. Tell the same tale at work, and to anyone else who asks.'

Ben nodded slowly. 'You're right. That's a bloody good idea.'

'I don't actually think you'll be embellishing,' David

sighed. 'I doubt that I *would* be a useful witness.'

'We should still be careful,' Ben said. 'It's awful, being suspicious of people we've known forever, but I don't want to trust anyone outside the family. Except you two and Chloe, and the cops. And Jackson, of course. And the Knights.'

His readiness to widen the circle was a concern, but at least he hadn't included Alex.

'What's the last thing you remember,' I asked David, 'on the Friday you drove down?'

'Having coffee at Gordano Services. Conor had rung me earlier, but for some reason that escapes me, I wanted a break and a think before we met.'

'We talked to the barista who served you,' I said. 'You rang Conor back.'

'Did I? What about?'

Although the doctors had cautioned against supplying lost memories, there was a chance this one would trigger his recollection of later events. I relayed what Brandon had told us.

'Fogle ...' The ghost of a memory flickered behind David's eyes. 'I think ... yes. That's so weird ... it suddenly flashed up. Conor was acting for Fogle, hoping I'd value an item ... wasn't he?'

'According to Conor. Any idea what?'

'None ... although ... whenever I happen upon a real find, something truly wonderful, it's a physical excitement. Visceral. Whatever he showed me that night, I think I felt that ...'

His voice trailed off. We let the silence lengthen, hoping he would conjure more glimmers from the darkness; but eventually he passed a hand across his eyes, frowning as if his head ached.

'I'm sorry. It's gone. And after Gordano, what I thought were memories have turned out to be nonsense. Alex Naylor throwing a brick through a window, for example, and a pavement covered in broken glass. Apparently, Alex was with friends the whole evening.'

'Mates he's known for years,' Ben muttered. 'Bet they'd lie for him, though.'

'There was no broken glass at the airfield,' I said, thinking briefly of the window smashed by Reece at Heron View. But that had been days earlier, while David was still in Ledbury. The incident must have been a dream, as David himself believed.

At this point, Ben asserted his authority as carer. 'I, um, think we should leave it there, as it's Dave's first day home.'

His brother was indeed looking tired. We said our goodbyes somewhat guiltily, David recovering enough of his usual spirit to wink as I shook his hand again.

I grinned. 'You don't give up, do you?'

'Make allowances, Kit. I'm an injured man.'

'Just as well.'

Although it might be a long road before he was his usual flamboyant self again, the attempts at banter were reassuring.

Ben came outside with us. 'Thanks so much for coming,' he said. 'And for what you suggested. I'll get on to it.'

'There's something else,' Lissa said. 'It might be important. Did you know Chloe's gran and her Uncle Guy changed their names when they left Jersey?'

'No. So what? I've got mates who've done that.'

'The real Finches died as kids,' I said. 'They're buried in a Jersey graveyard.'

He looked from one of us to the other, trying to process the information. 'OK, that's a bit sick.'

We shared with him our thoughts on the Finches adopting new names to escape a dark past. He recalled hearing the tale of a burglary from his Grandad Thomas, and conceded that would tie in with Ursula or Guy having originally stolen the rumoured antique. To safeguard Reece, we let him assume that Conor could have taken it either from Guy or during Ursula's house clearance.

'Will you tell George about the ID theft?' he asked, looking shifty.

'Of course,' Lissa said. 'Don't you want us to?'

'Not really. Chloe would hate seeing her gran arrested.'

'For Christ's sake, Ben!' I was furious. 'They won't care about charging Ursula for that, but it could turn out to be a vital lead – and what's more important, David's safety or keeping Chloe happy?'

'That's bollocks, you know I'd never –'

'Ben,' Lissa interrupted soothingly, throwing me a warning glare, 'we really need you to talk to Chloe and explain that we don't have a choice. If the Finches stole the antique, everything is linked.'

He held her solemn gaze, then turned to stare across the lane as if hoping to find the answers in tree and hedgerow. At last he said dejectedly, 'S'pose I can tell Chloe that.' He shot me a wary look. 'I don't want you and me to fall out.'

I didn't want that either. The emotional rollercoaster of the past ten days was getting to all of us.

'Sorry, mate, I was being a tosser,' I said. 'We know you wouldn't put David at risk.'

He smiled cautiously with relief. 'Right. We'll catch

up again before Friday, yeah?'

As the trip to Lundy was five days off, this was a safe bet. Less certain was whether, if Chloe confided her secret to Ben, he would pass it on. He might be committed to protecting David, but he was also a man in love – and if he betrayed Chloe's confidence, he could lose her.

I feared that he might keep quiet and hope for the best.

THIRTY-NINE

George rang that evening, rather than reply electronically to our message about the IDs. He suggested coming to see us in person. Since Thomasina would be home too late to cook, Lissa had offered to make dinner for all of us, so she invited George too. His eager acceptance may have been driven by the prospect of dining with Thomasina.

'We've found our vocation,' Lissa said, after he had rung off. 'First Ben and Chloe, now Tommie and George. We should set up a dating site. Sedgemoor Singles.'

Although she was joking, I liked the idea of fostering a romance between the handsome detective and our sexually supercharged landlady. They seemed a good fit. It would also take the heat off me. Lissa could trust me, and I trusted myself, but living under the same roof as Morgan Le Fay had its challenges.

The evening began well. George arrived with flowers for Lissa and Thomasina, and we served dinner in Greenways' startlingly Gothic dining room. Thomasina lit candles smelling of incense, which I thought an odd accompaniment to a meal, but George made an appreciative comment. We sat on intricately carved, black-backed chairs and chatted across a table adorned with a crimson cloth and a lighted candelabra. Dracula would have approved.

'Reminds me of my childhood,' George said.

'A blatant lie,' Thomasina teased him. 'This is nothing like your mum's house. I've been there, in case you've forgotten.'

He smiled into her eyes. 'I remember every second,' he said, adding with a glint, 'but I meant the vegetable curry. It's delicious, Lissa.'

The compliment was well deserved. She was a far better cook than I was. Left to myself, I would have lived on salads and takeaways.

'This is a real treat,' George added. 'We've been working all hours this week. Sorry to talk shop, but you two,' he waved his fork at Lissa and me, 'have substantially increased my workload. We weren't looking as far back as the 1920s, either here or in Jersey.'

'We thought not,' Lissa said. 'Why would you?'

'More to the point, why would *you*?'

We had anticipated awkward questions. She replied smoothly, 'No history of Netherzoy would be complete without the Naylors. We decided to include a paragraph on Ursula's background.'

'Good answer.' His tone was amiable, but his thickly-lashed dark eyes were narrow and alert. 'Can we talk about Zoyland House, Kit?'

'What about it?'

'All three emergency services arrived there last night to find they had missed the action. There were conflicting stories, so this morning DS Lampert and I called in, unannounced, after watching YouTube footage from the party.'

'Wild, was it?'

'Alex Naylor informed us – none too politely, as we'd got him out of bed – that when everything kicked off, he was downstairs and, in his own words, hadn't seen shit. When the boss asked to speak to Chloe, we learned that you drove off with her and Ben last night and she hasn't been home since.'

Lissa and Thomasina remained studiously silent. I was on my own with this one.

'Alex and Chloe had a row,' I said. 'There was some drama, and she rang Ben and asked him to pick her up. I was with him, so we took my car. I dropped them both back at Spindlewood.'

George pensively ate a forkful of curry. Chewed and swallowed. 'Impressive stunt,' he said, presumably not referring to the drive to Spindlewood.

'What, you think I was Spiderman?' I laughed at the thought.

George sipped his wine. 'You *have* seen the footage.'

'Guilty as charged. Ben showed us this morning.'

'Want to tell me what happened?'

I gave in with a sigh and confessed to my part in Chloe's rescue, hoping that would be enough to keep him on-side. George, however, was not a detective for nothing.

'What did Chloe and Alex row about?' he asked.

'According to Chloe, a private family issue.'

'No mention of ID theft?'

'Not a whisper.'

He finished his wine. Into the hiatus, Lissa asked whether they had interviewed Ursula since the baby's remains were found.

'We have, this afternoon. I can't say she made us welcome, but she told us quite readily that she had delivered Barbara Macrae's baby, the result of an affair with a guy in the village. The child was stillborn, and the mother buried it in the garden and begged Ursula to keep quiet, to save her reputation. Different times.'

'She's lying,' Lissa said.

'She may be, but as there's no evidence of foul play … Still, the grave wasn't the main reason for our visit. The boss asked Ursula why she and her brother stole the identities of two deceased children.'

This was as gratifying as it was unexpected. It might also mean that Lampert, too, suspected that the events of eighty years ago could be linked to recent crimes.

'Unfortunately,' George added, 'Ursula didn't appear to understand the boss's line of questioning. She became agitated and accused us of trying to prove she was dead. A nurse was sitting in on the interview, at Ursula's request, and at that point we were asked to leave.'

Lissa rolled her eyes in frustration. 'She played you.'

'We gave her the benefit of the doubt.' But his dry tone belied the words. He agreed with Lissa.

She stabbed a chunk of courgette with unnecessary vigour. 'Where will you go from here?' she said. 'Or can't you say?'

'I really can't. I told you about our visit to Ursula because the care home staff will let her family know, so the story would have reached you anyway.'

'How about the Jersey records?' I asked. 'Any unsolved burglaries from 1938, or crimes that the island's police were about to pin on a young woman and her teenage brother, before they both vanished?'

'Too tenuous. You're talking about a mention in an unknown file – even if the older records were comprehensive, which they're not. Some didn't survive long enough to be digitised. As for those that did, everything is kept until an individual's hundredth birthday – but that only came into effect in 2006, and it won't apply if the offender was never arrested or even cautioned, or if the original file went astray. Jersey was occupied by the Nazis.' He shrugged. 'What percentage of those records still exist? Your guess is as good as mine.'

Thomasina said ruefully, 'On the plus side, George, that frees you up to concentrate on the live investigation.'

'Indeed. One thing we plan to make public is that David and Conor may both have been hit with the same implement, a particular brand of tyre lever. The sharp end cracked Conor's skull. David suffered only blunt trauma.'

'So the killer came equipped,' I said.

'Do you need to find it to make your case? Lissa asked.

'Not necessarily. And overall, we're making progress.'

His quiet confidence could be a bluff, I thought, but the staff at Southampton General may have identified the man who had left David there. If so, my money was on Harry Diment.

With luck, Harry's footprints were also beside the rhyne. Although not conclusive evidence, that might scare him into a confession. If he incriminated his accomplice, Reece's testimony would never be needed, the lad could stop looking over his shoulder, and Lissa and I needn't feel guilty about keeping quiet.

'You're very patient, George,' Lissa was saying. 'I'm sorry we keep nagging you, especially about Ursula.'

'It's fine. Really, I get it.' His voice was gentle, because of Emily.

He wouldn't be so forgiving if he knew what we were holding back.

After dinner, we retired to our own room, to give Thomasina and George some privacy but also to plan the next few days. We wanted to book more interviews. It could be a while before David felt ready to start writing, but seeing a catalogued and indexed collection of documents, in soft and hard copy, would encourage him.

We had visited everyone whose phone numbers were

on the list, so on Monday we drove to Netherzoy and spent a couple of hours knocking on doors. Despite being mistaken occasionally for Jehovah's Witnesses, we made six appointments and completed three that day.

On our return to Burrowbridge, Lissa put herself in charge of wrestling with Mike Macrae's filing system again, setting aside two days to finish the job. I could never comprehend how she found such tasks enthralling, and was pleased to escape when she suggested I keep the Wednesday appointment by myself. We had always intended to split the workload, but so far had rarely done so, perhaps sticking together for moral support amid the chaos.

The interview went well. Old Mrs Pye contributed nothing about Ursula or Barbara, but she added some new anecdotes to our growing collection.

Satisfied with a productive afternoon, I turned up my collar against the chill and took a circuitous route back to the car. After sitting still for two hours, I needed a walk to loosen up, but Thomasina had been right about my injury being minor; I would be fit enough for hiking on Lundy. In fact I was looking forward to the prospect of a "lads' trip" with Ben, and remained sceptical about Alex's allegedly murderous plans.

I didn't hear the Rolls until it glided up alongside, matching my pace. The passenger window opened, and Jackson Naylor called from the driving seat, 'Kit, can you spare a minute?'

His expression was solemn, the twinkle noticeably absent. I got into the car, and he switched off the engine.

'I've just come from visiting David,' he said. 'He seems to be doing well. A relief for the whole family.'

'He was very lucky.'

Jackson nodded, his expression giving nothing away. Lampert must have approached him about the ID theft. I wondered if it had been news to him, and whether he had heard, via Chloe, that we were the source.

But that was not uppermost in his mind.

'I also called in at Spindlewood,' he said. 'Chloe extended her stay, but she's coming home tonight. She seems recovered from her ordeal.'

'Good to hear.'

'At the risk of descending into melodrama, I'm forever in your debt.'

'No, Jackson, please –'

'I planned to drive to Greenways to find you, so you've saved me the trouble. To be clear, if you ever need a favour, you only have to ask.'

'OK, well … thanks.' Since he was in a receptive mood, I added on impulse, 'There's one thing. It's not exactly for me, but it might be important.'

'All right.' Those astute blue eyes were boring into me. 'Fire away!'

'Chloe's got a secret that she doesn't feel able to share. It's the reason she and Alex fell out.'

His face went blank with shock. 'She's not pregnant?'

'No.' *Not to my knowledge.* 'This is some sort of family problem.'

'Really? I thought – I hoped – they both felt able to confide in me.'

'She's trying to protect you. Maybe they both are.'

He looked nonplussed, then sighed deeply. 'It seems I've reached the age where my kids feel responsible for me, instead of vice versa.'

'Shows they care, I guess.'

'They've both turned out well. I'm proud of them. But

I took my eye off the ball. If I'd been at home, that party would never have happened. I'll have a chat with them individually, try to get them to open up.'

'As long as they don't twig that I suggested it.'

'Have faith, lad. I've dealt with trickier operators than my two.'

I grinned. 'Sorry. Is your mum OK?'

'Most of the time, but she has bad days. I don't think she has enough to stimulate her mind. I'd hoped she would make friends at Cedar Lawns, but some of the residents have dementia, and the rest ... To be honest, I've heard they feel intimidated by her.'

'She's quite a character.'

'Mm. She'll be with us till Friday now, then Alex is taking her to Lundy. She'll enjoy that, and she likes his company. Says he reminds her of herself at that age.'

For all of their sakes, I hoped Ursula was mistaken.

'Well, I'll let you get on,' he said.

I had done all I could. At least he hadn't resented my interference in his personal life; or, if he had, he was too grateful for Chloe's deliverance to show it.

I returned to Greenways, to be awed by Lissa's efforts. Most of the boxes were now labelled, while our spreadsheet had grown to log every topic, cross-referenced with the names of contributors.

'Impressive.' I lifted the lid of *Box 1* to see an orderly collection of drop files with tabs.

'Isn't it?' she said. 'How was Mrs Pye?'

'Her dad was in the local cricket team. She's going to dig out some photos.'

'Excellent.' Lissa gave me a smile, which seemed a little forced.

'OK, sweetheart?' I asked.

'Fine. Shall we go out tomorrow? As a reward for hard work?'

Tomorrow would be Thursday. Our last day together before Ben and I flew to Lundy.

'Sounds good. Anywhere in particular?'

'Mystery tour. I'll drive.'

The hint of playfulness suggested she might be in the mood for another kind of fun. I would have pursued this agreeable thought, but my ringtone interrupted me.

Nathan Yandle was calling. I raised my eyebrows at Lissa, wondering whether to expect more revelations.

But it wasn't Nathan on the phone.

'Kit? Can you come? You need to come.'

'Reece? What's up?'

'He's going to kill him.'

'What? Who –'

'We heard Harry come home. He hasn't been back for days ... and Nathan stormed straight over there. I couldn't stop him.'

Swearing under my breath, I grimaced at Lissa. She was frowning in bewilderment, hearing only my side of the conversation. I put the phone on speaker.

'Is anyone else home? Your mum? Your sister?'

'No, they're still at Auntie's. You need to stop him. He thinks Harry knows who did for Conor. He'll make him talk, but he'll go too far and get sent down for life.'

'OK, Reece, you need to call the police –'

'You're joking me! They'll arrest him, won't they?' The boy was practically sobbing. 'Why are you being so useless? I thought you and Nathan were mates.'

'Not really.'

'He respects you. You could talk to him.'

Lissa was looking horrified. I knew how she felt.

'Reece, I can't. It won't work.'
'It has to. There's no one else.'
'How about Nathan's real mates? Or Conor's?'
'They'd help him put the boot in, wouldn't they?'

That had the ring of truth. As I hesitated, he added brokenly, despair in each syllable, 'Please, Kit.'

Lissa nodded once with decision and picked up her handbag.

'We'll go together,' she said.

FORTY

We made it in eight minutes. Along Honeysuckle Row, I was unkind to the car, bouncing it through the ruts while Lissa gripped the arm rest, but she didn't tell me to slow down.

'Straight to Harry's, right?' she said tautly.

'Yeah. We don't need to involve Reece.'

Outside the cottages, we crunched to a halt on the gravel, and Lissa was out of the car almost before it had stopped. I caught up with her halfway up the path to Harry's cottage and grabbed her hand.

'Hey, stay with me, OK? And stand well back while I knock.'

'Behave! We'll *both* stand back.'

The lights were on downstairs. I knocked (and stood back), but no one came. Not even Harry.

I brought Plan B into operation. 'Open up or we'll call the police!'

It was Nathan who opened the door. He was breathing hard, and the knuckles of his right hand were bloodied.

'You need to piss off,' he said.

'What's going on?' I said. 'Where's Harry?'

'We're having a chat.'

From the back of the house, Harry croaked, 'Don't leave! *Please!* He's going to kill me.' His pleas were interspersed with cracks like wood hitting stone.

'Let us in, Nathan,' I said pleasantly, 'or we really will call the cops.'

A grimace of regret crossed his face. 'Look, nothing personal, but you know I won't let you do that.'

To my horror, Lissa took out her phone. 'How about me? Are you going to beat me up as well?'

His dismayed expression was almost comical. 'What the hell do you take me for?'

She smiled. 'Let us in, then!'

Nathan rolled his eyes. 'Bloody Reece called you, didn't he? I'll kill the interfering little git.' But he had resigned himself to the inevitable. 'Whatever,' he said, and stomped back to the kitchen.

We followed him.

Under the stark overhead lighting, Harry Diment's plight made a shocking impact. He was seated on a kitchen chair, arms pulled around the back of it and presumably secured, while his ankles were tied with kitchen string to each of the chair's front legs. His lower lip was split, and his nose had bled down the front of a *Speak for the Trees* T-shirt.

At our appearance, he renewed his struggles, causing the chair to rock. The thudding we had heard had been its legs rising and falling on the quarry-tiled floor.

'Oh, my God!' Lissa threw down her handbag and knelt to untie his ankles.

'No!' Nathan started forward, but Lissa didn't even look round. She was assuming he wouldn't hit her.

I stepped between them and squared up to him. 'Don't even think about it!'

He shoved me with the flat of his hand. 'I don't hit women, all right? I've seen what bastards like that –' He bit off whatever he had been going to say. A revelation from his childhood, perhaps. *I've seen what bastards like that can do.* Instead he shouted, stoking himself up again, 'I know this tosser was there when Conor died.'

Harry burst out, the words whistling past a broken tooth, 'I saved David Macrae's life. I drove for seven bloody hours so that – so that no one would get to him.

I'm not a murderer.'

So that who wouldn't get to him? He had so nearly let it slip.

Nathan had noticed too. He roared at Harry, 'Who was it? *Give me a name!*'

Lissa had succeeded in freeing Harry's ankles. He flexed his feet, groaning, and stated with desperate bravado, 'Can't tell you what I don't know, can I?'

Nathan's fury exploded. Pushing past me, he dealt Harry a cuff on the head that rocked the chair sideways. Fearing for Lissa, I elbowed Nathan and lunged to save the chair. I missed, but she was already scrambling back, out of danger.

Harry and the chair crashed to the floor, his right arm and shoulder taking the impact. Very nasty, since his wrists were still tied, trapping his upper arm between the chairback and the floor.

We all heard the crack. Harry and Lissa both screamed.

Nathan stopped, literally in his tracks. This was no longer about throwing a few punches. Suddenly he was looking at GBH – and prison.

Without a word, he strode from the room.

Cursing, I squatted to deal with the string around Harry's wrists. He was in severe pain, gasping and swearing. Lissa scrambled to kneel beside his head, reaching for her phone.

'Kit's untying you,' she said. 'Don't try to move.'

He moaned, 'No cops.'

'Ambulance,' she said. 'If we drove you, it would feel horrible. The paramedics will give you something for the pain.'

He raised no objection to that. She told the call

handler that the casualty had rung her and her husband after a fall at home. He was in too much pain to say much, she said, and we didn't know whether alcohol had been involved.

By the time she ended the call, Harry's hands were free.

'Move this fucking chair!' he pleaded, close to tears.

Neither of us was keen to try, but if his circulation was restricted, and the ambulance was slow to arrive ...

We couldn't be responsible for him losing an arm. Lissa reached for his good hand, which startled him.

'It will hurt.' She tried to sound matter-of-fact, but her voice shook.

He nodded, and Lissa looked at me over his head. I tried to slide the chair towards me, down his body, but his weight was clamping the back of it down. The only solution was to raise his shoulders. Luckily, he was fit enough to help, but he made a lot of noise about it. While I supported him, Lissa pulled the chair away and set it upright.

Harry managed to sit up, with my help. He leant back against a kitchen cabinet, nursing his arm and groaning.

'You should press charges,' Lissa said.

'In enough trouble ... without that.'

He had a point. If Nathan was charged and convicted, Harry couldn't continue living next door to the Yandles. He may also have hoped that Nathan would appreciate the let-off, call it quits, and leave him alone.

I glanced at Lissa. 'Can you stay with him for a minute?' I said.

'Of course.'

I went into the hall. Nathan was sitting on the stairs, head in hands, a picture of well-earned despair.

'Good news,' I said drily. 'He's not going to bring charges.'

Nathan raised his head, trying to read my face. 'Seriously?'

'From the horse's mouth,' I said. 'Love thy neighbour, and all that.'

He rubbed a hand over his newly shaven scalp. 'Shit. Thought I was going down. GBH with intent. You can get life for that.'

The narrow escape had rattled him badly. I doubted he would try again, but there was no harm in making sure.

'I don't think Harry killed Conor,' I said. 'Nor do you, or you'd have finished him.'

'I wouldn't do that.' He slid a wary look in the direction of the kitchen. Since I had left the door ajar, there was nothing to see, but we could hear Lissa speaking softly. Nathan sighed. 'I just wanted a name.'

'You'd better go before the medics arrive. Tell Reece he won't be visiting you in the nick.'

He nodded dejectedly. 'How about you?'

'We'll stay till they turn up.'

'I wouldn't. Harry can say what he likes, but they won't believe he did all that from falling off a chair. They'll report it.'

'Let them. If they start giving me funny looks, Harry can put them straight.'

After Nathan had slouched off to his own cottage, I returned to the kitchen. Harry was still sitting huddled on the floor, his back to a cabinet. Lissa sat beside him, the two of them seeming at ease with each other, almost companionable.

She asked me anxiously, 'Has he gone?'

'Yeah. You might be a person of interest to the cops,

Harry, but Nathan's given up on you.'

'Tosser,' he muttered. 'This is what I get for being a bloody Samaritan.'

I grunted an acknowledgement but couldn't bring myself to heap praise on him. He had saved David from following Conor to an early grave, but his lies at the hospital had been misguided at best.

'You off too, then?' he asked, looking depressed at the prospect of being left alone. He was suffering, and most likely nervous in case Nathan changed his mind.

'We'll wait for the medics,' I said.

Unfortunately, he didn't reward us with a full confession.

At one point, Lissa asked, 'Do you think you'll be charged with stealing the Audi, Harry?'

'No.' He was defensive. 'If the hospital staff ID me, I'll tell Lampert that David asked me to drive him there.'

'Is that true? Was he conscious?'

'She can't prove he wasn't.'

'Ah ... and I suppose, if you ruined a pair of trainers in the mud, or even by falling into a rhyne, you'd throw them away, wouldn't you?'

He flashed her a startled look. 'Bag 'em up, pick a random wheelie bin on the next collection day. Who'd look twice?'

If nothing else, this confirmed his role in dumping Conor's body. His clothes must have gone the same way as the trainers.

'Harry,' Lissa said. 'We've helped you, haven't we? Will you tell *us* who got you involved?'

He gave her a twisted grin. 'No comment.'

'Because they'd come after you next?'

'No comment.'

So that was that.

As it turned out, Harry was lucky. The ambulance arrived within the hour. The paramedics received his fell-off-a-chair story with raised eyebrows and knowing looks, but they were friendly towards Lissa and me, especially after their patient enthused about how we had helped him. If anyone came under pressure later, it would be Harry himself.

We left them to it, let ourselves out, and sat in the car for a minute, taking stock.

'Well,' Lissa said, 'that was all a bit ...' Words failed her.

'You were amazing.'

'I didn't expect ... I've never seen someone ...'

Tied to a chair and beaten.

'No,' I agreed. 'Don't suppose Harry told you anything else while I was with Nathan?'

'I did most of the talking, about the carnival and the dismal weather. I was trying to keep his mind off things.'

We were driving back along the lane, more sedately this time, when she added, 'You know, I thought Harry was just a pathetic wannabe tough guy, but now ... I do get what Chloe sees in him. He might not have Ben's dimples and puppy eyes, but he's attractive.'

'Really?' I couldn't see it. 'Have you booked a room?'

'Not yet. I'll book two. You can bring your personal witch.'

I had thought it safest to mention my alternative therapy session before Thomasina did, and felt relieved that Lissa was willing to joke about it. We were more relaxed with each other than we had been a week ago, even if no nearer to finding a way forward.

Rather than talk any more about the violence we had

witnessed, I asked about our destination tomorrow, but she smiled and told me to wait and see.

I thought about Harry instead. From his response to injury, he was not as tough as he liked to pretend. It surprised me that he hadn't revealed the name of his accomplice.

There was only one conclusion to be drawn from that. However scared he had been of Nathan, Conor's killer frightened him more.

FORTY-ONE

When we set off the next morning, Lissa was still refusing to offer any clues, even when she exited the M5 at Junction 22 and headed for the Mendip Hills. In the village of Cross, we turned right towards Wells and Cheddar.

'The Gorge?' I hazarded.

'Later.' She checked the dashboard clock and sped up a little.

'Got a schedule?'

'An appointment.'

'Anyone I know?'

She simply smiled, though I detected signs of nerves in the faint flush at her throat and the way her middle finger tapped the steering wheel.

I reclined my seat and closed my eyes, feigning lack of interest. That tactic proved a dead loss. After a minute I sat up. 'OK, you win. I'll wait and see.'

'You're doing very well. I thought you'd be getting impatient by now.'

'Who, me?'

We drove through Cheddar itself, and on to a village called Draycott, where Lissa turned into a side road and pulled up outside a house built in the traditional local stone. It was a corner plot, hedged on two sides.

A young woman, business-suited and kitten-heeled, emerged from a Smart car parked across the road. She greeted us with a handshake and a professional smile. 'Mr and Mrs Pevensey? I'm Eleanor. Hills and Gorge Estate Agents.'

I met Lissa's eyes with barely contained anger, and her eyelids flickered: not quite a wince.

'It's just a viewing, darling,' she said.

We had last viewed a property the week before Emily was born, a two-bedroomed terrace that would have been our first step on the property ladder. Back then, we had dreamed of eventually owning a forever home to fill with a couple of kids and a dog. We had even talked about land for horses. Lissa still missed the gentle mare that she had grown up with. The old horse had spent her final years at an equine retirement home in the Kent countryside, close enough to visit.

The house in front of us was a good-sized family home – even if the horses would have to wait.

Eleanor's smile faltered as she picked up on the tension between us. 'If today is a problem,' she said, 'I'd be happy to reschedule.'

I forced a smile. 'It's fine. A misunderstanding.'

Reassured – or hopeful of securing a sale, regardless – Eleanor guided us along a path edged with rose bushes, all stems and thorns at this season, to the front door.

'As I mentioned on the phone, Mrs Pevensey,' she said, 'the property is unoccupied. The owners have moved north for family reasons, and the previous buyer pulled out last week. That's why they've dropped the price since it was last on the market.'

She didn't state the price, so I nodded as if I knew.

To be fair to Lissa, it was a great house, newly decorated and full of character, with four bedrooms. In Kent, it would have been way out of our reach, but after I landed the *Enigmas* contract, we had looked at Somerset prices and found them a lot less jaw-dropping.

Lissa was careful not to show enthusiasm to the agent, although her eyes were sparkling. I knew, with a sinking heart, that she had fallen in love with the place. I liked it too – but if we bought a family-sized home, I would be agreeing to try for a family.

We said goodbye to the eager Eleanor and watched her drive off. My scheming wife then turned to study my face.

'Are you very angry?' she asked.

'What do you think? When we pick a house to view, I'd like a say in it.'

She gazed at me, her beautiful dark eyes unreadable. Then abruptly she said, 'Get in the car!'

'Tell me you haven't booked another viewing!'

'You're safe. I haven't.'

I did as I was told, shutting the door harder than necessary and yanking at my belt to fasten it. Lissa slid composedly into the driving seat, executed an efficient three-point turn and drove north, back the way we had come.

Neither of us spoke.

When we reached Cheddar, I made no comment as she took the road through the Gorge, passing a few intrepid hikers. Finally, she pulled into a layby. On both sides the cliffs rose steeply, but not far above the road was a sloping patch of green, strewn with boulders, with a footpath leading up to it.

Judging from the number of marked parking spaces, this was a popular spot during the summer, but today the rain and cold had discouraged would-be picnickers.

Lissa looked me up and down, eyebrows raised. 'Have you finished fuming?'

In spite of myself, I nearly laughed. 'Just sulking, thank you.'

Her lips twitched, and she reached behind her to drag a shoulder bag through from the back footwell. 'Come along, then. I've brought lunch.'

We tramped up the path to sit on a flat-topped rock. The rain had stopped, but needles of icy wind probed beneath the neck of my leather jacket. I shivered, hunching my shoulders.

'I know Greenways would be warmer,' Lissa said.

'So would the car.'

'I want to clear my head. And yours.' She took two salad rolls in cling film from her bag, then a flask of coffee, setting them between us on the boulder. 'We need to talk.'

I regarded her with growing unease. This was about more than a contentious house viewing. 'OK,' I said.

She took my hand. Hers was colder than mine.

'We agreed that we don't want to live in Bristol,' she said, 'and this is a lovely area. I mean, look at all this on our doorstep!' She waved her free hand. 'Plus, we'd be a sensible commuting distance from the studios. And Draycott isn't touristy like Cheddar.'

'Mm.'

'Of course, we'd make any decision together.'

'I should hope so.'

She stroked my arm, her eyes holding mine. 'I'm sorry I didn't tell you about the viewing. I hoped the house would blow you away.'

I frowned at the wet road snaking away out of sight. The cliffs on both sides limited our view of the sky, but the clouds were dark, heavy with the promise of more rain to come.

'What's the asking price?' I said.

She told me. I had been right; an equivalent house in Kent would have been nearly twice as much.

I had no issue with Draycott as a location, especially if

Lissa had set her heart on it. As well as being convenient for Bristol, we would be less than two hours from Robyn, making day-trips feasible. Whether we needed four bedrooms was another matter.

'We could afford it.' Lissa spoke with authority. She knew our finances inside out, which was more than I could say.

Time for honesty.

'You're imagining us living there with our kids,' I said.

She lifted her chin, accepting the challenge. 'I'm hoping.'

'You know what the consultant said. Because Emily was born early, there's a higher risk of that happening again.'

'Because of how my body responds to pregnancy, not because we're cousins. Next time, the baby and I would be monitored every step of the way.'

I stared out across the Gorge, thinking of Emily being fed Lissa's expressed milk via a tube in her nose, and I didn't answer.

She said softly, 'You've always been willing to take risks.'

'Not with our baby's life!'

'We're not special or unique, Kit. There's no such thing as a risk-free pregnancy.'

'I know that. But I can't ... I couldn't bear for us to have another baby, just to ...'

To watch her die.

'So this is about you. You're scared.'

'Christ, Liss, who wouldn't be? Aren't you?'

'I want our baby.' Her voice trembled. 'If I was over thirty-five and we weren't cousins, would you think *that* was too dangerous?'

'Of course not.'

'The percentages are the same.'

I had no answer. Logically, she was right, but what I felt had nothing to do with logic. Although I knew that losing Emily had not been our fault, I was her dad. Every caveman instinct screamed that she had been mine to protect, and I had failed her.

Lissa said quietly, 'I'll tell you what *I* can't bear. Being given a glimpse of the future we hoped for, like … like a light coming on. And then that light going out. Forever.' She looked down at our clasped hands. 'Knowing that Emily was our one chance. Not because of some medical issue. I could have come to terms with that. But because you say so. And you know what scares *me,* Kit? That I won't be able to forgive you.'

Those final words … I couldn't let that happen. Couldn't throw away everything we had together. And that was what I'd be doing, unless I could face the chance, however small, of another loss, and more grief and guilt. A chance that thousands of prospective parents faced willingly, every day, with better and worse odds than ours. As Lissa had said, there was no such thing as a risk-free pregnancy.

Enough. The decision had to be made, here and now.

I met her eyes with difficulty, feeling as frightened as I had ever been.

'OK,' I said.

She blinked. 'W-what?'

'We'll try again.'

'But … just like that?'

'No.' I tried a smile. 'To save us.'

'Oh …' She looked across the Gorge, concentrating

fiercely on two birds of prey soaring above the cliffs. 'I didn't want that. To back you into a corner.'

'This is on me, Liss.'

She turned to me then, searching my face. Even though I had meant every word, I knew that they had sounded feeble, lacking conviction.

I said more firmly, 'You're right, I need to get my head straight. And I will ... but ...'

'But what?' she asked, suddenly afraid.

'Can we wait, maybe another month or two? I want ... I want it to be just Emily and us, Liss ... for a little while longer.'

'Oh, Kit.' She lifted my hand and pressed it against her cheek. There were tears on her face. Mine too, no doubt.

'My Amphelisia,' I said. 'If you're with me, I can face anything. Don't let me forget it again.'

She let out a hiccupping laugh and wiped her eyes on her sleeve. 'You always could deliver a line, Pevensey. Eat your salad roll.'

We sat with our picnic, cuddling close, Lissa telling me her own doubts and fears, and how she dealt with the sorrow that sometimes overwhelmed her. She also teased out of me a few more of the private thoughts that I had never shared. We both cried, but not with the despair that we had felt beside Daphne's grave. This time it felt like a release. For Lissa too, she said.

Rain swept up the Gorge. Seeing it blur the outlines of the cliffs, we hurried down to the car, gaining shelter as the first great drops splattered on the windscreen.

I leant back and watched them. Having taken such a momentous decision, I felt strangely calm. Panic might overtake me later; but whatever the future held, I would have to find the courage to deal with it, as well as to confront my own irrational demons – for both our sakes.

The next decision, however, was not scary at all.

'I like the Draycott house,' I said.

Lissa paused while fastening her seatbelt. 'Do you?'

I smiled into her eyes. Waited until she smiled back.

'Shall we arrange a second viewing?' I said.

FORTY-TWO

On Friday morning the sky was a uniform grey, the wind moderate. Average fare for November. To our untrained eyes, it looked flyable – but Thomasina, having been around pilots all her life, informed us over breakfast that Ben would not be happy.

'The wind's gusting eighteen knots, west-north-west,' she said. 'Almost at ninety degrees to the runway, at Merlin Park as well as on Lundy. The Jabiru can't cope with that.'

'So the whole thing's off?' Lissa asked hopefully.

'Unlikely,' Thomasina said. 'Alex has booked the Super Cub. It's bigger than the Jabiru. Not quite so sensitive.'

'Should we talk Ben out of going?' Lissa asked.

'You can try, but he won't want to let Chloe down.'

'Don't fret, sweetheart,' I said. 'Ben won't risk damaging his beloved Jabba.'

'I'm not actually worried about the plane.'

I promised to speak to Ben, while thinking privately that his decision might not be straightforward. Despite having studied the forecast in advance last time, he had relied on visual clues and the field's windsock to confirm the local conditions. Hardly an exact science, and this time his judgement might be skewed by his desire to please Chloe.

Thomasina's next words betrayed her own anxiety. 'The wind often dies down towards evening, but sunset can't be much after four. You'll need to be careful not to leave it too late.' She shook her head, as if to dismiss her doubts. 'But Ben's sensible. He'll err on the safe side.'

Lissa pushed away her cereal bowl, which she had

barely touched. 'I've got a bad feeling about all this,' she said.

'Sweetheart, I promise you, if it's too windy, or if there's any risk of landing in the dark, we won't take off.'

She didn't answer, because we were interrupted by a call from Ben. Chloe had sent him an update: Alex had phoned the island's office to notify them that he and Ursula hoped to land on Lundy at twelve-thirty. He had also requested a lift from airfield to village in one of the staff Land Rovers, which were usually employed to transport holidaymakers' luggage.

The perfect, caring grandson.

Ben wanted to land an hour after the Naylors. That was fine by me. No point seeking a confrontation, especially on an otherwise deserted airfield. The tourist helicopter used a helipad near the village, and Ben said visits by private planes were not a daily occurrence, even in summer.

Having worked the timings back, he told us he would be at Merlin Park at ten-thirty. If Lissa dropped me there an hour later, the Jabiru would be prepared and ready for take-off.

Thomasina wished us luck, then left for work. Lissa was quiet after she had gone. While we were filling the dishwasher, I caught her frowning to herself as if engaged in some internal debate.

'Penny for them?' I said.

She shook her head, in frustration rather than denial. 'We're going about this all wrong, keeping Jackson in the dark. It's irresponsible.'

'Chloe's not a child, and she spoke to us in confidence. We can't go running to her dad.'

'But what if I could persuade her to talk to him? To

tell him her fears about Alex, not the reason for them.'

'She won't be persuaded.'

'It's worth a try, isn't it? I could contact Jackson, request an urgent meeting, then invite Chloe to come along.'

'She'd hit the roof.'

'Well, I have to do something. I know you think nothing will happen on Lundy, except Alex being irritated because you and Ben have followed him, but we have to take sensible precautions.'

'Chloe's got it wrong, Liss. Alex might *prefer* his gran to keep her mouth shut, but if he was caught trying to kill her, he'd have thrown his whole life away. And for what? Chloe admits that their dad is bound to find out everything eventually, and any publicity would probably bring in more visitors to the museum.'

'Chloe doesn't agree, and she knows her brother.'

'Yeah, OK, but if she's right that Ben and me turning up will stop Alex in his tracks, there's no need to involve Jackson.'

'Unless Alex is so angry with you and Ben that he attacks you instead.'

'Give us some credit, sweetheart! We're not about to stand on a cliff edge, waiting to be shoved off.'

'Be serious, Kit! I don't want you to get hurt. Or Ben.'

Her mind was made up. She had had a bad feeling. When she tapped in Jackson's personal number, I reckoned that superstition rather than logic had been the deciding factor.

Jackson had no objection to meeting her but questioned the urgency. 'If you can make midday, I can spare half an hour then,' he said. 'Is it for David's book? I'm free most of tomorrow. I could give you more time then.'

'It's not that. I'm sorry, Jackson, I really do need to see you today.'

'Is there a problem?'

'Um ... It's too complicated to discuss over the phone ... but please could Chloe sit in as well?'

'Is this about whatever is going on between her and Alex?' His tone had sharpened. He was irritated, perhaps starting to resent our continued interference. 'I've spoken with them about last week and reminded them that they can come to me with any problem at all, any time. They've both assured me that they've made up and everything is fine.'

'That's great. I'm glad,' Lissa said, grimacing at me. ''But ... can we still meet today?'

A long pause. Then he said, sounding more puzzled than antagonistic, 'All right. Come to Reception at noon.'

Despite Jackson's annoyance, Lissa claimed to feel better for having taken positive action. She sat on our bed and watched me pack, which didn't take long. Since the Greenways scales had weighed me in at seventy-eight kilos, fully clothed, Ben had given me a two-kilo luggage limit, to include phone and wallet. This left no leeway for anything beyond basic toiletries, underwear and two T-shirts, all compressed into a bag-for-life. I was also forbidden to bring my leather jacket, the quilted one being lighter – but in a small act of rebellion, I exceeded my limit by taking *The Lundy Companion*, in case its hand-drawn map and descriptions of local landmarks came in handy.

'We still don't know where you're staying,' Lissa said. 'It seems odd that Ben hasn't told you.'

'Never mind, we'll see him in a minute.'

'Will you call me tonight? The pub has a signal,

doesn't it?'

'Ah, but there's a massive fine of a pound if you're caught using a phone.' She looked so indignant that I gave her a hug. 'I'm teasing, Liss! Of course I'll ring you, and to hell with the expense!'

She was not so easily pacified. 'You sound as if you're looking forward to it.'

'I am, a bit … but I will miss you, so, so much.'

Before she could tell me off for spinning a line, I kissed her at some length, as proof of sincerity. After a while I remarked that we had time to go back to bed for an hour. Having celebrated our reconciliation last night, I was more than ready to continue the private festivities.

'Or,' she said, with a mischievous smile, 'we could christen the garden.'

I laughed out loud. 'No! It's bloody freezing out there.'

'Don't exaggerate! I'm sure you'll manage, and I've never been seduced in a pagan shrine.'

She got her way. Ludicrously clad in only dressing-gowns and trainers, we ran outside hand in hand, giggling like teenagers. The grass was wet, the temperature less than ideal, but the back garden was hedged and secluded. We chose a flat green space, overlooked by a carved wooden bust of a smiling face with oak leaves in place of hair and beard. The Green Man, pagan symbol of rebirth.

The novel location was weirdly arousing.

'Like Celtic dogging,' Lissa said, spluttering with laughter.

We made love with an excitement heightened by the frisson of feeling slightly naughty – though Thomasina, far from being offended, would have found our antics hilarious – and in the process we created one of those unforgettable moments that give a relationship spice. If ever we passed Greenways again, even years in the future, we would glance at one another with secret knowledge, and smile.

Lying cocooned together in the dressing-gowns, now rather damp, to get our breath back, I found myself imagining the future that had once seemed within our reach. The family, the dog, the house full of love and bustle and chaos. An idealised vision, but our visit to Robyn and Ian had shown us the reality.

It may have been those memories, or the leaf-fringed smile of the Green Man, but I felt a flicker of the emotions that had driven me when I had been glad to agree with Lissa that we wanted children.

Time to find some courage. Since Emily died, fear of the future, and anger at life, had overwhelmed me. But that was not who I was. Having promised Lissa that I would get my head straight, the next step was to accept that I couldn't do it alone.

As if glimpsing this thought, she raised herself to one elbow. 'What is it, love?'

'Does your bereavement counsellor do video calls?'

She grew very still. 'I'm sure she would.'

'We could chat with her together, for starters.'

Lissa nodded once, blinking back tears. 'I'll contact her while you're away. I'll make us an appointment,' she said, and then kissed me with lingering tenderness, to let me know that she understood my turmoil, and how I would struggle with opening up to a stranger.

But today we were in danger of keeping Ben waiting. Returning indoors to warmth and reality, we showered and dressed, pausing now and then to kiss briefly, needing no more excuse than the accidental brush of hands or shoulders. I thrilled to her touch as if our new closeness had fired up forgotten nerve endings, and could tell it was the same for her.

Eventually, feeling cautiously hopeful, even mildly euphoric, I grabbed my two-kilo carrier bag and Lissa drove me to Merlin Park, the first leg of my trip to Lundy.

FORTY-THREE

True to his word, Ben had the Jabiru out on the grass in front of the hangar. As we got out of the car, he straightened up from checking under the fuselage and strolled to meet us. His disconsolate expression was all the more evident because he was clean-shaven.

'New image?' Lissa asked.

'Yeah.' Doubtfully, he stroked his smooth chin. 'Chloe talked me into it.'

Lissa said it suited him. I thought he would be showing pub landlords his ID for the next ten years, but refrained from saying so.

'We can't go yet,' he said. 'The wind's a couple of knots over the crosswind limit. It'll ease off a bit later.'

'How much later?' I asked.

'Before two, with luck. There's no fuel on Lundy, and we can't start with more than thirty-five litres because of the weight. That means making a pitstop at Eaglescott on the way. They're not open every day, but the guy who mans the bowser has agreed to meet us there.'

'And we'll still be OK for time?' I asked.

'Should land well before sunset, as long as we're away by two.'

Lissa hugged her arms around her. 'Have you heard from Chloe?'

'An hour ago. The Super Cub will be taking off any time now.'

'That's good – they won't be at Sedgemoor when we get there,' she said. 'We might as well all go together to see Jackson. It's too cold to hang around here, and we can buy lunch in the café.'

'See Jackson?' Ben echoed. 'What for?'

'We'll tell you on the way.'

Rather than waste time putting the aircraft away, Ben placed chocks under the wheels and tied it down with ropes connected from below each wing to stakes like giant corkscrews, wound deep into the turf. Then we drove to Sedgemoor Aerodrome, Ben choosing to ride with us, having already locked his bike and motorcycle gear in the hangar.

When Lissa explained her plan, he was predictably appalled. Hearing her reasons didn't make him much happier.

'I promise,' she said, 'I'll tell Chloe it's all down to Kit and me, and you were against it. But honestly, Ben, if we kept quiet and something went wrong on Lundy, Chloe would regret not talking to her dad – and she'd blame you for going along with it.'

'I'm screwed either way, then, aren't I?' he said.

'I can drop you at home if you like.'

He hesitated, then shook his head. 'I'll come with you. It's not like we really know anything. Chloe's bloody secret will be safe, won't it?'

This was the closest I had heard him come to criticising Chloe. He must have been deeply hurt that she wouldn't confide in him.

'But we can't take off later than two,' he added.

Jackson and Chloe were at the front desk, chatting with the staff there. Chloe broke off to watch us walk in, her expression coldly furious. She tapped Jackson's shoulder, murmuring to alert him, and he turned to greet us with smiles and pleasantries, asking after David and Alf. Although he had been expecting Lissa to come alone, he was too courteous to remark on this in public.

'Dad!' Chloe said between her teeth.

Jackson gave no sign of having heard, but ushered us all through a door at the back of the foyer, into a corridor that ran the length of the building. To our right, large windows overlooked the airfield, while on the left were three offices, each with glass from waist-height to ceiling, giving an impression of figurative as well as literal transparency. Ironic, in the circumstances.

His office, where we had met six years ago, came equipped not only with the usual furniture, but also a corner sofa and chairs around a glass coffee table, suggesting a preference for informal meetings.

At his invitation, Lissa and I occupied one side of the sofa, Chloe and Ben the other, though the girl pointedly edged along the cushion to put distance between them. She was nervous as well as angry, continually playing with a strand of her long hair.

Poppy, the young waitress from the café, had evidently been promoted to office duties. Jackson summoned her to take our orders for hot beverages, and engaged us in good-humoured small talk until she returned with them. Chloe maintained her glowering silence, causing Poppy to shoot her a curious glance before leaving the room.

Jackson had chosen to sit opposite us, ostensibly leading the meeting. 'This is quite a crowd,' he said amiably. 'Lissa, you implied there's a problem. Would you like to be the one to enlighten us?'

She sat up straight, lifting her chin. 'You might think this is none of our business, Jackson –'

Chloe cut in, 'Because it's not. I know what they're going to say, Dad, and it's all a stupid misunderstanding.'

'In that case,' he replied, 'now is our chance to clear it up. Let Lissa speak, love.'

'She doesn't know anything.'

'But you do?' he asked.

'No. What do you mean? Of course not.'

Lissa said in a rush, 'Alex and Chloe are keeping a secret. We think it's about your mum, Jackson, and they're terrified that you'll find out.'

'For God's sake, Dad!' Chloe surged to her feet, her voice high. She was close to hysteria. 'This is crap. Please don't listen!'

He stood up and put an arm around her. 'All right, love, you need to listen to me now. Whatever you or anyone else can tell me about your grandmother, I'm likely to have heard it before.'

Chloe stared up into her father's face, doubt turning to disbelief. 'What?'

'Sit down. Please.' Guiding her back to her seat beside Ben, he sat at her other side. 'DS Lampert came to see me yesterday,' he said, addressing us all. 'She asked if I was aware that Mum and Uncle Guy had assumed the names of two children who had died in Saint Helier in the 1920s. I expressed shock.'

'You already knew,' I said.

'Uncle Guy told me, years ago. They were born and raised in Germany, as Jutta and Gunther Vogel –'

'Fogle?' I interjected, hearing the phonetics without considering the spelling. He pronounced the *v* as an *f*. 'Like Conor's contact.'

'As you say. The name – V-O-G-E-L – is a German surname meaning "bird". The family owned a guesthouse in a small town near Munich. In the summer of 1938, Dad and Freddie stayed there. Mum fell for Dad and made up her mind to catch him.'

'And succeeded,' I said.

'Not initially. There was already talk of war. If Mum was in England when war broke out, she would have been interned as a possible spy – married or not. As I'm sure you know,' he nodded to Lissa and me, 'tens of thousands of German immigrants were sent to camps. Many were even deported to Commonwealth countries.'

'But that didn't put her off?' I guessed, thinking that a tiny snag like World War Two wouldn't have deflected Ursula from her chosen path.

'Mum was in love, and also keen to leave Germany.'

'She wasn't on board with Nazism? That was unusual, surely? And brave.'

Membership of the Hitler Youth organisation and its equivalent for girls, the BDM, had been compulsory, ensuring that the young generation was efficiently indoctrinated.

'Mum was happy to accept that she belonged to a superior Aryan race,' Jackson said, 'but Hitler also taught that a woman's main function was to breed more little Aryans. Mum didn't see herself in the role of, as she put it, a brood mare for the cause.'

I felt a grain of sympathy for the young Jutta Vogel. Not surprising that when an English landowner had cycled into her life, she had seen a desirable escape route.

'So,' Lissa queried, 'she asked your dad to create fake IDs?'

'They wrote to each other for months before that. But then Mum and Uncle came into a substantial amount of money, from an elderly relative with no children of her own. That tipped the balance for Dad. Zoyland House was, and is, expensive to run.' Jackson caught my cynical look, and laughed shortly. 'The course of true love runs more smoothly if you're not bankrupt. Arrangements were made. Mum and Uncle travelled overland through France, and from there to Jersey.'

'But,' Lissa put in, 'Guy – Gunther – was only twelve. Didn't their parents object?'

'In fact, he was fourteen. There were issues at home. Uncle Guy begged to go, and Mum took his side.'

'Your dad met them in Saint Helier?' I said.

Jackson nodded. 'He and Freddie had been to Jersey to search the parish records. Ursula and Guy Finch caught Dad's eye because of the surname, Finch being a bird. Guy Finch had been two years too young, but Gunther could pass for a tall twelve-year-old. Dad ordered copies of the Finches' birth certificates, which contained all the information needed to create a convincing set of documents, including passports. It was a lot easier in those days. No biometrics, no scanners.'

'If your dad had been caught,' I said, 'he could have been shot for treason.'

Before Jackson could reply, Ben spoke for the first time, his voice rough with outrage. 'So could Great-Grandad Freddie.'

'Regrettably, that's true,' Jackson said. 'But they were not caught. Mum and Dad were married, and Mum schooled Uncle Guy at home so no one would hear his accent and schoolboy English. There were gardeners and a cook, but he never spoke to them. His only friend was Freddie. But then the war came, and Freddie was killed.'

'He sounds a sad boy,' Lissa said.

'He may have been, but as a man, he moved into Heron View and found the peace he craved, painting birds and tending to the creatures who visited his garden. A form of therapy, I think. He struggled to come to terms with the past. He first confided in me when I was Chloe's age. Mum would be horrified, even now, if she knew.'

I recalled the words on Oscar's headstone: *I have kept the faith.* Freddie had put his life on the line for Oscar – but then, after Freddie had given that life for his country, Oscar had slept with his widow, setting in motion the events that had killed Barbara and their child. His generosity to Freddie's descendants had been his penance, his way of 'keeping the faith'.

And yet those who remembered Oscar said he had looked haunted. If he had chosen his own epitaph, I wondered how desperately he had tried to believe those noble words.

Chloe had listened to her dad's story in silence. She had stopped twisting her hair. Perhaps she felt relief that Jackson already knew their family secrets, but I thought Oscar's part in the deception could cause difficulties. His heroic war record had inspired the museum's creation. Jackson wouldn't want that record tarnished.

'You're trusting us to keep this dark?' I queried.

Jackson smiled his twinkling smile. 'I'd appreciate it. David never intended his book as an exposé of villagers' misdeeds, past or present.' He lifted his silver eyebrows at Ben. 'Do you agree, lad?'

'Course. I don't want people thinking Great-Grandad Freddie was a traitor. He wasn't, because your mum and uncle weren't spies.'

Jackson grunted. 'That's one way of looking at it.' He reached for his coffee, seeming relieved that the issue had been dealt with so easily. 'Does that answer all your questions, Lissa?'

'Not quite,' she said apologetically.

He paused, cup to mouth. Chloe also grew still, her wide blue eyes full of trepidation.

'Please, Chloe,' Lissa said, 'tell your dad what you told us.'

The girl no longer had a reason to hold anything back. Her father knew everything, and it hadn't destroyed him.

'I've asked Ben and Kit to fly to Lundy this afternoon,' she said.

Jackson was puzzled. 'Because?'

'I think Alex will try to ... to kill Gran.'

'Oh, for heaven's sake!' Far from being shocked, Jackson looked incredulous, as well as embarrassed that his daughter had involved us in her fantasy. 'I know you mean well, love, but this is crossing a line.'

'I don't want Alex to go to prison.'

Jackson raised his eyes to the ceiling as if praying for patience, then drew a long breath through his nose and tried again. 'Listen, Chloe –'

'No, *you* listen! He's doing it for you, and all of us, because he doesn't want Gran to start telling other people ... who she was.'

'That's not really a motive for murder, now is it? Did Alex actually *tell* you about this supposed plan of his?'

'He said she's out of control and we have to do something.'

'That sounds as if he was talking about her behaviour. We know your gran can be abrasive, and we've all heard her be rude to the carers.'

'Dad, I know what he meant.'

'Chloe ...'

'You don't believe me.' A fierce accusation.

'I believe you're sincere.' He paused to consider, then changed his approach. 'All right, let's say Alex is worried about your gran letting something slip. Wouldn't he simply warn her carers not to take her stories seriously?

Everyone is aware that she has memory lapses.'

Chloe was silent.

Her father pursued his advantage. 'Alex is devoted to your gran.'

'That won't stop him.'

Jackson regarded her steadily.

'Don't!' she said. 'Don't look at me like that!'

'What aren't you telling me?' he said.

She froze, startled, then let out a despairing little laugh. 'You know what? I'm sick of lying,' she said, and strode out of the room and into the one next door.

'That's Alex's office,' Jackson told us, frowning at the invasion of his son's domain but doing nothing to stop it.

We waited, watching Chloe through the intervening glass, Ben nervously stroking his smooth chin. Chloe stood on a step stool, ran her fingers along the top of a high shelf, and retrieved what must have been a key, which she then fitted into the desk pedestal.

She was looking for something specific and knew where to find it. With a padded A4 envelope in her hand, she marched back to join us, holding it out to her father.

'Conor stole this,' she said, 'from Uncle Guy.'

FORTY-FOUR

My mouth opened. Beside me, Lissa gasped.

Ben said blankly, 'That's the antique?'

Jackson took the envelope, looking up at his daughter in appalled disbelief. 'What is this? How did Alex come by it?'

'Uncle Guy rang him and said Conor had forced his way in. He seemed to know Uncle had this, we've no idea how. Conor even described it. He forced Uncle to tell him where it was.'

'Did Conor hurt him?' Jackson asked sharply.

'Just frightened him, I think. Alex confronted Conor about it and threatened him with the police unless he handed it over. So Conor brought it into work.'

'Alex should have gone straight to the police, regardless. Why didn't he?' Jackson's bewilderment was turning to anger. 'And why don't I know about any of this?'

'Uncle Guy begged Alex not to report it. He didn't want a fuss. He didn't even ring Alex till a day or two afterwards. Alex would have told you, but then Conor didn't turn up for work on the Saturday, and the police were all over us about David. Suddenly it was a mess, and Alex didn't want us caught up in it. The day of the party, after I'd come back from seeing Gran, he showed me *that*.' Chloe stabbed a finger towards the envelope. 'And he told me the whole story. And when we got home, it all kind of blew up. Just look, Dad!'

Jackson tipped the envelope's contents carefully into his palm. The object itself was concealed by a fabric cover, from which protruded two silver rods topped by elaborate silver-gilt swirls and four tiny bells.

I had imbibed a fair amount of knowledge from my antiques-obsessed family, before leaving home and choosing a different career, and perhaps a little of their instinct for the rare and precious had rubbed off. Looking at what lay in Jackson's palm, I felt butterflies in my gut.

He removed the gold-woven cover – the mantle – with infinite care, to reveal the miniature scroll inside, with its gold pointer attached by a chain. His expression never changed, though he grew so still that he barely seemed to breathe.

'May I see?' I asked.

He passed it to me without a word.

Out of respect, aware that whoever had used this would have taken care not to touch the scroll itself, I turned the silver rods to unroll it slightly, fearful of damaging the parchment even while I marvelled at its craftsmanship and exquisite calligraphy.

'This is a Jewish Torah scroll,' I murmured. 'Handwritten.'

'Would it have come from a synagogue originally?' Lissa asked.

'No. Miniatures like this are for personal use, at home.'

'Valuable, I imagine,' Jackson said.

'I'm no expert – and I've never seen one in real life, only a couple of catalogue photos – but this isn't gold and silver plate. It's the real deal. Could be centuries old.'

'Four figures?'

'Three, four, five. David or my sister might know, but I think even they'd need to consult a specialist in Judaica. Jewish religious art.' I looked at Chloe. 'When did Conor give this to Alex?'

'I told you, Alex said he brought it into work.'

'What day?'

'I don't know. What does it matter?'

It mattered a lot. Conor had shown David a beautiful artefact at Merlin Park, and Conor had never been seen alive again. He certainly hadn't been to work to hand the Torah back to Alex.

Had Alex tracked him down at the airfield and confronted him there? If Harry knew where Conor was going, he would have told Alex, under even subtle pressure. Harry owed the Naylors his freedom, his job, a chance to turn his life around. Alex's absence from the CCTV at the gate meant nothing, since the alternative route across the fields from Honeysuckle Row was common knowledge.

Ben said, 'If Alex was at Merlin Park ... but even if Conor and him fell out ... I mean, Alex wouldn't have hurt Dave ... would he?'

'Of course not,' Jackson said. 'Alex was nowhere near Merlin Park. He was with two friends all evening, gaming. I know them both. Very solid young chaps.'

None of Alex's friends at the party had seemed particularly dependable. If Alex had told the two in question a plausible fiction – about a date with a married girlfriend, for instance – they might well have lied to give him a less troublesome alibi.

There was no point in saying so. Jackson looked for the best in people, and made allowances for the worst. Where his children were concerned, that might render him wilfully blind, and right now he was busy convincing himself of his son's innocence. Challenging that would only make him defensive.

I went back to studying the scroll. Ursula and Guy had come to England from Nazi Germany the year before war broke out. Hitler had been in power for five years, brainwashing his people, instilling the lie that Jews were responsible for all of that country's economic woes. They were already being stripped of their rights, dismissed from jobs in most industries and denied access to schools and universities. The Nazis had called them *Untermensch*, sub-human.

'Do you know where your uncle got this?' I asked Chloe.

She nodded. 'He told Alex. The Vogels' neighbours were a Jewish couple, the Schneiders. They owned a successful clothing company. The government was forcing them to sell it to non-Jews really cheaply.'

'That was happening all over Germany,' I said.

'They were meant to hand in a list of all their personal possessions as well, but they left the scroll off the list. They asked the Vogels to keep it safe for them until they could escape to Holland. Uncle saw where his parents put it, and he hid it in his bag when he and Gran left for England.' Chloe looked deep into Ben's eyes, as if asking forgiveness for her uncle's crime. 'He believed the propaganda, that Jews were inferior, barely human. He told Alex it didn't even feel like stealing.'

'But when he grew up,' I said, 'he understood.'

'He was ashamed. That's why he hid the scroll away. He'd have hated for Alex to go to the police.'

I said thoughtfully, 'Conor told David that the seller was a Mr Vogel. If that was purely for his own amusement, using Guy's real name because no one would ever join the dots, how did he know …?'

I stopped. Took a breath. *The letters.* Conor had seen the German stamps and postmarked dates, and the return address on the envelopes would have included the name

Vogel. Also, the letters would have been signed 'Jutta', and she would have mentioned Gunther.

'Did your dad speak German?' I asked Jackson.

'He could order from a menu. What are you getting at?'

I decided to take a chance. 'You said your mum and dad wrote to each other for months. We've heard that Conor found letters in the house clearance stuff and chose to keep them.'

Jackson looked blank. 'What for? They'd be worthless to anyone but Mum. And who told you that? The Yandles? Harry Diment?'

'We've done a lot of interviews, and the grapevine is pretty efficient. Let's leave it at that. The point is, if your dad didn't speak much German, the letters would have been in English. Conor could have read them and worked out that Jutta Vogel and your mum were the same person. If she sent your dad a letter after she and Gunther left home, to finalise arrangements for meeting him and Freddie in Jersey, she may have mentioned that Gunther had taken the scroll.'

That seemed a neat way to let Reece off the hook.

'Whatever was in Conor's mind,' Jackson said, 'it's irrelevant now. We need to draw a line under all this. Alex didn't attack anyone, because he was never at the airfield … and I will take charge of that.' He held out his hand for the scroll, which I returned. 'I'll donate it to a museum of Judaica, claiming it was found in a box of wartime memorabilia, provenance unknown. And if Mum's carers ever query something she has said, it can be passed off as confusion.'

He paused, looking at each of us in turn, checking our reactions. 'Finally, Lundy. I don't think for one moment that Mum is in danger, but I'd like to set everyone's mind at rest. Chloe, you and I will message Alex to make him aware that the cards are now on the table, that he's not in trouble for concealing the scroll – and, since the pair of you are so determined to save me anxiety, that I'm on top of the situation.'

I met his daughter's eyes. Far from being relieved, she was distraught, still fixated on some inner scenario of doom.

What don't we know, Chloe? What haven't you told us?

'Do you still want us to go to Lundy?' I asked her.

She nodded miserably and looked up at Ben. 'Please, Benji?'

'Course. We promised we would.'

Jackson was taken aback. 'As long as you're not planning to make trouble for my son.'

We assured him that we were not. Chloe seemed cautiously appeased and said an affectionate goodbye to Ben before slinking back to her own office. Jackson apologised profusely for embroiling us in his family issues, and wished Ben and me a safe flight. Then he went to find his daughter.

Ben, Lissa and I retired to the museum café for lunch and tried to get our heads around the new developments.

Lissa scoffed at Alex's story of Conor handing him the scroll at work. 'I think Alex put it in his desk because he was trying to find somewhere safe,' she said. 'He could have been moving it around, trying to second-guess where the police might search if they turned up here or at Zoyland House with a warrant.'

'You don't buy his alibi, then?' I asked.

'Of course not. Neither do you.'

Ben continued to brood on whether Alex had attacked David. 'If I find out he did that ...' he muttered darkly. The Beast of Netherzoy was flexing his claws, at least in Ben's imagination.

'And there's Harry, too,' Lissa said. 'If Alex threatened to pin the murder on him, Harry would have known it would be his word against Alex's. He'd have been afraid everyone would believe Jackson Naylor's upstanding son. That could explain why he wouldn't give Nathan Alex's name.'

Ben stopped with a bacon roll halfway to his mouth. 'Nathan Yandle? What's he got to do with it?'

We told him, quietly enough to foil any eavesdroppers. His jaw dropped, not at Nathan's brutality, which appeared to come as no surprise, but at Harry's confession.

We let him ponder that for a while. Only when we had finished our lunch did I ask casually, 'What d'you reckon, then? Think Chloe's still keeping secrets?'

'No,' Ben said, quick to defend her.

'Yes,' Lissa said. 'She gave in too easily. I think she brought the scroll out to make Jackson think that was the big secret, when in fact she's still terrified of what could happen on Lundy.'

'Tell you what struck me as odd,' I said. 'If the Vogels despised all Jews, why would the Schneiders have entrusted them with a valuable family heirloom?'

Ben shrugged, but Lissa nodded slowly.

'You're right,' she said. 'It's more likely that Guy stole it from the Schneiders' house.'

'Yeah. The burglary that Barbara told her kids about.'

What did ring true was the Vogels' neighbours being ordered to list their belongings; but if they had hidden the scroll well enough to fool the authorities, how had fourteen-year-old Gunther happened to find it?

We had no answers to that conundrum. In order to lighten the mood, I asked Ben where we would be staying on Lundy.

He screwed up his face, anticipating my disappointment. 'Chloe said Alex was lucky to get Square Cottage, right? I reckon that was down to a cancellation. Everywhere was fully booked when I tried, but I've packed basic camping gear. Tent, sleeping bags, bed rolls.'

Camping in November. It was not an enticing prospect.

Lissa was heartlessly amused. 'How macho,' she said.

'We won't actually have to sleep outdoors,' Ben said. 'The Marisco Tavern stays unlocked twenty-four-seven, so that campers can come indoors if they need to. Course, it's really meant for if you're freezing and desperate, like – but that's OK. We'll put the tent up and pay for the pitch, then bring our gear inside when the bar closes. The camping field's officially closed in winter because it can get boggy, but all the staff are nice. They won't chuck us off, and they can't make us fly home in the dark anyway.'

'But what did they say,' Lissa asked, 'when you asked to book the campsite?'

'I didn't. When they told me there were no properties vacant and the field was shut, I said we'd just come for the afternoon.'

'Oh! I hope the staff are as tolerant as you think, or you'll both be sleeping in the road.'

Despite Lissa's lack of faith, Ben remained adamant that the pub would be available, and dossing there held more appeal than spending the night in a waterlogged field. It might even be a laugh, I thought.

As predicted, at one-thirty, the Met Office site showed the wind dropping by two knots. We returned to Merlin Park, and Lissa hugged me tightly while saying goodbye.

'Promise me,' she said, 'you won't do anything stupid.'

'I promise. Please don't fret. I'll ring you from the tavern.'

While turning to stuff my carrier bag into the luggage space – a few oddly-shaped cavities around the fuel tank, behind the seats – I marvelled at Ben's skill in finding room for camping gear. Our coats had to go in there too, because he had brought life jackets for us to wear as insurance for the sea crossing.

Once we were kitted out, I ducked under the door frame to manoeuvre myself into the passenger seat and buckle up, thinking that Ursula had done well to manage this. Unless the Super Cub had better access for the less agile, she would have needed to swallow her pride and accept help from her strong grandson.

Ben completed his checks out loud. Lissa stepped back as he opened the door briefly to shout, 'Clear prop!' before starting the engine. Then we bumped over the grass to the runway threshold. The process was familiar now, so I was resigned instead of impatient when we paused for the final into-wind checks. I blew Lissa a kiss through the side window, and she returned it before folding her arms again, hugging herself against cold and fear.

A sharp gust rocked the little aircraft. I looked a question at Ben, and his forehead puckered, but his voice through my headphones was untroubled. 'It's at thirty degrees to the runway now. We'll be fine.'

I remembered from last time how his demeanour changed when flying. Even then, under severe stress, he had been able to set his emotions aside and behave like a pro. Today he had the same air of calm confidence; he had followed procedures, phoned ahead, and checked the forecast.

I grinned and gave Lissa a final wave. We were on our way. No point worrying now.

FORTY-FIVE

The take-off was uneventful. With hindsight, we were lucky not to catch one of the intermittent gusts as our wheels left the ground. The only hint of the aircraft reacting to a crosswind was a slew to the left as the field fell away beneath us.

Heading west, we climbed to two-and-a-half thousand feet, high enough for the landscape below to whiten and blur. The town of Taunton, bounded to the south-east by the long ribbon of the M5, was a monochromatic sprawl amid the misty green and brown mosaic of fields.

The flight was pretty smooth, aside from one stomach-plunging drop over Exmoor. To pass the time, Ben lectured on the causes of turbulence, such as wind-rotor in the lee of hills, to which I had given no thought since Key Stage Three Geography.

On the final approach to Eaglescott, we descended crabwise to allow for the crosswind. Ben's jaw was set in concentration, and the grass zipping beneath us through my side window instead of the windscreen was not reassuring.

He made what must have been a textbook landing, using the rudder pedals to kick the aircraft straight a second before the wheels touched down. We rumbled along the strip and taxied to the fuel bowser, where Ben's obliging acquaintance was waiting. Several other aircraft were parked nearby, but there was no sign of their pilots.

We both had to leave the plane. A legal requirement during refuelling, apparently. We chatted with the fuel guy, who informed us that we were his only customers that day. Ben said the Super Cub could have completed the trip in a single leg, because the aircraft had a larger tank than ours, Ursula was light, and they carried no camping equipment.

When we took off again, it was still an hour before sunset, although the overcast sky threatened an early dusk. Ben was in buoyant mood, claiming to feel more comfortable now that we were fuelled up.

'You don't think we'll need the life jackets, then?' I quipped.

'Hope not. I've brought a locator beacon as well, though.' He indicated a palm-sized yellow gadget, like an old-style burner phone, tucked into his door pocket. 'Just in case.'

'Nice.'

He grinned at the sarcasm. 'I've flown to Wales. Never needed it.'

The North Devon coastline slipped away, while clouds swept gloomily overhead. On our left, in the south-west, a low sun peeked between layers of grey, sparkling on the sea.

Ben pointed. 'Lundy! Ten miles out, dead ahead. See it?'

I strained my eyes and may have glimpsed a darker shape in the murk. Then the sun sank into cloud, and sky and sea blended, the horizon no longer certain.

I reminded myself that we would never be far from the English mainland, and Wales lay about thirty miles to the north ... but we were heading due west, with no land in sight, and Lundy was only three miles long. Easy to miss in borderline visibility and dimming light.

Still, the small plane icon, which marked our location on the aircraft's GPS screen, was heading steadily towards the word *Lundy*.

Ben started our descent. The sea, which from higher altitude had appeared merely wrinkled, was now clearly choppy.

'OK for time?' I asked.

'A bit tight. Legally, I can land till half an hour after sunset, but I won't push it. They like you to buzz the field first, to clear any livestock, but we'll fly straight in if it's clear. Save a few minutes.' He nodded ahead. 'Four miles to go. See it now?'

The dark hulk of Lundy, familiar from photos online, was solidifying out of the murk. It looked closer than four miles away. We could see the cliffs, and breakers bursting into spray on the rocks offshore. A lighthouse – the South Light, Ben said – gave a white flash every five seconds.

I checked my watch. Four-thirty. The sun had set.

We flew in over the cliffs, revs too low now to scatter the few sheep that grazed there, pale in the dusk. The runway stretched ahead, marked by two parallel lines of white-painted boulders. It looked a lot rougher than the mown grass of Eaglescott and Merlin Park; and the wind, far from dropping towards evening, seemed stronger. The little plane lurched alarmingly as we crabbed downward. Ten feet above the ground ... five ... Ben kicked the plane straight. I pressed myself back into the seat, tensing every muscle.

The wheels touched down, bounced, thumped down hard, bounced higher – and this time Ben pushed the throttle lever forward, accelerating. We were airborne again, and gaining height. The top of the Old Light passed his window, and then we were over the cliffs and flying out to sea.

'Bit challenging,' I said.

'I'm going around. Least I know where that hump is now.'

It was unlikely to be the only one. Realising that my hands were clenched, I opened them, stretching out my fingers.

'There's no problem,' Ben said. 'If a landing starts going to shit, you put the power on, go around, start again.'

'Sure. All good.'

The plane banked around the south end of the island. On our left, the flashes from the South Light were bright amid deepening twilight. As we flew along the eastern cliffs and turned inland again, I had to peer to make out the white boulders edging the runway. Three dimly seen sheep completed a leisurely walk from right to left.

I glanced at Ben. He was composed, focused, but the angle of his jaw suggested his teeth were clenched.

Christ, he's twenty-two. He's a kid.

But a kid who had been flying this plane since his feet could touch the rudder pedals. I breathed deeply. I was not a nervous flyer. A good moment to remember that.

For the second time, I watched through my side window as we approached diagonally. The runway threshold rose to meet us. The Jabiru twitched straight, the nose flared, we came down hard – and stayed down. Ben braked sharply while the little aircraft bumped and juddered over the uneven ground.

I felt light-hearted with relief, almost euphoric. An adrenaline high, but none the worse for that.

'Great job,' I said.

'Thanks.' His voice was not quite steady. 'Didn't break the nosewheel. That's the Super Cub over there.'

The yellow plane was configured differently from the Jabiru, with two sturdy wheels at the front and a very small one under the tail. Less danger of collapse on a rugged grass strip, I supposed, although Alex would have needed to bring a portable step for Ursula.

We taxied to park alongside, avoiding two great tussocks of grass.

'The others must've been here for hours,' Ben said, his tone ominous. 'They're probably in the tavern.'

'We're going to play it cool, remember?' I said.

'Course.'

He was a little huffy, annoyed by my lack of faith, but that was no guarantee of restraint. For his own sake, I hoped he would behave. Chloe had been right about us, to a degree. If Alex started something, I would be able to land some telling blows, whereas Ben had got himself a tattoo to discourage the bullies. He might lash out under stress but he wouldn't last long in a scrap.

We unbuckled our harnesses and hauled ourselves out of the plane. Ducking under the wing, I stood upright and turned slowly, taking in the darkening landscape. Undulating heathland was intersected by stone walls, the silence broken by the chomping of a nearby sheep and the rustle of wind through the grasses. Westward, a lamp showed in a downstairs window of the Old Light, now converted to holiday lets. To the south, the top of a church tower, hard-edged against the twilit sky, peeped over rising ground.

In such an oasis of peace, it was difficult to accept that Chloe's suspicions had any validity, but Lissa's fears had begun to instil a few doubts in my own mind. My initial scepticism may have been naïve.

'The village and camping field are that way,' Ben said, nodding towards the church. 'Half a mile, maybe less.'

The expanse of grassland gave an illusion of distance. It was easy to forget how small the island was.

We turned our attention to practicalities. Ben produced chocks and the corkscrew stakes from behind his seat, and we secured the plane to the ground. Finally, having retrieved our camping gear, coats and meagre luggage, we stowed the life jackets in the Jabiru and headed for Lundy Road, the stony track that ran approximately north to south along the length of the island.

It was now fully dark. Ben had brought headtorches, which seemed a good idea but proved a mixed blessing, as they destroyed our night vision and threw the field's lumps and tussocks into deceptive relief. We set an undemanding pace and turned the torches off when we reached the road, eyes adjusting as we headed for the village.

Before we reached it, Ben steered me to the right, into a deserted camping field walled off beside the road. Erecting the tent took a few minutes. A pop-up would have been quicker but the wrong shape for the Jabiru's storage space. We left our bed rolls, sleeping bags and spare clothes inside the tent for later collection.

'The office will be shut now,' Ben said. 'We'll book in tomorrow.'

Tramping down the last slope towards the lighted windows of the Marisco Tavern, our footsteps were the only sound. The one small store was closed, the tourist helicopter had long since made its final flight of the day, and Lundy's visitors had evidently sought refuge in the tavern or their accommodations.

I recalled the online reviews about the island's time-warped ambience. An idyll of chintzy nostalgia and free-ranging livestock, where holidaymakers could retreat from the stresses of modern life. I could see the attraction and would be happy to return with Lissa next summer, but I was past the point of expecting our current stay to be a holiday, let alone idyllic.

With rising apprehension, I matched my stride to Ben's as we cut across the grass, taking the shortest route downhill to the door of the pub.

FORTY-SIX

The Marisco Tavern had two bars. The first was small and partially lined with bookshelves, while the main eating area beyond was high-ceilinged and spacious, looking out to sea. Every seat appeared to be occupied by diners turning pink in the warmth, amid a welter of discarded coats.

A quick recce confirmed that the Naylors were absent (unless both were in the ladies' toilets) but a glorious aroma of mushrooms and steak pie proved impossible to ignore.

'Next stop, Square Cottage,' I said. 'After dinner!'

'You want to knock on the door?' Ben was unnerved by the idea. 'Alex might kick off.'

'You think he'd take us both on, just for daring to turn up?'

Ben considered, then shook his head. 'S'pose not. He's full of crap, but he's not a nutter.'

'Good. We'll say we're looking them up because you told Chloe we were coming, and she mentioned they were here already.'

'He won't swallow that.'

'Never mind. We'll ask them to have lunch with us tomorrow. Great way to keep an eye on them – and better than Alex spotting us first and correctly assuming we're Chloe's spies. Then he really might kick off.'

Ben was glum at the prospect of lunch with Alex and Ursula. I clapped him on the shoulder. 'Let's find a seat!'

We approached a middle-aged couple at a corner table. Their coats were occupying what would otherwise have been vacant seats, so we used our best smiles while asking if we could join them.

They could hardly refuse, but they recognised me, which broke the ice. Introducing themselves as Frances and Henry, they obligingly stuffed their coats down beside the adjacent hearth and slid sideways on the bench seats to make room.

We played fair. I bought a round of drinks at the bar while ordering our dinner, then sat down again to answer their questions about *Enigmas*. They were a friendly pair, whose accents, poise and slightly tatty gilets hinted at unostentatious wealth. Over the meal, I took advantage of their willingness to chat.

'Friends of ours are staying at Square Cottage,' I said. 'Weird coincidence. A young guy and his grandmother. They flew in, like us.'

'Oh yes, we met them this afternoon.' Frances had weatherbeaten skin, a neat grey bob, and a habit of squinting over the top of her gold-rimmed glasses. 'We saw the plane come in, and then the Land Rover brought them here. Alex seems a pleasant young man. His grandmother was ... let's say, caustically monosyllabic.'

'Probably a little hard of hearing.' Henry jumped in as if used to neutralising Frances' outspoken views. His own manners were as impeccable as his slicked-back white hair.

'If you say so,' his wife conceded, with a glint of humour. 'Alex told us she's nearly a hundred. I hope I have a quarter of her spirit if I reach that age. They were planning a walk. Nothing too strenuous, but even so ...'

'Ursula's amazing for her age,' I said. 'Where were they off to?'

'Only the church, today. They're saving the south end of the island for tomorrow. Shutter Point might be too far, but they're hoping to reach Rocket Pole Pond. They'll be at the cottage now, I imagine.'

With luck. I excused myself and nipped outside to ring Lissa. The one-pound fine for phone use in the tavern was a symbol of disapproval, and I sensed that rebellion would be politely frowned upon by guests as well as staff.

After trying several different spots I found a signal halfway up the slope to the shop, and was pleased to hear Lissa's voice clearly.

'Hi, darling,' she said brightly, though I knew she was hiding relief. 'How was the flight? Have you seen Alex and Ursula?'

'Not yet. The flight was fine.' I paused, trying to identify the background noise at her end. 'Are you driving?'

'I'm in the car park at the aerodrome. There's a plane taxiing. I came back to speak to Jackson again, but I've just missed him. After you left, I kept thinking, what if we've got this the wrong way round and it's not Ursula's past that's the problem?'

'Whose, then? Alex's?'

'Why not? He and Chloe will run the show when Jackson retires, and they'll inherit everything eventually. What if Ursula knows something that would send Alex to prison, and he wants to silence her before she tells?'

'You think he killed Conor and confided in his gran? No, Liss, he'd never have told her. He's too aware that she can let things slip.'

Lissa said something in reply, but the signal was breaking up. I walked further up the slope. 'What was that, sweetheart?'

'I'm going to Zoyland House. Whatever's behind all this, I need to persuade Jackson to fly out to you tonight and take responsibility for sorting it out.'

'Wow. I'd like to be a fly on the wall.'

'Don't you believe I can do it?' she asked, with a touch of defiance.

'I believe you can do anything.'

She chuckled deliciously. 'Flattery, but I'll take it.'

While the signal held out, we exchanged some private, fairly explicit banter before signing off, but Lissa's sense of urgency about talking to Jackson left me feeling on edge. Alex and Ursula had taken one walk together already and, as far as we knew, no one had seen them since.

I returned to the tavern, to find Ben, Frances and Henry sharing stories of past holidays on the island. I explained that I wanted us to call on Alex and Ursula now, in case she went to bed early. Although it was barely seven o'clock, our new friends seemed to find this reasonable.

Once we were outside, I told Ben Lissa's plan while he was showing me the way to Square Cottage's front door. In the dark, this was far from obvious. Just along from the pub, a flight of steps led down into an enclosed courtyard, which gave access to four separate properties.

The Naylors' let showed a light upstairs, but the ground floor was in darkness. I recalled Chloe's description of the layout. Ursula might already be in bed downstairs, tired after an eventful day. If not, she had gone up to the living room after all, despite her failing heart – or they had left a light on while they were out.

I knocked on the door.

No sound from within. Not so much as a curious face at a window.

'Anywhere else they could be,' I asked Ben, 'apart

from the church, if they were there this afternoon?'

'There's the Old Light. It's converted to lets, but you can still climb to the top.'

'Ursula couldn't.'

'No.' Ben raked a hand through his curls, thinking. 'I was taken to a first-aid room once, as a kid. It was in the big barn, or near there.'

The barn proved to be just across the road, but it was in darkness. Having run out of ideas, we walked downhill to check whether the Naylors were revisiting St Helen's Church, which dominated the landscape south of the village – a monument to the thriving community of farmers and stonemasons who had lived and worshipped here in the nineteenth century.

The door was unlocked, but the place was empty. Ben optimistically called Alex's name, his voice echoing in the silence.

'Could we have missed them?' I asked. 'Is there another way into the pub from the back?

'Not from Square Cottage. It's only got one door.'

'OK, we'll try there again, and make more noise about it.'

We covered the ground at a run, and I hammered on the door, while Ben yelled, 'Alex! It's Ben and Kit. Open up, will you?'

Behind us, a female voice asked, 'Kester? Ben? Is there a problem?'

Frances and Henry stood at the top of the courtyard steps. Henry was frowning, uncomfortable with being seen to interfere. Frances was openly incredulous, eyeing us over her glasses. Such rowdy behaviour must have fallen well below the standards they expected, not only of Lundy holidaymakers but of Kester Pevensey, soon-to-be-presenter of *Enigmas*.

'Looks as if our friends have gone out again,' I said. 'We're a bit concerned.'

'Surely they won't have gone far in the dark?' Frances said. 'They'll just have popped out for a breath of fresh air.'

'Yeah. You mentioned a pond earlier?'

'Rocket Pole Pond. It used to be a small quarry – but that's half a mile away. Besides, Alex definitely said they're going there tomorrow.'

'Could have changed their minds. Ben and I will head out that way. Would you mind walking up to the north end of the village?'

'Of course not. We'll check the road to the helipad, too, and ask in the tavern. Someone must have seen them.'

'You're very kind. Sorry to mess up your evening.'

'Not at all. We're glad to be of help, aren't we, Henry?'

Henry agreed that they were, and they hurried away. It occurred to me that if Alex and Ursula were indeed taking an innocent evening stroll, neither would appreciate our increasingly public efforts to track them down.

We set off southward, the pale stones of Lundy Road visible without a torch. In front of the church, the road bore left. A short distance further on, as we walked around a gentler, right-hand curve, we could make out where it turned left again, curving around a stone wall to begin its switchback route down to the jetty.

'That's a crossroads,' Ben said. 'A track leads straight on to the old castle, but that's just more lets. The path to Rocket Pole Pond and Shutter Point goes right –'

'Wait! Who's that?' I stopped, taking out my headtorch, trying to locate the switch in the dark.

'Is it Alex?' Ben breathed.

The figure was the right height and build. Outlined dimly in silhouette against a wall, he stood alone and motionless near the crossroads, looking along the right-hand path.

I found the switch. The torch beam reached far enough to light Alex's face and white-blond hair as he turned, shielding his eyes.

We ran towards him, Ben calling out his name. Though temporarily blinded, he reacted to Ben's voice with disbelief turning to fury.

'What the fu –'

'Where's your grandmother?' I stopped at a safe distance from his clenching fists and scanned the grass path to the right, then swung the light back to him. 'Where's Ursula?'

'None of your bloody business! My bitch of a sister sent you, didn't she? Stupid interfering –'

'Where is she?'

His demeanour changed. He banked down the aggression to become the caring grandson. 'I don't know, all right? She was tired, confused, she went to bed early. I was upstairs for an hour or so, then I went down to check on her, and she'd gone – and her coat and walking stick were missing.'

'You were looking south. Think she'd go that way?'

'She might. We were going to do that walk tomorrow –' He broke off, hearing what he had said, then rushed on as if hoping we hadn't noticed. 'Look, I'm going crazy here. I don't know where to look first. She could have had a fall and be lying out there now.'

But he had referred to their plans in the past tense, as

if knowing the intended walk wouldn't happen. Now he was glancing from me to Ben and back again, his eye movements frantic, body language guilty enough to confirm my worst suspicions.

Whatever desperate motive was driving him, might he simply have knocked Ursula down and left her where she fell, to die of exposure? And if so, was he feeling remorse, or just regret that he hadn't finished the job?

If Ursula was out there, we might be in time to save her – and the village was so close, it would be quicker to summon help physically than to call the emergency services, even assuming a call would go through.

'Ben,' I said, 'go and alert the island staff, get a search party out!'

'Me? What're you going to do?'

'Start looking. Every minute could be critical.'

He nodded, turning to run.

In the torchlight, I saw Alex's expression change, panic giving way to vicious intent. He was between Ben and me – and he launched himself at Ben's back.

They sprawled heavily on the path, with Ben underneath. Alex started punching, but by then I was on him, dragging his arms backwards while he thrashed and kicked. His heel raked my shin and he reared his head back, missing my nose by millimetres.

Cursing, I rolled aside, pulling him with me. For a second I was beneath him; but before he could take advantage of that, I dug my heel into the stones and thrust us over again, then slammed him to the ground face down and straddled his prone body, gripping his wrists to keep his arms pinned.

The whole breathless manoeuvre had taken maybe fifteen seconds.

'OK, Ben?' I gasped.

He scrambled across the road and put a hand on the back of our captive's head, shoving hard. Alex jerked his head sideways, letting his ear take the impact to save his face. He yelled with pain and rage.

'Get off me! You've broken my ear –'

'Keep still,' I grated, 'or I'll break your skull!'

He stopped wriggling.

'Where's your gran?'

'I didn't kill her.' He started to cry, great gulping sobs of what sounded like real distress – and once again he was staring at the path going south.

It was all we would get, short of trying Nathan's tactics. I gave him a final, disgusted shove and stood up, and he bunched and scuttled a few steps on all fours, putting distance between us before scrambling to his feet. Then he ran off into the darkness, towards the village.

Ben sat down in the road. I shone the torch in his direction. The centre of his forehead bore a circular swelling, a classic 'egg', decorated with trickling grazes.

I winced. 'Shit! Were you knocked out?'

'No.' He touched the bruise gingerly. 'Ow!'

I gave him a hand up. Although clearly shaken, he was steady on his feet and seemed lucid. I checked his pupils. They were both the same size and reacted normally to torchlight.

'Feel up to going for help?' I asked.

'Yeah.'

'There's a chance Alex will hole up in Square Cottage, but he might spread the word about his gran wandering off, to cover his back. If he does that, go along with it for now.'

'He'll say we beat him up.'

'Tell them he knocked you down from behind. Anyone seeing you will believe that. Say he doesn't like you going out with his sister.'

Ben raised a rueful grin. 'I don't s'pose he does.'

'And take it easy. Don't run.'

I watched him jog towards the village, ignoring my advice, but after a few strides he slowed to a walk. Running would have jarred his head.

I hoped he wouldn't meet more trouble before he tracked down the staff, but it seemed more likely that Alex would be lying low, to get his story straight and prepare to play the injured victim.

Either way, there was no time to lose. Ursula was out here somewhere. I turned along the grass path leading south, sliding the torch strap over my head as I ran.

FORTY-SEVEN

To my left, a stone wall bounded the path. Beyond that, the land stretched away towards the cliffs. I kept turning my head to light the slopes in case Ursula was lying there, but saw no sign of her. Not too surprising. An old woman falling from a cliff, after supposedly clambering over a dry-stone wall, would not have looked like an accident.

After a short run uphill, I met an obstruction: two gates, the narrower one for walkers. Closing it behind me, I paused to listen. The path continued ahead, but now on the seaward side of the wall.

'Ursula!'

The cold wind flattened clumps of taller grasses inland, and a sheep looked up from grazing, eyes eerily reflecting the torchlight. Nothing else stirred.

I ran on, keeping in mind the hand-drawn map in Ben's book, as well as the satellite view on Google Maps. A sunken feature could be easy to miss.

Where the path split, I chose what seemed the main route. The rocket pole itself must be close; the landmark had given the old quarry pond its modern name. I slowed and looked around. Two more pairs of sheep's eyes glowed back at me, and beyond them the pole stood clear against the sky.

In the end, I had no problem finding the pond, even though it was obscured by low bushes. Three ponies were drinking there. Its granite banks were cut vertically, with occasional slopes and rocky outcrops descending almost to the current water level, allowing access for thirsty livestock.

At night, with a torch casting deceptive shadows, an

old woman might easily trip and fall into the water. If she didn't drown, the cold would soon kill her. A credible mishap, no blame attaching to her grief-stricken grandson.

I didn't think for one second that Ursula had come out alone. An episode of confusion, precisely when it suited Alex, was too convenient. He must have suggested a night-time stroll together, or even played on his grandmother's bloody-minded spirit, implying that she wouldn't be able to manage the mile round-trip to the pond and back, knowing that she would then insist they go there.

I shone my headtorch over rocks partly concealed by heather and long grasses, then across the water, from one end of the pond to the other. My mind flashed back sickeningly to Conor's bloated face. I steeled myself to see Ursula's dead eyes staring up at me, but the eyes that met mine belonged to the ponies, who raised their heads to regard me with interest.

A fish jumped, giving me such a start that I swore and leapt back. The ponies skittered sideways, whickering.

'Steady there,' I murmured. 'It's OK.'

Another sound reached me from the far side of the pond, almost like the cry of some small animal.

Almost.

I swung the torch that way, seeing only rocks and shadows.

'Ursula! Are you there?'

The sound came again, less a cry than a moan.

I had taken the dark shape among the rocks for another shadow. Now it shifted, and a thin white hand clawed upward, trying in vain to find purchase on a flat boulder at the water's edge.

'Ursula!' I sprinted around the bank.

I didn't hear him until he was almost on me, but at the last second, the thud of his feet cut through the wind. I whipped round in time to light Alex's face, contorted with rage, as he swung a fist at my head.

Instinctively, I ducked, throwing up my left arm and punching with my right, aiming for whatever I could hit.

Something that hurt more than a fist slammed into my left forearm, shooting pins and needles down to my fingers, but my blow connected somewhere on Alex's torso.

That or his own momentum threw him off balance. He cannoned into me. I staggered sideways, my right ankle turned sharply, and we both crashed to the ground, with Alex on top.

Landing on my side was better than face down, but the impact was hard and Alex was no lightweight – although, judging from his grunt of pain, he picked up a bruise or two himself.

Half-winded, I heaved him off and rolled onto my knees before he could recover enough to clout me again. The torch had slipped off my head and now lay on a nearby rock, tilted upward like a stage footlight.

Alex struggled up into a crouch. I flexed my left arm; nothing felt broken, but my hand was still weak and tingling. Luckily, Alex was breathing as hard as I was. He must have had a rethink and sprinted after me, fearing that I'd ruin his plan for the perfect murder. The chunk of rock in his hand could have come from any of the drystone walls that hemmed the fields.

I indicated his chosen weapon. 'Planning to chuck me in the pond ... after your grandmother?'

'Why not? Rescue gone wrong.'

I laughed on a breath. 'Another accident?'

'Tragic. I'm a mile away ... searching further north.'

'Think Ben will believe that?'

'Who'll care? No witnesses.' Despite his attempt to sound like a cold-blooded killer, his voice shook with the strength of whatever emotions were driving him.

That didn't make him any less dangerous. He had been sufficiently motivated to attack his grandmother. He wouldn't baulk at finishing me.

I risked a lightning glance at where Ursula lay in shadow. She had found enough strength to hook one arm over the flat slab. If I could get her to warmth and safety, she might have a chance.

Alex shifted, curling his fingers around the rock that should have cracked my skull. The element of surprise had worked with Ben, but now the odds were more equal ... except that Alex was prepared to kill. I only wanted to stop him and save Ursula.

There might be no way back for him, but for Chloe's and Jackson's sake I had to try. Moving slowly, wary of spurring him into action, I rose to a crouch, mirroring his own position. My ankle hurt but took my weight.

'Decision time, Alex,' I said. 'Screw up your whole life ... and cause your dad more grief ... or help me save your gran before she dies of hypothermia.'

His face went blank with shock. He turned his head to scan the pond, but I was between him and Ursula.

'She's alive?' he said.

'Just.'

'Shit! *Shit!*'

My earlier guess had been right. He must have run from the scene after pushing her into the water. Perhaps he couldn't bear to watch her die, or else he had been rushing to establish an alibi elsewhere. Either way, he would have known that Ursula couldn't pull herself out of the water. Only when he reached the crossroads had he paused, doubting himself, thinking that he should have made certain.

Leaving his grandmother here to drown or die slowly of cold and shock, alone in the dark, seemed to me more callous than if he had killed her outright. I could tell myself that she was a murderer, as ruthless as her grandson, but she was also an old, vulnerable woman fighting for her life.

'We need to act fast,' I said.

He shook his head, though his eyes glistened. 'I'll lose everything.'

'You don't have to.'

'I never wanted any of this. It's Dad's fault. If he'd let Gran move in with us, we could have looked after her.' Alex grimaced as if the thought was physically painful. 'Even if she needed a doctor, one of us could have been there, making sure she didn't say anything ...'

Didn't say what?

'Then talk your dad round!' I said. 'But for Christ's sake, help me now!'

Another headshake. 'Gran's had her life. I won't let her ruin mine.'

It had always been a long shot.

Never taking my eyes off him, I stood up and limped to the bank. 'Ursula?' I hunkered down and caught her hand. The bones felt fragile in my grip, but her fingers closed around mine. 'Hold on, OK? I'll get you out.'

'No,' Alex snarled. 'You won't.'

I was on my feet before he reached me. He still had his skull-cracking implement, but I hit him before he could use it – a decent punch to the ribs, but he was too warmly clad. The padding softened the blow. He reeled back, then put his head down and bull-charged me, knocking me off my feet. I grabbed a handhold, a flap of his coat, to swing him round, and we both went sprawling on the rocks beside Ursula.

Alex was closer but had his back to her. Hearing her whimper, he cried out and scrambled to his knees. Their eyes met. Hers looked black in the dramatic lighting, pupils dilated by shock.

I threw myself on him, grabbed his right wrist, and smashed his hand against the granite slab. He roared in pain, fingers jerking open, and I snatched up his weapon and hurled it into the pond. He rolled onto his back, still clutching his hand, and I drove a fist into his stomach.

He writhed over, coughing and gasping, then scrambled out of reach before staggering to his feet. We stared at each other, in my case with as much frustration as anger. He wouldn't stop. I saw it in his face. If he let me leave this place alive, Ben would corroborate parts of my story. It might not be enough to send him down for life, but he couldn't take that chance.

As soon as he moved, I sprang across the space between us. He leapt forward at the same instant, which increased the impact when I hit him.

I felt his nose break. His eyes registered surprise. Then his lids flickered and closed, and he slumped to the ground and lay still.

That gave me a bad moment. I felt for his pulse, but almost at once he stirred and groaned. I retrieved my torch and strapped it to my head again, turning it obliquely to avoid dazzling Ursula.

She lay motionless, still half-submerged. I knelt beside

her, saying her name and stroking her icy hand, and she murmured something inaudible.

'It's all right,' I said. 'I'm going to get you out.'

Easy to say. When I bent down and tried to lift her, agony forked across my lower back.

I froze, swearing through shut teeth, then tried moving as the pain slowly subsided. Everything still seemed in working order. I might hurt like hell tomorrow, but that was tomorrow's problem.

Focus, Pevensey!

Rethinking tactics, I lowered myself into the water to stand knee deep, before lifting Ursula into my arms. Even with her waterlogged coat, she couldn't have weighed more than fifty kilos. More than enough.

She muttered indistinctly, 'What're you doing? What's happening?'

'Ursula, it's Kit. Kester Pevensey.'

'Who?'

I laid her on the bank. Grass would have been kinder than granite, but it was out of reach. Climbing out of the water to kneel beside her, I talked to her soothingly, telling her what I was doing at every stage, propping her in the crook of my arm to unbutton the sodden coat and ease it off her shoulders.

'We need to get you warm,' I said. 'Are you in pain anywhere?'

'What d'you think? I'm ninety-nine.' The words were slurred, but the glimmer of spirit was encouraging. She was shivering, too. Another good sign. If her body began shutting down, that would stop.

She wore a woollen jumper and thermal vest. I managed to pull them over her head. She was pitifully thin, collarbones protruding, breastbone and ribs too close to the skin. I left her bra on for decency.

It was all taking too long. The wind must be chilling her to the bone. I glanced back along the path, then checked my watch. The face was cracked, but it still worked. Fifteen minutes since I had parted from Ben. Surely help would be here soon?

Shrugging out of my quilted jacket, I guided her arms into it. Her hand fluttered as if to brush me away, the movement random and uncoordinated. I chose to interpret that as reluctant permission, and zipped the jacket up to her chin.

When I began unfastening her trousers, she rebelled in earnest, with a high, keening wail. I let her keep them on. For all I really knew, bare legs might be a worse option.

Alex groaned again and swore. I looked round. He still lay on his back, head turned now to one side to watch me with glittering hate. His nose was bleeding heavily; the lower half of his face was dark.

'Fuck you, Pevensey,' he croaked.

No telling how long we had before adrenaline and desperation gave him the impetus to launch a fresh assault.

I said to Ursula, 'I'm going to pick you up again, OK?'

She frowned vaguely up at me. 'I fell in the pond. Stupid.'

Had she forgotten what had happened, or blanked out an unbearable reality? If she was protecting Alex, it was more than he deserved.

To avoid answering, I concentrated on the problem of how to carry her. A piggy-back was out; she was too weak to hold on. Instead I scooped her into my arms and staggered upright, using my thigh muscles to save my back. All the same, the effort hurt. Luckily, the village was only half a mile away.

With a little more luck, the cavalry would meet us before we got there.

FORTY-EIGHT

As I started along the path, Ursula was silent. Her shivers grew less noticeable, then stopped altogether. She was either warming up or sinking into hypothermia.

Speed was essential but impossible. My ankle was increasingly painful, not liking the extra weight or the uneven ground, and every limping step jarred my back. Also, I couldn't see my feet. After less than a minute I stumbled, causing Ursula to moan in protest.

'Clumsy Gunther,' she said.

I saved my breath for the job in hand. Thomasina's advice echoed in my head. *Gentle exercise and no more heroics.*

Silently, bitterly, I cursed Alex Naylor.

'Where's Oscar?' Ursula murmured.

It seemed kindest not to contradict her. 'In the tavern,' I said.

'Ah. *Natürlich.* La Folie Inn.'

I glanced down. Her skin had a greyish tinge and her lips were blue, but she was smiling.

'How're you doing, Ursula?' I asked breathlessly. 'Getting warmer?'

'*Ich bin* Jutta. Jutta Vogel. *Wo sind die Gepäcktaschen?*'

My German was basic, at best. In a moment of inspiration I panted, 'Remember ... to speak English.'

'Ah, very good. Where are our suitcases?'

'Safe.'

'Herr Schneider's face.' She chuckled softly. 'He couldn't believe I'd done it. Him and his silly wife.'

'Yeah?' I was humouring her, not really listening. There were tremors in my arms. I tried to shift my grip, and pain flared again in my back, forcing me to stop and lean against the wall to rest.

'Remember *Kristallnacht*, Gunther? All that glass.'

'What?' I looked down at her face. She was still smiling, as if reminiscing about that event gave her satisfaction even now.

I knew about *Kristallnacht,* the Night of Broken Glass. On 9th November 1938, a few months before war broke out, the Nazis had attacked and demolished hundreds of Jewish schools and synagogues, and thousands of businesses, even private homes, right across Germany and Austria. A lot of civilians had joined in. All the streets and pavements were covered in the glass from broken windows.

A memory came back to me. David, struggling to separate dreams from reality. *Alex Naylor threw a brick through a window, and I saw a pavement covered in broken glass.* But it hadn't been Alex. After seeing the Torah scroll, David would have identified it as antique Judaica. Had something Conor said inspired him to make a connection with *Kristallnacht*?

'They could have run,' Ursula – Jutta – said, 'but he wouldn't leave his money. Never heard me. Too busy at his safe. And I was quick. Quicker than gutting a fish.'

The chill that I felt had nothing to do with the cold. I staggered onward, but in my mind's eye, I saw Herr Schneider and his wife clinging together, thinking only of escape, hearing the yells of the mob outside, the windows smashing ... and then the man hesitating, making the fatal decision to go back for his cash, perhaps the couple's savings that they wouldn't trust to a bank ... and Jutta Vogel, light on her feet and utterly contemptuous, stepping up silently behind him with her knife.

'And Frau Schneider?' I couldn't help asking. Didn't

want to hear the answer.

'Stupid woman. She tried to run, you saw her ... but she was too old and fat.'

I tried not to imagine the woman's terror, or her brutal death. The two gates were ahead. This time the smaller one was ajar. Alex must have left it that way. I opened it with my fingertips, letting it swing closed behind me, and paused again there to lean against the gatepost. Couldn't go much further. My back was starting to cramp, and the voice of logic was goading me, *Just leave her here! She deserves it.*

But there was a world of difference between conceding that Jutta Vogel deserved death and abandoning a frail old woman to die of exposure.

Pushing myself upright, I set off again. The church looked close now. Not far to the crossroads.

'Don't tell Oscar,' she whispered. 'He mustn't know ... the Schneiders' money ... saved his precious estate.'

I got it then. There had been no convenient inheritance from an elderly relative. Everything that Oscar, and then Jackson, had worked to achieve had been built on the money that Jutta had killed for, to coax Oscar into marriage on the brink of war.

Avalon Sky was not unique in having links to Nazi Germany and the Holocaust. Plenty of far bigger companies, including some major household names, had glossed over their origins for that reason – but Avalon Sky's connection was chillingly personal, and its CEO was renowned locally as a man of old-fashioned virtues, a knight in all but name, while his father's war-hero status was integral to the brand. Alex must have feared, probably with good reason, that the company's fortunes would plummet if his grandmother's past came to light.

I had to find out the rest while she still thought I was her brother. 'Shall we tell Oscar ... about the Torah scroll?' I said.

'No. You made a bad mistake, Gunther. I told you ... leave it in the safe. Just take the money.'

'You didn't know I'd packed it to bring to England.'

Dummer kleiner Vogel. Silly little bird. Keep it hidden.'

We had reached the crossroads. It couldn't be more than two or three hundred metres from here to the tavern, along a road whose stones showed white in the torchlight. Piece of cake.

'Did Barbara know ... about us?' I said.

'Freddie was too loose-tongued. And the way she looked at me ... after the child ... I couldn't trust her.'

'You hanged her?'

'Choked her first. I protected us. Always.'

A Land Rover was approaching from the village. I heard the engine first, then the road ahead lit up – and the vehicle rounded the last curve, headlamps on main beam.

Newly energised by relief, I hobbled to meet it, preparing to hand over responsibility.

My right foot skidded on a stone and the sore ankle twisted savagely, throwing me to the ground. Somehow Jutta was still in my arms. She was clutching at me, her eyes half-closed.

'Gunther ...'

'It's OK.' But the pain was fierce. The whole of my lower leg was throbbing. I felt sick.

'Mustn't keep Oscar waiting.' Her voice was barely audible.

Lowering her head on to the stones, I sat up, breathing carefully. She reached for my hand and clung to it, bony fingers clamped around mine.

'Uns geht es gut, Gunther.' She smiled again, eyes closing. *'Flieg, kleiner Vogel!'*

The staff from the Land Rover were suddenly beside us, a man and woman, both young. They had brought a defibrillator. Nursing my ankle, I edged along to give them space. They wanted to know Jutta's name. I told them it was Ursula.

'Are you her grandson?' the woman asked.

'No. That's Alex. He had an accident ... by the pond.'

'Another casualty? How serious?'

'Concussed. He was coming round. Could be on his way here.'

My instinct was to tell them as little as possible. No one had seen Alex push his grandmother or attack me by the pond, and he was the one with a broken nose. He could accuse me of assault, which would end my career at the BBC before it started.

The young guy was speaking to Jutta, feeling for the pulse in her neck, then bending close to her mouth and unzipping her borrowed coat. 'No pulse, and she's not breathing. I'll try shocking her, but the defib might not work if her heart has stopped completely.'

I had never realised that, but he was right. The machine's computer wouldn't let him deliver the shock. He would have continued with CPR, but at that point, I recalled something Jackson had mentioned during our meeting in the Spitfire Café.

'She signed a form,' I said, 'not to resuscitate her.'

The man looked guiltily relieved. 'You're certain?'

'Her son told me.'

'Well ... I'm afraid she's gone, then. I'm sorry.'

We were all silent. I shouldn't have felt sad. She had

never shown the faintest flicker of remorse. Even her confession had been unintentional. But she had paid a heavy price if she had died knowing that the grandson she loved had killed her.

The young woman was close to tears. 'Poor old lady. She's wet through. Did she fall in the pond?'

'I pulled her out. Alex couldn't help.'

'But what was she even doing there, in the dark?'

'Don't know. Talk to Alex.'

'Oh ... yes. He's our next priority.' She pushed a few strands of hair off her face and took a deep breath. 'Sorry. You are ...'

'Kit.'

'I'm Mollie. This is Jacob. We need another vehicle, don't we? I'll drive to the pond to fetch Alex.'

'What took you so long to get here?' I hadn't meant to sound accusing, but it came out that way.

'Your friend,' she replied tautly, 'told the tavern staff that an old lady could be lying injured somewhere near the pond or Shutter Point. They radioed me. He also claimed her grandson had attacked him and it was the grandson's fault the old lady was missing.'

Mollie paused, raising her eyebrows at me for confirmation. I shrugged as if unable to comment either way, which fuelled her indignation.

'So I called another responder,' she said, 'to triage your friend. Then Jacob and I – did I mention I'd radioed for him as well? – we loaded up the equipment, a stretcher and so on, and here we are.' Her voice faltered, and she bit her lip. 'We did our best.'

I felt deservedly humbled, and thanked her. Jacob gave her a taste of the raised eyebrow treatment, and Mollie sighed, wiping away tears with her hand.

'I'm sorry, Kit,' she said. 'I shouldn't have gone off at you. It's great what you did, how hard you tried to save her. Have you hurt your foot?'

She examined it briefly, aware that Alex might need more urgent attention. 'It's very swollen already,' she said. 'Could be fractured. You should go to hospital. Come with me now, to pick up Alex –'

'No. Thanks anyway.' I clambered up awkwardly, sucking air through my teeth. 'I'll walk.'

'That's a really poor idea, Kit. I'm sorry to be blunt, but you could twist it again and do more damage.'

Anything was better than riding with Alex, and I didn't want to stay here until a vehicle turned up for Ursula. The wind was biting. I was missing my coat, though I would never want it back.

'It's no distance,' I said.

She gave up, clearly thinking me a macho idiot with something to prove. 'Whatever,' she said. 'I need to go. Wait here if you change your mind. I'll be coming back this way.'

Asking Jacob to stay with Ursula, she pulled a radio out of her coat pocket and ran back to the Land Rover.

None of us had registered the approach of a helicopter, but now it flew overhead, to hover some distance north of the village as if preparing to land. As Mollie drove south along the track, Jacob and I watched it descend out of sight.

'Privately owned,' he said. 'Heard one was coming in.'

It had to be Jackson. Although I wanted to intercept him before he heard Alex's story, the prospect was daunting.

Sighing inwardly, I thanked Jacob, though I wasn't

sure what for, and started to limp along the road towards the village. More of a lurching shuffle, really. There was a lot to be said for the painkilling properties of adrenaline. Shame it had worn off.

I checked my phone for a message from Lissa, but there was nothing. No signal, either. Would she have come with Jackson? We hadn't talked about that, but I allowed myself to imagine her running to meet me, then her arms around me and her lips on mine …

Please be here, Amphelisia.

In front of the church, the road curved right before running straight uphill through the village. A knot of dark figures was milling about near the pub, like disgruntled patrons ejected at closing time – except that the Marisco Tavern never closed.

The helipad was away to my left, but the group's focus of interest was on the continuation of Lundy Road, where it curved out of sight at the top of the village. Three people were walking fast towards us from that direction. Formless shadows, behind bouncing, dipping torches. The helicopter must have landed on the airfield, leaving the helipad free for an air ambulance.

Shivering, I pocketed the torch and propped myself against the tavern wall to wait. The nearest two onlookers, enviably clad in warm coats and hiking boots, strolled across to me. They would have taken me for any other visitor. It was too dark for my soaked jeans to arouse comment.

'Private chopper landed,' one of them told me, eager to share the news. 'We've been here seven years on the trot, never seen that before.'

'There's something serious going down,' his companion put in. 'The couple from Stoneycroft were going round asking everyone if we'd seen an older woman and her grandson since it got dark. Next, a young guy rushed in with a nasty head injury. Not the grandson, apparently.'

'Is he in there now?' I asked. 'The injured guy?'

'Probably. The Stoneycroft couple have kind of adopted him. You know what's going on?'

'No idea.'

The three helicopter passengers were close now. There was enough light to identify them ... Jackson first, then Chloe – and Lissa.

I took a halting step forward, into the light spilling from the tavern. One of the staff intercepted Jackson, and Chloe stayed with him, but Lissa called out my name and ran to me, exactly as I had imagined, except that her hug made it difficult to stand on one leg. I staggered, and she stood back a little, holding on to me.

'Darling! What's wrong?'

'Ursula's dead.'

'Oh, my God! Did Alex –' She broke off, stopped by whatever she saw in my face. 'Kit! You're hurt. What –'

'I need to speak to Jackson.'

'The staff are with him. They'll break it to him.'

'That's not –'

'We'll catch him when he's finished. Can you walk, darling? Come and sit down. Come on.'

I gave in. Sitting down sounded great. She helped me to a three-sided bench set into an alcove in the boundary wall. We could talk there without being overheard, so I told her more or less everything. She already knew what had happened initially, at the crossroads, because Ben had messaged Chloe.

By the end I was trembling from more than the cold.

'You're in shock,' she said, her hand warm in mine.

'I'm OK.' I raised a smile. 'Now.'

She kissed my shoulder, which for some reason choked me up.

'What am I going to tell Jackson?' I said.

'The truth.'

'I mean ... about the Schneiders, and the money.'

'Oh, I think he knows about that.'

'He doesn't,' I said. 'He can't.'

'You weren't there. When I told him we were sure there was a bigger secret, and that Alex and Chloe were scared it would have terrible repercussions, it was like a light went on in his head. He told me not to upset myself – I may have been a bit stressed – and before I knew it, he was making arrangements to fly a helicopter in. And here we are. Chloe and I refused to be left behind, of course.'

'So all that crap he gave us about his mum coming into money ...'

'She may have told him that, but he knew it wasn't true.'

So many lies and half-truths. I tried stretching out my leg to ease it. A waste of effort. Lissa squatted in front of me with her torch to see the damage.

'Oh, Kit! How did you walk on this?'

'Thought about you.'

She assumed I was joking and rolled her eyes, then spent a minute struggling with my wet laces and loosening the trainer, which had been pressing into my foot without giving the ankle any support: a miserable combination. After that she stood up to kiss my forehead and went off to find a first-aider who wasn't dealing with the Naylors' troubles. Since the only two staff within sight were in conference with Jackson and Chloe, she tried the pub and returned a couple of minutes later, sitting down again beside me.

'There's somewhere they call a recovery room,' she said, 'but you won't want to share that with Alex or Ursula.'

'Not really.'

'I said you'd rather come to the tavern, away from all the drama. They're fine with that.'

'Later, then. I have to talk to Jackson ... not just because of Alex.' Despair snatched at my breath. 'I failed, Liss.'

She squeezed my hand. 'My darling, you did everything you could.'

By tomorrow, I thought, that might be a comfort. I had wasted time trying to reason with Alex, and perhaps I should have scooped Ursula up and headed straight for the village, wet clothes and all ... but at least I had tried. Better than having to watch helplessly while a life faded away.

As if I had spoken aloud, Lissa said softly, 'Emily had the best care. If we had to live through it all again, would you do anything differently?'

'No.' I bowed my head. 'Why us, Liss? Why Emily?'

'I don't know,' she whispered, and we sat there quietly together in the dark and the cold, remembering our baby girl.

FORTY-NINE

There was no need to seek Jackson out. He and Chloe came to us. They sat on the adjacent bench, Jackson looking me assessingly up and down. He had aged since our last meeting. His jawline was slack, eyes sunken and shadowed.

'The rangers told me you were injured,' he said.

'I'm OK.'

'He's far from OK,' Lissa said. 'Thanks to your bloody son.'

I pressed her hand warningly. Aside from preferring to fight my own battles, I didn't want to fall out with Jackson. Fair-minded he might be, but he was also a concerned father – with, as his son had once pointed out, access to a good lawyer.

'I got to your mum too late,' I said. 'I'm sorry.'

'You've got nothing to apologise for, lad. Mum didn't die alone. That means a lot.'

His gratitude made me feel worse. Chloe, meanwhile, was watching Lissa and me broodingly, either feeling guilty or expecting to be blamed for the general carnage. It seemed only fair to let her off the hook.

'You did your best, Chloe,' I said.

She smiled uncertainly, as if trying out the required muscles.

'Ben is in the tavern,' I said. 'He'll be glad to see you.'

She went to find him, but her father stayed.

'The air ambulance will be landing shortly,' he said. 'Alex is conscious and alert, I'm told. The responders suspect fractured fingers, and his nose is broken. The staff seem to think he slipped while trying to rescue

Mum. Alex hasn't challenged that view.'

'Right,' I said.

'We'll talk properly later, Kit, but I need to know … Did Mum suffer?'

'She was cold, but more confused than distressed, I think.'

'Did she say anything?'

'She thought I was her brother. Her last words were, um … *Uns geht es gut. Flieg, kleiner Vogel.*'

'We're all right. Fly away, little bird. She used to call Uncle Guy that. In English, of course.' Jackson drew a long breath. 'I'll go and talk to Alex and make arrangements for Mum. I'll join you all in the tavern as soon as I can. Chloe and I will fly back to Sedgemoor tonight. There'll be seats for you two and Ben.'

Whatever Ben's view on that, I was thankful to avoid sleeping on a bed roll. Jackson headed off to find Alex, and I hauled myself up from the bench, only to discover that sitting for so long in the cold had been a mistake. The injured back muscles had set like concrete. Taken by surprise I groaned loudly, which was embarrassing and alarmed Lissa.

'Sorry.' I slanted her an agonised grin. 'Don't laugh!'

'As if.'

'You married a wimp.'

She didn't smile. Her face was screwed up in sympathy. 'Come along, my poor hero, let's get you to the pub.'

She took my arm across her shoulders, and we made our way down the slope to the Marisco Tavern as carefully and unsteadily as a couple of drunks.

Once inside, people from two different tables stood up to ask if we needed help. Lundy seemed to attract a particular type of visitor – courteous, respectful and full of community spirit, fitting naturally into their time-warped surroundings. Chloe emerged from the main bar, accompanied by a stocky, grizzled type brandishing a first-aid pack. A navy polo shirt identified him as one of the staff.

The kindly strangers went back to their dinner, and Chloe led us to Frances' and Henry's table, where the bar staff brought us chairs. Ben was there, holding an ice pack to the lump on his forehead. On seeing us, he displayed the damage with a blend of sheepishness and bravado, and was rewarded with an exclamation of horror from Lissa.

The grey-bearded first-aider did an expert job on my foot. No doubt he was kept in practice. The island's terrain must regularly have brought visitors hobbling to his door.

'Lot of swelling,' he said. 'Might be concealing a fracture.'

A cheery bunch, the Lundy team. I sighed deeply. 'So Mollie said.'

'You should get your back checked out, too. Suggest you cadge a lift in the air ambulance.'

Marvellous. Trapped in an enclosed space, far above terra firma, with a murderous bastard harbouring a grudge, a preoccupied pilot, and one or two oblivious paramedics.

Before I could reply more abruptly than he deserved, Lissa stepped in to explain that we were all flying back with Jackson.

Ben stopped kissing Chloe and paid attention. 'I'm not,' he said. 'I can't leave the Jabba here.'

'Of course you can,' Chloe said. 'It'll be quite safe,

Benji, and there's no way you should fly tomorrow. You'll have a terrible headache and you're probably concussed. Dad will help you collect the plane another day.'

So that was settled. The first-aider left, and we sat and waited for Jackson, letting time drift. Since Chloe had already relayed the news of her grandmother's passing, I found myself the unwilling focus of Frances' curiosity and obliged to field some awkward questions. I admitted only to getting hurt while trying to save Ursula, and was then offered strident but well-intentioned advice on the best treatment for sprains and strains.

It was all a bit full-on. Some peace and a stiff whisky would have been nice. I got neither. Henry bought a round of drinks, but no alcohol for Ben or me, because tea was better for shock. Ben informed me resignedly that this would be his second unwanted cuppa.

As my jeans dried, I felt warmer, though still not in the mood for Frances' determined small-talk. She meant it kindly, trying to lift my spirits by asking about *Enigmas*, then chatting with Ben about warbird restoration. She had more luck with him, the head injury having failed to dampen his new-found happiness with Chloe, but even he was flagging by the time Jackson returned.

'Sorry to be so long.' He drew up a chair next to Lissa and me, looking weary and haggard under the lights. Our new friends offered their condolences, which he received graciously. 'There's a lack of hospital helipads equipped for night landings,' he said, 'so the air ambulance will transport Mum to Sedgemoor Aerodrome.'

'Not your son?' Frances asked.

'Alex is at Square Cottage, in the care of a first

responder. Once I've delivered my party to Sedgemoor, I'll return for him, and then drive him to the emergency department in Bridgwater. He should be discharged after treatment.'

'Oh dear,' she said. 'You'll be up all night. Ben, couldn't you and Alex settle your differences so that you can all fly home together?'

Ben, Chloe, Lissa and I said emphatically, in unison, 'No!'

To Frances' credit, she accepted having overstepped some invisible line and backed off.

Jackson continued, 'Kit, a ranger will drive you to the airfield, along with anyone else who wants a lift. I'll meet you all there. Tomorrow, Alex and I will fly back here together and stay at Square Cottage. We'll both benefit from some quality father-and-son time.'

He couldn't fail to notice the collective reaction. Four of us were open-mouthed, while Frances and Henry wore expressions of tactful neutrality. All they knew of Alex was that he had attacked Ben and then left him to raise the alarm. I expected Frances to protest that he should be charged with ABH, not rewarded with a holiday.

But she took a different tack. 'I hope that's possible, Jackson. Henry and our two sons make a point of meeting for a fishing weekend whenever they can. It's always good to reconnect.'

'Absolutely.' Jackson summoned up a smile. 'You've been so kind. I hope our troubles haven't impacted your holiday too badly.'

Henry exclaimed that they had been glad to help, and Frances remarked how terribly sad it was, the way things had turned out, and would Jackson let them know whether, or where, they could send flowers for the funeral?

'I know we only met your mother briefly, but she was so brave, coming here at her age.'

No mention of the fact that Ursula had repaid their friendly overtures with rudeness.

Jackson took their email address, and we said our goodbyes. Frances appeared uncomfortable with Chloe's hug and patted the rest of us affectionately, as though we were well-behaved dogs.

Outside the tavern, Lissa and I leant against the wall to await the promised lift. Less of a trial than walking to the bench and back. The others lingered with us. It was not a bad place to talk in private, the earlier knots of spectators having migrated back into the pub.

Chloe asked in a small voice, 'Alex won't go to prison, will he, Dad?'

'I don't think so, love.'

Lissa muttered, 'Kit might have a say in that.'

Jackson turned to me with an air of getting down to business. 'Will you tell us what happened at Rocket Pole Pond, Kit?'

I omitted nothing, except for a few thoughts that the Naylors didn't need to hear. No one interrupted, but Jackson's shoulders slumped.

When I had finished, Chloe said defensively, 'This was always about Gran, you know. Alex never wanted anyone else to get hurt.'

'He planned to smash my skull,' I said.

'He didn't *plan* it. He was angry.'

'Alex found himself a weapon and tried to kill me.' I pushed up my sleeve and showed her my swollen forearm. 'This should have been my head. If he'd even knocked me out, I'd have ended up in the pond with your gran.'

Rather than protest that I couldn't know that, Chloe blinked her wide blue eyes and said nothing. For her sake, I hoped she believed me.

Jackson was a different proposition. 'A good defence lawyer would shred your testimony and Ben's without breaking a sweat,' he told me. 'Alex will say he and Ben had a fight, then you piled in. That would place you on a very sticky wicket. If you press charges for the later assault, Alex will admit that he was angry and followed you to the pond after you'd attacked him at the crossroads. He'll claim that he was unarmed and didn't realise you were trying to rescue Mum – that in fact he had no idea you'd found her – and that before he had time to do anything, you assaulted him again, blaming him for having left Mum to fetch help.'

'Is that what Alex has told you?'

'More or less.'

'You know it's bollocks.'

'I'm telling you what a lawyer would say.'

'And Kit's defence,' Lissa pointed out, 'could drive a bus through the holes in that fairy tale.'

'It doesn't matter, sweetheart,' I said. 'Jackson's right, I'd never be able to prove who struck the first blow. Nor would Ben. But you need to understand what Alex is capable of, Jackson. He's not like Chloe, just worrying about your finer feelings.'

'I know that,' he said.

'He thought that if the truth came out, he could kiss his golden future goodbye. Maybe he was right. Local opinion would have crucified you. But either way, he's crossed a line now. What he did to his gran may have torn him up, but he didn't give a toss about clobbering me. Anyone who crosses him in future will be taking a risk.'

Jackson was silent, frowning, unready to be convinced. I shook my head in defeat. What did I care, anyway? Everything hurt. Alex's bloody family could believe whatever the hell they liked.

Chloe was watching us with brimming eyes. Jackson hugged her into his side. 'Your grandad told me everything before he died, love. Your gran had confessed to him after they were married. It changed him. It changed *me*. I've done my best to atone.'

'But everything we have ... Everything you've worked for ...'

'The lifestyle we enjoy is not solely down to your gran. I've worked hard all my life and been fortunate with some investments along the way. A lot of good causes have benefited – but I'm not man enough to go public, nor to give your inheritance away. You'll have to make your own peace with that.' Jackson looked at me. 'Alex will be held accountable. I'd planned to retire next year, but Chloe and I can run things between us for the next ten years – can't we, love? I'll keep Alex close until then. After that, we'll see.'

Ten years. Not a prison sentence, but still a punishment that Alex would find nearly intolerable. Next year he would have been CEO of Avalon Sky, but now he would be working for his father until he was thirty-five, with no guarantee of eventual promotion – and Jackson's threat to 'keep him close' implied that he wouldn't give his son a glowing reference to start afresh elsewhere.

Jackson Naylor was not so soft after all.

Lissa asked quietly, 'Don't you want justice for your mum, Jackson?'

That hit a nerve. He grimaced. 'It seems not. One more thing I'll have to live with.'

'Justice has been done,' Chloe murmured.

Jackson was shocked. Even if the death sentence had not been abolished decades ago, execution without trial would be vigilantism, not justice; and Ursula had been his mother, after all.

But on some primitive level, and despite having battled to change the outcome, I was with Chloe. After eighty-plus years, Ursula Naylor – Jutta Vogel – had finally paid for her crimes.

I knew what Lissa would say, too; that Barbara and baby Daphne, and the Schneiders, could rest in peace at last.

FIFTY

We saw the air ambulance rise from behind the barn and wheel away towards the mainland and Sedgemoor Aerodrome. Ursula was beginning her last journey home from Lundy.

Jackson headed for Square Cottage to check on Alex before leaving, while Ben and Chloe went to collect the gear from the camping field. All of us would then meet at the airfield.

Lissa and I waited for the Land Rover, which was driven by Mollie. By the time she dropped us beside Jackson's helicopter, Ben and Chloe were already there, staring at his phone screen.

'Have a safe flight,' Mollie said, turning in her seat as Lissa helped me struggle out of the vehicle. 'And Kit, go to A and E!'

Not being a fan of unnecessary hospital visits, I grinned ruefully and made no promises, and with a resigned headshake she drove away. Ben and Chloe walked over to us, the screen lighting their faces from below.

'Message from Dave,' he said. 'Must've come while we were in the tavern.'

'Is he all right?' Lissa asked.

Ben showed us the screen, and David's words danced in front of my tired eyes. The message was brief and to the point. *I know what happened at Merlin Park.*

Ben tried to text him back, but predictably it failed to send. Jackson turned up a few minutes later and had no issue with Ben using the phone in flight, but by the time we took off, it was after ten-thirty. David would be in bed, so we wouldn't learn more until the morning.

The flight to Sedgemoor must have been smooth,

because I dozed off for half of it and woke as we landed. The air ambulance had already unloaded Ursula, so Jackson went to carry out whatever grim administrative tasks could be achieved at that hour. He planned to snatch a few hours' sleep afterwards and go back for Alex at first light. Meanwhile, Ben cajoled Chloe, against her better judgement, into driving him to Merlin Park to collect his bike.

Lissa and I finally arrived at Greenways well after midnight. All the lights in the bungalow were off, and the place felt empty. Even Bormo was out, and it was a safe bet that Thomasina had gone to Spindlewood to keep Alf company.

I had no energy to wonder about tomorrow's revelations. The day had begun to feel endless.

The night seemed longer still. I filched two of Thomasina's paracetamol and fell asleep from sheer exhaustion, but every unconscious movement jolted me back to painful awareness. By the morning I felt wrecked, as well as grumpy about needing Lissa's help to dress myself – and Thomasina's magic touch was unavailable. Ben messaged to let us know that it was her weekend to work. She had gone to the practice straight from Netherzoy.

He also invited us to Spindlewood for breakfast, to hear David's story. I would have made the effort, but Lissa asked if they would come to us instead.

So the three Macraes turned up at Greenways, laden with ingredients for a 'Full English'. When they trooped into the living room, I was sitting along one of the tapestry-covered sofas to keep my foot elevated, while a fringed cushion behind my back tickled any exposed skin it could find. Fidgeting crossly, I caught Lissa's wry glance, stopped scowling, and forced a smile for our visitors.

David now looked a lot better, but Ben's appearance was shocking. His entire forehead was grotesquely swollen and several shades of purple.

'Christ!' I said.

'It's fine. Chloe dragged me to Minor Injuries after we got back from picking the bike up. They gave us a leaflet on head injuries and told her to keep an eye on me overnight.'

'Which she did?' Lissa teased him.

He blushed, adding to the array of facial hues. 'It was practically morning by then anyway.'

'Well, good for Chloe!' she said. 'We were too tired to bother last night, so we're going this afternoon.'

This was news to me.

'We're not,' I said.

'You'll do as you're told,' she countered with a beatific smile, and kissed the top of my head.

Frowning mutinously, I noticed an oddly-shaped plastic receptacle dangling from Ben's hand, alongside the grocery bag.

'What's that?' I said.

'Bacon, sausages –'

'No – *that*.'

Mischief tweaked at the corners of his mouth, and he held the item out for my inspection. 'It was Dad's. He found it handy on long flights, when he got caught short. I thought it'd save you getting up.'

'Are you taking the piss?'

Ben looked down at the apparatus in his hand and convulsed with laughter. Alf kept a straight face, but David hid a smile behind his hand, and even Lissa met my eyes with an apologetic sparkle.

I grinned in spite of myself. 'Sod off and cook, Ben!'

While he and David made a start on breakfast, Lissa perched on the sofa arm and Alf sank into an armchair, regarding me with approval.

'So you put Alex Naylor in hospital, eh?' he said. 'Bloody good job. You need to hear Dave's story. Put him right on a thing or two.'

We had to contain our impatience until breakfast was served. We ate from trays on our laps, mostly for my benefit, but Alf said he always preferred an armchair to a hard seat.

David fetched us some orange juice and made a business of polishing each glass with a tea towel, inside and out, as if playing for time.

'You don't have to tell us, David,' Lissa said.

'No, I do.' He sighed, taking the last unoccupied chair. 'I owe you that. To be honest, I didn't think it would ever come back, but as soon as Ben told me about the Torah scroll, a picture of it flashed into my head. I could almost feel it in my hand, along with that flutter of excitement, the sense of holding something rare and very special.'

'You remember Conor showing it to you?' I said.

David nodded. 'In the caravan. He'd told me on the phone that he wanted it auctioned for a friend named Fogle, but ... well, I wasn't born yesterday, and I know Conor. As soon as I saw the scroll, I wanted to know its provenance. He became quite huffy, so I said that it wasn't really for me and he should try an expert in Judaica. I once saw a similar item sell for eighty thousand pounds.'

I whistled.

David smiled. 'Exactly. Conor said Mr Fogle was a friend of Jackson's, as if that would change my mind. You can imagine, by this time I was smelling an exceptionally large rat.'

'Was Harry Diment there?' Lissa asked.

'No, only Conor. But then ...' David paused, watching for our reactions. 'Alex Naylor arrived.'

Lissa gasped, and I swore under my breath.

'He didn't have a car, so he must have used the footpath. He was absolutely incandescent. He accused Conor of stealing the scroll from his uncle and ordered him to hand it over – although in stronger terms. Conor insisted it belonged to a Mr Fogle, and that's when Alex totally lost it. Of course I know why, now. I suppose Conor had told *me* the name because it was true, in a way, and he may have hoped that would convince me the scroll had provenance, but I'm sure he told Alex to imply that he knew the whole story.'

'Did Alex kill him?' I asked.

'No. He was shouting, asking who else knew about the scroll. Conor said he hadn't told anyone, he wasn't an effing idiot.'

Conor must have thought he was being clever. The fewer people he told, the safer he felt. But he had been wrong.

'Of course,' David said, 'I was unaware of the background, although Alex's attitude, and something Conor said, made me wonder. The Nazis stole an immense quantity of treasure from the Jews, as I'm sure you know. Many of those items are still unaccounted for.' He paused for a sip of juice, then went on, 'Regardless, all I wanted at that point was to leave, but Alex and Conor were between me and the doorway, squaring up to each other. Maisie was barking and running around their feet, thinking it was all a game ... and then Conor kicked her out of the way and pulled a knife on Alex.'

He stopped, looking down at his plate with sudden revulsion, then set the tray aside, continuing more shakily, 'I didn't give a thought to the knife. I grabbed Maisie up and pushed Conor away. He tried to hit me, but I was holding Maisie. She nipped him, I think, and he swore and lashed out again. I thought it was his fist, but ... Maisie made this awful sound ... and I saw the blood.'

'Oh, David,' Lissa breathed.

'I started yelling at him, screaming I suppose, and someone – it must have been Alex – hit me across the face, and Conor snatched Maisie and ... broke her neck.' He dropped his head in his hands. 'I think I actually saw red ... and I was trying to take Maisie back. I hit Conor ... I've never struck anyone before ... and then there was a sort of crack, and he was on the floor. Dead. And then everything went black.'

'You didn't kill him,' I said.

David looked up, his eyes tortured. 'I punched him.'

'And you heard a crack afterwards, right? You and Conor were both hit with a tyre lever. Alex must have brought that in case Conor refused to hand over the scroll – or else he'd planned to silence Conor anyway, and you were collateral damage.'

David rubbed a hand over his face. 'It really wasn't me?'

'It really wasn't.'

He drew a shuddering breath. 'Thank God! At least I know, even though Alex will never be charged ...'

Alf stirred himself. 'That's not right. The bastard should go down.'

'It'll never happen, Unc,' David said. 'What jury would convict him on the word of a man recovering from amnesia? A half-decent lawyer would pulverise me. And

Harry can't afford to upset the Naylors. He'll never testify that he followed Alex's instructions to collect the Audi and help him dump it.'

'And Harry doesn't know about the scroll,' I pointed out. 'Or the Finches' real identities. On the plus side, Alf, Alex will spend the next ten years under his dad's thumb, with nothing guaranteed at the end of it. And he loved his gran. I think what he did will haunt him forever.'

Alf looked dissatisfied, and Lissa asked David, 'Is that enough for you?'

'Oh, yes. I'm incredibly relieved that I didn't kill Conor, but after what he did to Maisie, I'm not sorry he's dead.' David shot me a troubled look as a thought occurred to him. 'You should steer clear of Alex, though, Kit. You've made an enemy for life there.'

'He'll blame his father, not me,' I said, as if I believed it. 'And he must know he'd be the prime suspect if Jackson died suddenly. Lampert will guess we're all lying about what happened on Lundy. She might even promote Alex to the top of her "murder wall" for Conor.'

'What if he comes after you instead?' Lissa murmured.

'And risk Jackson's wrath? No, I'm safe, sweetheart.' *Fingers crossed.*

It occurred to me that Alex might be the one looking over his shoulder, if Nathan Yandle ever found out that he had killed Conor; but we could reassure the Yandles that Reece was safe, without revealing how we knew. Alex wouldn't chance trying to identify a possible witness whose silence to date implied that he had seen nothing incriminating.

But I had been wrong about one thing. Alex hadn't crossed the line when he pushed Ursula into Rocket Pole Pond. He had become a killer the night he struck down

Conor Yandle.

'How about Harry?' I asked David. 'His defence for taking your car is that you asked him to drive you to a hospital.'

'Well, I don't want him going back to prison on my account. He did save my life. I'll tell George that I may have come round and begged him for help. Perhaps I did.'

Harry himself had suggested otherwise, but what the hell? He had already suffered for his mistakes – and with Conor gone and Alex under scrutiny, maybe he really would go straight.

The Macraes stayed to chat for a while, sticking to happier topics like the village project, and Ben's plans to take Chloe away on holiday next year – firstly to Lundy, then on a motorbike tour of Europe.

'Good idea,' Alf said. 'I'll enjoy a bit of solitude for a change.'

'You wouldn't mind?' Ben asked.

'I haven't had a nightmare this week. I won't count my chickens just yet, but things could be looking up.'

'That's great, Unc,' David said, 'but I'm sure Tommie and I can keep you company between us.' He turned to Lissa and me. 'How about you two? Any plans? It won't take you till January to finish my research.'

'First of all,' she said, 'Kit needs to get fit, and I need to land a new job. And then ...'

She paused. I looked up into her eyes, finding them watchful, a little anxious, challenging me to finish the sentence.

But I knew, finally, where my priorities lay.

'We're buying a house,' I said.

THE END

About The Author

Jill Todd was born in Eastleigh, Hampshire. Her parents taught her to read and write at four years old to occupy her during a long illness, and she has been writing stories ever since.

After completing a historical novel (published in 1988), she then rediscovered a social life, married and had a family. Whilst working as an Admin Assistant at a local secondary school, she still managed to continue writing as a hobby.

Her first contemporary novel, *Echo of Bells*, was published in 2016. Since retiring in 2023, she has been able to write full-time, and intends her new thriller, *Avalon Sky*, to be the first in a series.

In 2000, her husband and four fellow pilots won a microlight aircraft kit in a magazine competition. The build took three years, and the little plane (or a fifth share of it) became part of the family, which inspired one aspect of the plot of *Avalon Sky*.

Holidays in Somerset and on Lundy Island supplied more material, and the island remains one of Jill's favourite places.

https://jilltoddnovelist.wixsite.com/books

www.blossomspringpublishing.com

Printed in Dunstable, United Kingdom